FORT CASS SHOWDOWN

"You have no choice," Hervey said, laughing at Fitzhugh. "You just git your skinny butt outa here, you and your Cheyenne woman. Your wagons with all those geegaws and pretties—well, I just took 'em!"

Fitzhugh's Hawken lay in its beaded sheath, but he knew by the time he drew it, cocked the hammer, and aimed that Hervey would have pulled him off his horse. But he had his Bowie at his belt, and with a sudden blur his hand held it.

"I just as soon stick a man so he feels the blade slice his kidneys," he said. "You steal my trade goods and I'll kill you."

Hervey didn't laugh and Fitzhugh judged that he'd made his point. But still he didn't move, sitting mean-eyed on his restless horse. The knife felt sweaty and good in his knotted hand, and the muscles in his arm, shoulder, and back were stretched tight and ready—ready to explode!

ENJOY THE OTHER THRILLING ADVENTURES OF THE ROCKY MOUNTAIN COMPANY

by Spur-award-winning author
Richard S. Wheeler

THE ROCKY MOUNTAIN COMPANY: FORT DANCE
0-7680-1469-5 Available September 2002

THE ROCKY MOUNTAIN COMPANY:
CHEYENNE WINTER
0-7860-1470-9 Available November 2002

THE ROCKY MOUNTAIN COMPANY

Richard S. Wheeler

PINNACLE BOOKS
Kensington Publishing Corp.
http://www.kensingtonbooks.com

PINNACLE BOOKS are published by

Kensington Publishing Corp.
850 Third Avenue
New York, NY 10022

All Kensington Titles, Imprints, and Distributed Lines are available at special quantity discounts for bulk purchases for sales promotions, premiums, fund-raising, and educational or institutional use. Special book excerpts or customized printings can also be created to fit specific needs. For details, write or phone the office of the Kensington special sales manager: Kensington Publishing Corp., 850 Third Avenue, New York, NY 10022, attn: Special Sales Department, Phone: 1-800-221-2647.

Pinnacle and the P logo Reg. U.S. Pat. & TM Off.

First Printing: March 1991
10 9 8 7 6 5 4 3 2

Printed in the United States of America

For Elizabeth S. Wheeler and the late S. Lawrence Wheeler

Chapter One

Upon these people Guy Straus was betting everything he possessed. And more: everything he could borrow. From the beginning, Yvonne had been the Cassandra, begging him not to do it. But he was doing it. On its surface, the Rocky Mountain Company had seemed much too risky. Actually, he'd concluded, it was opportunity, and the difference between catastrophe and success lay in those who had joined him in the dark, burnished salon of Straus et Fils, on Chestnut Street. A fortune awaited those who knew how to trade for buffalo robes, but it took the right men to do it. Rough men like these, and their wives, gathered here to create a company.

One of those men, who would run the northern post on the Yellowstone, stood across the room, favoring his bad leg and looking acutely uncomfortable. He glared about with hawkeyes, from behind a carrot-colored beard, saying absolutely nothing and missing nothing.

The other, the brown-haired toothpick of a man who would run the southern post, slouched comfortably near the sideboard and the sweets, absolutely at home in any place, with anyone. But Guy knew his amiability could be deceptive, and that this one, in danger, could explode like a howitzer full of grape shot.

Each of them had spent fourteen years in the mountains, a thought that comforted Guy. The success of the Rocky

Mountain Company depended on the wariness and experience of these two. And their beautiful dusky wives.

It seemed the right moment, something to be seized or lost and not likely to appear again. The beaver trade had died. John Jacob Astor had seen it coming, watched the silk top hat come into vogue in Europe, driving out the heavier ones made of beaver felt, and had sold out. Pratte and Chouteau, here in St. Louis, had bought his Upper Missouri Outfit, and Chouteau was now doing a modest trade in buffalo robes with distant tribesmen. And far out the Santa Fe trail, on the rim of Mexico, Bent, St. Vrain survived as an outfitter for the traffic on the trail, trading for a few robes on the side. Yes, there was opportunity, he thought, for a company dealing in robes.

On this May 15, 1841, the grass was greening on the prairies to the west and the muscular Missouri was rising toward its June crest far to the north. The date was reckoned by their calendar, that of his two partners and one of their wives. It was Yvonne's as well. His calendar was more ancient. The other woman present in the salon reckoned time by winters, each with its own name, each committed to memory by old men. But it was not the dates, but the times that mattered, and the times were as good as they would become.

Neither of his partners—they weren't actually partners yet, but would be in a few minutes—looked as if he belonged in these burnished offices that Guy Straus had shaped to his elegant tastes. If he'd had the slightest suspicion that they and their wives were comfortable here among these amenities, he would have chosen not to do business with them. This would be a new business, actually, but a logical outgrowth of the business Straus et Fils had been doing in rude St. Louis since 1795. His parents had arrived then, from Paris, a whisker ahead of the guillotine, condemned for the sins of moderation and past acquaintance with royal finance. Up until now, Straus et Fils had been a house of arbitrageurs and brokers, trading the unruly coin of the frontier—pesos, francs, reals, dollars, cents, pounds, ducats—for something else, always for a small fee. It had expanded into commodity brokering as well—dollars for prime beaver plews, or Witney trading blankets for wolf pelts or Crow elkskins, or whatever else rough unlettered men floated down the endless mysterious river out of uncharted lands across a continent. A perfect prelude, he thought, for what would come.

For these unusual skills, as well as a staggering investment, he would own two-thirds of the Rocky Mountain Company, as they all had started to call the new firm of Dance, Fitzhugh and Straus. That was exactly the percentage kept by Pierre Chouteau Jr.—*le cadet*—of his giant Upper Missouri Outfit, the rest going to his brilliant managers out at the posts. A good model, Guy thought. Already he had invested in tradegoods—brass kettles, fishhooks, hoop iron, fusils, hatchets and axes, blankets, awls, bolts of bright tradecloth, traps, beads of every rainbow color, gay ribbons, tin mirrors—and another item that slid delicately from mind, as if the thinking of it would alert General Clark to its presence, and jeopardize their new trading license and two thousand dollar bond. The pure grain spirits were already en route by back trails to their destinations.

Nor was that the end of his investments. Among his purchases were a dozen Conestogas in fine condition, yoke and harness for them, oxen to draw them, and equipage for the trading post that would be built in Mexico, perhaps on the Purgatoire River, near Bent's Fort. More costly still was the chartering of the *Platte* from Captain Joseph LaBarge, the only opposition steamer available to carry tradegoods up the Missouri to the Yellowstone, and as far up that unnavigated tributary as the draft of the steamer would permit. And not even that was the end of it, for in a few hours he'd be paying wages to thirty men, mostly French engagés.

Yvonne stared at him stiffly from an uncandled corner of the salon, anxiety written upon her olive features and downturned soft lips. It was not that she disapproved, he thought, but that visions of failure and bankruptcy and debt and grinding poverty terrorized her. But that would not happen, and the rough men and barbarous women she viewed with such dread were his assets, as capable as any on earth of turning that frightful outlay into untold riches.

His slave, Gregoire, of bituminous flesh and New Orleans breeding, served chocolate-hued chicory-coffee to them all in priestly fashion, ritually pouring from silver service into Haviland teacups. Guy Straus watched Gregoire bestow a filled cup nested in its saucer to Robert Fitzhugh and his wife Little Whirlwind, a name he had amusingly converted to Dust Devil. Guy Straus wondered, idly, whether either could hold a cup and saucer properly. Indeed, he wondered whether Fitzhugh would survive the afternoon in these civilized confines. He had the look about him of a keg of black powder with a hissing fuse. He had not been out of the mountains for eleven years. No one called him Robert. He had been Brokenleg in the mountains, and indeed Brokenleg here. His left knee no longer flexed, and his leg stood rigid from hip to ankle as a result of an ancient folly when Fitzhugh's world was young and green. Guy Straus smiled. He knew his man.

Still . . . Brokenleg Fitzhugh had his weaknesses, Guy thought uneasily, his mind turning to those casks of grain spirits being carried on six packmules far to the west of the frowning American army at Fort Leavenworth. And yet another weakness too, he thought, his eye upon the comely young Cheyenne bride standing beside him in velvety white-chalked doeskin that clung deliciously to her slim figure. In a minute, Fitzhugh would own one sixth of the Rocky Mountain Company. But just now, the six-foot carrot-haired, amber-bearded scarecrow looked like he was about to snap the saucer in two.

Gregoire administered his sacraments to the other partner in this enterprise, Jamie Dance, who lounged lazily in the bay of a vaulting window that lit the salon and opened on Chestnut Street. The man stood loose as a cat, his every gesture a minimal expenditure of energy. His very tongue was as lazy as the rest of him, so that he drawled out his words in a soft slur. But there was more to Jamie Dance than his aversion to work. Among the free trappers in the mountains he'd become a legend. He always showed up at a rendezvous, or trading posts, with more beaver plews than anyone else, even though few of these were the skins of animals he'd caught himself. Not unless he was utterly desperate did Jamie Dance bait his traps, plant them in icy streams, haul beaver out of cold waters, skin, flesh and dry the plews. Instead, he purchased quantities of gewgaws from traders each year, along with fresh decks of cards and a few jugs of spirits, and then rode into the wilderness equipped with the means to allow others to do his work for him. He was, in fact, a born trader, who would go from village to village among the Indians, bartering away gunpowder, mirrors, ribbons, and sometimes a furtive cup of grain spirits, in exchange for heaps of valuable furs. And among his trapper colleagues, he employed his deck of cards, playing Euchre or Old Sledge, and achieving the same result.

Of his two partners, Guy thought, lazy Jamie Dance might prove to be the more productive—if he could stay out of trouble, which gathered about Jamie like the flies of summer. And no trouble haunted the new company so much as the one surrounding the new Mrs. Dance, until recently Teresa Maria Antonia Juanita Obregon, daughter of the alcalde of Taos, Juan Santamaria Obregon y Castillas, and his wife Luz. Guy could understand the elopement perfectly: before him stood a woman who dazzled the eye, a wild fiery thing, slender and vivacious, with flashing eyes and tawny flesh and buxom chest, who radiated energy even as

Jamie seemed to absorb it. It had been a scandal, and it might keep the Rocky Mountain Company from obtaining the Mexican trading license it needed, especially if the company's southern rivals William Bent or Ceran St. Vrain applied pressure in Santa Fe.

Outside, the church tolled the hour, the fourteenth of that day, and Guy Straus realized the moment had arrived to begin the business at hand. He tugged at his black broadcloth frockcoat, making it fit smoothly over his burly frame, out of ancient habit. He looked like a balding bag-eyed Spaniard, which in fact he was, after a fashion, but of the Sephardic variety that had been driven out or underground by Queen Isabella centuries before. The Strauses had lived in Amsterdam for generations, before drifting into France.

"Gentlemen, and my ladies, let us begin," he said, stopping conversation in the salon.

He eyed the young men almost paternally, though the date of his birth, 1798, wasn't so far removed from the dates of theirs, 1810 for Fitzhugh and 1811 for Dance. Fitzhugh settled himself awkwardly, his stiff leg stabbing under the walnut table, while Dance slid into the ladder-backed chair as loosely as a wineskin. The ladies congregated in chairs along the windowed wall, as was proper, along with Guy's children, David, Maxim, and Clothilde. Guy thought he'd hasten things along before Fitzhugh exploded.

"On this memorable day," Guy began, "we organize ourselves into the Rocky Mountain Company, or more properly, Dance, Fitzhugh and Straus. It is a great day, eh? A little like marriage." He smiled. "For richer or poorer, in sickness and health, till death do us part, eh?" His jest won him a few nervous chuckles.

"Before you," he continued, "is an agreement, copied out by my clerk, Monsieur Ribeaux, which I trust is nothing more or less than what we arrived at by handshake last November. Monsieur Fitzhugh, perhaps you would read it?"

"Who, me?" said Brokenleg, startled.

Guy smiled.

"I'd rather wrestle a grizzly," Fitzhugh said, staring wildly at assorted ladies and almost-grown children.

Guy waited, letting the silence thicken. He preferred that Fitzhugh read. Dance didn't know how, except to cipher numbers to some extent.

"Well, if it's how we figured, me and Jamie with a sixth and you with two-thirds . . . You know." He stabbed the air unhappily. "Gimme the nib and I'll just sign the thing."

"Yeah," said Jamie Dance. "I'll just put my mark on. You'll do the provisioning and accounting, sell the robes, and me and Brokenleg run the posts, that's all I need. You got that down on that parchment, and I don't need nothing more."

Guy laughed. These two would rather ride a fresh-trapped mustang than commit to paper and contract. The handshake had counted, not this parchment. Guy knew that, and had organized the company and committed funds on that handshake last fall.

"I'll read it anyway," Guy said. "It's just a few paragraphs." And he did: The firm of Dance, Fitzhugh and Straus would be organized this fifteenth day of May to engage in the buffalo robe trade, and whatever other peltries and usable items—buffalo tongues in particular—might be obtained from the western tribes. Straus would capitalize the company and dispose of its product as well as provision the two contemplated posts with necessaries and tradegoods. Dance and Fitzhugh would operate the posts, conduct the trading, and ship the returns as soon as feasible each spring, and appear in person for the company's annual meeting each July, when trade was slack.

"Is that it, gentlemen?" he asked.

"Sure 'nuff is," Dance replied.

Guy plucked one of his steel-nib pens, made by Josiah Mason in England, and dipped it into the pot of India ink and scratched his name on the three copies. He handed the small instrument to Fitzhugh, who scratched his signature so violently Guy feared the pen would snap or the parchment would be plowed through. But except for a widening pool of black on one copy, nothing untoward happened. Guy handed Brokenleg a blotter. Next, with a small helpless grin, Jamie made his careful mark, an X, and Guy printed Jamie's name behind it and he and Fitzhugh initialed it.

"Guess we're married," Jamie said, beaming. "I ain't much of a husband and I'm a worse wife."

"Madre Dios, you're no husband at all," retorted Teresa Maria.

Jamie chortled, enjoying some secret that lay veiled from the rest of them.

Guy let the contracts dry on the freshly-beeswaxed table. "We'll uncork some champagne to celebrate. But now, gentlemen, we've business to attend. Captain LaBarge is ready to sail. He's got the southern outfit in the forehold, and the northern outfit aft. He says the sooner the better, even tomorrow, so he can catch the June rise of the river, *oui?"*

Guy hoped that news would translate into action later in the afternoon. "I'm assured by Waddell and Smythe that the wagons are waiting at Independence, along with the livestock. Monsieur Dance, I trust that your southern outfit will be unloaded from the *Platte* and reloaded in the Conestogas as swiftly as possible, and I trust, Monsieur Fitzhugh, that the wagons and mules destined for the Yellowstone will be loaded on the foredeck as fast as you and your engagés can manage, eh? LaBarge has other dunnage waiting at Independence, and a lot of passengers."

"I reckon we'll have all our truck shifted in half a day. If not, we'll burn the torches," Fitzhugh said.

"We're already days behind the American Fur Company

packet," Guy said. "They'll have their goods shelved at Fort Union before we arrive in that country."

"Once I git there, I can move fast," Fitzhugh said. "I don't have to build a fort."

That had been a key factor in their plans. When the beaver trade dwindled, American Fur had pulled off the Yellowstone River, abandoned its Fort Cass at the confluence of the Big Horn, and did a desultory business in robes and peltries from Fort Union on the Missouri, a place not very accessible to Mountain Crow and Cheyenne. All Fitzhugh needed to do was move in, and contact his Cheyenne relatives, and he'd be in business, butting against Pierre Chouteau. But Jamie Dance was going to have a tougher time, and they'd worked out a fluid strategy to deal with it. The first obstacle would be a trading license from Governor Armijo at Santa Fe. If that proved impossible—and well it might, given Jamie's reputation—he was to establish a post on the United States side of the Arkansas River and avoid trading in Mexico. There were none to move into, and it would have to be built from adobe or cottonwood. During that first year, they wouldn't have much of a post at all: Jamie intended to drive his wagons out to the villages and trade there. William Bent was already doing that, but Jamie felt sure he could best Bent at his own game. Jamie would deal primarily with the dangerous Comanche, Kiowa, and Lipan Apache, because Bent's wife was a southern Cheyenne, and Bent, St. Vrain had a lock on the Cheyenne trade.

All this the three future partners had discussed by the hour over coffee, or sometimes bourbon, at the Planters House that winter. Today's events were more ceremony than substance, and Guy didn't suppose they would alter things much.

"You've each picked out a trade outfit you think is suited for the tribes you'll be dealing with. Are you quite satisfied with it? We have a few hours to add or subtract. Our rivals are wily men, *messieurs.* Nothing—truly nothing—escapes the attention of Cadet Chouteau, or Monsieur Bent and his *frères.* But I keep hoping you might think of something, some *petite entrée—* "

"Wall, as a fact, I've got me an ideah," drawled Jamie Dance. "Not so much for my outfit as Brokenleg's. Them tribes up there haven't got much choice for bow wood. They make their bows outa juniper or chokecherry mostly, and it's poor doing compared to osage orange. They trade most anything for a good stick of osage orange, from this country here, just so they can have them a first-rate bow. I don't think the big outfits ever cottoned on to it—I mean, how much those warriors lust for a stick of osage orange. But I reckon we'd get a dressed robe for a stick of it."

Bois d'arc! A tanned robe worth four dollars for a stick of wood that grew so commonly in Missouri it could be gathered by the ton. The very thought excited Guy. "Where? How?" he asked.

"Best groves of it are over the other side of the state, east of Independence. That's where the Osage tribe cut the wood. I'm thinkin'—to save time—when LaBarge sends his deckmen to shore for a wooding, we can put our engagés to work cutting the osage orange sticks. I'll show 'em what's good sticks and what's poor doin's. Most of it should go up the Missouri with Brokenleg, but I'll fetch along a few hundred myself. It's got to dry six months, so we don't be makin' a robe killing until next year."

"Ah, *mon cher* Monsieur Dance, that is the edge, the advantage, we've been looking for, eh? A robe for a stick of wood?"

"Should work," Dance replied. "Most of those warriors can't afford a parcel of robes for a fusil, but they can spare a robe or two for a prize bow wood that let's 'em put an arrah thirty yards further than their best wood bows."

"Only for the Cheyenne!" spat Dust Devil, from a shadowed corner. "Never to the Absaroka dogs!"

There, right there, lay one of the Rocky Mountain Company's potential weaknesses, and Guy thought to deal with it—again.

"Madame Fitzhugh," he began amiably. "A trading post makes a profit, and guarantees its safety, only by observing the strictest neutrality. The *bois d'arc* must be available to all who wish to trade for it, I'm sure you and your husband will agree. For your own safety."

He wasn't so sure they agreed. Dust Devil had made it a life mission to fight the traditional enemies of the Cheyenne, especially the Absaroka, or Crows, but also the Assiniboin. She was a Suhtai Cheyenne, and thus of the special clan that largely governed the tribal religion and its sacred symbols, including the medicine hat. Fitzhugh himself was more Cheyenne than European these days, speaking his wife's tongue adequately, and favoring her people in all tribal matters. If the post made its bias too obvious, it would collapse—and sink them all.

"I reckon I'll trade where the trading is," said Brokenleg quietly, overriding Dust Devil. "That's how it's got to be."

They toasted the new company uneasily, knowing the risk even better than they knew the reward. The Cheyenne problem in the north. A problem with Mexican licensing in the south—a license they needed to put them close to the Kiowa and Comanche. And looming like a rumbling volcano over them all, the ruthless competition of two giant firms with deep experience in the fur and hide business, Chouteau in the north and Bent to the south.

"I'll tell Monsieur LaBarge we'll be aboard at the fifth hour," he said. "Have your engagés ready by the fourth, with their packs. He will wish to sail at dawn. Mrs. Straus and I will board this evening and say *au revoir* to all of you and our sons at Independence.

Eighteen-year-old David would be Dance's clerk, reading and figuring for the trader; sixteen-year-old Maxim would clerk for Fitzhugh. Guy had fought it fiercely, fearing he might never see his dear flesh and blood again, but acceded at the last: what papa could stand in the way of sons whose eyes gazed toward the shining mountains?

Chapter Two

A red ball of fire rolled across the broad Missouri valley ahead, so that the black waters of the river seemed to rise out of a cauldron of fire. Not a tree lined the banks to catch the gold of the setting sun, but only grass, glowing ochre in the last light. Already the sky above the bluffs had turned indigo.

Before them, the river vibrated with life as an endless stream of black buffalo swam north like some giant snake out of the skies. Brokenleg's senses demanded noise; demanded the thunder of a vast herd on the move; insisted at least upon the splash and froth and bawling of a thousand animals, a column a hundred yards wide, swimming a half a mile of water en route to summer grass. But he heard no noise. Countless buffalo, backlit against the dying sun, swam as patiently and silently as beaver, scarcely disturbing the powerful river. On occasion this vast black bridge bowed downstream, toward the idling *Platte*, which lay anchored in still waters away from the main channel because there was not a stick on shore to tie it to.

He couldn't fathom the silence. Not even when the water-blackened beasts clambered up the slippery bank gleaming orangely off to the right did they shake and bawl and thunder the earth. Instead, the great procession slid across grassy bottoms and up an apricot bluff and vanished into the dark sky, like a mirage. He could see no end to them in the south; no end to the humped beasts that dominated the short-grass prairies from Mexico far into the English possessions to the north. If the parade continued much longer, LaBarge would probably stay the night here, no doubt irritable because the nearest woodyard lay far ahead and he'd anchored too close to the current.

It seemed an omen, all these buffalo, as common as ants, rippling the sunset light before him, making the river hump and shatter into silver splinters that seemed to bounce off a few high wisps of cloud above. He'd come to have the same instinct about the sacred animals as Dust Devil, seeing them as something much more than meat and hide, clothing and tools, glue and horns. The buffalo was more; it was holy; the gift of the One Above, Dust Devil would have said, for the use of the People. He waited, trying to fathom in himself whether the silence of tens of thousands of buffalo was a sign of welcome—or something else. He needed that welcome, though he would never admit it. He glanced covertly at Dust Devil, standing beside him up on the hurricane deck beside the texas where they could see, and sensed her fierce anger. A bad omen, then, all those sacred buffalo marching up into a great hole in the sky.

They'd been stalled for two hours there in the land of the Santee and Yankton Sioux. These buffalo were the first they'd seen this trip, though they'd been looking ever since the stop at Bellevue, where the army performed its final inspection to ascertain whether the packet contained nefarious spirits. It found none except normal ship's stores for passenger use. Not until they'd reached a certain woodyard below Sergeant Bluff one moonless evening had spirits in wooden casks appeared in the low hold. None of the passengers knew it save for himself, young Maxim Straus, and Dust Devil, who frowned at it all. Those plus Captain LaBarge and his mate and two crewmen. Without those illegal spirits, the whole enterprise would collapse. With them, they had a fighting chance against the giant American Fur, with all its ruthless power and subterfuge—and vast stores of the illegal commodity.

At first some of the passengers and his own engagés shot at the buffalo, killing a few, which were snared by the crew and hauled aboard, rivering water and blood. But the shooting palled, especially when dead bloody buffaloes spun and bobbed silently downstream in the opaque aquamarine water, useless meat. The boat lay on the soft-lit river as silent as the ghostly herd that shook loose of the clawing stream on the north and trotted up into the night.

He didn't speak. No one spoke. He hadn't heard a word for an hour. He liked being there. For the first time in moons, he felt right. He'd started to feel right back near Bellevue, where the Platte, a mile wide and six inches deep and mostly rolling sand, debouched into the Missouri. And where the bankside forests thinned, finally surrendering to grass. And where the moist oppressive air gave way to something drier and cleaner in his hungry lungs, and the scent of prairie replaced the fetid odor of hardwood forest. Above the Platte, the color of the river changed from chocolate to murky green. Below Bellevue, the trees had hemmed him like prison bars.

He'd borne St. Louis only by large infusions of corn spirits, quietly, nightly, staving off the demons that choked and throttled him until he bolted up in the night, sweating and cursing. Somehow he'd survived, eyeing the denizens of that rich city as narrowly as they must have eyed him, in his velvety fringed elkskin britches and calico shirt, his unkempt beard, and a red mane flowing from a half bald crown of skull down to his shoulders. He'd had to do it, and he did it.

Straus had booked a cabin for him on the *Platte*, but even though it was the most spacious available it closed in on him until, scarcely out of St. Louis, he'd fled out onto the boiler deck, and vaulted up the companionway and rolled into a buffalo robe on the hurricane deck, just aft of the texas. Dust Devil hadn't joined him. She had taken to her cabin as if it was a fine eighteen-hide lodge, with slaves who'd bring her tea or coffee at the slightest wave of her hard hand. She liked slaves, and had never ceased pestering him for some, especially a few Crow women she could persecute.

The sun slid behind a bank of clouds along the northwest horizon, gilding their tops until Brokenleg thought for an aching moment they might be the western mountains, snow-capped, blue and royal. But they weren't, and it was much too soon to entertain such thoughts. It left him disappointed in the graying light. He felt almost right, but not quite. These prairies were tallgrass and thick, dampening him almost as much as the dank forests. Not yet free, not yet. But better than St. Louis.

Odd how Guy Straus had sensed it in him and sympathized, although not a word had passed between them. On several occasions Straus had offered his carriage and trotters for a jaunt out of town, and Brokenleg had taken him up on it, driving hard out Market or Chestnut or Washington into the wooded hills to the west. But it never helped. Sometimes Straus took him to the comfortable, decaying Planters House to dine with Robert Campbell, legendary fur man who'd come out to the rendezvous with the Sublettes, Fitzpatrick, Bridger, and all the rest. They'd whiled away an occasional afternoon over thick aromatic coffee and fiery French liqueurs, talked of men they both knew like Joe Meek or Milt Sublette or Davey Jackson, and icy rivers and shining mountains and lupine-strewn meadows they'd both seen, and that had helped. He'd learned, then, that Straus had borrowed from Campbell to help provision the Rocky Mountain Company. But in the end, nothing helped much, nothing save for this, a flight out to the high and lonely lands, disturbed by nothing but the wind.

Above, in the pilot house, he heard the voices of the master, LaBarge, and his pilot, Roux, making fast the packet for the night. The boiler fires had long since died, and with the soft chuff of steam from the escapement, so the packet lay like a dead thing upon the water, anchored for and aft. Below, the dinner gong sounded, and Brokenleg knew he'd have to face the companionway, always a torture for a man without a good knee. Deck passengers, including his ten engagés, were on their own for meals, but cabin passengers were served on foldaway tables set in the men's saloon, forward on the boiler deck, a tobacco-stained public area between the banks of port and starboard cabins. Fresh buffalo hump, boss ribs, tongue tonight, he knew. Wordlessly, Dust Devil drew her shawl around her and slid off to the companionway, heeding the bell.

"It's not a place I'd choose for an anchorage, Mister Fitzhugh." The voice eddied down from above, and Brokenleg saw LaBarge peering down at him from the pilot house. "These crossings have been known to last for a day or two. We may be here a while."

"Just seeing them—just seeing—" he stopped, unable to convey something that burned in him in ways beyond the captivity of words. Why did everyone want to talk? Couldn't they just leave him to his silence?

"And an arrow's shot from shore," LaBarge continued. "Shallow enough for them to wade most of the way out here, too. The Yanktonai, I mean. Here we are, stalled, in the only country where we've had trouble for years. And I've got only three cords aboard, and most of it green cottonwood, so I'll need the rosin. Let's hope all that banging didn't reach the wrong ears."

Fitzhugh said nothing.

"If you're inclined, Mister Fitzhugh, you might put one or two of your engagés on watch tonight, up here on the hurricane deck."

"Do it myself," Brokenleg said.

"I'll have some roustabouts on the foredeck, watching

for sawyers or driftwood all night. They can snare the firewood and keep watch."

"Last of the herd's swimming right now. You could get up steam and go a mile or two before it gets pitch dark."

"How do you know that, Mister Fitzhugh?"

"Just know it."

LaBarge laughed softly. "I believe you. My pilot and I know this river the way you men of the mountains know the wilderness. But I suppose we'll wait; take our chances with the Sioux."

Below, amid the motley crowd on the main deck, his engagés performed their evening chores. Oxen, horses, and mules, packed tightly into a temporary pen lashed to the foredeck, were being watered and fed with precious hay and oats stowed down in the hold. Many nights, when LaBarge was able to anchor at an island, the animals were led out to pasture or picketed on grass beside the packet under careful guard. But not this night, with the packet riding a backwater eighty yards from shore. The scrape of shovels and the acrid scent of manure told him his men were cleaning the pen in the dusk, dumping the waste overboard.

Beside the corral hulked the three Pittsburgh wagons they'd decided on. These were high-wheeled monsters with watertight boxes to protect the cargo while fording streams, useful for hauling tradegoods out to the villages and returning with the robes. They stood now without their sheets, their bows naked in the twilight. These giants had proved their worth on the long flats of the Santa Fe Trail, but none had ever been brought into the rougher country of the northwest, and Brokenleg considered them a gamble.

Every one of his ten engagés was a Creole, and every one had experience on the great river. He'd asked his old mountain friend Samson Trudeau, back there in St. Louis, to put together a seasoned crew for him, annual contracts at twelve dollars a month. Brokenleg knew almost none of the engagés, but he'd learn about them soon enough, and probably fight a few of them, too. And he supposed that one or two were being paid by American Fur to report everything to the powerful men up at Fort Union. He'd weed them out soon enough, with fists if necessary. Those things didn't stay hidden forever.

Dance had the larger crew, twenty teamsters drawn from the small settlements near the Missouri and the Mississippi. He had to haul his entire stock of tradegoods and furnishings out the Santa Fe Trail, a task that ate up men and wagons—and capital. The Rocky Mountain Company was investing far more in its southern post than in his, on the Yellowstone.

The dinner bell gonged a second time.

"The second bell, Mister Fitzhugh," said LaBarge from the pilot house. "You'll miss the boss rib and tongue."

Fresh buffalo meat! The first since last fall. The lordly buffalo's flesh was hard, tough, chewy—except for the soft, delicious humpmeat, which made a roast better than any beef he'd ever tackled, or the tongue, sweet and moist and flavorsome. It set his stomach to growling, and he limped toward the companionway, wishing he could hurry his bad leg.

The hollowness that Guy Straus felt in his heart was something new in his experience. It felt as if he'd lost everything except life itself. That wasn't the case, he reminded himself, and the chances were excellent that, far from losing, he'd win a fortune. But not even Yvonne's steadying presence in that rude Independence inn allayed the underlying dread that possessed him.

They'd taken the *Platte*—LaBarge's packet—as far as Independence, along with all the rest. They'd return to St. Louis on the next riverboat heading east, one of the dozen that plied the Big Muddy between St. Joseph and Independence and St. Louis. He wanted to see everything, every wage-man his capital had engaged, every Conestoga he'd contracted to buy and have refitted here; every ox and horse and mule. There were sharpers at every hand in this robust village sprawled at the edge of Indian lands. Independence thrived as an outfitter for the Santa Fe Trail; the place to buy mules and oxen, Conestogas and Pittsburghs, and light wagons; the place to collect yoke and harness. The place to warehouse hides and furs for transshipment down the river. The goods he'd purchased in St. Louis and here, and the men he'd hired back there and here, had cost him more than the entire available capital of Straus et Fils. And with everything riding on an investment as terrible as that, he had ridden the packet west so that he might examine every spoked wheel, every hickory or ash tongue, every watertight box, every wagon-sheet waterproofed with linseed oil, every fat and well-shod ox and mule.

He trusted Dance and Fitzhugh utterly, but they were new at aspects of all this, inexperienced in business, and certain facets of provisioning and selling would depend on him alone. He had to see, see with his own eyes, the whole of his investment; judge with his own seasoned grasp of human nature the quality of the new employees of the Rocky Mountain Company.

And there was still another final, overpowering, gripping reason for him to come upriver this far. Maxim and David. He could delay a little longer the wrenching loss of his two slim, thoughtful, adventuresome sons; one heading southwest, the other northwest, both into wild barbarous lands with dangers lurking at every hand. He did not know how he'd endure it, and wondered why he'd succumbed to their constant badgering, their demanding, their shining hopes. True, Dance needed a clerk; someone to read correspondence and keep the books and tally goods and sort prime robes from poor ones. Who better than his own David? God knows, the young man had danced through his studies, mastered four tongues and could understand a fifth, and had a business sense in his young head that delighted his father. But Maxim, Maxim, only sixteen, a stripling boy. If David could go, nothing less suited Maxim, and between them, his sons had worn him down. Even dear Clothilde, thirteen, had begged to go, at least for a season, but there he'd put his foot down firmly.

Not everything had gone smoothly. Jamie Dance's idea of collecting osage orange bow wood had come too late, and they'd gathered only a few dozen suitable sticks bank-side while the packet crew was fueling at the woodyards. These few were given to Fitzhugh because the wood was prized so highly up on the Yellowstone. And the wagons awaiting them at Independence were to be equipped with spare tongues of suitable hardwood, but his inspection revealed that none had been supplied. He'd uncovered a wheel with cracked felloes, too, and other defects. Three of the men engaged for the Mexican post failed to appear, and a search of the rough dramshops of Independence revealed no trace of them. No replacements could be found; it was already late in the shipping season, and those bound out the Santa Fe Trail had departed long since.

In spite of all that, the two outfits were assembled swiftly. It took only a day for the rest of the Yellowstone provisions to be loaded in the cramped hold of the *Platte*, and only one more for the Mexican outfit to be assembled and loaded into the giant wagons gathered at Westport, well up from the levee.

The first bad moment came at dawn, when LaBarge's roustabouts were firing up the boilers, and heavy black smoke from the twin chimneys lowered down upon them through a gray fog that the sun would soon burn off. He and Yvonne had stood on the levee watching Fitzhugh's men drive the bellowing oxen and whickering mules aboard and pen them. Maxim, his son, his flesh and blood, stood beside them, too excited to notice the grief etching the faces of his parents. But at last, when all was stowed and steam chuffed from the escapement above, Fitzhugh had limped over to Guy, given him a rough mountain embrace, just the sort of emotional hug that had always faintly embarrassed Guy, and said his goodbyes.

"Adieu, papa, maman," Maxim had bawled, his eyes bright. "See how well I'll do!"

"Be careful!" Yvonne had cried, reaching for Maxim as he'd danced off. "Listen to Monsieur Fitzhugh!"

"Go with God, Maxim," Guy had yelled at the skipping lad, feeling desolated.

Moments later the whistle shrilled, and deckhands hauled in the manila lines. A violent shudder shook the riverboat as the sidewheels cranked into water, and the boat edged from the bank, a writhing thing off to its doom in an unmapped, unknown land.

"Don't let him go, Guy! Stop it!" she'd cried, grasping at his arm. "We'll never see him again. My baby. He's too young. Oh, why did you ever—" She stopped suddenly. She'd started to accuse him, he knew.

He watched the riverboat churn up the slate-colored river into the morning fog, and vanish silently and mysteriously. About him, rough-dressed men and a handful of women turned off the levee and wandered up the bluff and back to Independence, a sprawl of log houses, frame stores, and a few brick buildings that were signs of permanence out there at the edge of the Indian country. He felt emptied; half his fortune riding the dangerous river; his youngest son plunging into a wild land.

Over at his camp, Jamie had been too busy even to attend to this parting. He'd said his goodbyes to his old trapping partner the previous night, when the last of the Mexico outfit had been offloaded. Guy had sighed, hollowly, and led Yvonne back to the Republic House, dodging pigs and chickens, long ox-trains in the rutted streets, and sinister scarecrows of men who looked like they belonged behind bars rather than free on the streets. No matter how he had tried, the vision of profit, of returns, of comfort, the thing that had sustained him in all this, wouldn't return to his mind, and he had chastened himself for getting snared into this mad enterprise.

The departure of the wagon train had gone a little easier two days later. Santa Fe and Bent's Fort and Mexico were known locales beyond the far horizon, and this outfit would roll to a place on earth he could fathom, unlike Fitzhugh's outfit, which would drop off the rim of the world. And David had reached eighteen and manhood, ready to begin his life, unlike Maxim. Still, when he watched the other half of his fortune, and his other son, rattle off into the west that morning—all alone, because Yvonne decided not to venture out to the camp—he'd felt shaken. Too much could happen. For any Comanche warrior, David's scalp would be as much a trophy as any other.

Now they waited at Republic House for the next eastbound packet.

"Are you satisfied?" Yvonne asked, accusingly, over breakfast.

"Our sons will come home men," he replied.

"Will they?"

"With a fortune in hides, if I can sell them well."

"But we didn't need a fortune. We've been perfectly comfortable."

"The west is there, waiting. A continent, wrapped in beauty. It sings its song to every man in this village, and our city down the river, Yvonne. I could not resist, and neither could our sons and neither will Clothilde when she's a little older. Men climb mountains simply to say they did, and I—and our new partners—wrest wealth from the unknown world just because we must. I'll go see it next year. Not just now, *bien-aimée.* I've so much to do. But soon. It lures me. I listen to Campbell or Pratte or young Chouteau himself sing the songs of the shining mountains, or our own Brokenleg talk of his in-law Cheyennes in all their savage strength, and I'm lost."

Yvonne smiled bitterly.

Chapter Three

Well before dawn, gray light skidded along the hurricane deck, slid over the humped form of Brokenleg, and into his face, prying his eyes open. He awakened instantly. Years in the mountains had taught him to sleep lightly, and respond to the subtlest change in the rhythms of the night. Twice he'd awakened last night, reacting to something, but it had been the night-noises of the deck passengers far below, men relieving themselves over the coaming.

The buffalo robe wrapped around him failed to protect him from the dawn chill, but he was used to sleeping cold. Dew whitened the hurricane deck, and even the robe, which he wore skin-out for protection again the sudden night breezes, felt cold and damp to his hand. He studied the misted shore, knowing how tribesmen loved to pounce at this hour when their victims lay sleep-drugged and quiet in their robes. But he saw nothing across the shallow waters.

Below, out of sight beneath him, men stirred, and the clang and thump of a day began. The cook would be starting his fire in the galley stove. Deckhands would be scraping mud out of the boiler, if they hadn't the night before, and screwing the manhole cover back in place. The river carried so much silt that the boiler had to be opened each day and the mud scraped out, lest the pipes clog and the boat blow itself to smithereens. A solid clank below told Brokenleg that the cover had been slammed shut and was being wrenched down. He'd smell the cold smoke of half-burned wood soon.

Men and animals stirred. The Rocky Mountain Company's oxen, milch cows, mules and horses stomped restlessly, waiting for water and hay, unhappy at their close confinement. A mule kicked, and all the beasts in the pen milled, threatening to burst through the fragile lashup that held them to the foredeck, just back of the capstan behind the duckbilled bow.

Time to get up. His bad leg hurt as it always did after the night had stiffened it. He could never figure which was worse—the pain of morning, or the pain of evening, after he'd spent a day worrying and abusing the torn muscle and cartilage and badly mended bones. He clambered to his feet and rolled up his robe, a good thick winter-hair one that had served him for years. Dust Devil had given it to him, tanned and softened by her own hard hand. Nothing she touched remained in its original form, including himself. She'd tanned him about as well as the robe, he thought, pounding his brains and liver into his unrepentant hide and then working his rawhide soul into something more tender and useful. He picked up his heavy octagon-barreled Hawken and wiped dew from it, checking to make sure a cap embraced the nipple. Pinpricks of rust pitted the old mountain weapon, just as they pitted him, he thought. If his lock had been flint and frizzen, he'd have changed the priming powder in the pan on a morning like this.

Smoke belched from the twin chimneys just forward, and lowered malevolently upon him, slowly turning the packet into a living thing. Tribesmen thought the fireboats were alive, were giant beasts that could fight the current and the wind; and not a few infants along the great river had been named Steamboat. He limped toward the forward companionway, facing the ordeal of a one-footed descent to the boiler deck and then the main deck so that he could relieve his bladder in one of the privy closets that hung out from the coaming just aft of the eighteen-foot paddlewheels.

"Well, Mister Fitzhugh, we escaped the attentions of the Yanktonais after all," said Captain LaBarge, from his open door at the texas. "Now all we have to do is find wood."

"If they're around, they're chasing buffler."

"Let's hope they do. I've wood enough for six or eight miles, depending on the wind and current. Woodyard's about five. If they're around the yard, we've got problems."

"Woodcutters there?"

"No. Too dangerous. We'll cut our own. It's a good bottom full of cottonwood and willow."

"Deadwood?"

"We've girdled a lot of trees over the years. I should say, American Fur captains have. We're getting the advantage."

"I'll put my men on it."

LaBarge smiled. "I was going to put them on it. Every man, crew and passenger."

"I'll get Dust Devil up here with a carbine. She's some shot, and she's got Injun eyes."

"Obliged. But with her I'm never sure which way she'll point the barrel."

Brokenleg grinned.

A muffled voice erupted from the speaking tube in the pilot house, above. "Steam's almost up, sir. Two minutes."

An erratic chuff of it popped from the escapement pipe behind them. LaBarge nodded to the pilot, who peered down at him from over the wainscoting of the pilothouse. On the main deck, the mate organized crews, one at the forward capstan to raise the wrought-iron anchor chain, the other at the rear to muscle up the smaller stream anchor. Somewhere below, two muffled bells rang and a shudder vibrated through the boat. Deckhands weighed anchor, winding chain around the capstan. The freed boat suddenly swung loose and began drifting. Then the paddles cranked over, bit water with a powerful splash, and the *Platte* exerted its own living will against the seductions of the river.

"You're off before breakfast, Captain."

"We can eat any time. On the river, time's of the essence, Mister Fitzhugh. I prefer to be off well before this, as soon as we can see ahead. Now—if you'll permit me—"

Brokenleg watched him swing up the narrow stairwell to the lofty pilothouse atop the texas. He felt a new rhythm, more disciplined and violent, as the packet eased into the main channel, a vicious aquamarine flood that meandered from bank to bank, as icy as the mountain snows that formed it. He limped forward and braved the first companionway, preferring to clamber down facing the stairs and hanging onto both oak rails. He had to do it one-footed, a series of small leaps to lower steps. Whenever he landed on his bad leg, pain shot ruthlessly up it and exploded in his brain. It was easier to climb the stairs.

On the boiler deck he changed his mind, and limped instead through the glassed doors into the gloomy men's saloon where a youth wearing a white apron was unfolding tables for breakfast. The place was redolent with the residue of a thousand cigars, the scummy swamps of unemptied spittoons, and the more acrid odor of spilled spirits. Now it lay dead and dank, but each night the saloon blossomed under bright lamplight shattered by cut glass chimneys, and the usual poker and monte games drew the crowds.

He tried the door marked eleven, knowing it would not be locked because Dust Devil never locked it. If it was locked, then the underwater spirits could not escape. On land, she never closed doors or fastened the lodge flap tightly because under-the-earth spirits might be trapped, and evil come upon them. He was less worried about escaping spirits than about invading mortals.

She lay bare-shouldered under her rare, cream-colored buffalo robe on the bunk, watching him disdainfully, her straight hair loose and silky about her face. There was always disdain in her eye for whites and for any tribesmen other than her People. She'd never gotten accustomed to sheets and pillows and blankets, but she welcomed the cotton lint mattress joyously. She didn't disdain that, at least, even if those who invented it were beneath contempt. He grunted, set his Hawken in a corner, threw his robe beside it, and pulled the white-enameled metal chamberpot from its nest under the bunk, and turned his back to her—why, he didn't know. A white man's modesty. Cheyenne modesty. No northern tribe was more puritanical. He rather preferred it: Dust Devil would be disdainfully faithful all her days. In a few moments he felt relieved, and ready to cope with the day.

Beneath them, under the deck, the boiler thundered and groaned and snapped hydrophobically, straining at its thick rivets. That was half the reason he couldn't sleep in here—all that pent-up violent power just below, like a buffler stampede.

"I will make the coffee come," Dust Devil said, rolling out of her robe. She wore nothing, and the sight of her slim, lithe body and velvet belly, as bright as apricots, caught his eye and flooded his loins with need. She knew exactly what she was doing to him—the mischief in her disdainful black eyes betrayed it—but she ignored him and reached for her whited doeskin dress, lifting it over the jet hair which hung loosely over her naked shoulders. Her raised arms lifted her wide breasts, and drew her belly taut.

He caught her just as her mocking face vanished behind her skirts, and the fringes of the hem slid over her breasts. He clamped her to him, like a kicking fawn in a sack, sliding his hard hands over her smooth back, feeling the corrugations of her backbone under his eager fingers.

She snorted. "I will make them bring coffee," she said from somewhere inside of a writhing mass of velvety doeskin. "You sleep up there in the sky instead of here, while

I wait all night. Maybe I should go up there on the hurricane deck."

He laughed, and pressed her closer, his hands rounding over her hard small buttocks.

"I must greet Sun and pray, or—the underwater spirits—" He tugged at her dress, reconquering lost ground. "I'm Suhtai," she reminded him earnestly.

"I ain't anything except male," he retorted, tugging the dress back over her blue-black hair, leaving wisps of it on her face and under his searching lips.

"Is this any way to greet Sun?" she whispered, her hands tugging at his elkskin shirt, lifting it higher. "It is better in a warm lodge in the winter. Not a cold cabin in a fireboat. You wait."

He laughed, feeling the change in her.

"You need more wives. When we get back to the good land of Sweet Medicine, I will find you more wives from my clan. Or slaves. We need slaves. Assiniboin women. I will make them tan robes," she whispered. "And come to you at night. I get tired of this. Why can't you be Cheyenne?"

"What do Cheyenne do?"

"Make war, not love," she breathed in his ear. "Bring me some Crow scalps."

He laughed. "This is how I count coup."

But she had ceased struggling. He felt the packet quarter around a bight or an oxbow, sliding sideways with the current in a strange, uncontrolled motion that paralleled his own. Now her swift fingers loosened his fringed buckskin britches and pulled at him eagerly, tugging him not toward the narrow lower bunk but the floor. She'd lived with his bad leg for years, and knew the ways to cope with it, and practiced them on the hard planking of the cabin.

"Oh, you longknifes," she muttered. "What a way to greet Sun."

* * *

The woodyard lay ahead on the right, an enameled green streak of forest half a mile distant. Brokenleg squinted at it through eyes tortured by summer sunlight lancing off the reckless waters, marveling at the astonishing sight of woods in the grassy trench they'd navigated for a hundred miles. The high-plains light affected everything, burning the sky azure, almost black; careening off the white-enameled packet, magnifying the mountain people crowding the foredeck.

He turned to Trudeau, the competent engagé who would probably be second in command at the trading post. "Samson, the captain wants every able-bodied man aboard to cut wood. Fast. His deckmen will hand out axes and bucksaws when we land. The Yanktonais have been stirring up trouble for two years."

"I'll tell our men. We cut wood so fast we don't get any arrows in us, *n'est-ce pas?"*

"Cut long lengths. Just get the wood aboard and they'll cut it to length. That firebox eats wood—eighteen cords a day, LaBarge tells me."

"What about the Indians?"

"The pilot'll be watching from the pilothouse. You come running if you hear a shot, or the ship's bell. I'll have Mrs. Fitzhugh watching from the hurricane deck. She's got eyes I wish I had."

"Maybe we should be armed, *oui?"*

"No. You'll be carrying saws and axes we can't afford to lose."

Trudeau grunted, gesturing toward the hold. Among the Rocky Mountain Company's tradegoods were hundreds of axes and hatchets.

"The engagés, they won't like having no rifles."

Fitzhugh peered at the other passengers milling on deck, trappers and traders of one sort or another, he thought. Two squaws, both wives of traders at American Fur Company posts. Half the bearded motley crowd carried rifles and not a few had Arkansas toothpicks or Green River knives as well. A rough and murderous lot who shot before they asked who they were shooting at. Fitzhugh felt a certain empathy. It was live or die in the mountains, and the difference between the two could be split seconds, or who saw whom first. Still—these buckskinned, greasy, hirsute, gaptoothed ruffians could get them into trouble fast.

He felt the throb of the two steam pistons change, and heard a new rhythm as the pitman rods cranked the paddlewheels slower. Deckhands gathered at the starboard gangway, ready to lower a stage to the muddy bank. At the bow, a man with a marked pole stabbed at the water, shouting depths up to the pilot. The *Platte*, loaded, drew four feet. As the packet slid out of the main channel into turbid backwaters, a great peace settled over it, as if it enjoyed a moment of leisure in the slackwater.

At about three hundred yards, LaBarge, up in the pilothouse, scanned the shore with his spy glass, and then stiffened. Fitzhugh heard him yelling down the tube to the engineers, and caught the clanging of bells as the paddlewheels ground to a tentative halt. The boat settled low, barely moving. Fitzhugh squinted toward shore, wondering what had stalled the boat, but the glare of the river under a June sun dazzled his eyes to tears.

"Mister Fitzhugh," yelled LaBarge from high above. "Please come up."

He did, swinging his bad leg up the companionway furiously, using his powerful arms to avoid steps altogether. He stopped at the hurricane deck, his lungs burning. LaBarge had descended that far, spyglass in hand. Wordlessly he handed it to Brokenleg.

"Yanktonai," the master announced dourly.

Fitzhugh adjusted the focus to his leaking eyes and peered through the bobbing circle, unable to hold the glass steady because of his violent exertion. He saw thirty or so bronzed men, most of them wearing only a breechclout and coup feathers.

None painted. All armed; mostly with bows, but three or four with fusils or muskets of some sort. Hard to tell.

"For all practical purposes, we're out of wood. We can make the opposite bank anywhere in the next mile or two," LaBarge said darkly. "After that we hunt driftwood."

"They're not concealing themselves and not painted, captain. I think we both know what they'll say."

"I do," LaBarge replied crisply. "And I don't have much choice. We're out of wood, and they can beat us to the next woodlot—and the next. And I don't know of any beached driftwood or islands along here."

"Why'd you summon me?"

LaBarge smiled quickly. "You're a known man, Brokenleg. You've a hold full of tradegoods—and I need some gewgaws . . . at reasonable cost. You're in command of ten good Creoles—seasoned Indian traders. And you'll avoid war—which is the only thought burning in the heads of those mountain cretins on deck. And that's not all. You can speak Siouan dialect, and know sign language. We'll negotiate. I need your help. My mate will keep an eye on those ruffians brandishing their rifles on the foredeck. And I'd like your sensible engagés to keep watch as well. I want no shooting."

Fitzhugh grinned, a vast amiable understanding growing between himself and Captain LaBarge. But the captain didn't wait. He barked commands, and as Fitzhugh sprang painfully down the companionways, he felt the wheels bite into the river and guide the packet toward the fated bank.

On the main deck the mob had spotted the Yanktonais now, and men crowded the starboard rail brandishing rifles. On the closing shore, knots of tribesmen stood alertly, bows in hand but not drawn. Thirty or forty, Brokenleg thought, with more—boys probably—holding horses back among the cottonwoods.

"I'm going to get me that red nigger chief," bragged a graying man in grease-blackened buckskins. He eased his mountain rifle down to the rail, and squatted behind it.

"Gentlemen!" bawled a voice from above. Fitzhugh turned to see the master, LaBarge, leaning out of the pilothouse, a megaphone at his lips. "Put your weapons up. We're going to parley for some wood. These are Sioux—Yanktonais—and they'll want a few trinkets for the wood from their land."

Trudeau gazed anxiously at Brokenleg, who nodded.

Most of the rough assemblage lowered their rifle butts to the deck. But not the old braggart, who peered down his barrel from heavy-lidded eyes.

"Mate!" yelled LaBarge, and pointed.

Catlike, the mate yanked the rifle upward and out of the old mountaineer's hands. The gray giant leapt up, yellow murder in his eye and an Arkansas toothpick in his hand faster than Fitzhugh was able to see. But he found himself surrounded by deckmen and engagés, and slowly slid his glinting weapon into its belt sheath, his expression lethal.

"Look to your duties," LaBarge yelled from above. Ship's hands gathered at the companionway to lower a stage, and readied manila lines to anchor the boat to stumps along the bank.

Brokenleg didn't like it. He was about to walk down that gangplank and parley with the chiefs, and if any of that undisciplined mob on the main deck so much as lifted a rifle, the first arrow would pierce his own guts.

It wasn't hard to pick out the chief now, as the boat slid into shore, riding stilled paddles. The headman wore three coup feathers, carried a new rifle, and sported a grizzly claw necklace, formidable medicine. He stood almost six feet, and all of his honey-colored flesh stretched thinly over a massive bone frame. The headman's gaze sought him out and their eyes locked in a testing of wills.

The headman wasted no time on preliminaries. Even as the boat nestled into the shore, he addressed Fitzhugh, who stood at the opened gangway. "You cannot have our wood. It is ours. You have killed our trees," he said in his Siouan tongue.

"What do you want for it?" Fitzhugh replied.

"You cannot have it."

"We will find some across the river, then."

"I will come onto the fireboat and talk."

Fitzhugh nodded. "Lower the stage," he said to the hands. "The chief will parley." And then to the headman: "Just you. No others. You will be safe; I declare it."

The chief held up two fingers.

"Two, then."

Forward, a deckhand tossed a manila hawser to a warrior, who wound it around a stump, anchoring the boat. Fitzhugh didn't like it until he spotted the slipknot around a kevel. The stage thumped into grass, and the chief, followed by a powerful subchief with battle scars puckered across his left arm and ribs, walked fearlessly onto the main deck.

"I am Crow Beak," he said, not introducing his colleague.

"Robert Fitzhugh."

"Brokenleg," the chief said.

That was no surprise. His bad leg seemed to travel before him from one campfire and village to the next. "We've stopped for wood."

"It is ours. You must not kill our trees."

"We will pay for it. A mirror and vermilion for each man. And some powder for you."

"One rifle for each of us. And two handfuls of balls. And much powder. And a keg of the spirit-water-that-makes-men-crazy."

"No. Too much. We will go to another place for wood."

Crow Beak studied the diminished pile, down to a dozen long sticks, near the firebox, and smiled. "It is as I said. These things you will give us for our wood."

From above, LaBarge called down. "We're running out of time, Mister Fitzhugh. If I'm to make the far shore and safety, we must be off. Offer them a cask of spirits."

Fitzhugh grinned. "Make the ship fast, Captain. Forget the steam. Me and Crow Beak here, we're going to have us a party."

Chapter Four

11 juin, 1841

Cher papa,

It will be a long time before this reaches you. I will give it to Captain LaBarge to take downriver with him, and I suppose you will read it when you pour coffee for him in our salon and get his news. But perhaps it will arrive sooner, if we meet the American Fur Company packet going downriver, and I can give this to its master.

Until today, we had an uneventful trip. I am trying hard to learn all that there is to know about the trading business. Monsieur Fitzhugh patiently answers all my questions, even though I ask him many. Do you know what a split robe is? That is one that is composed of two halves, sewn together, and it is not as valuable as a whole robe. A buffalo is a heavy animal, and sometimes it is hard for the squaws to peel the hide off in one piece, so they slice down the backbone as well as the gut, and take two pieces.

Even though you bought me cabin passage, I like to sleep on the main deck like the other engagés. M. Fitzhugh has made Samson Trudeau second in command, and I think that is good. M. Trudeau has *savoir-faire* and is good with the engagés. M. Fitzhugh knows French, but his accent is atrocious, so he mostly gives his instructions to M. Trudeau, who passes the word to the engagés. There is only one engagé I don't much like, Emile Gallard, and he seems always insolent and crafty. There is work to do each day, such as feeding and watering the livestock, and taking them to shore to graze whenever we can, especially evenings. There's no time for it when we stop for wood, which is often.

We sleep mostly under the three Pittsburgh wagons on deck, and when the weather is bad we put up the wagon-sheets and have a perfect tent that suits our needs. When we are cold, we can stand next to the firebox or boiler and warm up fast. I am taking care not to catch a cold, so don't worry. Sometimes violent thunder showers pepper the river and the packet, so we all take cover somewhere under the boiler deck. The rain and hail are so thick at those times I wonder how the pilot can even see. But M. LaBarge never stops, except at night when no one can see the river.

I have learned that the Missouri is a treacherous, changing beast, and never the same month to month and year to year. It is full of logs and driftwood M. LaBarge calls sawyers, and if one strikes the hull it can poke a hole in it. Then we must head for the nearest bank and make repairs. So far, the water has been high, but soon we will be hitting sand-bars, and then we must work past them with spars. I can hardly wait to see that.

I am proud that I am living on deck, as an engagé, rather than living in the cabin. All the engagés have been employed up the river, and they tell me lots of things about the Indians there, and the weather, and all the tricks used by American Fur Company to drive out the opposition. And here I thought I liked M. Chouteau. He's always been so kind and neighborly.

I don't think Mme. Fitzhugh likes me much. She is such a beautiful woman that I always tremble when I see her. But she looks at me as if I don't exist, and she doesn't know how much I admire her diamond-shaped coppery face, and long black hair with tints of blue, and her perfect white teeth. The engagés tell me that her people, the Cheyenne, are proud and fearless and make beautiful art with quills and beads and paints. But she is haughty, and I know she scorns all people except her Cheyenne, and thinks we are all nothing more than maggots. I think she even has that opinion of M. Fitzhugh, though I shouldn't say it, and you will scold me for thinking it. But when she talks of the Cheyenne, her face lights up, and that look in her eyes, the disdain, goes away. Oh, I could fall in love with an Indian woman as proud as that! Perhaps I will come home with a beautiful mountain bride. That would shock you, *papa,* and especially *maman.* But I like her better than the silly girls of St. Louis because she is dignified and doesn't giggle. You would approve of a wife like that.

And now I will tell you what happened today. We were almost out of firewood. M. LaBarge tells me the *Platte* burns eighteen cords a day—think of it! And there is so little wood here, where nothing but grass grows in the river valley. But now and then are flats full of cottonwoods, and the crews of the packets stop and load up. Everyone must help cut and haul wood, all passengers, or else it takes forever before the packet can go again. Well, *papa,* this is a dangerous country because a Sioux tribe called the Yanktonai are making trouble for the *bateaux,* demanding things and sometimes even shooting. They don't have many rifles—mostly smoothbore fusils—but they can send a hail of arrows if they want.

Well, *papa,* today the woodyard was full of Yanktonai, more wild Indians than I've ever seen before, and all armed. I was afraid, and so was everyone else. All the passengers rushed to get their rifles and pistols, and it looked like a bad situation. We had to stop for wood; it was a dilemma for M. LaBarge. One old fool in greasy buckskins even lowered his Hawken to the rail and crouched down, about to shoot, but the mate knocked his rifle up. The man was very angry and had a knife, but our engagés and the deckhands stopped the trouble. I think if he'd shot—he was aiming right at the headman as the boat slid toward the bank—it would have started a battle, and maybe I wouldn't be here to write you about it. I wanted to be brave, and be a man, but all I really wanted was to hide from those bows and arrows.

M. LaBarge asked M. Fitzhugh to negotiate, because he's a seasoned trader and experienced here on the upper river, and knows the minds of the wild tribesmen. It was in Sioux, and I could not follow, but he stood before all the Yanktonai, unarmed, talking easily and showing no fear through the *rencontre,* and then suddenly he grinned and said to M. LaBarge to tie up because they were going to have a party. And that made things better almost at once. He sent M. Trudeau for some of the pure grain spirits—ship's stores, of course, *papa*—and a kettle. And then he made trade whiskey. Do you know what that is? Ugh! It is one-fifth pure spirits, the rest Missouri river water, a pound of rank black tobacco for flavor, black molasses, and a few red peppers just to burn the tongue a little.

When this was done he picked up the kettle and walked right down the stage to the shore, as calmly as could be, and grinning all the while, as if thirty Indians didn't have bows with nocked arrows in them. He seemed to know just what to do. He dipped a tin cup into the pot and handed it to the headman, a burly, mean-looking warrior named Crow Beak. Well, *papa,* M. Crow Beak drank and sputtered and gasped, and smiled, and gulped it all, right down, and quietly sat on the grass. M. Fitzhugh gave a cup to the next, and the next, and they all sputtered and gasped, and pretty soon they were all jabbering and laughing and making the sign-talk with their fingers. M. Fitzhugh drank some himself. I shouldn't say some. I should say two cups. Only he just got more and more quiet, unlike all the Yanktonai, and began to smile, and listen to them politely, like some Buddha. And pretty soon he turned around and yelled to M. LaBarge, back on board, that Crow's Beak wanted us to have all the wood we wanted, forever, as a friendship gift from the Yanktonai.

Well, *papa,* you can bet that M. LaBarge wasted no time, and soon everyone—his hands, our engagés, and even I—spread out in the woods and began cutting trees, and hauling long logs back to the boat, sweating and cursing while M. Fitzhugh sipped that awful stuff and smiled. I think his leg stopped hurting and that is why he smiled. I can always tell when his leg hurts because his face shows it, but after two cups of mountain whiskey, his leg didn't bother him at all. And so, *papa,* he saved the day, and kept us all from being hurt or killed, and the boat invaded, and all our goods down in the hold stolen away. He's a trader, and he knew what to do. He didn't want a fight, the way some of the passengers did, bragging they could whip any band of Yanktons any time. *Papa,* we have a good man for our *bourgeois.* I don't have much experience, I know, but I could see it, see him smiling and brave and ignoring all those arrows. It cost us a few centime—he gave each Yanktonai a twist of tobacco before we left—but M. LaBarge said he'd reimburse the Buffalo Company, because this was part of the expense of running the packet.

Peu a peu we had our wood, more than eighteen cords, but all in long logs that needed cutting, and most of it dry, too. It all took only three hours, through the middle of the day. And then M. LaBarge told M. Fitzhugh the hour had arrived, and the fire was burning and soon we'd have steam. And Brokenleg—forgive me for using the familiar form, *papa*—got up, handed out the twists, gave Crow Beak a big bearhug, and walked back on board, while all the Yanktonai howled and bawled and waved and wobbled, happy as could be.

Papa, all this is a lesson you probably wish a young man of my age didn't learn. I know your thoughts. But even if I'm not yet grown, I am trying to keep a wise head and listen and learn. You implored me not to take chances and to heed all warnings, and I am doing that, *papa.* I will be safe. Before you know it, I will come down the river to the board meeting next summer, and you will see a different son.

Next is Fort Pierre, three days up the river, and I am eager to see it. But first we will go around a giant horseshoe bend that will take hours for the boat to negotiate. It's only a mile or so across at the neck, and passengers like to walk overland and wait for the boat to catch up. I've never seen a fur post, and I want to examine everything so I can learn and maybe improve. It is one of Chouteau's posts, named for him, so we will see how they treat us, the Opposition.

Love to you and *maman. Shalom, Papa.*

Maxim

Brokenleg Fitzhugh hated to admit how much fear clawed his belly. They'd rounded a gentle bight and now Fort Pierre lay ahead, baking in a hot June sun on the west bank. He knew approximately what would happen at this proud trading post of the American Fur Company, and it sandpapered his nerves raw. He didn't like fear, though he grudgingly acknowledged it had kept him alive a few times back in the beaver days when he and Jamie Dance snatched plews from under the noses of Bug's Boys on the Three Forks. But this ritual that lay ahead unnerved him, and he thought he'd rather wrestle a grizzly again than endure it.

The blistering sun cooked the decks so hot he could feel the heat burn through his moccasins. Fort Pierre wobbled in the heat waves like a living thing across the water. The fierce summer sun had yellowed the grasses on the bluffs, except for the coulees and gulches, where the better-watered grasses obdurately remained green. Clustered about the fort were Sioux lodges of buffalo cow skin, their peaks and wind-ears blackened by smoke. The midday sun was too hard even for the hardy squaws to endure, and they had abandoned their robe-tanning until a milder hour, and lay within their lodges enjoying the occasional promise of cool that eddied under the rolled-up lodgecovers.

He stood in the shade of the boiler deck promenade, watching this island of civilization startling up from a grassy wild, a thing that didn't belong here—any more than the fort he would soon occupy belonged on the confluence of the Yellowstone and Bighorn Rivers. Two Stars and Stripes flew, one from each log blockhouse at opposite corners—a Yankee presence in an alien land. The log stockade appeared to be shaped in a perfect square, and he could see the peaked roofs of civilized and carpentered buildings within. This post was no rude log affair, but one painfully transported from downriver, and well settled after a decade of service and refinement. He liked the place: it had that quality of amiable welcome to tribesmen, combined with a business-like military bearing that announced flatly that it could deal death and pain to those who misbehaved. The fort made a statement without words.

He felt the packet settle into quiet waters, suddenly released from the turbulent power of the main channel, and at the same time heard muffled bells and a metronomic slowing of the great steam pistons that drove the gouging paddles.

"Your first gander at an upriver fur post," he said to the youth beside him.

"I want to learn everything inside. Will ours be like it?"

"Some. I've got my ways, and American Fur has its ways. But fetch a look at how it works, Maxim."

"But will they welcome us? I mean, we're the Opposition."

"Oh, I imagine. There's a kind of rule out here that a post welcomes any white man and offers vittles and a bunk. I suppose it's because there's so few. Back in the beaver days, trappers'd drift in for a winter, and the fort'd make do. Buffler meat's there for the asking, usually. Mostly, the booshways are as itchy for company as anyone can get . . . out here where there's none to be got."

"You mean they want us?"

"Of course. Guests're big doings. Most booshways, they'll put out a spread if they've got it. By spring they're out of most everything. By May or June, they're desperate for coffee and sugar and airtights of vegetables."

Maxim eyed him sharply. "The engagés told me that the company will hurt us any way it can. Even—bloodshed. How are you so sure that—"

"Wait and see. I don't know who's the trader here, but he'll probably have a French name and a fair-enough smile. All but one. There's one of the top AFC men I'd rather not tangle with."

Maxim waited, obviously wanting a name, but Brokenleg didn't see fit to supply it. Last he knew, Julius Hervey hunkered up on the Missouri somewhere. No man in the robe trade seethed with as much hatred, imagining slights and inventing grievances even while he rode roughshod over others, red and white alike. He'd killed men and brutalized others, and made a mocking game of it all, a sort of plaster god out beyond the reach of law, discipline, and ordinary decency. It would be something to watch out for.

"You're a wise lad to be thinking about that, Maxim. Chouteau's got his ways."

"Is it safe, Mister Fitzhugh? Is it safe to land?"

The youth's urgency struck Brokenleg. He selected his response carefully. "First, lad, call me Brokenleg or Robert, like any other man—"

"But the French are more formal, sir—"

"Whatever way you prefer, Maxim. No, it's not safe. That's something to learn about the mountains and the country here, up the river. Nothing's safe. We'll put in here, and maybe there'll be trouble. All the time I trapped beaver and watched how the stick floats, I never felt safe. And the ones that did, lad—they went under."

Maxim turned silent, watching the looming post soberly as the packet slid toward the levee. From the near blockhouse a boom erupted, followed by a puff of white, and a percussive aftershock.

"Mountain welcome. Six-pounder."

"This isn't the mountains."

"That's how it's all called back here."

A mob gathered at the levee, engagés, tribesmen in breechclouts, squaws in bright calicoes, bare-armed and some barefooted, scampering golden children. And out of the front gate, back from the river, a burly graying man running to fat, his white hair riding back upon his shoulders, made his gouty way down the soft naked slope.

Brokenleg grunted. "Ulysses Chardonne," he muttered.

Maxim peered, uncertain what that meant.

"The booshway. Good enough trader," he said. "And good company man," he added tightly.

The escapement pipe of the *Platte* erupted, the steam shrilling the boat's own welcome note before evaporating in the dry air. The paddles halted their labor like resting oxen, and the boat slid close to the bank. In a flurry, deckmen tossed hawsers to waiting hands on the bank, and the packet was made fast.

"Well, Maxim. Come along now. We'll have us a little palaver with old Chardonne, and you'll learn a few things—such as how much the fur company knows about what we're doing. A lot. You'll discover ol' American Fur Company knows what we've got in the hold, where we're going, and what tribes we'll be trading with."

"How can they know that?"

"Because on the upper Missouri—they're God."

"Ah, *mon ami* Fitzhugh, it is you!" bellowed Ulysses Chardonne as they stepped off the stage onto dusty ground. "Come along, come along. We will make the talk, eh?"

"You're looking well, Ulysses," Fitzhugh replied, limping as badly as the gout-tormented factor.

Chardonne grunted. "Neither of us is exactly, what is the precise word—new. In new condition."

"Ulysses, this hyar stripling is Maxim Straus, Guy's boy. Come to help me."

"Oh, I know." The jowly factor stared at Maxim. "The country's not safe for a lad like you, well-educated, prepared for a life in finance. Maybe you should stay here, wait for the company boat to take you down."

"Maxim can made up his own mind," Fitzhugh said hastily.

They pierced through a gate in the looming stockade into an inner yard surrounded by frame and clapboard buildings of unpainted milled wood that had been hauled a vast distance upriver. Engagés' barracks occupied one side; dining, kitchen and storage rooms the other. In the warehouse, robes had been gathered into bales of ten, and filled the air of the yard with a pleasant redolence. Before them stood Chardonne's own house and offices, a peak-roofed structure that looked as if it had been ripped from the east somewhere and planted here.

No sooner had the *bourgeois* led them into an ornate parlor with red silk settees than an Indian woman—Sioux, Fitzhugh thought—emerged silently, carrying a tray with a decanter of brandy, and wide snifters. He could only guess at her relationship with Chardonne, but one thing was certain: he had an eye for beauty.

"Ah, a little something to make wet the throat on a day like this. We were resupplied three weeks ago when the company packet came in, and for a while, now, we'll make a few luxuries. . . . Young master Maxim, would your father permit you some brandy, or shall I have Ix-ta-sah bring some tea?"

"I am permitted a few sips, M. Chardonne."

The *bourgeois* smiled. "A French boy."

Fitzhugh sipped from the proffered glass, and felt the fire scour his tonsils and clear his nose.

"And what is the news, my *bon ami* Brokenleg? It is the Opposition, yes? Tell me about it all. Here you bravely tackle M. Chouteau, and off to the south, you engagé Bent, St. Vrain. A penchant for bloody noses, I'd say."

"Buffler robes ought to fetch more than beaver, Ulysses."

"But the market, she is already flooded. What are they good for? Carriage robes. And how many of those can all these fur companies sell? What else? In Europe, they don' like the buffalo, and like the fleece of the sheep, yes? And what of the rawhide. No one makes a decent shoe or boot from the buffalo. No one can make the tan so the leather's just right, not too soft, not brittle. So—it is a great mystery, why you and M. Straus and that wildman Jamie Dance, you get together and do this crazy thing."

Fitzhugh realized that the wheezing *bourgeois* had not wasted a minute, and would be getting to the point shortly. "That's for Guy Straus to work out, Ulysses. I'm just the coon that exchanges a few gewgaws for robes."

"Ah, and what makes you think you can offer what we can for the robes, or pay as little as we do for the tradegoods, eh?"

"I imagine we'll give it a whirl."

"Ha. Madness. The tradegoods disappear. The hides rot or get wet or bugs eat them. There are great calamities on the river. A tribe trades with you one day, and makes grief the next, he? It is not a game for little companies, but only giants that can absorb the losses, eh?"

"We'll take our chances."

"Ah, Fitzhugh, indeed you will. Do you trust the savages? Will they never strike when you are away from the post, out on the prairie somewhere, with a wagon of goods they want, or a wagon of robes you've traded for, plus a few horses, eh? They strike, and you die only once, and then what?"

"I suppose it's plumb unsafe, Ulysses," Fitzhugh said,

thinking to help this little waltz along. He slid some of that fiery brandy down, to keep his whistle wet.

"I'll tell you how to be safe, *bon ami.* I'll tell you how to avoid the heartache, the loss, the awful feeling when the news comes that the packet, she is wrecked with all of a season's returns on board, eh?" He leaned over, swilling the brandy around in his snifter. "M. Chouteau has authorized me to buy your entire stock of trading goods at cost plus ten percent. A true profit, a handsome profit, eh? And of course, retire from the business."

Fitzhugh let it hang for a moment, but he had known this would come and how he'd reply. It was the standard offer, but only half of the proposition.

"I reckon we'll take a stab at the robes. There's a profit in them, oh, hundred to five hundred percent, if we get the robes downriver next spring."

"Ah. If. Big if. *Le grand* if. But you Opposition fellows, you hardly ever do, eh?"

Chapter Five

LaBarge would not tarry an instant longer than necessary, not with a third of the river left to conquer. As soon as the few passengers bound for Fort Pierre had debarked, along with their meager belongings, the packet's whistle shrilled, catapulting flocks of magpies into raucous flight. The stop had consumed only twenty minutes.

Brokenleg hurried through the post, prodding the gawking boy before him, and down the soft slope to the river. It had been much as he'd expected, and he'd have to think over some of the things Chardonne said. That was the way of American Fur: amiable hospitality on the surface, but something else flowing beneath.

They hastened aboard, the last passengers, and the deckmen lifted the stage and coiled the hawsers that had tied the packet to posts at the levee. The *Platte* shuddered and belched black smoke, its wheels churning placid water, gathering the strength in its loins to tackle the brutal current of the channel.

"M. Chardonne treated us kindly, don't you think? I like him." Maxim said.

Fitzhugh grunted.

"He invited me to stay, and was concerned about my safety. I shall tell *papa* that some of the company, at least, are very civil people."

"Maxim—you'll find that sort of hospitality at any post, American Fur or Opposition, including ours. It means little."

"Mister Fitzhugh, surely you take a dark view of an amiable man."

Fitzhugh sensed that no matter what he said, the youth would take it wrong. It would be best not to say anything. Some things couldn't be told, but had to be experienced. And the youth would remember only Chardonne's easy smile and affable talk, and not realize the swift talk over a slug of brandy had been business and worse—a series of threats. Oh, indeed, how AFC would love to have young Maxim, the son of the Opposition's key financier, as its guest—as its hostage. And Maxim didn't know that once Fitzhugh had refused the company's usual buyout—its standard offer to any opposition outfit coming upriver—the catastrophes that Chardonne had delicately warned of would begin to happen, and they wouldn't always be accidents.

"Stay alert, Maxim, and watch." Fitzhugh didn't have the fancy words or the grace to describe what really had transpired, and he feared he'd only harden the lad's favorable view of Chouteau's men and methods.

He left the boy on the main deck, where engagés huddled in the shade escaping the furnace heat of the sun. Then he limped and sweated up the companionway's two flights, and emerged into the blinding glare of the hurricane deck. He saw her there, standing alertly, leaning forward as if to hasten the packet in its progress. She wore a hip-length white blouse cinched at the waist with a blue quillworked belt, and full skirts of bottle green. She smiled, and he discovered ease in her chiseled features he'd not seen there for months. Her sharp, eager gaze took in the vast panorama before them, the distant yellow bluffs and the treeless plains humping and rolling toward a vast emptiness beneath an enameled blue sky. Not far to the west rose the Black Hills, and Bear Butte, where Sweet Medicine had received the Four Arrows sacred to the Cheyenne people. This was the eastern edge of her people's land, and the sight of it had transformed her.

Instinctively he slid an arm about her waist, in spite of the fierce heat, and she responded softly, sidling closer to her man as they watched the shore creep by. Then, just as impulsively, she pulled free and fixed him with a disdainful gaze that told him that he and this packet and all aboard it were invaders and trespassers. A part of him accepted that, and a part resented it. He'd married into the Cheyenne tribe, and had bonded himself to them, and become a part of them. The land of Sweet Medicine had become his own; he felt much more possessive of this vast lonely country than anything back east where he'd come from. Dimly he recollected upstate New York, his innkeeping parents Nathaniel and Bethany, his brothers and sister, the intimate green vales of that settled country. It would never be his again. Neither would the civilities that went with it. His family would find him harsh, violent, uncouth now, acid of tongue and direct of eye. This land of Dust Devil's, of her people, of Sweet Medicine, held upon it all he had.

" 'Bout home," he said.

She eyed him scornfully and pulled free. His eyes were watering from the glare, so he left her there and limped around to the small stair that led to the pilothouse, and gimped up it.

"Sorry to weigh anchor so fast, but the river's already crested, and I'll be fighting sandbars all the way back," LaBarge said.

"I know."

"Chardonne try the usual?"

"Cost plus ten percent and an agreement not to go into opposition."

LaBarge nodded. "When they found we'd had the *Platte* built, they wanted to charter it exclusively. They were provoked when my brother and I declined, and warned us of all the usual hazards on the river. One never knows, does one?"

"You've made serious opposition possible, Joe."

The master nodded. Up until now, opposition companies could ship tradegoods upriver on American Fur packets only at exorbitant rates which gave the monopoly all the advantage in trade.

"I don't doubt that some of my crew have been bought. But I've not spotted anything—yet." He peered earnestly into Fitzhugh's eyes. "You'd be wise to run a daily inventory of your tradegoods down in the hold—and take a close look at your wagons and stock every day."

"I'll teach Maxim. That's a clerk duty that he can learn."

"I wouldn't do it that way," LaBarge said, sharply, and didn't elaborate. But Fitzhugh caught the warning.

"Sandbar," muttered Roux, pointing at a long swell of water angling out from a bight.

LaBarge's attention shifted totally to the coiling river, which was working its way around a broad oxbow studded with prickly pear and a little yucca. The channel ran between visible snags tilling the water on the right and the glassy swell of the bar arrowing toward them on the left.

"La-haut," he said to Roux, pointing at a patch of darker water scarcely thirty yards wide. The pilot, who was manning the helm himself at this hour, turned the duckbilled prow a bit to the right. LaBarge pulled the bellcord, and a moment later the packet slowed to a lazy crawl into the upwelling torrent.

A giant hand seemed to rise from the river and clamp the vessel in its grasp. Fitzhugh stumbled forward on his game leg into the wainscoting. Below, cargo shifted, and men yelled. The boat stood stock still while the river sucked by, gurgling at the intrusion. LaBarge pulled the bellrope, a series of tugs, and from below came a clanging of metal, and a thrashing of paddles in reverse, churning aquamarine water into white froth. But the bar didn't yield its prey. After a moment, LaBarge tugged the bellrope again and the paddles quieted. He leaned out of the pilothouse and nodded to the mate, far below.

"We'll grasshopper," he said to Fitzhugh. "There was no bar here last year. This is a bad one, and we're thirty or forty feet onto it."

Down below, deckhands lowered the front spars, normally used for lifting heavy items out of the hold, into the water until they settled into the sandbar. They rigged manila lines that ran from cleats on the foredeck to pulleys at the top of the spars, and back down to a capstan on the foredeck, and then, with a long rod through the capstan, began the slow twisting that wound the line around the capstan, lifting the whole front end of the packet upward on its spars, like a grasshopper rising on its legs. The spars themselves had been set at an angle, leaning forward to give the vessel a push when the moment came. The packet creaked and the rope hummed and spit spray as the prow inched upward.

Roux nodded, and LaBarge yanked the bellrope hard, and a sudden roar of the steam pistons echoed. The eighteen-foot wheels churned, driving the packet ahead on its spars until the angle was too great and the packet settled back onto the sandbar, but twenty feet forward of its previous position. Fitzhugh had seen it before, and marveled at its ingenuity as much now as when he'd first witnessed a riverboat being eased over shallow water. It took two more grasshopperings before the packet slid free on the far side of the bar, and danced on the sparkling waters like a manumitted slave while men cheered down below.

LaBarge smiled. "It can be worse than this," he said. "Sometimes we must shift cargo to the rear, or forward, and the crew hates it."

"I reckon the river gets shallower and tougher every time we pass the mouth of a creek," Fitzhugh said.

LaBarge snorted. "It's the June rise that counts. I've always thought there's water deep enough to go to the great falls of the Missouri on the June rise. But no one's ever been there. Too many rocks and rapids."

"I'd take it kindly if you'd push on up the Yellowstone

far as you can. The Bighorn's a long ways up, and I hate the thought of three or four wagon trips from wherever you drop us, and that mountain of stuff sitting unguarded out there."

"We'll find an island. A place where you can store your goods while you're hauling. Lots of them on that river, M. Fitzhugh. Some of them separated from the riverbank by a gravelly bottom with only a few inches running over it—easy to ford. I wish we could just anchor and wait, but we'd never make it back down."

"We'll manage," he said, "But I don't have enough men to do it right."

LaBarge smiled tightly. "M. Chardonne warned about calamities," he said softly. "It'll depend on whether the tribes on the Yellowstone know about us."

Maxim took his new duties seriously. He had grown up solemn by nature, not given to laughter and lightness, and inclined to see life as a series of crushing responsibilities.

M. Fitzhugh showed him how to check inventory. Each morning, as the packet toiled up the endless miles of the great river, the *bourgeois* swung down the ladder into the low hold carrying a coal-oil lantern and his cargo manifest. Maxim could stand, but just barely, in the five-foot-high hold, but M. Fitzhugh had to crouch, which wasn't easy with his stiff leg.

"Now this'll take time. It's slow and tedious, but we've got to do it each day, boy."

Maxim nodded as Fitzhugh limped to the closest freight, oblong crates. Maxim could hear the water gurgle and suck at the hull, and slide beneath the bottom. Above, the thunder of pistons rumbled softly.

"Hyar, hold the lamp now. This crate's got axes in it, fifty according to the waybill. Now first you look at our manifest, and find out how many axes we're taking for trade.

Hyar, now. A hundred. Have we two crates? Hyar we are, two crates. Now look and see, here, whether they've been pried open. If someone's filching axes, he's got to open the case. Try it with your hand, eh?"

Maxim did, discovering that the lid remained tightly attached.

"Petty thief'll fool you; he'll make it look like there's been no tampering, so look sharp and use your hands."

And so it went. Maxim learned to look and feel, and check off the boxes and bales and sacks, and to use his hands as well as his eyes because thieves would deceive. He learned how to spot-check, too. There were too many boxes of blue-and-white glass trade beads to examine, but M. Fitzhugh showed him how to make a random check, and look at something new each day.

It took much of the morning, and once they ran out of coal-oil and had to grope back to the forward hatch where a little light lit the shadowed hold.

"Always be careful with this lamp," Fitzhugh warned. "If you drop it and that coal oil spreads and burns, you'll cost us our goods, Mr. LaBarge his riverboat, and maybe kill us all. Now one more thing. Don't bring that lamp close to these casks of grain spirits. But do check the spirits first of all. There's the temptation, both to crewmen and our engagés. They'll draw what they need from a bung, and then put water in to compensate, so you can't tell by weight. Not even a seal works. A thief wanting spirits will auger through the back of a cask if he must. No, the secret's camouflage. This one's marked vinegar, eh? That one's turpentine. Another's marked lamp oil. And check twice a day. Do that, and maybe we'll have enough left when we get up to the Yellerstone to start a robe business."

All this had happened the very day they'd pulled away from Fort Pierre and Ulysses Chardonne, and Maxim knew that it was because Brokenleg had turned down the American Fur buyout, and now feared sabotage. It ate up his mornings, and he hated the dark, pungent hold, and the fearsome creaking of the boat as it slapped through rapids and around bends. His dreads gripped him there, especially when rats scurried along the bilge ahead of his lantern, blurred sinister movement. He ached to be out upon the deck, watching this strange barren country roll slowly by, with its occasional copse of cottonwoods along the bottoms, amber bluffs, antelope, buffalo, and even an occasional Indian watching silently from shore. It tugged at him, but so did the weight of his responsibilities.

He'd promised his father he'd watch and learn, and contain his own impulses. And his father had gravely charged him, that last night in St. Louis, with the task of being Guy Straus's eyes and ears, and more. "You will be my representative; the member of Straus et Fils present on the post," he said. "You'll want to hunt and fish and have fun—and that's fine. But business first, Maxim. Business first. For your mother, and me, and Clothilde and David."

Each day's venture into the cavernous hold turned out to be the same. He swiftly learned where the beads and hatchets and brass kettles were; where the crates of fusils lay, and the casks of powder and bars of galena were stored. He eyed the DuPont unhappily, keeping his lamp far from it. He knew how many bales of Witney point blankets there were, woven in England especially for the trade. And he knew exactly where the hoop-iron lay—iron the tribes used to make metal arrowpoints and spear points too. He knew there were three cartons of tin mirrors, and six of colored ribbons, and whole bales of tradecloth and calicoes, kept well above the bilge, along with the bales of blankets. He learned where the awls and files were, and the rolls of canvas duck, and the packets of needles.

Each morning he checked diligently, checking off his cargo manifest; and each day he found things exactly as before, except once or twice when they'd hit sandbars and cargo had to be shifted. After those episodes, he'd checked all the more carefully, not wanting to let his *papa* down, or M. Fitzhugh either, by some foolish lapse.

He imagined what it would be like to miss something, to have something vanish for days on end before it was discovered—by someone else. He dreaded that. He dreaded being called just a boy, not old enough to clerk for the Buffalo Company. He dreaded the day when he might have to run to M. Fitzhugh and tell him that something or other was missing. And then they's search together and probably find it, because Maxim had been young and hasty and eager to bolt up to the main deck and the sunlight and the comic banter of the engagés. Indeed, they teased him, and called him a mole, but they did it kindly. They liked the grave boy who talked French, and knew he was doing what all fur company clerks do.

"Where's the spirits, eh?" they had asked, half humorously.

"Coming, coming, *messieurs,*" he had replied. "Soon you will carry it on your backs into the hold."

A fib. It bothered him to do it.

They arrived one lusty summer day at Fort Clark, high in Dakota. Like Pierre, it was an American Fur Company bastion, but somehow different, perhaps because it stood hundreds of miles farther up the endless river from St. Louis. Nearby were the Mandan and Hidatsa villages, tragic ghosts now because smallpox had destroyed their populations, and reduced these quiet, stable, crop-gathering tribes to handfuls. And along with them, Fort Clark had declined in importance, but still traded for robes. A few years earlier the Mandans had been a proud and happy people, living in great earthen lodges that housed several families and supplied warmth and shelter, cultivating vast fields of corn.

Just a few passengers, mostly metis and their squaws, debarked there, carrying their few belongings. Even so, they were AFC people and Maxim watched them sharply from his post beside the gangway, his eyes studying every bag and parfleche leaving the boat. Then Brokenleg took him to meet James Kipp, the partisan there, who bantered a bit, as Chardonne had done many leagues downstream. Maxim liked Kipp, and saw a clear eye and a face unburdened by craft. Was the famous skulduggery of AFC unknown to this amiable man? It puzzled Maxim, this meeting a man he expected to loathe, and finding instead a commanding trader who enjoyed guests, enjoyed the Opposition, and wished Brokenleg and Maxim success.

But even as they talked, the boat's whistle blew, erupting steam into the light transparent air of the upper plains. Captain LaBarge would not waste a minute. Maxim hastened toward the riverboat, having trouble keeping up with Fitzhugh who limped like a charging bull. He paused on the levee, peering about suspiciously at a few crates and the motley crowd, mostly metis and a few young Hidatsa dressed brightly in tradecloth blouses and skin leggins. He spotted nothing amiss. Fort Clark had been resupplied a few weeks earlier by the fur company steamer *Trapper*, the very one that had brought the whitemen's plague with it a few years earlier.

A few hours later Fitzhugh summoned him to the railing and pointed. Far off on a golden bluff lay the village of earthen mounds that once thrived as the home of the Mandans. It looked forlorn, even in the golden warmth of summer, and indeed, the cornfields down on the bottoms looked untended and going to weeds and cottonwood saplings. He wished Captain LaBarge would stop and let him explore the dark village, let him find souvenirs, if any remained—surely arrowheads, bows, pots, fired clay bowls. The farther he traveled from St. Louis, the stranger everything had become. He wanted bits and pieces of it. He yearned to draw and paint, so he could send folios down to *papa* and *maman,* with the barren grassy hills showing, the broad flood of water that lay blue in the bright daylight but turned green and gray in shadowed times, the powerful tall native people he'd seen—he couldn't tell one tribe from another, but M. Fitzhugh had rattled off names. How could the man tell? For the life of him, Maxim couldn't see how the *bourgeois* could separate one tribesman from another.

The air had changed. They'd climbed steadily from St. Louis, though never visibly. This land lay about sixteen hundred feet above sea level, which made the skies a more intense blue than he'd experienced in St. Louis. The river occasionally narrowed now, and the bluffs rose closer. He marveled at the flow of water, the steady flood that boiled out of the distant fabled mountains in a volume beyond fathoming. And yet, he'd never seen the mountains, and M. Fitzhugh told him he wouldn't. There was still a vast wilderness to conquer.

The next morning he lowered himself into the dark hold and began his inventory by the pitiful light of the coal oil lamp. That's when he discovered the shortage. Trembling, he began a hunt, pushing cargo, peering down the two aisles, fear clutching at him, wondering how long he'd let this terrible loss escape his attention. Twice he toured the hold, stem to stern, but the bales were not there. He stooped down to the bilge, wondering if the missing goods lay in the rocking water, and saw nothing in the oily light. The blankets! Good Witney blankets, brought all the way from southern England to New York, and then shipped to New Orleans and up to St. Louis. Witney trade blankets, used by Hudson's Bay and all traders, made in one-point, two-point, and three-point sizes, with bars on them to tell tribesmen the approximate weight—and cost. A three-point blanket weighed about four pounds, and ran six feet long. They'd been baled into twenty-blanket lots and carefully set high above the rest of the cargo to keep them from the bilge. Gone! Fifteen bales of blankets, three hundred of them, the entire year's supply for trading—gone. Terror cramped Maxim. He wept, feeling too young, too much a boy, as he probed the hold once again, half afraid some vicious man would jump out from a dark corner with a knife. But no. The blankets had vanished. Each one had cost around two dollars, higher or lower depending on weight, imported from the Early Company in Witney, west of London. By the time they reached the new post on the Big Horn they'd cost the Buffalo Company over four dollars, most of it for shipping. More than twelve hundred dollars gone. They'd fetch from one to five robes apiece, depending on weights and qualities.

He paused, the lantern clutched in his sweating palms, engulfed in misery. The missing blankets would have traded for around a thousand robes, each worth about four dollars back east. Over four thousand dollars. Tears welled up and streaked his cheeks, and he wished desperately he'd never come up the great Missouri.

Chapter Six

The boy looked like he wanted to die. "I've let you down," he cried.

Grimly, Brokenleg followed him down to the main deck, and into the hold, and they began a systematic search. An hour later Fitzhugh knew for certain that the boy had it right: fifteen bales of blankets, each weighing about fifty pounds, had vanished overnight.

They'd anchored at a wooded island, a half day's travel from Fort Clark and the Mandan villages. There'd been a new moon, which meant the night had been as black as nights get. Most of the deck passengers had debarked, leaving only a handful bound for Fort Union or the post at the confluence of the Yellowstone and Missouri.

That meant that fewer people were sleeping on the deck these days. Most of the remaining deck passengers were the Buffalo Company's own engagés, sleeping under the Pittsburgh wagons. The others usually slept along the boiler, well back of the hatch and foredeck. The blankets had been a perfect choice, he thought. The loss of one of the most important trade items would paralyze their operation and drive tribesmen to the American Fur Company posts, which were well supplied with them. And they'd been the quietest item to steal, soft so that they didn't scrape and bang while being hauled away, or splash much if they were eased into the river. And nicely bundled in bales a man could handle easily—or two men, one below in the hold and the other receiving the bales and dumping them gently into the black current, all but invisible in the night.

But were they dumped, or would they show up on AFC shelves somewhere? Ditched, he thought. The *Platte* had anchored at an island small enough to make a cache of them risky, especially with engagés gathering livestock in the morning. On the other hand, these Witney blankets were identical to those used by AFC and Hudson's Bay, and could be put into AFC trading inventories without being noticed. But he doubted it. AFC didn't operate like that, selling stolen goods. It had other, more pernicious ways of dealing with opposition—such as this.

"I should have checked sooner," Maxim said, miserably. "I should have caught them."

Brokenleg sighed, not knowing how to ease the guilt that flooded the youth. "You're sounding like it's your doing," he grumbled. "Like you snatched them blankets. Like you weren't watching. Fact is, you didn't snitch them; thieves working for Chouteau did. Fact is, you checked exactly as you should—and I wanted—and because you checked, we found out fast. Whoever done it's on this boat. And I'm going to get him."

"Maybe they've been taken back to Fort Clark," Maxim said.

"Maybe. But I doubt it. The company don't work like that. They're all choir boys in white robes. More likely there's three hundred blankets bumping along the bottom of the river scarin' fish, below that island somewhere."

"We're ruined," Maxim said. "I let you and *papa* down."

"You didn't let nobody down. Get that through your haid."

The boy looked unconvinced, and Fitzhugh knew he couldn't help the young man further. He'd have to wrestle with it in his own mind now.

"What are you going to do?"

"I'm thinking on it. Could be, those Witneys weren't

dumped over the side, but stuck in a cabin somewheres. I'm thinking I've got to talk private with Captain LaBarge, and we'll do a quiet search abovedecks, including the crew cabins and all the staterooms, as well as storage, and all that."

"It'll attract attention."

"I'm thinking on that. If we do it right, hardly anyone'll notice. Except the one or two who done it. Say—I guess I'd better check to see who's on board and who isn't. Could be we got shut of someone back there."

"It's no use."

"I've been in darker holes, Maxim, and with six feet of sod over me, too. You get yourself together and be thinking how we'll earn a profit and whip American Fur so good they don't know what hit 'em."

"We hired traitors," the youth said bitterly.

"Could be. But there's other passengers and crew on board, too. I'll see to them first, before I'll start suspecting our own men—good Creoles, I think."

They walked glumly toward the patch of light where the forward hatches lay open. "Now, Maxim, plaster a smile on that mug. And don't talk to anyone for now. Not to Samson Trudeau, not to the engagés. I'm going up to palaver with LaBarge. We've got to have a quiet look into every corner of this packet first, before we get down to cases."

He hated to leave Maxim just when the lad wallowed in grief, but he had to. He hurried the boy ahead of him up the ladder to the deck, and nudged him. "Smile, boy," he said, and limped up companionways, not smiling a bit himself. He found LaBarge up in the pilothouse and beckoned to him. The captain nodded, and trotted down to the hurricane deck, which was already roasting in the morning sun.

"Lost some goods," Brokenleg began, peering about sharply. They stood alone up on that burning deck.

LaBarge waited, intently.

"The blankets. All fifteen bales of Witneys. Between the

time Maxim checked the hold yesterday, after we'd got loose from Fort Clark, and this morning. They were missing this morning."

"Are you sure?"

"I went down there myself and tore the place apart. They're gone."

LaBarge sighed. "I'm not surprised."

"Last night was perfect. Dark. Not so many deck passengers. Bales easy to lift and ease into the river. And by gawd, Joe, it near ruins us. I thought to send an express down to Straus for more, but he's got to order from England. We'll have none this year. Not even to wrap our cold carcasses this winter. Not until next year."

"—Unless they're on the boat. That's what you're wanting to find out next."

"Had it in my haid, yes. Lots of places—crew cabins, lockers, engine room, pantries, on the main deck; a lot of cabins and staterooms on the boiler deck."

"I'll start a search. Do it myself."

"That'd be too obvious. I'd just as soon keep her quiet for a while so I don't burn my hand on this hyar skillet. I'd hate to start accusing engagés I hired and still trust—at least until I got some more facts."

"The mate, then. Hugh Clowes. He can wander anywhere; he's got keys to everything, and he won't draw any attention because that's what he does anyway."

"That's a start, Captain." Brokenleg ran a bony hand over his bald crown and into the thinning carrot hair behind, perplexed. "I don't figure we'll find one wooly blanket, but we need to know."

"You still planning to open trade?"

"You bet. And I'll be sending down the returns on this boat next spring."

LaBarge smiled wryly. "They knew what to take," he muttered. "Knew how to hurt you. How to hurt us both. I think I'll start taking some precautions of my own." He peered up at the pilot-house atop the texas. "Monsieur Roux, please call the mate," he yelled. A head peered over the half-wall and nodded. Fitzhugh heard a voice swallowed up in the speaking tube to the engine room, and waited.

Hugh Clowes showed up on the hurricane deck a minute later, panting and sweating from his fast vault up the companionways. LaBarge outlined what was wanted and what had happened, and the mate nodded gravely.

"I won't miss a trick," he said, and vanished down the innumerable stairs to the main deck. It would take a while.

"Can he be trusted?" Fitzhugh asked dourly. He had visions of a conspiracy, with someone like Clowes at its center. At the moment he didn't trust anyone, including LaBarge.

"He's been with me for years, on half a dozen packets, and I've never seen disloyalty in him. He's doing some piloting, and knows he'll be piloting for me soon. Pilots are lords of the river, Mr. Fitzhugh. Clowes is not a man to throw away a chance to earn a thousand a month."

"They earn that?" It astonished Fitzhugh. His engagés earned about a hundred fifty a year.

"Some earn more. Roux earns twelve hundred. Often he nets more than I from a trip up this river."

Far below, the main deck looked deserted in the mid-day sun although Maxim huddled on the railing at the prow, looking stricken and staring at the murky water. It would take time for Clowes to inspect an entire packet, open every locker and bunker and cabin and poke around. While he waited, Brokenleg tried to force his mind to deal with this; figure out how to draw tribesmen to a post without blankets to trade; how to root out the thieves from among his engagés; how to report this mess to Guy; how to lift the weight from Maxim, down there. And the more he wrestled with it, the gloomier he became.

"Fitzhugh, you'll fry if you stand here on this deck. Come

up to the pilothouse. We can talk freely there. Roux's at the helm this afternoon."

The pilothouse was particularly hard for him to get to, but Brokenleg didn't argue, and lifted himself up the narrow stairwell with crowhops and the power of his burly arms. He loved the lofty shaded commandpost of the packet, high above the shimmering river. A white summer haze veiled the brown bluffs from his eyes, and blurred the infinitudes beyond. A free land here, rolling and rising endlessly to the horizons, toward the unseen mountains to the west, lifeless from a distance but teeming with humans and animals on closer inspection.

LaBarge interrupted his reverie. "Whoever did it's on board," he said gently. "Have you made any plans?"

"Not yet," Fitzhugh replied curtly.

"We might start with a rollcall," LaBarge said.

"We might, and if someone's missing I'm getting off this boat and kill him."

"Chances are, whoever did it's on board."

"If he is, I'll get him. I'll string him up by the thumbs and flog him."

Captain LaBarge smiled faintly and said nothing.

"If he's one of my engagés, I'll tear him apart. And if he lives, I'll see to it he don't ever work up the river again."

"With that leg of yours, I don't think you should—"

"Let them try me. It hasn't stopped me yet."

"I have Clowes if you need him. A human battering ram. He always has to settle a few challenges, each trip."

"I won't need him."

"Deal with your engagés first, Mister Fitzhugh. And if it comes to nothing it'll be my turn to tackle my crew—and the last of the passengers. If I were to make a stab at it, I'd say one or two of the passengers. Men bought and paid for by American Fur, just biding their time until the right moment—which was last night."

A line of snags arced off the west shore like sharkfins,

and LaBarge and Roux turned back to sparring the river. Brokenleg stared dourly, not seeing a thing, hot-tempered and ready to explode, the way he'd spent his months in St. Louis. He peered down from the hurricane deck, glaring red-eyed at deck passengers below. One of them would feel his fists and boots before long.

No blankets. The tribes would catch on in a hurry, and take their robes to Fort Union. The more he pondered the future, the more his spirits sagged. American Fur—he never doubted what lay behind this—had dealt him a killer blow. And soon he'd receive another offer from them, this time for less than the cost of the remaining tradegoods. But enough to salvage the company, especially if Jamie Dance did well in the south. Maybe the thing to do was deal as soon as the *Platte* reached Fort Union. Sell the rest of his outfit to Alec Culbertson or David Mitchell for a decent price—if he didn't strangle one or the other first. He thought he might even break even—and let the engagés go. If not that, hire LaBarge to take it all back down the river. Brokenleg supposed he'd never go to St. Louis again and the Buffalo Company's northern operations died aborning.

An hour or so later, Roux exclaimed, and pointed at a distant column of smoke miles up the river valley, its source obscured by cottonwood-choked bends. They closed on the smoke with a speed that puzzled Fitzhugh, and then the single column of smoke became two, and the twin chimneys of the *Trapper,* heading down to St. Louis with the annual returns from the American Fur posts, appeared first, followed by the white packet itself. It was steaming fat and arrogant, its belly laden with packs of buffalo robes, riches beyond imagining wrested from a wild land. The glistening vessel, which looked much like the *Platte*, awakened both curiosity and loathing in Brokenleg.

"Shall we flag it?" Roux asked.

"Downriver mail," LaBarge said.

A series of short blasts of the whistle followed, and a sudden softening of the vibration rising from the bowels of the packet, and the *Platte* slid to the extreme edge of the narrow channel, waiting for the American Fur vessel. The *Trapper* slowed, less able to govern its trajectory going downstream, and then drifted alongside LaBarge's packet, paddlewheels halted. Down on the main deck, Hugh Clowes hefted a canvas bag, while deckhands on the closing boat hefted grappling hooks. The mate heaved, and the duck bag sailed safely into the arms of a crewman on the St. Louis-bound vessel, and with ear-splitting blasts of their whistles, the two ships parted company.

"There," said LaBarge. "Maxim's got a letter to his father in the bag. Guy'll have the news."

"If they deliver it," Fitzhugh said dourly.

The ship's master laughed. "There's honor among rivermen," he said, but Fitzhugh didn't feel like believing him.

LaBarge left him to his brooding while the rest of the afternoon sagged by. Sometime later—Fitzhugh noted suddenly that the sun had swung north of west and dropped some—Crowes appeared in the pilothouse.

"Not a bale of blankets on the boat," he said quietly. "I didn't miss a thing. They're either on the bottom, or cached somewhere. I'm sorry, sir."

Brokenleg felt like a cinnamon bear with a foot in a trap, alternately helpless and in a rage. He had to talk to the engagés, and couldn't put it off. He gathered them on the foredeck at dusk, after they'd completed their livestock chores, noting sharply that all ten stood before him. He couldn't discern the slightest alarm or sullenness in them, and that somehow relieved him a bit. He'd try his own harsh upriver English on them this time, and let Samson Trudeau translate.

He ticked them off: Larue, Lemaitre, Bercier, Brasseau,

Courvet, Dauphin, Guerette, Provost, Gallard, and Trudeau. Every one of them built like an ox and capable of incredible toil. He'd pound every one of them into the deck if he had to.

"Now listen," he began roughly, "last night sometime the trade blankets were taken from the hold and either pitched into the river or cached on the island. Or perhaps carried off in a canoe or yawl. Who's to say?"

His men turned solemn suddenly, their gaiety vanishing with the news. And they began peering at each other, suspicion flaring among them.

"Fifteen bales, three hundred blankets gone. Some son of a bitch has tried to ruin the company. If I find him, I'll kill him, but not until I hurt him bad. If you saw or heard anything, you'll tell me because I'm going to find it out. If it wasn't one of you, then it was the crew or the passengers. No one's left this boat and no one will until I find out. We've now searched above and below decks; I've examined the hold; Hugh Clowes the rest. The blankets are gone. I hope it wasn't you, but if it was, by God, watch your back."

They stared sternly at him now, wondering about their own fates, as well they might.

"I don't like threats," said Gallard. "If you want to make the fight, I'll fight."

"All right, Gallard, step forward."

"No, no, Monsieur Fitzhugh," Trudeau interceded. "A fight gains you nothing. I know these men; I hired them. I trust them. If you blame one, blame us all."

"Maybe I damn well do."

"Monsieur, that's unjust." Trudeau's level unwavering gaze bored into Brokenleg.

He felt the heat drain out of him, the fuse on his powderkeg pinch out. He met their flinty glares with his own, not yielding anything but not accusing either. It occurred to him that maybe he'd lost the respect and solidarity of his own men.

"I don't figure we can bring in much trade without blankets in our inventory. They're woven in England and can't be replaced in time for this season. I don't know what we'll do. We may not trade. I'll know better after I talk with Culbertson, or whoever's running Fort Union. The Buffalo Company may have to let you go there, buy out your contracts."

"Leave us there, monsieur?"

"Likely you can engagé with American Fur, and I'll try to make arrangements with Monsieur LaBarge to carry you back down. I don't know at this point."

"But monsieur—" it was Trudeau speaking—"we have other things to trade, *n'est-ce pas?*"

"Yes. And where will the chiefs take their villages when some of the warriors and squaws want blankets—which will be every time they want to trade?" He left the question unanswered. "We'd be lucky to get a thousand robes."

"Monsieur Fitzhugh. We signed for a year, and we will stay with you. And you will employ us. *Sacre bleu,* are we going to wait for the chiefs to come in to our fort, or are we going to go out with these grand wagons and trade in the villages, eh?"

Trudeau's stout courage pierced Brokenleg. He suddenly knew he'd lost his temper and maybe their loyalty and he'd better pull himself together fast. He'd spent more winters in the mountains than he could count, and now, on his first attempt at being a *bourgeois*, he'd let his anger conquer him. It jolted him.

"Reckon you're right, Trudeau," he said wearily. "I'd better find a way."

"We'll find this *batard.* We have our ways, Monsieur. Let us prove ourselves to you. I will strangle the *batard* and throw him to the fish if I find him. And so will the rest of us."

Fitzhugh nodded. "Do it, then," he said.

"Tonight, we will spread our bedrolls on the hatch. Nothing goes in or out, *oui?*"

That struck Fitzhugh as a sensible idea, and he smiled grimly.

"We'll go to the villages, *oui?* The ones the traders never go to. The ones too far south—Cheyenne, Sioux, Crow. We'll take these big Pittsburghs, these *bateaux* of the prairies, full of goods, and come back with robes. These *hommes,* monsieur—are *hommes* to make the robes."

"That's winter travel you're talking about."

Trudeau's face eased.

Something in his engagés buoyed him. Still feeling shamed by their loyalty, he left them and clambered painfully up the long stairways to the hurricane deck. Dust Devil always watched the sunset from there and he wanted to share it. LaBarge was pushing hard these days, and the *Platte* still furrowed the channel, heading toward some anchorage the captain knew of ahead. The day had been hell, but the indigo twilight brought a peace of its own.

He found her with a shawl drawn over her shoulders, her lovely face set toward the west, a new patience upon it. She watched him limp toward her as she clung to the rail, a gentleness upon her he hadn't seen except when she stayed in her own village.

"Sweet Medicine," she said.

"Still a piece to go."

"You talked to the engagés?"

"Yes. I told them I'd find the thief and kill him with my bare hands. I was ready to, but Trudeau stopped it. He said they'd do their own hunting. The Creoles like to deal with their own. They're like a pack of catamounts. They won't quit and they won't let me quit."

"You were quitting?" Amazement laced her question.

"I figured I've got to sell out at Fort Union."

"What did they say?"

"They said they'd drive the wagons out to the villages and trade, blankets or no blankets, all winter. That's cold work fit for a slave."

"All you do is roar like a bear," she said. "You should let Samson Trudeau run the post. He knows how and you don't."

She was right, he thought. His explosive temper could get him into deep trouble.

Chapter Seven

The crown jewel of the American Fur Company, Fort Union, lay about two miles above the confluence of the Missouri and the Yellowstone. From there, Pierre Chouteau ran his Upper Missouri Outfit, operating several sub-posts farther up the great river to entice the trade of the Blackfeet away from Hudson's Bay in Canada. Brokenleg had not seen it in a decade and wondered whether it retained any of the glory of Kenneth McKenzie's day, when the fort did a massive trade in beaver plews, and McKenzie was called the king of the Upper Missouri.

But the beaver days were long gone, along with McKenzie, and only a modest trade in buffalo robes kept the fort profitable. When Brokenleg had seen it in the mid-thirties, it had been a startling island of civilization in a vast wilderness; a place where French wines graced the table, along with fresh greens from its gardens, milk and eggs from its flocks, and dainties shipped from St. Louis. The *bourgeois* himself and his top men had dined in black frock coats, attended by a bevy of gorgeous Assiniboin women in bright cottons sewn into the latest Parisian fashion.

That July afternoon the *Platte* pushed its way past the braided confluence of the Yellowstone and Missouri rivers, between looming reddish bluffs, while everyone aboard watched the various colored waters, the aqua of the Missouri and green of the Yellowstone, mix and streak. But Fitzhugh was watching something else, the ruin of old Fort William just there at the confluence. No one occupied it now, though once it had been the pride of Rocky Mountain Fur, the only major opposition American Fur ever had. But the beaver days were gone, and now the decaying fort belonged to Pierre Chouteau, Jr., who bought it to keep it out of the hands of opponents.

The old ruin saddened him, and his thoughts turned to the joyous day of the free trappers, of the Sublettes and Bridger and Campbell and Fitzpatrick, the wild rendezvous when a man would squander a year's hard-won plews for a jug of mountain whiskey, a few new traps, and enough powder and ball, sugar and coffee, to keep him until the next one. This robe trade lacked the joy of the old days. The trappers had vanished from the high lonely mountains, all except a few who hung on, earning nothing much; and now the fur companies bartered for buffalo robes, and scarcely noticed when a man brought in a pack of beaver. He and Jamie Dance had hung on, surviving somehow, building up an awful thirst because they couldn't afford mountain whiskey, or even aguardiente, the famous Taos lightning that cooked a man's innards. Oh, those lost days, when it lifted a man's heart to be young and strong in the western wilderness, a thousand miles from a settlement or a fence or a loaf of bread or a lawyer or a deacon.

His reverie was cut short by the sight of Fort Union itself, shimmering in a brutal heat, its American flag limp on its staff. The fort seemed as startling now as it had ever been, with its stockade of silvered cottonwood logs surrounded by the perennial lodges of tribesmen, bright-painted cones in a sea of ochre and rust-colored rock. Now, at the height of the trading season, whole villages of Assiniboin, Cree, Blackfeet and River Crow—violent enemies elsewhere—had collected here to push soft, brain-tanned robes through the trading window and collect the shining manufactured goods on the shelves.

Within, the peaked roof of the factor's house—once

McKenzie's palace—poked above the stockade, along with the shingled roofs of warehouses, barracks, and kitchens. It had been laid out like the rest of the fur posts, with bastions at opposite corners—defenses never used because no tribe dared antagonize the supplier of its powder and ball, hoop iron, pots and kettles, and all the rest. But towering there anyway with slits in their brooding rock walls to permit riflemen a shot along any side of the stockade—just in case—because no army would come to a rescue, and no law existed save for American Fur's own.

This, indeed, was an occasion. On the distant levee tribesmen gathered, while engagés came running down the steep grade to the river. A boom roared out upon the water, followed by a puff of white from the near bastion, and a sudden thump of air—the fort's salute. Scarcely ever had Fort Union witnessed two riverboats in a single year; and never had it seen an opposition packet.

He felt the sudden change as the *Platte* cut away from the swift current of the channel and into slackwater, riding easily on its flat hull. He heard the descending wheeze of steam pistons slowing and the languid splash of stilled wheels as LaBarge and Roux angled the packet toward shore. Down on the bow, Maxim looked a bit frightened. Curiosity consumed Fitzhugh: how had the passing of the old world, the beaver days, and the rise of the new robe trade affected the great old fort and its ways? And, too, what about Alexander Culbertson, the bearded senior man here, newly married, they said, to a fifteen-year-old Blood girl closely tied to the chiefs of that tribe, a pretty thing named Natawista. He'd never met Culbertson, but like very denizen of the upper Missouri, he knew the name.

A mob of passengers lined the rail, and Fitzhugh realized there still were many on board, both deck and cabin class. Few of them were employed by American Fur, he surmised. Most of those had come upriver on the *Trapper* a few weeks earlier. No, these rough sorts, some with squaws, were free men of the mountains, no different from what he and Jamie had been only a few months ago—men who'd never go east, just the way he'd never go east because he couldn't breathe there. He could scarcely imagine how he'd borne St. Louis as long as he did. He stared sharply at them, memorizing faces one by one, wondering which of these ruffians and mountain savages had taken coin to wreck the Buffalo Company. Someday he'd find out, and there'd be a reckoning in blood. He got no clue, though some stared back from weathered eyes as sharp as hawks', and with unsmiling visages that dared Fitzhugh to make something of their deadly gaze. Mountain men. Forever fearless, and forever afraid. He knew the feeling, how it was to live ruthlessly in wilderness, afraid of nothing—except what might happen next.

Deckmen tossed hawsers toward the levee, and the manila lines were snatched by white and bronze hands, and wrapped around posts driven there. The *Platte* had arrived, and announced its presence with an insolent shrill of its steam whistle, as if to say that not all power and law and wealth lay on the shore. Fitzhugh grinned. Whoever pulled the whistlecord had let it howl a few seconds too long. LaBarge himself, he thought; once the pilot of company riverboats; now the master of his own packet.

He waited patiently while crewmen lowered a stage at the gangway and the most eager of the passengers bolted to the levee, loaded with duffel. This would be an overnight stop, he judged, seeing no firemen tending the ravenous flame under the boiler. Tomorrow, the *Platte* would retreat the two miles back to the confluence, and head into the virgin waters of the Yellowstone river, probing cautiously, no doubt with a man at the prow sounding the bottom with a marked pole.

He watched the passengers disperse, knowing one or two might be men he'd gladly strangle. No reunions, he noticed. No waiting women, cries of joy, handclasps, hugs. Rough men stepped onto land unmet, and uneager to talk, and vanished toward the fort or out into the sea of cowhide lodges. Chiefs and headmen waited and watched, knowing they'd eventually be invited, two or three at a time, to tour the fireboat and receive a twist of tobacco. The forward hatches remained closed, and the second mate stood guard there. The few items destined for here had long since swung to land with block and tackle strung from a spar. No blankets. Fitzhugh had watched it all, red-eyed. So had LaBarge, from above, and Hugh Clowes, standing right at the gangway.

When at last the crush of passengers and half the crew, freed by four-hour shift, had boiled toward the gray palisade, a brown-bearded man in shirtsleeves, with a demure Indian girl clinging to his arm, stepped forward, an engaging smile upon his amiable face. Culbertson, of course. Fitzhugh knew the man at once. LaBarge did, too, racing down the companionways to welcome the top man in Chouteau's Upper Missouri Outfit. Brokenleg found himself liking the man on sight for reasons he couldn't fathom, and wished it were not so. They would talk on board, then. He nodded to Maxim, who still sulked around the prow, and then to Dust Devil, who stood disdainfully, eyeing all these enemies of the Cheyenne, white and red, with the same expression she reserved for dog-vomit.

"Joe LaBarge!" exclaimed Culbertson, with such gladness in his voice that Fitzhugh bridled. LaBarge bawled his delight, with a handshake and mountain hug.

"And you're Fitzhugh. Brokenleg Fitzhugh, our Opposition," Culbertson continued, extending a warm hand.

"I reckon I am. And this is my Dust Devil," he added. She nodded slightly, with tolerably decent manners for one who supposed she was among coyotes.

Within moments, they'd met Natawista, whom Fitzhugh found shy and beautiful. The girl spoke no English but plainly understood it, following the conversation with her brown eyes. And Brokenleg had dourly introduced Maxim, who stared solemnly, afraid to speak.

"Let's go on up to the saloon and have some spirits," LaBarge said. "It looks to be a madhouse out there."

"Height of the trading season," Culbertson said, following LaBarge up to the boiler deck. "We've hardly had a night's sleep since we were resupplied."

Fitzhugh followed irritably, flanked by Dust Devil and Maxim, irked by LaBarge's plain delight at this reunion, and wondering darkly if the whole world had conspired against the Buffalo Company. The men's saloon glowed amiably in the late sun. A cabin boy brought out tumblers, decanters and water and left them, while the ship bobbed quietly, a slumbering water-beast tethered to the levee.

"Ah, Mister Fitzhugh," said Culbertson amiably. "I know you, though we've never met. Not a man of the mountains speaks ill of you. And here you are, starting an Opposition post, you and my friend Guy Straus, and Mister Dance," He smiled. "We'll have a worthy opponent this time, Mister Fitzhugh."

"Make an offer," Fitzhugh blurted. "That's what you came here for; make an offer, damn ye."

Time snagged on a bar. Joseph LaBarge stared, amazed, at the hot-tempered young man beside him. Alec Culbertson paused, sipped whiskey, and glanced at Fitzhugh, weighing words.

"Why, Mister Fitzhugh. We were just resupplied," he began slowly.

"I already know your reasons," Brokenleg shot back.

The response puzzled LaBarge as much as Culbertson.

"Perhaps you'd better explain, young man," Culbertson said, carefully.

"You've wrecked us and now you're workin' around to a low bid."

Alec Culbertson drew into a bewildered silence, obviously not wishing to exacerbate matters. Fitzhugh glared at him, daring him to say a word.

"I think," said Captain LaBarge, "I should do some clarifying, Alec. Mister Fitzhugh, here, and his new company suffered a grievous loss downriver, near the Mandan villages. Someone onboard managed to dump fifteen bales of Witney blankets overboard—we think it was overboard—in the dark of a moonless night. We haven't the faintest clue—"

"Hell we don't," Fitzhugh interrupted. "American Fur done it. You done it." He glared at Culbertson.

"Mister Fitzhugh, I assure you I haven't the foggiest idea who . . ." Culbertson's voice trailed off. "It doesn't matter what I say. We're convicted."

"Make your offer. If it's good enough, you'll get the outfit. That's what you wanted."

LaBarge bridled at the harshness he was hearing, and the vicious glare in Fitzhugh's eyes, half mad.

"I had no intention of buying your outfit. We're well supplied. Most items, anyway."

"You can have it for what we have in it."

"But, sir, I told you—"

"I know what you told me."

Maxim stared at the floor and wouldn't lift his gaze. Dust Devil sat stone-faced and impenetrable. LaBarge sighed, unable to balm the hurt moment. "I think Mister Fitzhugh sees all this as a conspiracy by American Fur, Alec. At Fort Pierre, Chardonne made your company's usual offer, along with some veiled threats. Now Brokenleg's upriver without a key trade item, knowing it'll be twice as hard to buck your competition. I think he was expecting the coup de grace from you."

"Mister Fitzhugh, this is a large company, and things happen that I'm unaware of. But I can promise you this: if I find the culprits who stole your tradegoods, I'll have them punished. If it was something done by one or another branch of American Fur, I'll resign my post here. I plan to defeat your opposition, sir, by every means available to me—that's honorable."

"You ain't making an offer?"

"No. Under other circumstances, I might have bought some of your tradegoods. We're already short of some stock. But not under these conditions. We've a few blankets I'll sell you at our cost, sir."

That struck LaBarge as an unusual offer. "There, Brokenleg, Alec's doing what he can."

"It's just a way to get more robes outa us."

"Mister Fitzhugh," LaBarge said gently, "the cost of shipping your entire outfit downriver would be ruinous to your company."

"Maybe you're an AFC man."

"I'm my own man," LaBarge snapped. "And this is my own packet. And if you deal with me, or Alec Culbertson, or the tribesmen you wish to barter with in this fashion, you're doomed before you begin. I think Guy Straus made a mistake about you."

"No, he didn't!" cried Maxim miserably.

"Some sneak dumped the blankets, and it wasn't so he could get rich trading them. He did it to hurt me."

Alec Culbertson drained his glass and stood. "I think I'd better attend to my duties, gentlemen. My sincere regrets, Mister Fitzhugh. Captain, Natawista and I would enjoy your company at dinner, eight o'clock. You'll hear the bell." He paused, wrestling with his own instincts. "And you, my friends. I trust you'll join us?"

He peered at Fitzhugh, Dust Devil, and Maxim amiably.

"You go, Maxim. Me, I'm not walking into that thieving fort."

The boy stood gravely, troubled to the core. LaBarge was irked.

"I'll come," Maxim said.

"Very well, then, Mister Straus. You come along with Captain LaBarge."

LaBarge accompanied his guests down the stairs to the main deck, and saw them to the stage. He didn't much care for American Fur, but Alec Culbertson was another matter altogether. He knew no finer man. "I'm sorry about this unhappy occasion, Alex," he said, shaking hands. "It's been my pleasure to meet you, lovely Natawista."

She smiled and said something in her Blackfoot tongue.

Over on the levee, the headmen waited. They always did. These were nearly naked in the hot sun. Some he knew, such as Bear Ears of the Cree, and Standing Buffalo of the Hunkpapa Sioux. There was a Crow headman here too, standing amiably among his mortal enemies.

"Mister Clowes," he said, "bring them on board by threes."

He always enjoyed this because a fireboat was magic to them. It had become a ritual for pilots and masters to permit them—but not other tribesmen—to gawk and touch, and explore, and to receive the peace-offering from the company, the tobacco twist. He adjusted his doublebreasted blue uniform, wishing he could be as naked as the headmen in the boiling summer heat, and smiled as the first three, two Assiniboin headmen and a lesser Crow chief, spread out on the deck.

He motioned them up the companionways, until finally they reached the pilothouse, where the chiefs could peer down upon the world below like lords in castles. They touched the gleaming brass of the compass, and tugged at the helm, and exclaimed at the twin black-iron stacks before them. He couldn't explain anything—their tongues were beyond him—but he didn't need to: they'd entered a wonderland, fantastic beyond the imaginings of tribesmen, and needed no explanation of the actual utility of instruments.

Quickly, then—a dozen bronzed headmen waited politely on the levee—he led these three down to the boiler deck and the saloon, intending to show them a few staterooms. They plunged through ornate doors into the men's saloon, and discovered Fitzhugh and Dust Devil still there, the stiff-legged trader with an empty glass in hand and a look about him of drunken anger. And beside him, Dust Devil, utterly sober and looking like a wasp's nest.

Brokenleg simply glared, unfathomable thoughts ticking through his saturated brain. But not Dust Devil. She stood, examining the headmen with those disdainful eyes of hers, reading tribe from the shape of moccasins and the set of feathers and the decor on breechclouts.

"Aiee, Assiniboin dog-vomit and Crow horseturds," she said in English, and repeated it with the hand-language of the tribes. "It's bad enough to have a Crow on board, but Assiniboin dogs too. We will never trade with you."

The headmen froze, understanding the insult perfectly, and recognizing a Cheyenne woman before them. They eyed her menacingly, but did nothing. The Crow, Walks at Night, memorized her with glittering eyes, and then studied Fitzhugh with contempt.

"Mrs. Fitzhugh, that will be quite enough." LaBarge snapped. "These headmen are guests of the LaBarge Brothers, and I'll not have them insulted."

"What you bawlin' about?" Fitzhugh muttered, rising up on his stiff leg.

"You're not in any condition to discuss the matter, Fitzhugh. And if you want my opinion—which you don't—you've just destroyed your hope of trading with two important tribes up on the Yellowstone."

He herded his guests out onto the deck before real trouble erupted, suddenly aware that Guy Straus's company was doomed. He had contracted to haul their outfit as far as he could up the Yellowstone, and he would do that. And leave the whole pile there along with the angry drunk and the fanatic Cheyenne and their hopeless engagés. He was going to have to talk with Guy Straus when he got back to St. Louis—and perhaps spare that good man further loss and grief. Maybe he could talk Maxim into going back as well. Or Alec Culbertson could. Fitzhugh was too small of heart to fill a trader's shoes.

Chapter Eight

Brokenleg knew they'd come as far as they could, even before Captain LaBarge told him. For two hours he'd watched crewmen in a yawl sound the rapids ahead, peering at boulders that cleaved the water viciously. It wasn't much of a rapids, but enough rock lay in it to daunt a master of a packet.

"Mister Fitzhugh," the master said curtly, "this is it. I see no islands, so I presume you'll wish to unload on the south bank,"

The master's curtness, ever since Fort Union, irked Fitzhugh, but he ignored it, "Any spit of land or something we can defend?"

LaBarge shook his head. "Good cottonwood grove a mile back," he said.

"No chance of your laying over for two weeks, I suppose."

"None. The water's dropping daily and I'm in danger of getting caught. In fact, sir, I will be starting at dawn."

"Back to the woods, then," Fitzhugh said. He hated to lose ground. They'd come only about seventy or eighty miles up the Yellowstone, and needed to go about two hundred fifty. It'd be a long hard haul from here; and they'd have to do it twice, and maybe send one wagon back a third time, to carry all the goods in the three Pittsburghs. "We'll need to hide the goods and hope some band or other doesn't follow the wheel tracks."

LaBarge nodded, and began instantly to wheel the packet around in the narrow, rapid channel, a tricky business. An hour later they anchored along a thickly forested bank, with towering cottonwoods that screened the area from a river trace a half a mile away that ran along the foot of the bluffs. It had taken some doing. They needed to find a slot where the great wagons could escape the woods; where the packet could glide close to the shore, and where the mountain of tradegoods could be hidden, because it would be guarded by only two engagés while the rest drove the loaded wagons to old Fort Cass, a distance of about a hundred and eighty miles. Fortunately, they'd seen no sign of a passing village, probably because it was still the trading season, and most bands were camped close to the trading posts.

They ran the wagons down the stage first, and then began lifting goods out of the hold, using a spar and block and tackle, and bit by bit the hold emptied and a heap of goods, looking oddly vulnerable and out of place, grew on the grassy bank. At nine in the evening, when all that was done, they loosed the livestock and herded it to shore, the last task. The bawling of the oxen troubled Fitzhugh; he wished the whole thing could be accomplished in perfect silence.

At once LaBarge ordered his crew to prepare to sail.

"You're not staying the night?" Brokenleg asked, amazed.

"We can make ten or fifteen miles. Especially with that moon," LaBarge said, pointing to the orange globe perched on the eastern slopes.

"I could use the protection."

"Mister Fitzhugh, I'll be running on sand as it is. Have I fulfilled our agreement?"

". . . Yes."

"Then I'll have you sign this document saying you've taken possession of your goods."

Brokenleg signed it unhappily, scratching with the goose-quill nib the master gave him.

Swiftly, deckmen raised the stage and retrieved the hawsers that had pinned the *Platte* to the bank. And then with barely a splash, the paddles wheeled over, cut into water, going with the current now, and the packet ghosted out toward the channel, silently so as not to alert any curious ear. Slowly it merged into the murky golden light of the summer's eve, vanishing by degrees rather than sliding around a bend. Fitzhugh watched it go, a wraith returning to civilization some infinitude away, the vibration of its engines dulling into deep silence. Dust Devil stood beside him watching the vessel slowly vanish, and the engagés watched too, filled with a strange solemnness that comes upon a group suddenly isolated and utterly alone.

"Load the wagons," Fitzhugh said quietly. "I want everything that can be rain-damaged—the ribbons and tradecloth especially—under the sheets right away. That, plus the fusils, powder—and those casks of turpentine and vinegar. We'll load tonight, and leave at dawn."

But no one moved. The wilderness closed about them suddenly, a chill on the hot summer's air. He heard crickets. Something splashed on the river, a dusk-hunter. After the daily hum of the boat, comforting in its way, the smallest sounds of nature seemed alarming. Even the snort and snuffle of horses grazing made him jumpy, and set engagés into spasms of watchfulness. Far away, up on a bluff somewhere north, a coyote barked just once. Men peered fearfully into the surrounding cottonwoods, whose thick canopy plunged the ground at their feet into blackness.

"Monsieur Fitzhugh," said Trudeau softly. "I think while a bit of light remains, the men might reconnoiter the woods, and the grass here, and see what is best to hold the livestock. We don't have hobbles."

"Do it," Fitzhugh snapped. He'd had the same notion himself, getting oriented, probing outward, looking to defenses. Ten men, even armed with good percussion locks, weren't much of a force.

Dust Devil watched them all disdainfully. She looked utterly at home here; in fact, everything had reversed. She'd been uncomfortable in St. Louis and on the riverboat but once she set foot on land under the benign watch of Sweet Medicine, all that had changed. It suddenly occurred to Fitzhugh, as he watched her wicked grin, that she would come to him one of these nights full of fierce passion and joy.

"Monsieur Trudeau," he added, as men fanned out quietly, "we've all spent our lives in places like this."

They were back in ten or fifteen minutes, having probed out to the looming bluff and the silent trace below it to their satisfaction. The golden moon afforded enough light to load up the wagons with the important and vulnerable things to be taken on the first passage. The livestock settled down to contented grazing, freed at last of the miserable confines of the packet.

By the time the day faded into a faint blue memory on the northwestern horizon, they'd made a camp of sorts. But not a comfortable or cheery one because he'd banned fires, and mosquitos whined like bullets around them. The Creoles brooded, which was quite unlike them. He'd expected quiet humor, small ribald jokes. Still, they'd done what they could. He'd appointed two men to each of the watches and made sure they were well armed. He himself would take the third watch. There'd be only five hours of true darkness in this northern clime, this time of year.

It irked him that LaBarge had pulled out so fast. That the captain had been cool to him ever since Fort Union. Brokenleg resolved to tell Guy Straus about it. There wasn't even a parting drink, a round of spirits, a warm clasp of hands, a big hooraw, the way it had happened at the rendezvous when things were breaking up until the next year. No. Just some tart, hasty au revoir. He got the feeling that the master didn't like him. Well, too bad. Maybe he didn't like that master and his thieving blanket-stealing crew.

The river glittered by, bouncing stars off its oily surface, on its long, mysterious passage to the sea. Somewhere to the south and west snow from the gulches of towering mountains, the backbone of the continent, melted into rivulets that found their way to tributaries and finally to the Yellowstone—the Elk River, the Crows and Blackfeet called it—and on to the Missouri, still snow-cold and crystalline. And then at some unfathomable moment, having tumbled down a continent, these waters flowed, warm and muddy, into the Gulf of Mexico at New Orleans. A light steamer could come the whole distance bringing goods from anywhere. From England. From Europe. Independence lay some unspeakable distance down its path, and beyond it St. Louis, farther than a man could walk in many months. The rivers were a golden cord stretching from this silent wilderness back to a land of brick buildings and frame houses, places he didn't like much, but whose steel and gunpowder he badly needed.

"Sweet Medicine," said Dust Devil, breaking into his sad reverie. "Ah, it is good. My people aren't far. Maybe along the Powder. I can almost tell you where, even though I can't see them. See, Fitzhugh, this is the place where Sweet Medicine sees me. If Crow dogs come, we will kill them."

"I reckon we won't," he retorted. "We're gonna trade fair and square. You got to cut that out."

She laughed, disdain back in her throat. "Well then, we'll kill Assiniboin. Or Blackfeet. Or Gros Ventre. Or Hidatsa. All dogs."

"You're a bloodthirsty whelp tonight."

"Tonight I am home."

"I reckon you are, and I reckon there's a few around hyar who'd like to lift your scalp."

"Not as much as they'd like yours—what's left of it, redhair."

"I ain't got me enough up front to scalp."

She laughed, a child's glee silvering out into the night, caught his hand with one of hers, snatched up their robe with the other, and dragged him along the bank to a hummock where tall grasses grew thick.

No tribulation on earth could stay the swift blossoming of Brokenleg Fitzhugh's soul. It began, actually, with the departure of the *Platte*, although he'd been too irked and worried to notice. But the next day broke upon joy, and not even the maddening difficulties and delays involved with yoking oxen and harnessing mules, assigning engagés to wagons, and choosing the two who would stay behind, could arrest the sweetness of this life in the wilds that began to percolate through his hot blood.

They made sixteen miles that day, by Fitzhugh's reckoning, along a trail that had never seen a wheeled vehicle. The trace along the south bank of the Yellowstone had been cut by buffalo and other animals, widened by horseback Indians, and rutted by the poles of countless travois. Only now and then did sagebrush or juniper or a fallen cottonwood log impede their progress. And none of these bothered him in the slightest.

He didn't understand what pressures he'd been wrestling with until he no longer felt them. Even the riverboat, that last vestige of polite society and manners, had managed to bottle him up, force him into a taut silence, and build in him a dour, rank sullenness. He scarcely paused to consider his own mood. Overland travel had been torture for him ever since he'd ruined his left leg. He had a special saddle with a long left stirrup to accommodate that stiff limb, but it didn't save him from pain. He could take only two hours of that sort of torture, and then he had to tie his horse to a wagon, and slide aboard until its jarring had tortured his leg in new ways.

But the odd thing was, he didn't mind it. He scouted ahead as much as his leg permitted, and when pain drove him back to a wagon, Dust Devil automatically rode ahead, her skirts hiked high and her jet hair blowing wild as the wind. His attention had returned to an older, atavistic, primitive knowing of the land. He read the circling bald eagle with his eyes, spotted a purple summer thunderhead off to the south, watched a pair of whitebellied antelope skitter up a long slope and then pause on its crest to watch the strange procession of carts, things new to antelope-eyes. Once he watched the two spare horses lay back their ears and stare into a cottonwood copse, and he knew intuitively they'd scented or sensed a catamount in there. That day, like the ones before it, burnt hot and breathless through the afternoon, but the dry air sucked the sweat away as fast as it formed, and he scarcely knew discomfort.

By that evening he should have been exhausted, but he wasn't; he felt elated. His engagés were savvy about the ways of the wilderness and didn't shy from the toil it required. Like Brokenleg, they belonged here and knew what to do without being asked; knew how to remove obstacles from the trail, how to sound a bottom and a ford, how to rest the sweating, lowing oxen and comfort the nervous mules. He let Samson Trudeau choose the stopping place, and the engagé did it expertly, on a grassy flat in a vast side-coulee where bluffs would conceal their fires and the livestock could be easily herded. The place lay higher and drier than the Yellowstone bottom, and there was not a mosquito to torment them. Men and stock would sleep well.

"You are happy," Dust Devil said to him in the lavender twilight.

It startled him. "I cain't rightly say I noticed it. My haid's been full of stuff. You know. Getting the goods shelved, fixing up the old place, getting word out to the—the tribes. Sending the wagons back for the next. Who should go, who should stay. Trading. Gettin' that first robe through the window and giving out something for it. We'll be manned pretty thin—but, yeah, I'm feeling perky at that."

"It is because you're here. You don't like it back there with all the whitemen and the cities. Not even the riverboat."

"I reckon that's it."

"I hardly know you back there. You were different. Now you're Cheyenne like me."

"Reckon so."

She'd put it into some sort of words for him, and after that he knew what was happening inside of himself each day and they toiled west and south, day by day. They hit a hailstorm one day and soggy ground the next, which mired the iron tires and exhausted the oxen and mules. They had a bad time fording the Powder, quicksand sucking at hooves and wheels, and had to double-team once to drag a mired wagon out. They saw a barechested horseman atop a bluff on the north side of the river one day, and knew they'd been observed. One day they couldn't make meat, and gobbled down oat gruel boiled from precious stores. Four of the oxen were rebellious and troublemakers, and the engagés fought among themselves to avoid having to use them. Brokenleg established a system of rotation, so that the troublesome beasts were inflicted evenly on each pair of engagés. And through it all, Brokenleg felt restraints falling away like dead leaves, and he was discovering that even the annoyances didn't bother him.

One day while he was resting on a wagon, Dust Devil rode back to him with a wild joy illumining her face. "A village of the People ahead. They're gone now but they were there."

He rode ahead of the wagons with her to the bank of the Tongue River, and she showed him the site. It'd been some village all right. The grass was clipped down; white bones lay about; teepee rings remained in large concentric circles across the open flat.

"How do you know it's the People?" he asked.

"I know."

"Could be Sioux. They're some like your Cheyenne."

"It was the People."

"You figger out how you know, cause I want to learn it. Maybe it smells right."

"Smell! Smell! The People don't smell. Whitemen stink. Crows smell like dog-vomit."

He laughed. "You smell some, at least on Sundays and Tuesdays," he said, but she whirled her spotted mare and rode off, indignant. Before they'd gone down to St. Louis, they'd spent many of their waking hours insulting each other and laughing. He hadn't even been aware it had stopped, or that it had started up again.

They'd planned to camp at the Tongue that night but pushed on two extra miles to get to fresh grass. That made another night without meat because whoever'd camped there had driven it miles away.

Through the fat long days of July they toiled westward, fording the Rosebud and then Sarpy, closing in on the place where they would start a trading post. The oxen were thinning down but the mules showed little sign of their long toil. Fitzhugh eyed the stock warily, hoping it'd last out the return trips. He worried about the mountain of goods left behind, and the two left to guard it; but he could do nothing, and it didn't pay to let a thing like that nag at him.

They made their last camp about eight or ten miles from the Bighorn, he reckoned. One more day, at any rate. That evening they stopped right beside the Yellowstone, surrounded by thick brown grass, with scarcely a tree in sight. Some places along the wide river were like that. He'd shot a buffalo cow there; a good, careful shot that struck right behind the shoulder, where his fifty-two-caliber ball would have the greatest effect, and had it half butchered when the wagons pulled up. That seemed fitting enough—a buffalo feast on the last night out, to celebrate the start of the Buffalo Company's new post. The engagés rejoiced but Dust Devil turned solemn, and he couldn't fathom it.

"I don't want any," she said, and refused to touch even the succulent humpmeat, or tongue.

He shrugged, wondering if it had to do with that mirage way back down the river, when they stood on the hurricane deck and watched all the buffalo march into a hole in the sky.

"It's sacred!" she cried, angrily.

The next day, a rare overcast one in which July seemed to vanish and the Moon when the Chokecherries Ripen replaced it somehow, she remained sullen and stayed by herself, as if the company of whitemen was as loathsome as the Spirits she feared so much, which lived under the earth. The chill day delighted the engagés, and made life sweeter for the livestock, and they made good time. Trudeau, who knew the country well, thought they'd reach Fort Cass by mid-afternoon.

Brokenleg didn't sense that anything was amiss until he began to smell woodsmoke, faint and pungent and elusive, on the air rolling out of the west, upriver. A village, he supposed, right there on the confluence of the Bighorn and the Yellowstone, always a choice place to dwell, with its ample fuel and grass. He hoped the good buffalo grass around the fort and the nearby hills wouldn't be eaten off by the herds of whatever village it might be.

By noon the woodsmoke smell had grown stronger, and Dust Devil had grown more sullen.

"Absaroka," she muttered, and he couldn't imagine why she said it. Certainly a little smoke in the air didn't provide the clue. The engagés smelled the smoke, too, and looked a little fearful.

"Trudeau, tell them to relax. We're traders, not soldiers. They can be armed if they want, but I want those weapons sheathed."

Trudeau walked among the wagons and the gaunted teams, giving the solemn engagés the word.

They'd been discovered now. Horsemen up on the hills

above the broad valley watched and waited, in twos and threes.

"Absaroka!" Dust Devil spat, a loathing underlying the name.

Nonetheless, Fitzhugh led the wagons upriver, even while knots of almost naked warriors rode out to escort them, smiling, pointing, guessing at the contents of the giant wagons, exclaiming at the strange sight of yoked oxen and harnessed gray mules dragging the giant boxes toward the village.

"I reckon they're camped around Fort Cass outa habit," he said to Trudeau. "We'll just drive on up to the fort and claim it, and you and the rest can start unloading while I palaver with their headman. Stroke a luck, actually. We got us a whole blooming Crow village to trade robes with, fast as we can get the stuff on the shelves."

They rounded a last headland looming up on the south, and beheld a vast village, with lodges everywhere, dimpling the broad flats under a low gray sky. A skim of gray smoke layered over the encampment. He glanced at Dust Devil, who stared at the sight angrily, withdrawn into herself, like a nun in a bawdyhouse, he thought, amused. From everywhere, Crow people tumbled out to see the amazing sight, these white-sheeted monsters pulled by slavering whitemen's buffalo. A happy crowd, he thought, enjoying the bright children, the little lads naked but the girls in skirts, and the broad-cheeked young women, laughing and pointing and obviously guessing at the mysteries within the wagons.

They rode down a sort of street, exciting yellow curs, which barked at strange sights; past smoke-blackened lodges of cowhide, with medicine tripods before them, the doors of the lodges all facing east to greet Sun and bless the lodge.

Ahead lay Fort Cass, on barren land stripped of the cottonwoods that once surrounded it, the palisades silvery in the gray light. It excited him. The post! They'd restore it, renew it, clean the cobwebs and rattlers out of it, sweep the dirt floors of its warehouse, chase away the small wild things that had taken it over . . .

It flew two flags.

It took him a long, dark moment to register it. One was the familiar Stars and Stripes. He closed his eyes, half-wild. The other pennant was the familiar ensign of the Chouteaus.

He paused on his slat-ribbed horse, his leg aching suddenly, staring at this apparition. Fort Cass had been put back into service. Its giant doors had been rehung. The hard-used grassy meadow around the fort had been ground down to tawny dust. His heart sank at the sight. This was no Crow village; it was Fort Cass doing a booming trade with the Crow nation.

As he sat his horse, gaping, a brown-bearded man emerged, a man with bright black eyes and a sharp cruel twist of lip. Julius Hervey.

Chapter Nine

Oh, the waiting was hard. In spite of all his careful planning, he hadn't counted on this, the daily toll upon his health and mind simply from waiting for news, and keeping his imaginings under control. Guy Straus had a vivid imagination, especially when it came to calamity—shipwreck, Indian trouble, pox or cholera . . .

He'd kept busy, of course. Most days brought some business, in the form of currency exchange. His ability to change reals and pesos into dollars was valued in frontier St. Louis, as was his ability to convert buffalo robes into gold, or wolf pelts into iron kettles. The thrust of business kept him from worrying too much about his sons, especially Maxim, out there in a land no one but a few trappers knew. But he had bad moments, especially when Yvonne's worrying undermined his own optimism, most often at night as they snuffed the last candle and the torrent of doubt flowed from her like ink into the dark.

Oh, there'd been things to do. He'd contacted a French-Osage métis and offered him fifty dollars to cut five hundred selected sticks of osage orange, all prime bow wood, and deliver them bundled into hundreds to his agent at Westport. The thought of trading a prime buffalo robe, worth four dollars in the east for a stick of supple yellowish wood worth a few cents, pleased him. In fact, it tickled him because it gave them an edge, at least for a while, against

Pierre Chouteau *le Cadet* and all his numerous family and Creole relatives and allies by marriage, and loyal retainers.

And he would soon need to be writing Charles Early, at Witney mills in England, ordering next year's trade blankets for delivery in St. Louis by April 1, 1842. He debated whether to raise the order, and decided against it. He had no information suggesting he should. But he did write Cabot Mills, in Lawrence, Massachusetts, wondering whether that firm might weave a blanket suitable for the Indian trade. American blankets were dyed in drab colors, lacked the stripes and brightness the tribesmen loved, and also lacked the bars, or points, that instantly told them whether the blanket weighed two, three, or four pounds. Worth a try, he thought. A lot cheaper to ship Yankee blankets than English ones.

Often he dined with Robert Campbell at the rambling Planters House just to talk about the fur trade, and worry together. The affable Scot had been a part of it for years, an important person with Rocky Mountain Fur. What's more, he'd been out there, out to the wild rendezvous back in the beaver days, out the long Platte River trail to the roof of the continent. He'd been there; he knew the ropes—and he'd been a partner in several fur ventures that opposed the giant octopus, Chouteau.

"It all boils down to the men you send out there," he said over thick aromatic coffee. Guy had heard him say it before, and believed it fervently. "Put the right men out there and you'll do well, barring calamities and acts of God. But nothing'll squander a man's fortune away out there faster than bad judgment, stupidity, or some weakness or blindness. It's a crucible, that wilderness and all its hardships. It burns away the dross and only the pure mountaineer survives."

"I think I've got the men," Guy responded.

"Do you?"

The way Campbell said it sent a chill through Guy. "Are you suggesting I don't?"

"No, mon, I'm suggesting I'm not sure. It's a gamble, They both could turn out fine, as solid as Milt Sublette or Jed Smith."

But his caution, and his eyes, suggested something else.

"Tell me what you see, Robert. In confidence, of course."

But Campbell had smiled easily. "I would not have invested a farthing if I felt they weren't top men, both Fitzhugh and Dance."

But something hung there, in the smoke-laden air of the Planters, that disturbed Guy.

News came at last in late July. The first scrap of it arrived with the *Trapper*, the AFC steamer, back from Fort Union carrying the year's returns for the Chouteau interests. Its master, Jacques Raval, had sent a second mate to Chestnut Street, hand delivering Maxim's letter. Guy read it with vast joy, delighting in Maxim's enthusiasm, glad of the youth's critical assessment of Brokenleg and relieved that the frightening episode with the Yanktonai at the woodyard had turned out well. Or mostly well.

Within the same week he got a brief note from David, delivered by eastbound Mexican traders they'd encountered on the Santa Fe Trail. All was well; no disease; several breakdowns of the wagons which had forced them to stop for repairs; no reports of Comanche or Kiowa trouble ahead; and Jamie a good man, a natural leader out on the trail, a big grin forever cheering his teamsters.

These Guy showed to Yvonne, who found cause in them to worry all the more, until Guy gently teased her about it. And then the waiting once again.

And so things revolved until early August. One hot day when scarcely a breeze stirred a leaf, a fine black-lacquered chaise drawn by a gray trotter drew to a halt before Straus et Fils. Its driver, a trim, bearded man in a doublebreasted blue suit, clipped a carriage weight to the trotter's bridle, and let himself into the foyer.

"Joe LaBarge!" exclaimed Guy, upon discovering his guest. "You're back! It's good to see you, my *cher ami.* Come, come, come—" He steered the master back toward his own walnut wainscoted office. "Tell me everything. Everything! How goes the *Platte*? And tell me—everything!"

Captain LaBarge settled into the settee covered with watershot yellow silk, and accepted the aperitif Guy splashed generously from a decanter.

"Back in one piece, Guy. Fast trip down, and profitable, though not exactly lucrative."

"Here's to your successful return, Joe!" Guy lifted his own glass, and the captain did also, sipping slowly for a moment.

"The trip was very successful for the LaBarge Brothers," the master said, amiably. "We made Fort Union in good time, in spite of low water; delivered a few of Chouteau's goods along the way—things that failed to make the *Trapper*. After that, *mon ami,* we probed up the Yellowstone—a lot less water, and narrow channels, you know. But we pushed ahead. As far as Wolf Rapids, maybe seventy or eighty miles up. That's what the old beaver men called the place when they drifted down the river in their bullboats or mackinaws, carrying bales of plews. That was it, Guy. Boulders there, and a narrow channel. Wide enough, actually—close to eighty yards, but with that current we'd have had to run lines and winch it through from the banks. I decided no; that was it, with the river dropping an inch or so every day.

"I put Fitzhugh off on a wooded bank, along with the goods and wagons. And Maxim, of course. A rare lad, Guy. Earnest. Serious. Conscientious. Too much so, but that's not a fault. He wants to do well, as a sixteen-year-old lad must. We left at once, the Yellowstone shrinking like that—say, this is some bourbon, Guy—and fought sandbars all the way to the Platte River. I picked up a little downriver dunnage—mostly robes for Chouteau. Some of the posts took advantage of the chance, even though the new season'd hardly begun."

"My company—all is well, then? They are off to Cass?"

Joe LaBarge hesitated. "Off to Cass, yes. The livestock, the wagons, the engagés in good shape. About the tradegoods, Guy—"

"What, Joe? Some difficulty?"

LaBarge nodded, looking stern. "Theft. Or sabotage. No one knows which. But the fine hand of your rival down on the levee."

Guy felt his spirit grow small and still. He set his tumbler down on the beeswaxed desk, and settled into his armchair, preparing for the worst. "What, then?"

"The Witney blankets. All fifteen bales. Vanished. The night after we'd stopped at Fort Clark and the Mandan villages. We'd anchored at an island, as usual. Maxim discovered it the next morning. He did the daily tally, you know. Toiled away by the hour down there, every morning, counting everything."

Guy sat, stunned, sorting things, absorbing loss. "The blankets. I'd sent three hundred up the Missouri, and two hundred out with Dance. I suppose it'll affect Fitzhugh's trade badly. A key item. And a profitable one—three to five robes a blanket, Joe."

LaBarge said nothing. Guy sipped, letting the implications seep through him, his alert mind asking questions.

"What measures were—"

"Everything. My mate conducted an aboveboard search. Both my first and second mate asked a few of my trusted crew—ones that've been with me for years—to watch and listen. Fitzhugh . . . well, he dealt with it—his own way."

"Which was?"

"Roared at his men. Left the accusation over them all. Promised to butcher the guilty party or parties."

Guy didn't like the sound of it, and it was plain from LaBarge's compressed lips that the master shared his view. Guy sighed. "He's not experienced with men."

"No," LaBarge agreed, "he's not. It took Trudeau—he's made Trudeau his second—it took Samson Trudeau to keep it from blowing up. Trudeau told him the engagés would handle it their own way."

"How did Maxim handle himself, Joe?"

"A boy's guilt. Undeserved, I assure you. But he tortured himself for not watching closer."

Straus nodded. "What do you make of it, Joe?"

LaBarge shrugged, "Not fatal. Trudeau—always Trudeau—simply told Fitzhugh they'd need to get out to the villages more, with those wagons, and trade that way. If it got down to trading at forts, the bands would go to American Fur posts where they could get blankets, rather than your post—where they couldn't."

"That was Trudeau's idea?"

"It was, Guy."

Guy stared out upon Chestnut Street, watching a carriage rattle by. "Is there more, Joe?" If there was, he scarcely wanted to hear it. "Did Fitzhugh want more blankets expressed up there?"

"No. Not American ones. The tribesmen won't trade for them. He didn't write a report for you, either. I suppose he thought I would tell you. And—Guy, yes. There's more. He . . . obviously has trouble—dealing with spirits. But that's not as bad as Mrs. Fitzhugh's passionate allegiances. At Fort Union, our Cheyenne lady managed to insult Assiniboin and Crow headmen, and would have kept at it if I hadn't taken measures. She's hurt the trade of Dance, Fitzhugh and Straus worse than I can tell you. I've dreaded bringing you this news. I debated with myself all the way down the river about it. To say something or nothing. For your sake, I'm saying something. I'm sorry, Guy. I'm going to give you a candid opinion you may not relish. Brokenleg Fitzhugh—despite all his admirable skills—isn't the right man, and I foresee grave losses and difficulties."

Guy sat quietly, thinking of Yvonne's steady drone of pessimism, and sighed. "Joe," he said. "Tell it to me again, all of it—every nuance. I need to know everything. And plan to stay for dinner, *cher ami.* I'll send word to Yvonne. And I'll snare Campbell if I still can. And—forgive me, Joe—I quite forgot that you'll want time with Pelagie . . . We must have her also. And tell us about the river, Joe. The river that goes two thousand miles to nowhere, eh?"

Guy blamed it on the cloying night air that left his nightshirt soaked, or perhaps it was the dinner wine, or the keen excitement evoked in him by Joe LaBarge's anecdotes. Or maybe it was the other matter, the incompetence of Brokenleg Fitzhugh . . . Whatever it was, he tossed and fought the coverlets, and rocked the fourposter.

"You're not sleeping, Guy," Yvonne said wearily, peering at him in the comfortable darkness.

"I'm troubling your sleep, Yvonne," he replied guiltily.

She reached out a hand to him and caught his, squeezing it. "It's the Buffalo Company."

Guy squeezed back, finding pleasure in the touch of her hand clasped in his. It had been like that from the beginning, gentle and affectionate love, especially in their private moments. She was innately a pessimist, and seemed astonished and delighted when she listened to his love-talk; as if such a good thing couldn't possibly be happening.

"It could be the river, Yvonne. Joe comes to dinner and talks of the river, and I hear magic and music. I see the boat skimming upstream, its wheels doing what wind and muscle can barely do, up into a land I've never seen, a land I must visit some day—"

"It's the Buffalo Company," she said.

He laughed softly, but his laughter perched on the honed

edge of truth. She twisted under the light blanket until she nestled close to him. They rarely made love any more but something sweeter in its own way had replaced it, this nestling and touching and talking of two mortals long accustomed to each other, and well versed in each other's follies. French men and women knew how to be friends, he thought. The Yankees and English had never learned how, and each sex peered at the other across a chasm. Ah, but the French . . . In truth, she clarified his thinking and her pessimism had always been a valuable check on his occasional enthusiasms. And his sunny faith in the goodness of life had a way of lifting her when she needed a boost, he knew. They'd learned not to spar, but to be plain, even blunt. He considered that a phenomenon in a Frenchwoman.

"I suppose it's the blankets," he said. "It's not just the loss, bad as that is. Three hundred of them, worth—with the shipping—over a thousand. It's the rest. It's what Chouteau's done; what'll be the next thing; whether they can get some robe trade without—"

"It's more than that, Guy." She was staring at him, he knew, though he could barely see her. "I always knew it wasn't right."

She alluded to the Buffalo Company itself, which she had opposed on the ground that the other partners, Dance and Fitzhugh, weren't the slightest bit capable. And now he had some confirmation of her view in Joe LaBarge's careful, dour assessment of Brokenleg and his Dust Devil, an opinion that Guy had not divulged to Yvonne even though she seemed to sense it. He debated telling her the rest of LaBarge's news, but thought it'd lead only into one of her bouts of pessimism.

"If it was only blankets, you'd be snoring. It's that Robert Fitzhugh and that savage he's bedded with, and poor Maxim, in danger out there. You can't do a thing about the man. He's your partner and not your engagé. As you said, it's a little bit like marriage."

She had an uncanny way of getting to the center of things she knew nothing about, he thought. She'd always done that. She'd been born a Diderot, in the family of the great encyclopedist, and like his own family, hers was neither Louisiana nor French Canadian, but a transplant from Europe. Like all the Diderots before her, she came equipped with a dazzling mind and an incisive way of probing into things and drawing conclusions.

"I don't know who's the worse savage," she continued. "Fitzhugh or Little Whirlwind—it's loathsome that he calls her Dust Devil. He has no respect for a woman. You didn't see him, Guy. You didn't observe. But I observed. Every time I saw him, I observed. I saw the wild light of his eyes. His eyes are like the bore of a cannon full of grapeshot. His receding hairline is the mark of an imbecile. His stiff leg maddens him. His brow is the brow of an ape. He has taken a savage squaw who turns upside down the theories of Jean Jacques Rousseau, yes? I formed an opinion. And it's grounded in scientific observation and rational study."

He laughed, but uneasily. "Your rational study and scientific observation are famous, *cher* Yvonne. And they always lead to one conclusion—nothing works!"

"But it is so, yes?"

"No."

"What is it that Joseph told you about him, Guy?"

"Told me?"

"Yes, told you. You are no good at secrets, Guy. When you are silent about something, it is because you are keeping a secret. All night at dinner you and Joe LaBarge talked about everything but your partner Fitzhugh and his squaw. And so I knew."

He chuckled, though he didn't want to. "I have more hopes for our Mexican post than I do for the Yellowstone one," he said softly.

"So! Even our Maxim could run it better than that drunken madman and his bitchy little squaw, Guy."

"We'll see, Yvonne," he said. "All we can do is wait. If I misjudged, we'll be hurt."

"And Maxim might be killed."

"That's not very likely."

"I worry about it."

"The Fitzhugh you saw here is not the Fitzhugh that will run the post in the wilderness, *cher amie.* He was a caged tiger in St. Louis."

"And an uncaged tiger on the Yellowstone, yes?"

He sighed. He didn't have half her acuity and wit when it came to these bouts. "My little Diderot," he muttered, "you have a mind fit for an encyclopedia, but not for the Yellowstone."

She laughed. That had always been the fun of it. From the day he'd met her in his youth, that cheerful laughter had galvanized him, even though his strict parents had done their best to head off the liaison.

"Go to sleep now," she whispered, and kissed him squarely on the stubble of his cheek.

"I'm going to prowl," he replied. "Tonight I'm the uncaged lion."

He slid out into the damp cool dark, feeling his cotton nightshirt cling, and wandered out of their bedroom, feeling her bright, curious brown eyes watching his departure.

He did not go downstairs, but instead shuffled toward the empty bedroom on the east side of the house that had housed his boys, passing Clothilde's quiet room on the way. The boys' window opened out across rooftops to the Mississippi river, as wide as a sea, and to the levee and wharves along the bank, where white packets lay ghostly in the night. A little to the north, the vast flood of the Missouri debouched into the Mississippi, staining the waters chocolate all the way to the sea. The river lay inky, perceived as a vast streak of nothingness.

He wanted to go up the river. He wanted to see for himself how Maxim fared, how Fitzhugh had repaired old Fort Cass, how many good robes lay in the warehouse, and whether they were properly protected from water and bugs and wild creatures. He wanted to see what goods lay on the shelves of the trading room, and see Fitzhugh's records, a line for each transaction: three robes for one brass kettle; six robes for a pound of powder and a bar of galena and five sheffield knives . . .

He admitted, as he thought about it, that he didn't wholly trust Robert Fitzhugh now. He wanted to see for himself. He wanted to make corrections if such were necessary. He wanted to find out whether Dust Devil had truly driven away the trade of other tribes, especially the Crow, beoause Fort Cass lay in Crow country, and Crow robes were prime, better tanned and softer than most others. He needed to know. He needed to bring Maxim home, if all had failed. He needed to measure Fitzhugh, before he ordered more blankets from Witney, before he mailed letters to the east, committing to a mountain of tradegoods, and another mountain of debt.

And, he admitted, another reason lay in his heart: the wild lands drew him like a magnet, just as they'd drawn a host of men before him. He wanted to go up the river just to see it; to see Sioux and Crow and buffalo and mustangs and a sea of grass. If only he could know . . .

But going over two thousand miles up the river without the help of steam engines was almost beyond his imagining. He could indeed catch a river packet to St. Joseph. And perhaps a rare packet would go even higher this late in the year—maybe even to Bellevue, though he doubted it. the rest would have to be by horseback. The thought encouraged him. With a few packhorses, he could take some blankets for trading. American blankets, to be sure, but at least something. He could visit his post on the Yellowstone and come down in a mackinaw, one of the flatbottomed boats carpentered upriver to float furs and men downstream. Maybe be back before the worst cold set in, before December.

He stood at the window, watching the inky river, yearning, aching, needing, and knowing it could not be. He could not abandon his business, Straus et Fils, for so long a time. No. He would have to trust. Trust his own judgment, trust his partner and his partner's wife, trust his sixteen-year-old Maxim, trust the engagés they'd employed. He had no other choice. What happened up there, so far from his control, would rock his family or it would prosper them all.

He felt an ancient need, the communion with the Source of wonders and wisdom and courage. He felt the nakedness of his head, and wished he might find his yarmulke before he prayed, but he knew God would hear and care.

Chapter Ten

Everything happened too fast. Brokenleg scarcely had time to grasp that he could not simply move into Fort Cass and set up trade, before Hervey fell upon them, striding across the flat like a lord. The new *bourgeois* of the fort radiated power. Brokenleg had known him for years, and wished he hadn't.

The wilderness affected men in various ways. In Julius Hervey, a life far from the restraints of law and moral authority had swiftly stripped away all inhibition until the remaining creature had become pure whimsical will, with not even a shred of the softening of civilization. His powerful hulking body had become a bully's tool, used indiscriminately against anyone, red or white, who got crosswise of him.

Even as Brokenleg sat his ribby horse bracing himself against Hervey's assault, he watched the man's smoldering eyes survey his wagons with a rapacious glance, study Maxim, who sat in the first wagon looking pale and stern, eye Dust Devil, and then settle mockingly on him.

"It's you, Fitzhugh. I've been expecting you."

"Didn't know American Fur had set up here again."

Hervey smiled, slowly. "Run your wagons into the fort and we'll unload," he said.

It was a command. "I reckon we'll go somewhere else, Julius."

"Bring your woman, too. She's something."

Brokenleg realized that Hervey was already possessing her. His eyes did that. They made no distinction between seeing and owning. Hervey had made a long career of taking away the wives of engagés, usually by force, and daring them to do anything about it. Those who dared to resist he had pulverized, or murdered.

"Reckon we'll be on our way."

"No, you won't. You'll enjoy Fort Cass."

"You heard me, Hervey."

But Julius Hervey simply grinned. "You!" he said to Trudeau. "Drive them wagons on in and shelve the goods. American Fur's bought them and bought you."

Samson Trudeau stared helplessly at Fitzhugh, and Fitzhugh saw utter terror in the engagé's eyes.

"Samson, turn the ox teams west," Fitzhugh said quietly, far more quietly than he wanted to speak.

Julius Hervey looked amused as Trudeau fearfully began tugging at the lead yoke of oxen. Then, with a single catlike dart of his hand, he grasped Dust Devil's bridle and began dragging her mare toward the fort.

"Come along, Fitzhugh, and I'll give you payment. We're short of tradegoods; didn't expect so many Crow. Traded everything in two weeks. Waiting for resupply, but Culbertson's short hisself."

All the while he tugged on the mare's bridle, while Dust Devil yanked her reins and resisted. "I'll kill you, white dog," she snapped.

Hervey chuckled. Fitzhugh knew he had to catch her fast, and that was just what Hervey wanted—a chance to pulverize Brokenleg.

But Dust Devil had her own notions, and leapt free of the horse, stumbling out of Hervey's swift reach, and when she turned toward him, a lethal silvery blade projected from her fist.

"Sometime soon, Little Whirlwind. I always take what I want," he said. "Unless Stiffleg there says yes. I don't like gifts. A little squaw with a knife." A moment later he was shoving Trudeau aside and grasping a lead ox by its nose.

Fitzhugh peered around unhappily. A mob of Crows was gathering, drawn by the wagons and the new traders. Most of them would side with Hervey, partly from fear, partly because he'd already traded with them. They were forming a wall around the wagons, one that would pen and frighten the oxen.

Hervey turned the ox and let go, laughing at Fitzhugh. "You've no choice, Brokenleg. No where to go, and all these nice gewgaws and pretties sitting there. First thing we did was burn the other posts, what was left of them. Lisa's place, Benton down the river. You try building a post around here, and these Crow'll be thinkin' on that Cheyenne devil you got, and your own Cheyenne ways, and maybe they'll skin your hide back, if I don't do it first. Now you just git your skinny butt outa here, you and your Cheyenne woman, and leave the wagons and men. I just took 'em."

Brokenleg wanted to say it wouldn't work. Not even Pierre Chouteau would permit that. But Julius Hervey had ways of making it work, all of them deadly.

"I reckon you'll have to kill me right now, Hervey, because if you don't, you aren't getting these here of my goods, and my woman . . . and my men."

His Hawken lay in its beaded sheath, and by the time he drew it, cocked the hammer, and aimed, Hervey would have pulled him off his horse, but he had a Bowie at his belt. He chose that, and with a sudden blur his hand held it and his arm poised to throw it. He reckoned he could plant it in Hervey's gut without any fuss.

Hervey paused and laughed. "Now, that ain't sociable, old Stiffleg." The threat of a poised knife, held by a master, didn't seem to faze the man.

"Hervey. You steal my tradegoods and I'll kill you. You touch my woman and I'll kill you if she don't. You wreck my fort or kill my men, and you won't see daylight. You whip up these tribes against me, Hervey, and it won't be me that'll feel it, but you—and your American Fur." He felt a roughness in his throat that he'd forgotten lay inside of him, all those months in St. Louis. He'd become a wilderness child too, with more years of it behind him than Hervey. Some wild joy blossomed inside of him as he watched Hervey's alert embered eyes shadow and the faint wings of death feather across Hervey's square face.

"I never forget," said Hervey. "A man makes a threat on me, and I figure I've got a right to do what I must. Even if it takes a year or two."

"I'm making a threat."

"And here I was going to break out your trade whiskey and have us a party tonight, with a squaw for everyone." Hervey still mocked, as fearless as any man on earth.

"After stealing all I got."

"Not just you, Stiffleg. It belongs to Guy Straus and Jamie Dance, too—remember?"

Fitzhugh didn't answer. Instead he stared relentlessly at Hervey, his knife hand poised and ready. "Trudeau," he said softly, not taking his eyes from Hervey, "turn the oxen. We're going up the Bighorn a piece."

"Better make it a big piece," Hervey said. "All the way back to St. Louis. I'd hate to see anything happen to Straus's boy there. Dumb thing for the man to do, send his boy out to get hisself scalped." He beckoned at Maxim. "You. I heard you was coming up the river. You better get into the fort there where you're safe, and then we'll get you back down to your pappy."

Maxim hesitated, subdued by the sheer force of this strange, menacing man. "I'll go with Mister Fitzhugh. I think I can help him."

"It's your scalp, kid."

Maxim peered back grimly.

"That reminds me, Hervey. You lay a hand on him, you set Injuns on him, you steal from me, you do that and you better watch your back every second of every hour because you're not worth coming at from the front. Out here, I don't pay no attention to things, just like you don't. Just as soon stick a man so he feels a blade slice his kidneys afore he knows who stuck him."

Hervey didn't laugh that time, but subsided into a feral watchfulness. Fitzhugh judged he'd made his point and it was time to go.

"Git," he snapped to Trudeau, never taking his gaze from Hervey.

Behind him he heard the curses of the teamsters, the crack of whips, the bawling and slobbering of oxen, and finally the heavy rumble of the Pittsburghs, threading between silent ranks of Crow people who stood solemnly after watching the confrontation. But Fitzhugh didn't move, and sat mean-eyed on his restless bay, his bad leg jutting right at Hervey, like a sort of lance, his knife feeling sweaty and good and hard in his knotted hand, and the muscles of his fore and upper arm, his shoulder, his back and the cords that stretched down upon his chest ready to explode.

Hervey had stopped smirking, stopped doing anything except staring at that arm, that glinting blade, and the murder written in Fitzhugh's relentless eyes. Nothing changed. The afternoon sun had stopped, along with the breeze. The flags on Fort Cass lay limp. Several hundred Crows stood frozen, like a waxworks display. The smell of rank green cowpies lifted to him from the place where the oxen had stood. But Fitzhugh waited, listening to the distant rumble of the wagons, putting distance between his party and Fort Cass. When he couldn't hear them any more, and only the songs of meadowlarks filtered to his ears, he slid the nose of his horse to the south and touched his moccasins to its ribs.

He walked his nervous pony through the crowd, and then past hollow silent lodges, some with medicine tripods before them bearing Cheyenne scalps. And finally out upon a meadow, stripped to dust by Crow ponies, and at last out to a virgin valley, thick with cottonwood, much narrower than the miles-wide trench of the Yellowstone, but formidable in its own right. Before him the silvery Bighorn rose ever southward toward a place where it pierced through a vaulting yellow canyon. But he wouldn't go that far. He'd build his fort on the east bank of the river, close to good trails used by the Sioux and Cheyenne, trails that led down the east flank of the Bighorn Mountains into some of the best game and buffalo country on the continent. He'd find a grassy park near the river, protected by high cliffs, with abundant cottonwoods for building his post and for fuel, and for winter horsefeed. It would be a sunny place, he knew, bright and clear skied, and well away from the blackness at Fort Cass.

Dust Devil knew exactly where the new post should be. Only three sleeps to the south, up the Bighorn, lay a broad sunny bottomland where the Little Bighorn flowed into the Bighorn. It was not far from the mountains, and thick with game, and a favorite haunt of buffalo. And it had always been a place favored by her people when they wandered north in the summers to hunt. All this she explained to her man.

"I'll ride ahead and find the People and bring them there to trade and protect us," she said to Brokenleg, after they'd put Fort Cass behind them.

"Too far from the Yellerstone, Dust Devil."

"But it's where my people come—"

"We got to think of supply, of gitting the robes out and down the river. Of staying close to the steamboats."

"Close to Fort Cass? And all those dogs?"

"That's how she's got to be. I've got to send the wagons back at least once just to get the rest of our truck. Build a post here and then steal Hervey's trade, right under his nose."

"But—that Julius Hervey will murder you. And those Absaroka dogs. I couldn't stand them. I will have a sweat to take the stink of them out of my nose. They're nothing—they're cowards and liars and their women are unfaithful."

"Hope to trade with 'em, Dust Devil. They got good robes."

"Not as good as the People. And they're enemies."

"I reckon we'll fort up on the next good flat. I want three, four miles between us and old Hervey anyways, but no more'n that. In fact, we're coming on a likely spot by my calculations."

The news amazed her. They'd come only a little way from Cass, and she could smell them all behind her, the stinking Crows, the stinking engagés. They all stank, including Brokenleg. Not a one smelled as fresh and fragrant as her people, who smelled as sweet as sagebrush and new-tanned leather, and juniper smoke.

"But—my people won't come here. Next to these filthy Absaroka. The Dakota won't come either."

"Just about every trading post I seen, they get along good enough, leastwise around the place."

"You like them more than the Tsistsistas. More than me. More than my clan and my mother's clan and my grandmother's clan. More than the Suhtai."

For an answer he grinned, and steered his bay closer to her mare. "Reckon yer an idjit," he said.

She hated that, the way he always made light of her, as if she were a child he was addressing. Whitemen did that with women of the people, a sort of unconscious condescension. With him it didn't seem to matter that she came from an important family that tended the sacred medicine hat, Issiwun, in its special lodge on the south side of the village circle. And even if he made fun of the Tsistsistas, he shouldn't make fun of her Suhtai, who were a sacred people who joined the Omissis band and others not long ago to guide them and share the greater medicine of the Suhtai. Brokenleg was nothing but a smelly barbarian, and she didn't know why she put up with him. Maybe he would divorce her, but it'd cause a scandal and her people would turn their faces from him because marriage was a sacred thing. Maybe that would be good! Then the Tsistsistas would know about the whitemen and all their evil ways—worse than the lecherous Crows—and all the things she saw in St. Louis with her own eyes. So many whitemen. Like the leaves on a cottonwood. And how they all smelled. Oh, she would need ten sweats with sweetgrass and sage smoke to cleanse herself of St. Louis and the riverboat!

"You smell bad," she said primly.

"Not as bad as Julius Hervey," he said, his face sober.

They'd reached a broad meadow around an oxbow, a place where sandstone bluffs would stay the northwind and catch the winter sun; a stretch of level ground flanked by massed cottonwoods to the south, and west along the riverbank. All the signs announced that it had been a favorite camping site of countless villages of various tribes for generations. Teepee rings filled the meadow, and here and there ancient firepits still held charred sticks and ash. The cliffs tamed the wind, and subdued the winter, and caught the snow to make the good grass in the spring.

She knew what he was thinking, and hated it. If they went a few sleeps more, they would be close to her people.

"I reckon if I have to choose a place for a new fort in a hurry, hyar it is about as god as it's gittin'."

She said nothing, glaring at him with disdain.

"We're four miles from Cass, I reckon. Two, three miles up the Bighorn. Lotsa meadow and water. Cottonwoods for building and burning and feed. Loose rock all over them bluffs, yeller sandstone to build us some chimneys—I didn't figure on building a fort, and didn't bring a stove, Dust Devil. This hyar earth looks pretty soft—like we can scratch up a garden for some greens. And this hyar's one of the most traveled traces around—everything from buffler to—"

"Absaroka! Assiniboin! Cree! Hidatsa! Gros Ventre! Blackfoot! I will warn my people about the ones who will come here."

"I reckon you're right. Good traffic. Lotsa everybody. That's what it takes to make a post. I reckon your folks'll be first to put robes through our trading window, eh?"

"I will tell them it's bad medicine. That under-earth spirits live here. That Sweet Medicine doesn't see this place; that—"

"You're needin' a husband," he said. He always said that as a rebuke. She stared back, disdainfully.

Behind him, the oxen sagged in their yokes. They'd come far this day, to Fort Cass and then another few miles, dragging massive wagons over a trace that was full of humps, hollows, rivulets, and juniper thickets that choked progress.

"Trudeau. We'll camp here. Good grass. I'm thinking we'll stay here—it's a likely enough place."

Samson Trudeau surveyed the site, which lay glowing in an apricot light from a bedding sun, and nodded. "Monsieur Fitzhugh, it is suitable. Not as magnificent as Cass, there on the Yellowstone where ever'one comes. This is—a bit apart, yes."

"You got any better notions?"

"Maybe go back down the Yellowstone a way. To the Tongue. That is closer to our goods."

"I wanted to fetch us a spot as far from Fort Union as I could," Brokenleg said. "So we get a good trade."

"Ah, monsieur, Fort Union, she has come to us here." He laughed easily, but Fitzhugh didn't.

"We'll build a fort here, I think."

Trudeau sighed. "With ten men? We need fifty to make a fort. And these ten, we need most of them taking the wagons out and trading."

Why was it, Dust Devil thought irritably, that Brokenleg

would listen to another whiteman but not her? She glared at him while he and Trudeau exchanged ideas politely. Why could she never get him to listen like that? He though he knew more than the People, that's why. He really listened to the color of their skin.

"I been chewing on it since we come on up hyar. I figger we'll just build us a little cabin, enough to fetch the tradegoods out of the weather and keep ourselves warm. Then we'll go out with the wagons and trade."

"Six wagonloads—or seven—of goods, plus ten men, plus you and Mrs. Fitzhugh, and all the robes we bring back, in this petite cabin, *n'est-ce pas?"*

"Wall, I was thinkin' mostly we'd be out tradin'."

"Monsieur, let me ask you this: we unload the wagon here and go back for more, *oui?* We leave—on the grass here—a great heap of things that go bad when it makes rain. Bolts of tradecloth—calico, gingham. Ribbons. Iron and steel that rust. Kegs of gun powder that maybe don' keep rain out. All this we leave here, on the grass, and most of us go away for a month and bring a load, and then we go away for one more month and bring a load. And all this time, she never makes rain or hail, and it stays warm. And nobody comes by that steals anything, *oui?* Or makes war, *oui?"*

She watched her man turn old, and saw the fleeting shadow of despair flick across his face. He hurt; she knew that. His bad leg tortured him. He'd been on that horse for hours.

"I think maybe we can put the stuff that needs cover in one wagon and leave it here, and you go on back for the rest."

"Monsieur, we need a fort or a trading house. It has come August now, and in a few weeks it makes frost. And with only two wagons, we make three more trips back there. By then, ever'one knows where we come and go. And they see all the tradegoods sitting in the field, like a baby buffalo without its *papa* and *maman.* Wolves, they see the infant and lick chops. Maybe a few of us against a hundred Blackfeet, *oui?* Not so safe any more."

"I'm fresh outa furs, Trudeau."

The engagé shrugged. "Then maybe sell to Culbertson for what you can. Better something than nothing."

"I'm too tired to make decisions," Fitzhugh said shortly. "Maybe we ought to scout around. There's been four, five trading houses put up hyar. Old Lisa's post back in ought seven; old Benton. I forget the others."

"Hervey, he burn them."

"He says he burned them. I think we should see."

She said, "He burned them. I saw when we came. I was watching for them."

He turned to her, pain weighing his face now. "I reckon we should look anyway, Dust Devil."

"You don't take my word or trust me."

"I'd like to see myself, I guess. Maybe you missed something."

"Do what you want!" she cried. "I can help if you want. But you don't want! I could go find my people and bring them. I could find my village. We can store all the tradegoods in the lodges and they will be safe. No Absarokas will come and steal them because the Tsistsistas are strong. We can live in the lodges too, and be comfortable. They'll trade—they'll bring good robes, better than the Crow-dogs' robes, and take away these things. I'll tell them to meet you where the Bighorn and the Little Bighorn come together."

Her man assessed her wearily. "How long you figger it'd take to track them down and git yur people there? Or hyar?"

"A moon maybe."

He sighed. "We got only two men and most of our stuff at Wolf Rapids. Can't wait so long. I reckon we'd better see how things look in the morning, because they don't shine now."

He'd rejected her offer, she thought.

Chapter Eleven

Fitzhugh woke up with a mind as stiff as his leg. He knew what he would do, and no one would like it, including himself. A little before dawn, a dew had settled, wetting his good buffalo robe and silvering the bunchgrass in the meadow. August, he thought. The Moon When the Berries Ripen. And the sun was a little slower to make heat and comfort cold flesh. In the mountains, weather controlled everything, including the choices he faced this late summer day.

He peered about in the gray light. The oxen grazed nearby, hobbled. The mules and horses roamed from clump to clump of good grass, some on picketlines, others hobbled. Dust Devil pretended to sleep in her robe, but was furtively watching him, the way a cat watches the one it permits to feed it. Maxim lay in his blankets, curled into a ball against the coolness. And near the three ghostly wagons, eight engagés fought the dawn.

Just standing up was an ordeal, one he faced at least once a day. He'd learned to pull himself up from his right side, using his Hawken as a staff. He hobbled around, driving the badness out of his leg, something that had become a morning ritual. Dust Devil's gaze followed him, like a panther sizing up its prey. He'd skip breakfast, he thought, limping out toward the bay on the picketline. He studied the animal carefully, not from any love of horseflesh but because a horse was a useful machine, a conveyance for a lame man, and needed proper handling. The stallion yawned, baring yellow grass-stained teeth. A lame-man's horse: low, stocky, quiet-natured, rather slow. Not a horse with which to escape a war party. Saddlemarks left a sheen on its slick hair.

He threw a buffalo-skin apishemore over the back of the animal and then his Santa Fe saddle, and drew up the latigo.

"Where are you going?" said Dust Devil, who materialized beside him. "It is too early. We have not greeted Sun."

"Cass," he said. "Stay here. Keep them here."

"I know," she said.

He expected a question, several questions, but she didn't ask them. "I'll wake Hervey up. He likes to sleep late."

"Dogs," she said. She gathered a shawl over her shoulders and headed toward the line of cottonwoods along the river. She had the primness of Cheyenne women. He watched her slim form grow distant and then disappear in brush, and felt an ancient pleasure at her lithe grace.

He had to mount from the off side and swing his stiff left leg over the animal. This horse was used to it, but it could be a problem with a horse unfamiliar with his ways. He settled himself in the cold leather, feeling it through his britches, and then walked the horse slowly north, aware that most of the men in camp were awake and staring.

He wanted coffee. It helped him think. But there was nothing to think about, and coffee would take a half hour. He would do what he had to do. The choices had narrowed down. He'd been dumb, supposing they had a fort at their disposal. American Fur usually burned a post it was abandoning, precisely because the old structures were a temptation to opposing companies. All the forts along here, Lisa's old post, Joshua Pilcher's Fort Benton, and old Fort Van Buren, now lay in ashes. So he would do what he had to. It could be the ruin of him; the ruin of Dance, Fitzhugh and Straus, but he pushed those thoughts aside, savagely.

When the choices narrowed down, you took the best of a bad lot.

An hour later he raised Fort Cass, which lay somnolent in the horizontal light. Most of the Crow lodges had vanished, but a dozen or so remained, the last stragglers. The Crows must have welcomed the trading: it'd been years since they had traders close by, and no doubt they had plenty of those magnificent soft-tanned robes to exchange. No tribe tanned better than the Crow.

He rode straight to the fort, scarcely arousing a dog. Most Indians slept late; most traders did, too. Its gate lay on the shadowed north side, facing the glinting river. He steered the bay close to the massive gray planks of the door, and then hammered on the door with the back of a trade hatchet he kept on his saddle, and which he could throw as well as his knife. Nothing happened, and he hammered again, sensing the noise was swallowed up in the quiet of the dawn. Then at last the door screeched open a crack on its iron hinges, and Hervey himself peered out.

"You."

"Me."

A faint rising amusement spread across Hervey's face, and the gate swung majestically on its old hinges. Harvey wore britches and an undershirt, and his free hand held a fifty-two caliber trade rifle, cocked.

"There's no witnesses," Hervey said.

"Reckon that's true."

Brokenleg heeled his bay and steered the horse through the widening aperture, down a narrow corridor and into the yard. He'd been in this place before, back in the beaver days. It had never been much of a fort compared to Union or MacKenzie or William up on the Missouri, or Laramie on the Platte. A rough palisade of thick, adzed cottonwood logs surrounded a miniscule yard. All the fort's buildings lined the palisade. A warehouse on one side, and around the rest a stone magazine, a trading room beside the gate, barracks for a handful of engagés, and the trader's house, also of log and crudely made. A hand-dug well in the yard drew water from the high water table there, seventy yards from the Yellowstone.

Brokenleg dismounted stiffly, a business as tricky as mounting with his game leg. Hervey's rifle followed him around as he stomped to put some blood in his bum limb. Then he limped over to the warehouse and found a heap of robes within, some of them pressed and baled up into the standard packs of ten, others in the process of being graded, and lying in mounds. Good winter robes. A few summer robes. A smaller heap of special robes, mostly amber or tan colored, which might bring a premium. The smell of leather, and smoke, and the more pungent smells of the tanning media, brains and liver and urine, clung to them.

Hervey stood behind him, the trade rifle aimed squarely at his back.

"Lots," said Brokenleg. "I reckon the trading room's mostly empty."

Hervey grunted.

Fitzhugh lumbered toward the trading room to confirm it, while Hervey, still amused, followed behind carrying murder in his arm. Brokenleg pushed open the squeaky door and peered into a brown gloom, lit only by a tiny foot-square pane of glass that didn't admit much of the morning's glow. But he pushed the door wider and walked in, letting in more light with him. He saw at once that the room had been largely stripped of goods. A well-supplied trading room could be a wondrous place, with bright blankets, scarlet and green and sky blue on the shelves; trays of beads; racks of shining rifles; beaver traps in lots of a dozen; gleaming brass or copper kettles; bolts of coarse tradecloth, or finer calico or gingham, joyous as rainbows.

These rooms were where it all happened, where a tribesman pushed his robe through a small window onto a counter, where it was assessed for quality and credited. And then the tribesman or woman would select the whiteman goods: a good robe would fetch sixty loads of powder and shot. A trade rifle was worth six to ten robes. A robe would fetch two gallons of shelled corn, or three pounds of sugar, or two pounds of coffee. It would be worth a hank of beads of a yard of tradecloth or flannel. And blankets went for a robe a point, just about the way the beavers traded in the old days, a plew a point.

But most of the shelves were bare.

"That's what I thought," said Fitzhugh. "They pretty near cleaned you. And you aren't getting any resupply."

"I could steal yours," Hervey said. He poked the trade rifle higher, until the bore leveled at Fitzhugh's heart.

"Want to sell the fort? I don't figure you'll do much business rest of the year, but it'll cost plenty to keep you'n your men hyar. It's a loser."

Julius Hervey laughed.

"Pay a hundred robes for her."

"Go home," said Hervey.

"It's a fool waste, you manning this empty logpile whiles we go on tradin'. You could build you a mackinaw and float your returns on down to Culbertson."

"We're good with flint and strikers, Stiffleg. Should have burned it long ago."

"I'm building me a post about four miles around the bend."

"Your heirs will, maybe."

"You got some coffee?"

Hervey nodded. "For you, a robe a pound, and the beans ain't roasted."

Brokenleg stared. "Got some whiskey?"

"Never heard of spirits where its illegal. American Fur got into some devilish trouble about that, and's real careful now."

Fitzhugh laughed.

Outside, the sun caught the inner west well of the stockade, and whirled white light through the yard and into the trading room.

"If you aren't going to sell the place, maybe you'll rent it."

"Not to Dance, Fitzhugh and Straus. That's what I'm here for. To keep you from doing business. Easiest way's to pull the trigger."

"You aren't drunk enough."

Hervey chuckled.

"That warehouse. It's got a good watertight shake roof. I'm thinking I might rent her to store my goods until the first of the year whiles we build us a post around the bend."

Hervey's grin grew. "It ain't rentable."

"Five months, from now—August the sixth—to January the sixth, for ten percent of my tradegoods across the board. Give you some trading goods. I got four more wagonloads coming. You'd be liable for damages and loss—usual agreement."

"I'd steal them all. Bury the witnesses."

Fitzhugh glared. "A deal?"

"You'd never see them again. You'd all die trying to fetch them. And I'll trade your entire outfit anyway."

"It's a deal, then," said Fitzhugh. "Shake on her. I'll have the boy—Guy Straus's son—fetch the inventory and we'll divvy up. Git the wagons hyar in an hour or two."

Julius Hervey smiled, and shook. But Fitzhugh didn't like the feel of his hand.

Maxim Straus was beset by layer upon layer of alarm. The news that Fitzhugh had ridden to Fort Cass filled him with foreboding. He didn't expect to see Brokenleg alive again, and he wondered what would happen to all those goods, brought here at such great cost. Then Brokenleg had come back, looking cheerful, and began issuing incredible instructions: the engagés were to unpack the furnishings and tools for the fort, and then take the tradegoods back to Fort Cass, where they would be warehoused. Back there into the jaws of American Fur Company! Back there, into the hands of the most frightening and menacing man Maxim had ever encountered!

He studied Fitzhugh as the man sipped coffee and breakfasted, and felt the worm of suspicion crawl through him, and despair knot his insides until he couldn't eat or think. Maybe the man was betraying his father. If not that, then certainly his business judgment was sorely wanting. Maxim noticed he wasn't alone, either. The engagés were straining and muttering, unloading tools and yoking oxen, all the while glancing darkly at Fitzhugh. And Dust Devil was snapping and glaring at her husband. Maxim knew he was not yet a man, and maybe he didn't understand all things, but the longer he sat at the breakfast fire, the more he was eaten up with worry.

But Brokenleg merely grinned, and looked for all the world as if he'd just conquered the world.

Maxim felt a hard knot in his throat, and didn't even know if he could talk, but he was driven to try. Maybe Fitzhugh would swat at him as if he were a horsefly, but he had to try.

"Mister Fitzhugh," he said, his voice a creaking soprano, "why are you—"

"Why, Maxim, it's the best I could get. We're in a hard place."

"You've sold out!"

"Whoa up, boy. I haven't sold out. We got us a roof for a few months whiles we build us a post."

"A roof?"

"Yep. Shakes nailed over tarred canvas, nailed onto sawn plank. Keeps rain and snow off good robes, and it'll do the same for our tradegoods. Bolts of tradecloth, gingham, calico, iron stuff, kegs of powder—it needs a roof."

"We'll never see it again!"

"Oh, I think we'll see it, leastwise what we're keeping."

"You're giving them some?"

"Ten percent, Maxim. We don't have to get it outa there until after the first of the year."

"Ten percent! Ten percent of everything my *papa* spent, and got together and shipped, ten percent of that, and the blankets gone, and—"

"Lucky to get a roof for that. You know of any other roofs around? Nearest one is Fort Union, maybe two hundred fifty miles down the Yellowstone. And that isn't no more friendly than Cass. After that, I'm plumb outa roofs. Unless we go another few hundred miles to some Hudson's Bay outfit. There's Wyeth's old place down on the Snake. Hudson's Bay now. Will and Milt Sublette's place down on the Platte, where the Laramie runs in."

"We could find a cave!"

"Try again."

"We could make a roof in a day or two."

"Oh, we could make a roof, but not in a day or two. Easy to talk about, but the making is harder. I could put every man here, including you, to work with an ax and an adze and a saw, and we wouldn't have much of a hut even in a week. And it'd leak."

"But we could use the wagonsheets! For a big tent!"

"Reckon we could, but I won't."

"But why? They'd protect the tradegoods from rain."

Brokenleg tried to explain: "Well—boy—we didn't figure so good. Maybe I didn't figure so good. I figured we'd just waltz into Fort Cass. It's not just a roof we need, but walls. A fort. We could rig up a tent, but what if a couple hundred Blackfeet came along? Just the few of us against all of 'em? They'd help themselves to everything we got; everything your pa bought for an outfit. Wagonsheeting don't stop bullets and arrows and hatchets none, and it's nothing a man can hide behind, neither.

"All that stuff—it's safe at Cass. We got Hervey to deal

with, but he's got men above him he's responsible to. Like Culbertson. You know any other way to keep our outfit safe? We got a fort to build—that or curl our tail betwixt and 'tween our legs, and git us down the river. We got us only ten, eleven men to build us a fort. American Fur, when they build a fort they use fifty men and some hunters to feed 'em."

But Maxim wasn't a bit mollified. "We are housed in Independence for fifty-seven dollars a month! Not ten percent of everything!"

"Well, I'll just set you to findin' us a fifty-seven warehouse."

Brokenleg was toying with him, and he hated it.

Dust Devil joined in: "We could put everything in my people's lodges," she said.

"We could," he agreed. "We could. But we won't. And them cowskin lodges aren't all that dry, comes a blue norther. Nope. We're storing at Cass. I got Hervey over a pretty good barrel. He sold out faster than he figured, account no one's traded with the Crows much for years. And he don't expect no resupply soon, if ever. But he has to stay put. If he pulls out and burns Cass, he'd leave the Crow trade to us. I got that figured, anyway."

"But my people—they'd trade for everything—"

"Hush now. You know how it is. How the trading's going to be."

None of it made any sense to Maxim. "Hervey's going to steal everything and kill you. Kill everyone. I don't want to die. We'll never see any of it again."

But Brokenleg had grown weary of the interrogation, and was drifting off, eyeing wagons, checking the pile of axes, saws, shovels, kitchen utensils, sacks of beans, coffee, sugar, and all the rest.

"Leave a wagonsheet here," he said to Trudeau. "That'll be our camp tent. We'll unload at Cass, and then send six men back for the rest. That'll make a strong party, hooked up with the others on the Yellerstone. You take the stuff down to Cass and then come on back here, Trudeau. We got us a post to build before we get so cold we can't do nothin'."

"Monsieur, I'd rather face the devil than Hervey. Are you sure—"

"We got this hyar devil by his tail, Trudeau. I'm sure."

Maxim wasn't sure at all. He'd lost. He'd been the sixteen-year-old in Fitzhugh's eyes. He stood sullenly beside the heap of goods on the meadow, watching Trudeau ride off, and the engagés whip the bawling oxen into a lumbering walk back down the Bighorn to its confluence, and then down the Yellowstone.

"Well, Maxim, let's go pick us a spot to build a post."

Maxim followed sullenly. As soon as he could he would write a letter to his father, and entrust it to Trudeau. He was the Straus family's eyes and ears. He couldn't imagine why his father ever trusted Brokenleg Fitzhugh with so much. They could save some of it by going down the river, now, before it got cold. They could save a lot of it, and maybe get some robes, too, trading as they went. But no . . .

"Now let's see here, Maxim. A post has got ta be right where lots of Injuns come, sorta convenient to them. It's got to be up enough from the river so's it don't flood, like when icejams bust loose upstream and send a mile-wide sheet boiling down, tearing out cottonwoods and all. Now this hyar plain looks pretty good, don't you reckon? Lots of meadow for them to pitch lodges. Pony grass. Yonder on the river, lots of cottonwoods and some willow too. Wood for the post. Wood for cookin' and keepin' our bones from freezin' solid. Lots of loose sandstone yonder, easy to pry out."

"Sandstone?"

"We got to build a fireplace outa somethin'. We didn't bring no stoves along. Sandstone and mud mortar, makes us a decent fireplace or two, and some chimneys.

"We should go home."

"Reckon we should? You're plumb right. We should. We haven't got the men or the stuff to make forts. But we'll do her."

As fast as Fitzhugh talked, he limped along even faster, and Maxim was amazed at the man's speed. Every little while he stopped, eyed bluffs, studied grass, peered at the nearby woods. At last, he paused on a slight rise, a gentle lift of the meadow perhaps a hundred yards east of the Bighorn River.

"Got her," he muttered. "What do you think we should name her?"

"Dance, Fitzhugh and Straus," Maxim said sourly.

"Nah. Too much of a mouthful. Down on the Arkansas, it's not Bent, St. Vrain and Company Fort, it's Bent's Fort. And up there on the Missouri, it isn't Pratte and Chouteau, or Chouteau and Company, or American Fur Company—she's Fort Union."

"Whatever you want. We won't have anything to trade anyway, since you gave it all to Hervey."

"Aren't you a worrywort. I don't much like calling a trading place a fort. Sounds like some battle. Let's call her a post. Or house. I always liked that. Hudson's Bay, they got Rocky Mountain House up younder on the Saskatchewan, and it sorta tickles me. Maybe like Bighorn House. Or Bighorn Post."

"Whatever you want."

Fitzhugh laughed. "Go fetch you a sharp ax. And me, too. I got to get it staked out. We don't have no time for a palisade, knocking down a few hundred trees and skinning them flat on two sides and planting them. No, with all the men we got, we got to build us a big house, you know, for tradin' and storin' robes and the like, and then a couple of little houses, and maybe a polefence to keep the livestock in."

"We should go home."

Fitzhugh laughed. "You're going to raise some blisters, boy."

The thought of cutting down even a single tree, limbing it, dragging it to this site, seemed utterly daunting, once Maxim thought about it. How could they possibly build a whole post with so few men, and most of them gone for another few weeks?

"Mister Fitzhugh," he said miserably. "We thought there'd be a fort. All we'll do now is destroy everything my father and grandfather built, with a lot of suffering—more than I can explain to you; *you* wouldn't know—over many years."

Brokenleg paused, obviously aware of Maxim's misery. "Son," he said quietly. "It's lost for sure if we go back. We haven't got a way to take seven wagonloads back in three wagons; haven't got replacement livestock when the oxen and mules wear out. If we make us a flatboat to float down the river, we abandon the wagons and livestock. And those mackinaws got a way of crackin' up and leakin'. Maxim—son—we got us into a hard place, and I'm doin' all I can to get us out. And besides, son. We're just gettin' going. We're gonna make us a heap, for your pap and mam, and for me and my lady. Your pa's a rare and fine man. I think the world o' him. Last thing I'd want to do is give him a hurt. Now fetch the tools, son, and we'll see what we can do betwixt now and cold weather."

Chapter Twelve

That ~~warm August morning~~ Brokenleg Fitzhugh was more worried than he let on to Maxim. He hadn't counted on building a fort. That had been dumb, and he cussed himself, but here he stood, two thousand miles from anywhere, and he had no choice. All he had by way of tools was what he'd brought for maintenance at Fort Cass. A couple of axes for firewood; a maul and wedges; a bit and auger, a good two-man saw, a carpenter's saw, a crowbar, a chisel and an adze. He didn't have a nail or a hinge or anything for a roof. He had more axes and hatchets coming in the next load, trade items actually, but he could sell them used as well as new.

But that wasn't the worst of it. He needed forty or fifty men to build a regular fort, and he had only ten—ten plus a boy and a cripple. And of those, eight would be gone for several weeks, bringing in the next load. He'd sent back enough to make a strong party, well armed, guarding the valuable tradegoods. He'd asked them to bring everything in one trip, even if the wagons groaned under a mountain of goods and the ox and mule teams were abused. And come back slow, sparing the livestock as much as possible. But he wouldn't see them until September some time. And meanwhile he'd have only himself, Maxim, Trudeau and whichever engagé Trudeau brought with him, and Dust Devil. That plus a few stray horses that would need constant herding.

He expected Trudeau back soon; Hervey would make it easy for them, no doubt. He didn't trust Hervey, but he'd deal with that later. He'd get over to Cass and keep an eye on his merchandise. But if there was going to be trouble, it'd come at the beginning of January, when they went to fetch their tradegoods. If Hervey shut him out then, there'd be a war. And some repercussions back in St. Louis. But he didn't figure it that way: out here in a wild land, traders followed certain semi-honorable codes, and Fitzhugh was counting on them.

He was going to have to make himself the post hunter, and the engagés might resent it. But with his bad leg he wouldn't be much good at building, and he knew more about bringing home meat than most of them. Keeping ten hard-working men well fed when they were toiling from dawn to after dark would be a task in itself, and by the time he sawed up buffalo or elk into quarters and packed or dragged it back each day, he'd be as weary as the rest.

He limped across the open meadows, feeling the sun warm him and zephyrs toy with his red hair, enjoying the fine summer day. He wanted to inspect the cottonwood groves close to the river, see where to start cutting. He was juggling so many ideas in his head that it ached. He didn't even know what sort of place to build, but he knew he lacked the men to put up a regular stockaded fort with bastions and buildings within. It'd have to be something simple, where they could store tradegoods and robes; a base they'd need, even if they did their trading out in the villages, hauling wagons out to the winter camps. By God, he wouldn't even be trading for the first robe until after the beginning of the year! But maybe that wasn't so bad; he'd start trading just about when Chouteau's outfit would start running low on tradegoods. The forts were usually cleaned out by March or April, right down to the bedsheets. No, maybe it wasn't so bad to start trading late.

Everywhere he trudged along the river, the cottonwoods

towered majestically, with trunks three feet in diameter, dividing crookedly into thick limbs that erupted outward toward a giant crown of leaves. The sight dismayed him. It'd take several men with several axes a whole day to fell one of these lords, and then the logs would be too big to drag to the site, hoist, and fit into a wall. Some willows nearby looked better, but they were too few. Dourly he stared at the unpromising groves, wondering if he'd have to move upstream, to a different meadow.

Maxim showed up carrying two axes, and looking solemnly at the noble trees.

"This hyar's not good for building a post, boy," Brokenleg said. "Too big and too crooked. We may be needing to move a piece."

Maxim looked relieved.

"Well, let's see what we got for rock," he muttered, limping away from the river toward the tan sandstone bluffs a quarter of a mile distant. His leg bothered him. It always did, but he swore it hurt more when he was puzzling things out, as if his brains were in his bad knee. They passed the supplies lying nakedly in the grass, while Dust Devil watched them skeptically, and trudged slowly up a soft grassy grade toward the rock. "Watch out for rattlers. This here's what they roost in when they're in rattler heaven."

Maxim walked warily.

Fitzhugh liked what he saw. At every hand he found stratified rock, weathered and rotted loose by frost and water and wind, lying in slabs that were there for the taking. More tan treasure than he could ever use. Enough, laid up with mud mortar, for good strong wind-tight walls; enough for a flagstone floor some day. And best of all, something that could be laid up almost without tools. "I think we're going to build us the Bighorn House outa rock. I think we can lay up more good wall in a day than if we wrestle them giants down."

"There's nothing here!" cried Maxim. "How can we build a house out of nothing? Where's the windows?"

"Oh, we won't have real glass windows, at least not this year, boy. We're gonna have them someday, though. But we'll have windows, and they'll let light in; light enough, anyway."

Fitzhugh was getting notional the longer he stared at the loose rock. A building grew in his mind, a long rectangle with yellow rock walls and wide fireplaces at either end, a peaked roof with a good layer of sod over the poles since he lacked nails and anything else to build a nice shake roof. Maybe the following year they could strip the sod off and make a better roof. But this year, his choices ran from bad to desperate.

Maxim grasped a slab of sandstone and tried to lift it, but couldn't. He wobbled it but couldn't even raise it an inch. He turned to Brokenleg, a question in his eyes.

"Oh, you're goin' to be the mud boy. The mortar man. We'll have some strong men here to pry these loose; haul them on a stoneboat—gotta build a couple of stoneboats—and you'll be there at the post, mixin' mud faster than they can lay it up."

"Will mud work?"

"Well, we don't have lime for mortar. When settlers chink up a log cabin, they throw in some horse manure, and maybe grass, to make it stronger. But this clay's all we got, and that's what we'll use with the stone."

"I could do that."

"You'll be plumb sick o' running mud, but yes, Maxim, you could do that. We got to build a few tools today. A couple of stoneboats, and dig a pit near the river where you can mix up mud, real nice, accordin' to yur fanciest Frenchie recipe, and haul buckets. I got to make some wooden trowels, too, to spread the stuff."

"Have we got buckets?"

"One here, and a couple comin' in with the load."

For the first time, Fitzhugh thought, Maxim didn't look completely overwhelmed. "I reckon we can have the walls up by the end of October, and we can hang some wagon-sheets for a roof over part of it whiles we roof the other. There's lots of yeller jackpine up yonder, and that'll make good roofpoles—not straight like lodgepole, but good enough."

"What'll the inside be like, Brokenleg?"

"Why, I reckon we'll have the tradin' room over on one side, and storage for robes behind it; and the other side, we'll all squeeze in for bunking and cooking. That's why we'll have a fireplace each end, one for the business area, one for the livin'. Then we'll have to build us some pens out back for the stock—and lots of stuff. Sheds and all. And that don't cover half of it. We got to cut hay off these flats and get in firewood afore we get snowed under."

Off to the north, he spotted two horsemen approaching slowly and he realized he didn't have his Hawken in hand, and thus had violated the most basic rule of survival.

"Let's git," he said sharply, limping toward Dust Devil's little camp.

"That's the first rule," he muttered to Maxim. "And I plumb forgot it, my head's so full. You don't go anywhere without you got yur rifle. Mostly this hyar is friendly country—Crow people. But it just could be Bug's Boys, and they could just take a fancy to your topknot."

"Bug's Boys?"

"The Devil's Boys. Blackfeet. Sorta everyone's enemy around hyar. Including us, unless maybe we can try some tradin'. But they dicker mostly with Hudson's Bay up in British country, and some with American Fur, and use all that lead and powder they git on the rest of us."

"How'll I know?"

"I can't rightly explain now, but you'll learn soon enough, or leave your scalp on a medicine tripod."

The lead horseman was Trudeau. He had Emile Gallard

with him. Gallard always evoked thoughts as elusive and fragile as the dust on butterfly wings, something he could never pin down in his head. He wondered at Trudeau's choice—whether there had been design in it.

He found his Hawken back at the camp, propped up against the cask labeled vinegar, just where he'd left it. He lifted it anyway, just to get rid of the naked feeling that beset him when his fingers had nothing but air to grasp.

Trudeau pulled up, and slid off the gaunt pony. "Ah, Monsieur, it is done. We unloaded the wagons, and I have sent them on their way, as you instructed."

"Hervey cause you trouble?"

"Non, Monsieur. He just stand and smile like a cat, and peek at everything we pull out of the wagons. We haul it all into the warehouse, into the rear corner, and then we do the division. We count the bolts of tradecloth, and he takes a tenth. *Sacre bleu!* He takes the best colors! Red! We count the kettles, and he takes a tenth. I stand and grieve, watching his engagés take away the tenth into the trading room. He asks where the trade blankets are, and I say we lost them, and he says, is that so, and I nod, and he smiles like a man making love to a virgin. But after we are all done, I make him sign the paper, that he is storing the rest—the inventory list here—and he takes away the tenth. It is what you wished?"

Fitzhugh examined the inventory list, and Julius Hervey's signature on the receipt, and the separate list of Hervey's share. Brokenleg sighed. American Fur was now back in business, and using Dance, Fitzhugh and Straus trade items. It irked him, and filled him with a helplessness against the ironies of fate. He nodded curtly.

"The wagons are off? The men well armed and provisioned? The wagons and stock in proper condition?"

"Oui, Monsieur. And I bring Gallard here because he is strong and can help make the fort."

"But he's our best teamster—has a way with the oxen, Trudeau."

Trudeau shrugged. "Ah, indeed. But I think to myself, here is a man to build a post, *n'est-ce pas?"*

Something lay unsaid in all this, but whatever it was, Fitzhugh couldn't fathom it.

"All right then. Hyar's what we're going to do," he said.

They toiled through the hot August days making pitiful progress. Everything had gone harder than Brokenleg had visualized. Just making the stoneboats turned into an ordeal because they lacked bolts or nails to anchor any sort of platform or crosspieces to the runners. But they had rawhide, and a bit and auger to drive in pegs, and gradually the two cumbersome sleds took shape.

He put Trudeau and Gallard to work at the bluff, prying rock loose and knocking the larger pieces into smaller ones with the maul so they could be handled. Maxim learned to drive the horse dragging the stoneboat. And Fitzhugh, along with Maxim, tumbled the rock off the stoneboat at the building site, chafing their hands in the process. The result seemed pitiful. A stoneboat worked well in the winter, on frozen ground, snow or ice, but not on dry meadow. So the dray couldn't pull as much, and the pile of rock pried loose by the engagés grew faster than the rock at the building site.

Each time Fitzhugh helped Maxim drag the rock off the stoneboat, his bum leg tortured him. The mid-day August heat sucked water out of them all, and hung oppressively in the valley, but Dust Devil didn't come bearing cold river water. In fact, she disdained the whole business, and tended camp silently, glaring at the sweating, slaving whitemen around her as if they were mad. There were times, too, when Fitzhugh had to saddle up and make meat, and when the hunting went badly he disappeared all day, further slowing the progress. And yet, in spite of their difficulties, the heaps of dun slab rock piled along the site of future walls grew bit by bit. Brokenleg wanted a mountain of it ready, within easy reach, for the time when they all laid up the walls.

And so they labored, from before dawn until darkness choked off their progress. But even then work didn't cease. Maxim learned to wipe down his weary horse and balm the flesh with tallow where the harness had chafed it. And each morning, the boy had to unhobble the horse, brush it carefully, and begin the long business of harnessing, easing on the collar, the surcingle, the tugs, the bridle and reins. Maxim worked silently, his skinny frame growing even thinner under the terrible duress of brute labor. Fitzhugh watched, worried, because the lad's spirit had sunk back inside somewhere, and no one had the faintest idea what Maxim was thinking. Fitzhugh's days didn't end with the darkness and cool either. Often after his evening meal, he stood on his aching legs, got an ax, and trudged down to the wood areas along the river to girdle trees. They'd need dry wood later.

Only Trudeau and Gallard seemed to prosper during the ordeal. Like most engagés up the river, they were used to brutal toil day after day, and asked little more than a pipe of *tabac* at the day's end. Fitzhugh watched Gallard closely without quite knowing why, but detected no signs of disloyalty. The man's gaze seemed direct enough, and his manner steady. Fitzhugh never asked Trudeau about the engagé, having learned back on the *Platte* to let the Frenchmen deal with their own, the way they chose.

Frequently tribesmen came by—usually Sioux or Crow—and that delighted Fitzhugh because word of the new post would spread swiftly. He would begin trading when the winter was coldest, when the sun scraped the southern horizon, when the nights were longest. He gave the headmen twists of tobacco, hoping it would last, and made the finger-talk with them while Dust Devil sulked and glared. Only once did a party come through painted for war—Sioux, going on a horse raid against the Crow. They stopped, stared at the Hawken cradled in Fitzhugh's arms, studied the growing rectangle of tumbled rock, peered covetously at camp goods, especially the keg labeled vinegar, almost as if knowing what was within it, and then walked on. Like most horse-raiding parties, they were on foot. They planned to ride back to their village.

All this cut into work time, but still pleased Brokenleg. The lower Bighorn valley was a great highway, and the highway led straight past his new post. But if it delighted him, it obviously displeased Dust Devil, who saw only enemies of her people among these visitors, and peered at them with such hostility that they took notice, and eyed her thoughtfully with long, silent looks.

One morning Julius Hervey rode in on his buckskin stallion, his bright eyes surveying the heaps of yellowish rock forming a rectangle where future walls would rise.

"A rock house, and nothing inside," he taunted, as Fitzhugh labored at a stoneboat.

Brokenleg stood slowly, feeling his leg torture him and sweat collect at his waist. "Permanent," he replied.

"Make a nice barn after you leave. All that labor for nothing."

"I reckon it won't burn."

"You chose a good place. Now, if you had something to trade, you might get some robes. But you won't. Do you think you'll ever see all that stuff again?"

"I reckon."

Hervey laughed. "We were resupplied. Mackinaw poled up from Fort Union. I sent twenty bales of robes back. We're fixed for the year. With the stuff you gave us, and ours, and all the rest of yours sitting in my warehouse, if I feel like dickering for it."

Hervey was needling him, he knew. Maybe even looking

to murder him. One never knew about Hervey, except that when he was in fine fettle, as now, he got cocky.

"Reckon you would," Fitzhugh said.

Maxim looked stricken. Fitzhugh shoved the rest of the sandstone off the boat. "You git on over there, boy," he said roughly. Maxim stared bitterly at Hervey and then hawed the horse, snapping its lines over its croup.

Hervey grinned. "City boy. He'll make some muscle, if he survives."

Fitzhugh stood, wearily. "Rest of my stuff's due in a day or two, at least if they didn't have no trouble. From Wolf Rapids. We'll keep it at Cass like the rest."

"And I get a tenth. I'm giving it away, Stiffleg. I'm bribing whole tribes with your stuff. And after I give away the ten percent, I'll mostly give away the rest." Hervey's bright eyes bored relentlessly into Fitzhugh.

"Always comes a bill of reckoning, Julius. I'm an old reckoner."

Hervey's gaze went cold, and then slid back to mockery.

"I admire your industry. It's amazing what a man will subject himself to for a fool dream. That's all it is, you know."

Fitzhugh had wearied of the taunting, and peered out upon the golden meadow, and then up into a cloudless sky with a blue so intense it hurt his eyes. Somewhere to the east, and close now, three heavy wagons were slowly rolling toward him, along with eight men. He'd have them together, his whole crew. And then things would happen.

"Had some river Crows come in yesterday," Hervey said. "They'd been down the river, trading at Union, when your packet came in. Seems that pretty squaw of yours insulted a headman named Walks At Night. Those Crow, they got a bit huffy about it and told me they'll stick with American Fur, right to the last robe. Now was I you, Stiffleg, I'd ditch her. Pitch her right outa the lodge. In fact, was I you, I'd give her to me. I'll use her good."

Dust Devil glared at the man on horseback. "Good! Crows all dog dung. We trade with Cheyenne."

"Feisty, ain't she," Hervey said. "I'll take her off your hands, Stiffleg. Show her who's a man around here. I'll even keep her for ten percent."

Fitzhugh got hot, but wouldn't let himself get riled—and murdered.

"There went your Crow trading, Stiffleg. And those Cheyenne, this here is a far corner for them. You're going to have trouble with the Crow. In fact, you won't have a horse or ox or mule around here within a month."

"I'll remember that, Hervey. And I'll know who put it in their haids."

Julius Hervey laughed heartily, reined his horse around, and trotted off toward the north, like some prince of darkness.

Chapter Thirteen

Brokenleg Fitzhugh sat his horse beside the gate of Fort Cass, watching his Creole teamsters whip and curse the yoked oxen and the mule team into the yard within. His oxen had become bilingual, he thought, responding to the cussing of two tongues. The creaking Pittsburghs groaned under their excess weight, their sheets flapping in the gusty breeze.

They'd made it. The stock seemed none the worse for wear, either, apart from the usual gaunting up from long hard use. Hervey's engagés directed the wagons toward the warehouse, and then stood idly while Fitzhugh's men began the sweaty task of unloading tons of tradegoods.

"Now I have it all, and you'll never see it again, Stiffleg." Julius Hervey stood solemnly at the gate, watching the Opposition's goods slide into the bowels of his fort, while Brokenleg oversaw the unloading.

"Reckon that's possible."

"Let's go in there: I want my ten percent. Not that it matters. It's all mine, Stiffleg."

Fitzhugh slid his bum leg over the croup, and eased down to the packed earth from the off side of his animal. His leg hurt. It always flamed into pain when he first put weight on it. Outside the gate, a crowd of Crows gathered to see the sights. More of them now than a few weeks ago. Cass had been back in business, drawing trade from all the Mountain Crows, and one village of Shoshone.

"Maybe I'll keep your wagons, too," said Hervey. "Now that I've swallowed up everything. I'm the whale, and you're Jonah."

"Reckon you could."

"Not could. Will. This isn't St. Louis."

"I've got some stuff here that's fort supplies, not trade goods."

"Ten percent."

"That stuff's stayin' in the wagons and coming with us."

"Glad you think so, Stiffleg." Hervey looked almighty pleased with himself.

The warehouse eave dropped too low to permit Fitzhugh's men to drive the lumbering Pittsburghs in, so they were unloading at the door, sweating mightily as men in the wagons lowered crates into the arms of others on the ground, while oxen stood restlessly, muttering and stinking.

"Mule work," said Hervey.

Charles Brasseau, the black-haired engagé Trudeau had put in charge of this second trip, handed Fitzhugh the cargo manifests, and Maxim's inventory lists. Brokenleg paged through them, until he found the separate list of post furnishings.

"Hyar's what I'm takin' out," Fitzhugh said. The list included sickles, scythes, manila rope, a plow, oakum, skillets, tea pots, percussion caps, wash basins, skimming ladles and forks, soup tureens, tumblers, yellow jugs, brown havana sugar, shaving soap, ground salt, black pepper, a coffee grinder, coffee boiler, candle molds, twenty pounds of candlewick, a small iron strongbox, spoons, knives and forks, a barrel of rice, barrels of molasses, sugar, crackers, and dried apples—and a lot more of the things that were the daily tools of life at a trading post.

"Ten percent." Hervey looked gleeful.

"We'll see."

"Plows and scythes and sickles. You must think you'll stay long enough to plant a garden and cut hay."

"Reckon so. Maybe we'll be selling you vegetables."

Hervey chuckled.

When at last the first wagon was emptied, the sweating men paused while Hervey wandered among the wooden crates and pasteboard boxes, taking his tenth of brass hawk bells made in Leipzig, beads made in Venice, Pennsylvania trade muskets, steel strikers made in St. Louis, DuPont powder from Delaware, French calicos, Sheffield knives and awls, and all the rest, checking lists with Brasseau, and putting his heap to one side. Fitzhugh hated it, and knew Maxim would hate it even more. He felt like he'd opened an artery. Which is why he kept Maxim back at their camp, along with Trudeau and Gallard, guarding the place. Maxim had accepted dourly.

Hervey chose his tenth well, with a knowing eye for the best colors of calico, the bluest beads, the most sought-after sizes of Wilson butcher knives. When numbers didn't work into tenths—such as taking his share of forty-eight trade rifles—he took a dollar credit or debit from the inventories and applied it to other items, choosing with the skill of a seasoned trader on intimate terms with the tribesmen he dealt with. Brokenleg watched silently, rarely objecting, knowing that Hervey would love to taunt him into doing something reckless. Brasseau peered at him from liquid brown eyes, a look that asked whether Brokenleg was crazy, or merely demented. And so the taut afternoon unraveled.

Late in the day, the engagés finished stacking the impressive mountain of goods in a far corner of the warehouse, while Hervey's men toted their plunder into the Fort Cass trading room, and his clerks settled it on shelves there. Each item on those shelves would sell for six or eight times its price back in the states, in part because of the costs of transporting the item so far. The prices at Fitzhugh's post would be about the same.

"Friendly of you to bring us tradegoods. Now we can

put you out of business in three months instead of six," Hervey said.

But Brokenleg was studying the warehouse, making sure it was tight, hunting for signs of leakage from the roof. He saw no stain of water on the handsawn planks overhead, no dried and cracked mud in the earthen floor. If rats didn't eat up his tradecloths and anything else they found tasty, his goods would be as safe as he could keep them in a wilderness. "Load up them housekeeping goods," he said to Brasseau.

"Those stay," Hervey said, his eyes mocking again.

Fitzhugh nodded to Brasseau, and the Creoles began dumping the scythes and pots back into the nearest wagon, with fearful glances toward a man they knew could easily murder them at a whim. But Hervey just smiled, stalking the warehouse like a joyous catamount surveying a carcass.

"Sign this," said Fitzhugh, shoving at Hervey the manifest of goods being stored. The factor grinned, nodded, and beckoned Fitzhugh toward the trading room, where he scraped his signature on the document without looking at it—which bothered Fitzhugh almost more than Hervey's threats.

"I'll be back end of the year," Brokenleg said.

"Try it," Hervey retorted.

Out in the yard, where the sun lay flat and pummeled the east wall with yellow light, the engagés had turned the weary yokes of oxen and headed the lightened Pittsburghs toward the gate.

"Let's git," said Fitzhugh.

They whipped and cursed the slavering animals until the oxen hunkered down into their yokes, and lifted the wagons into a slow roll, raising dust. And then they stopped.

"Monsieur, *la porte* . . ."

The doors of Fort Cass had been closed.

Fitzhugh's pulse rose. He peered around sharply. The yard was empty. Meat smells drifted from the kitchen. Cass's engagés had vanished. But Hervey stood in the shadow of the warehouse, leaning idly against the doorframe.

"Open it up, Hervey, or we will."

Hervey smiled and said nothing.

Fitzhugh peered around, studying the barracks, the offices, the spare rooms, looking for signs of war, and finding none. Orange light caught the American flag waving langorously above the gate. It came to him they'd either leave peaceably or dead. No conduct was beyond Julius Hervey, including mass murder and theft of the Opposition's trading goods. But Fitzhugh guessed the man was bluffing, intimidating. Usually, a strange honor prevailed out here in a wild land, even among or between trading opponents. But that didn't apply to the burly, mocking brown-eyed man with fists that pulverized whatever he chose to ruin.

"I reckon we'll let ourselves out then, Hervey."

Fitzhugh nodded to his teamsters. None of his engagés carried their rifles. Not when they needed whips in hand to goad the oxen and mules. Ahead, Brasseau fearfully walked toward high, roughhewn doors made of heavy sawn plank and bolted together with iron. No one stopped him. He found the doors unlocked, and began shoving them open. They creaked like gallows timbers in the hush.

"It's after trading hours, Stiffleg. We lock before supper in the summer, sundown in the winter." Hervey's mocking voice told him that the truth was otherwise. "Not that it makes any difference. Say goodbye to everything now, and enjoy working on your rockpile."

"I'll be back, Hervey," Brokenleg said, as the Pittsburghs lumbered out into flat light, and turned toward the Bighorn.

Work quickened at the construction site with the return of the engagés. Fitzhugh put Lamaitre and Bercier to prying up rock from the bluff; Courvet and Dauphin to running the stoneboats to the site; Brasseau and Larue to cutting roof poles and beams and sawing plank; and Guerette, Provost and Gallard to laying up the walls, using mud mortar mixed by Maxim. The boy was hard pressed to mix enough mud to keep three men supplied. When Fitzhugh wasn't hunting, he helped Maxim with that crucial task.

They'd dug a pit beside a cutbank on the river, at a place where there was abundant moist gravelly clay. There the young man spaded clay into the pit, added buckets of water, and hoed the mud into a thick pudding. It was risky work. He had to pluck out oversized rock, and balance water and mud to get the right consistency. Provost or Guerette usually showed up with empty buckets before Maxim was ready, and helped with the final mixing. Within an hour on that first day, Maxim had reached his limit. Fitzhugh said nothing, let the boy recover his strength, and continue doing what he could.

Still, in spite of the lack of manpower, a thick rectangle of stone began to rise, day by day, but with a frightful slowness as Fitzhugh eyed the autumnal skies warily and men drew their blankets tighter around them at night. There were never enough men. The pile of poles brought in each day on the woodcutters' wagon, one of the Pittsburghs with its sheet and bows removed, grew steadily, but not fast enough.

The erection of the post was only one of several pressing problems troubling Fitzhugh. He needed to put the whole crew to cutting prairie hay with the scythes, and stacking it. He'd need plenty of winter feed for the livestock. And firewood. He'd need a dozen cords to start with, and more as the winter progressed. And it had to be dry wood, from dead trees. The oxen, mules, and horses had to be guarded constantly, and the camp tended, and Dust Devil didn't have enough time—or the inclination—to do it all. But the most troublesome problem of all was simply keeping his large crew fed.

Daily, before dawn, he saddled up his horse, and haltered a packhorse that tolerated a load of bloody meat, and rode out to hunt. He had found precious little of it, perhaps because game shied from the intense activity around the construction site, but also because the tribesmen camping at Fort Cass four miles away were also hunting, and perhaps because of something else—Fitzhugh had the feeling that someone was deliberately driving game away; someone employed by Hervey to do just that. Fitzhugh had found an occasional fresh pony track threading through lush bottoms where game usually lingered. A buck or doe a day wasn't enough to feed his ravenous men. He had to add an antelope to that, or a wild turkey. He found no elk or bear. Each dawn he ranged as many as six or eight miles looking for meat, and when he found none, he repeated the whole thing in the evening, ranging south up the Bighorn river through bottoms that should be crawling with deer.

Once or twice he brought back two; most of the time he came back emptyhanded. His bum leg had made it difficult for him to limp far from his horse, or tie the animal somewhere and stalk game out of a thicket. He was tempted to give up hunting, turn it over to Bercier, who loved to hunt, and work on the construction himself—but with his leg, he'd be less useful there than out hunting, his old Hawken across his lap. As soon as he rode in with a carcass, Dust Devil wrapped its hind legs with thong, hung it with rope, and sliced down its gut. She could butcher any animal with astonishing speed, muttering and laughing as she yanked back hide and sawed at meat.

Almost daily, small parties of Indians rode in and stared at the construction. These were mostly Sioux hunting or trading bands, en route up or down the river trace. If Fitzhugh was in camp, he'd give their headmen a twist of tobacco, and invite them to come trade when the days were shortest and the cold had come. If Fitzhugh was out hunting, then Trudeau did the same thing. There was little danger, except to the horses, which were a temptation to any plains warrior of any tribe. A new trading post meant more goods, and competing prices, and they welcomed it. Still, Fitzhugh noticed, the Crow stayed away, and that became yet another thing to worry about. Neutrality was the only real safety a post had, a reality he'd never been able to pound into Dust Devil's skull.

One night parties unknown had attempted to steal the stock, but the shrieking of a nervous mare, plus careful picketing and hobbling, had prevented it. The engagés had boiled out of their robes and fired random shots into the dark, and then checked with a lantern. All animals were accounted for. But that added to Fitzhugh's worries: His stock was critically important, not only for construction but also for the trading strategy he had in mind, driving wagons out to the villages all winter.

By mid-September, a rectangle of sandstone rock rose about three feet, broken by a front and rear door and notched at either end by the fireplaces. Sun and wind dried the exposed mortar into light tan hardness, but Fitzhugh knew that back under the rock, the mud stayed as wet as ever and would be drying for months, emitting a dank smell all the while, that would make the post unpleasant until the mortar froze solid in the cold. The weather was changing. The sun rose lower and fled earlier, robbing them of daylight hours. The heat vanished, turning each autumnal day into a perfect climate for hard work, but also plunging the camp into a deep pre-dawn chill, with an occasional skim of ice.

He watched his men carefully, studying each, fathoming character. The loss of the blankets still rankled, and if it had been done by some traitor in his midst, he intended to root the man or men out. But he discovered nothing. None of these hardy French, used to brute toil, was sloughing off his tasks; indeed, they worked with a cheery optimism, making small jokes, enjoying a pipeful of *tabac* in the evenings, doing their assigned tasks without being asked, knowing that any slacking hurt the enterprise, and burdened the others. His only suspect, Gallard, showed no less enthusiasm than any of the rest. He watched Maxim, too, wondering whether the lad's enormous task and somewhat pessimistic outlook would lead to discouragement, or worse, sickness. He had no physician here except for Dust Devil and her medicinal herbs, and no shelter either, save for the pitched wagonsheet, or two wagonbeds.

One day just after the equinox, Brokenleg rode south, up the valley, under a low gray sky driven by a sharp northwind. He raised no game, and decided he'd find none on the bottoms that day, so he turned his bay eastward, toward a notch in the bluffs, thinking to ride out on the humped prairies above and shoot some antelope. The notch afforded a buffalo trace, winding through thick juniper and sagebrush growth into a dish in the prairies, its buffalo grass cured tan now and bobbing in the stiff northwind. He saw no white rumps or bellies of antelope, but what he did discover excited him more. Thirty or forty dark buffalo grazed to the east, facing into the wind, unlike cattle. He'd been lucky. If he'd come upon them a little north of where he saw his pony, his scent would have reached them.

"Buffler!" he announced to the wind. "Buffler! Eats for weeks, if she stays cold. Horns, hide, and tongue. Boudins, humprib, and backfat! Damn my bad leg, if I don't drop two or six."

In fact his bad leg would keep him from the most effective way to shoot them. He should work his way around to the south, tie the horse out of sight, stalk to within two hundred yards or so, and then shoot the sentries, resting his battered piece on crossed sticks. But he could no more stalk than a bull moose could stalk. But maybe the wind would work for him, masking the sound of his passage. That plus their weak eyes.

"Dang it now, horse, if I don't lay a few buffler to rest, it'll be because you aren't daintyfooted," he whispered. "Now you git a sneak into your walk, like that gray wolf yonder, lookin' for dinner—I never seen a mess of buffler without a gray wolf or two wanting handouts—and we'll git around south a piece."

He backed off a hundred yards or so, and then eased the bay around the edge of the basin, staying below the skyline. There buffalo ignored him, attacking the grass with a herbivore's greed. Minute particles of sleet, as fine as sand, and invisible to the eye, slapped at his beard. That suited him fine too. The meat would keep.

A sentry cow watched his slow passage around the perimeter, but sounded no alarm. She'd be his first target if he could just ride another fifty yards to give himself a good heart-lung shot. He spotted several calves, strategically surrounded by adult animals which could form a perimeter against wolves in moments.

Fitzhugh reached a likely spot and eyed the sentry, which stared alertly now. He wondered whether to dismount and try a prone shot, the type most likely to kill. But he knew himself, and his leg, and his awkward contortions getting off a horse, and decided he had to shoot from horseback, an event that the bay anticipated by laying back its ears and sidling, which made accurate shooting all the tougher.

"Now, dang it, horse, you mind your bad manners. What I don't want is worse manners."

He slid his Hawken from its quilled elkskin sheath, and checked the percussion cap. The bay sidled beneath him."Quiet now, or I'll shoot you, too."

Then he lifted the heavy octagon-barreled rifle, and drew a careful bead on a hat-sized spot behind the cow's shoulders. But the horse danced. He full-cocked the hammer, and waited for the nervous animal to stop it, cussing because the cow turned slightly toward him. He jammed the butt deep into his shoulder, aimed and waited. At last the bay paused for an instant, and Fitzhugh squeezed. The wind whipped the boom out of his ears, but he felt the jolt to his shoulder, and saw the cow shudder, shake her head, and slowly sag to the earth, forefeet first, her rump up like a surrendering flag.

The other buffalo didn't stop their mowing.

"Hyar's supper," he said, digging around in his possibles for another ball and a wad. He poured a guessload of powder from his horn down the barrel, drove the patch and ball down with the rod stowed under the barrel, and then slid a tiny cap over the nipple, after checking to see whether it had been fouled.

A restlessness swept among the buffalo. In some sort of synchronization, they all shifted their positions a few yards, out of some primal purpose beyond the reckoning of man, and then settled down to eating again. With their sentry down and spasming, they'd lost their guard.

The second shot was easy, right behind the shoulder of a small cow that had started some dark winter hair. The third shot missed the lights of a large cow, and she began bawling and blowing blood from her nose, mincing in a frenzied circle. It took another shot, this time while the bay was skittering sideways, to kill her. It struck her in the neck, and pierced an artery, which began gouting. That's when the nervous herd bolted off to the east, with the slinking wolves behind it.

Fitzhugh rode warily out to his three carcasses, knowing how often a dead buffalo wasn't really dead. Three cows! He exulted. Three tongues, three robes, three humpmeat, more boudins that a man could swallow, and hot liver, too, ready to devour mountain-man style. He'd allow himself that, he figured. And maybe haul a tongue back.

He slid to the ground, feeling pain shoot through his bad leg, made worse by the deepening cold and the needling sleet, that seemed to increase every minute. They looked plumb dead, but a man could never be sure, so he kicked one and then another. The third shivered, so he avoided her. He eyed the skies unhappily, and gave up on cutting one open for the liver. Instead, he pried one's mouth open and sawed away at the massive, hot, wet tongue. Even that turned out to be a mean task, with his hands going numb from the cold. He wished he'd dressed better. But at last he yanked the rough-textured meat from the mouth, and clambered stiffly aboard the bay, glancing sharply at the horizons to see whether he'd been watched. He saw nothing, and discovered that the farther hills were veiled by falling snow. He had to get back—a two-hour ride—and fetch two wagons fast. Before the early blizzard engulfed them.

Chapter Fourteen

Her man rode out of a whirl of snow and dismounted awkwardly, staggering on his bad leg. Then presented her with a buffalo tongue, thick and heavy and not yet frozen.

"Where?" she asked.

"Two hours. Maybe six or seven miles."

The terms confused her. "Is that far?"

"Yes. I'll get some men and a wagon."

"How many?"

"Three. Unless they get et up by coyotes before we git there."

"I will come. Whitemen don't know how to cut."

"It'll be cold."

"That's good! It will freeze the meat."

"Let's hope it don't freeze before we git to it."

That was something to worry about. Three frozen carcasses would be hard to handle. But the snow would be something to worry about, too. It came in cruel gusts now, driven out of the north in a dull white blur, coating her man and his horse, building up on the chest-high walls of the post, numbing fingers of the engagés.

"I'll get knives," she said, leaving her cooking fire. She would take her blanket capote as well, along with gloves because her fingers would get stiff, and she might hurt herself sawing at the half-frozen meat. Three buffalo! It gladdened her heart. It would make her life simpler for a while.

"Throw an axe in the wagon," he said. "So we can chop froze-up buffler if we got to."

She eyed the low opaque sky nervously, and dug into her parfleches for her winter moccasins, with rawhide soles made from the skin of a bull, and rabbit fur lining. Wind rattled the canvas tent they'd made of a wagonsheet. It was all they had.

Her man stared into the whiteness, looking for men he could spare. He chose the three who were laying up the walls.

"Reckon we've got some meat to make," he said. "Six, seven miles south. I downed three buffler. You'll have yourself some humpmeat and boudins tonight. But we'd better git, before the snow builds up."

Guerette, Provost and Gallard abandoned the masonry at once and began digging in their kits for capotes and gloves.

"Next yoke comes in with a stoneboat, take them. Let's have three yoke, just in case it gets skiddy. We got to yank that wagon up a snowy grade."

They understood his English well enough, though they didn't speak it much, and soon had the six oxen hitched to an empty wagon. But the remaining oxen would have an easier time, skidding the stoneboats over snow. Her man would keep the woodcutters and rock-diggers busy, even in the mounting blizzard.

How like cattle and horses whitemen were, she thought, contempt building in her. Pulling and sweating in a harness made of words and commands. When her father had given her to Fitzhugh, she accepted it, thinking she would become the woman of a great warrior and fighter, but he turned out to be like all the rest of the whites, slaves, doing woman's work. And now these white cattle were going out to butcher buffalo, just like the women of her village. She wished Fitzhugh would go kill Crows and steal Blackfoot ponies instead of—this. Then she could be proud, instead of ashamed.

Maxim showed up from the riverbank, carrying a bucket of mud. He set it down, after seeing that work had been abandoned, and watched the preparations, expectantly.

"Brokenleg, I want to go too," he said.

"I reckon we need someone to tend camp, keep a fire cracklin', cut us some firewood. It's gettin' plumb mean."

"I want to learn the business. I want to see the buffalo, and what you do, and how you get the hide off. That's what I'm here for."

Fitzhugh grinned. "Well, git your winter duds on, and fetch you a knife and ax. And dump that mud so it don't freeze in the bucket."

"I didn't know it got so cold so soon."

"This hyar's just a fall blow. We got good weather yet."

They struck south, with the northwind harrying them along. Fitzhugh rode his snowcaked bay, looking cold, but Dust Devil chose to walk beside the lumbering wagon to keep warm. The oxen, their breaths steaming, had no trouble dragging the empty Pittsburgh, with its chattering wagonsheet, through two or three inches of snow, but coming back would be an ordeal for them if it kept falling out of the sky. Maxim huddled under a blanket in the wagon, looking cold, and the sight awakened her contempt. Why were whitemen such weaklings? It was growing colder, she knew, because Winter Man ruled the world this day.

She felt the soft snow compress under the rawhide soles of her moccasins, and heard the wagonwheels squeak and hiss as they cut a long thin line through the powder. Once they struck a small drift, and the oxen had to lower in their yokes and drag the lumbering wagon through. The cold bit her calves and stung her ears and numbed her fingers, and she drew her capote tighter, and tugged its hood forward. Ahead, the engagés trudged beside the six oxen, breaking a trail for her.

At long last, her man turned them left, toward the river bluffs, and onto a steep trail to the top of them.

"Just beyond the top there," he said. "I ought to git on up and chase off the coyotes and crows."

But the grade rose too steeply for the oxen, and they began churning snow into brown muck, skidding and stumbling as the deadweight of the wagon dragged them backwards. The engagés pushed from the rear, while Maxim whipped, but still the oxen made no headway and churned up the foot-deep snow. Then two went down and couldn't get up because of the grease underfoot. Guerette had to release the front yoke from the tugs, while the rest eased the heavy Pittsburgh back a little, before the downed oxen could stand.

Dust Devil watched contemptuously. A horse drawing a travois would have climbed the grade easily. A few squaws, with a few ponies and travois, could have done what these whitemen didn't know how to do.

"I guess that's it," Fitzhugh said. "Ease the wagon back down there and unhitch them yoke. We'll take the oxen up top, and then drag the buffler down with 'em."

The engagés unhooked the oxen and then eased the wagon backward a way, a tricky job that had them sweating and cursing and riding the wagon brake so that it skidded slowly. But at last they had the wagon parked in the Bighorn River bottoms, and walked the yokes of steaming oxen to the top of the bluffs and out into the dished prairie. Fitzhugh looked bewildered for a moment, because the black buffalo carcasses were nowhere to be seen, but eventually he found them, buried in the deepening snow, as white as the terrain around them.

It didn't take long to pin their front legs together with thong and attach tugs to the beasts. The cows had not yet frozen, and would slide in a limber way over the snow. In fact, when they reached the downgrade, the carcasses tended to slide into the rear of the oxen, and engagés had to grab their tails to keep the carcasses from careening out in front of the ox yokes.

"Maybe we should just pull these hyar buffler back to camp," her man muttered.

"No, you will make the hair bad. We got good robes," she said.

"You can tan 'em, since you haven't got enough to do."

"I will!" she retorted hotly.

At the wagon, the engagés unhitched the yokes from the carcasses and hooked them to the wagon again. The animals responded sluggishly, stumbling through the heaped snow. Dust Devil knelt beside one cow, and began her buffalo prayer.

"Thank you buffalo cow for your meat, giving me flesh to eat, like your brothers and sisters," she sang in Cheyenne. "May your spirit be happy in the next world, knowing you have given me your flesh."

Maxim was staring at her, but it didn't matter. The big cow lay on its side, a lump of cooling flesh too heavy to handle. She pulled out her shining knife and began sawing through the brisket, feeling the resistance of the thick hide as she cut and hacked. Snow landed on her bare hands and didn't melt. It mixed with the red gore and iced there, driving sensation from her fingers until she could scarcely tell that her knife was in her hands. She knew the danger, and hoped to warm her hands within. But the carcass had cooled too long, and her hands met only with sharp cold when she forced them inside the belly of the cow. Still, it had to be done. She wanted the offal out before it froze there.

"Help me," she snapped at Maxim. The boy was worthless, but she needed more hands to pull out the guts.

He stared at her, horrified, and then reluctantly pulled off his mittens and plunged his reddened hands into the cavity, looking half-sick.

"Don't throw out them boudins," Fitzhugh said from horseback. His red beard had collected a load of snow.

She snorted at him. "Do you think I don't know how?"

At last the innards lay in the snow, too cold to steam,

and she turned to the next cow, already exhausted. It grew colder, and the snow had become stinging pellets that would torture them all the long way back. She could not even feel her hands, and feared the knife might slip as she sawed into the brisket again.

While she wrestled with the second cow, the engagés wrestled with the gutted one, trying to lift it into the wagon. Its weight was too much for them, and it didn't help any that the Pittsburghs had no tailgate at the rear of their waterproofed boxes. Fitzhugh dismounted, cursing as he landed on his bum leg, and added his own strength to theirs, to no avail.

"Reckon we'll have to quarter it," he muttered.

"Take the hide off first," she demanded.

But he ignored her and pulled the ax out of the wagon. "We better do this fast afore it freezes up and we do too," he said. And with that, he sunk the ax deep into the carcass, severing muscle and bone. It angered her, even though she knew they had to do something fast. She wanted the robes.

The light dimmed. She didn't know whether daylight had played out, or whether the lowering clouds had grown darker and thicker. She wondered if they'd get back to camp, and whether anyone had brought a steel striker and a flint. She sawed furiously while Maxim pried the stiffening brisket apart. And then it happened: the knife struck something hard, recoiled in her numb hand, and slashed deep into Maxim's thumb. He jerked his hand back as bright blood gouted out, and mixed with the pink slime on the carcass and the snow.

"Ow!" he cried, jumping up. Blood sprayed everywhere.

She stood swiftly on numbed limbs and grabbed at him. "Let me look," she said crossly, half-believing it had been the boy's fault for trying to help with something he knew nothing about.

Fitzhugh and the three engagés had finished quartering the cow into huge bloody, snowy chunks, and were loading the last of them. It took three engagés to lift a quarter over the back of the wagon and into its belly.

"My thumb!" cried Maxim.

She caught him at last and pried his good right hand from his slashed left one. She could barely see the trouble because of the scarlet blood. But it welled from a deep gash below the lower knuckle. Maxim held back tears and looked frightened.

She didn't know how to stop that much bleeding.

Fitzhugh limped over to them, cursing the snow and his pain-lanced leg. He stared a moment. "Got to stop that fast," he muttered. "Tourniquet. Sew it up. But we want a needle and thread." He peered about, looking for something. "Put a hot knife to it, maybe," he muttered. "You got starter?"

She shook her head.

"Somebody's got a flint," he roared. The engagés who crowded around Maxim now, shook their heads.

"Hyar, now," he said, digging in his kit for an old calico shirt he was using as rifle patching. He tore a generous strip of the green cloth and wrapped it hard around Maxim's hand, while the boy winced. Tears built under his eyes. Red swiftly spread out upon the green. Then Fitzhugh tore a broader strip and wrapped it around the boy's upper arm and began twisting it tighter and tighter.

"It hurts," Maxim cried.

"We got to plug up the bleeding. This'll set you back, some, boy."

"I'm bleeding to death!"

"Go fetch us a good stout stick so's we can twist it tight," Fitzhugh said to Provost. The engagé nodded and walked toward a juniper shrub, ax in hand.

Blood oozed through the bandage and dripped into the snow. Maxim looked pale. Dust Devil stared angrily at him, and then turned back to her butchering. Whitemen were weaklings, she thought, as she began sawing through the brisket again. Time closed in on her now; she had to gut the cows before they froze. Behind her, she heard them working with Maxim, tightening the tourniquet with the stick.

"I'm going to tie this bandage tight with some whangs," Brokenleg said. "And then git into the wagon, boy, and outa the wind."

When she'd opened up the second cow she plunged her numb hands inside and began tugging at guts, which finally tumbled out and into the snow. Then she turned to the third buffalo and began the whole thing over again, feeling her flesh goosebump and the snow rob the heat at the center of her body. She made little progress because her hands weren't working right, and it angered her. Maybe they had offended the spirit of this one.

Brokenleg saw her struggling, and the pathetic cut she'd started in the freezing animal. "Git aside," he said roughly. She glared and delayed as long as she could as a matter of pride, and because it felt good to resist him. But finally she stood up, knife in hand, her skirts covered with frozen bloody muck.

"Guerette, Provist, turn her on her back," he said. The engagés grabbed legs and pulled at the cow. Fitzhugh's axe slashed down, chopping straight into the chest, and then he whacked his way down the brisket with savage strokes, opening the cow in seconds, the stiffness of the half-frozen flesh helping him complete the crude cut. Then, with a grim determination, he hacked out the innards, and began quartering the cow, completing the whole business swiftly. They loaded the snow-caked quarters, while Maxim huddled at the front end of the wagon, and without a moment's delay, Provost began whipping the reluctant oxen into the northern gale.

She knew she must walk, move, run before she froze. The wind didn't seem terribly cold, but the snow had wormed its way into her hair, and down her moccasins, and up her legs, and down her neck, melting into icy water that sucked heat from her. Heading into the storm felt terrible. The oxen bawled and rebelled, not wanting to walk that direction, but slowly the burdened wagon creaked through snow, leaving sharp trenches behind it.

Ahead, Fitzhugh on his horse broke trail on one side, while Gallard, beside him, broke trail on the other. As light dimmed they pierced into the mouth of the storm, grimly northbound up the bottoms along a vanished trace. After a while Fitzhugh halted, letting the oxen sag in their yokes, and clambered painfully into the wagon.

"I got to let some blood through, Maxim."

She peered into the gloom, over the pile of meat, and saw him loosening the tourniquet.

"How does it feel, boy?"

"It prickles. I'm so cold."

"Let's see that paw."

Fitzhugh examined the bloody bandage. "Plumb froze up. It ain't bleein' anyway. You'll be all right."

"I feel sick."

"Well, that's natural. We'll git on home, if we can see our way."

"What's home?" Maxim asked bitterly.

"I reckon they've got another tent rigged up and some dandy fires roarin'. And the other wagon's got the sheet on it too. It's not a house, but it'll do. And this'll blow off in a few days."

Fitzhugh twisted the stick tight again. "You can do this yourself, boy. Every fifteen, twenty minutes. Let her bleed. And if your hand don't start up leakin' again, maybe you can quit the tourniquet pretty soon."

"I'm so cold. And hot."

"Stomp around some. Walk when you can."

But Maxim didn't respond.

Guerette and Provost whipped and hawed the snow-caked oxen again, driving into a deepening dusk, and the wagon creaked forward. Once the wagon lurched violently, tilting to the left and then slowly righting itself. A wheel had dropped into a snowfilled hole. She wondered if they knew where they were going. How easy this would have been with a few horses and travois, she thought angrily. They struck a mass of trees and veered away from it, a sure sign they were no longer on the well-worn trace. The snow ceased to sting her face, though it whirled in, and she realized her skin had ceased to feel. Even her eyelids caught the hard flakes and held them.

An ox fell, dragging its yokemate down also. Engagés poked and prodded, but it lay in the snow unmoving and uncaring.

"Get shut of it," Fitzhugh commanded. Weary engagés, floating like ghosts in the last light, unhooked the front yoke to get at the middle one, and freed the downed ox from the heavy wooden collar twisting its neck as it lay on the ground. Not even when freed did it stand, and neither did its mate. It took precious time, and the last of the light, to work the wagon and remaining yokes around the unbudging ones.

"I'm ridin' ahead to git some help," Fitzhugh said. "Don't whip these others too much. We got to save them so's we can git out and trade. We're not far now."

He vanished into a cavernous gloom while the rest stood around, not knowing whether to keep walking and stomping and running to stay warm, or whether to crawl in beside Maxim, where at least the stinging wind didn't probe through every layer they wore. They crawled in, stumbling over the mountains of meat, and collected at the front of the box in the icy calm.

"I want to go home," Maxim mumbled.

She settled beside him, discovering not warmth but at least respite from the brutal blowing snow, and not comfort but less pain. Right now, she thought, they could be in the warm, lined lodges of her people, sitting around crackling fires, listening to the wind chatter the smoke flaps. They could have traded all they brought to her people, and have a great pile of fine robes to take back to the whiteman's world. And her people could have been well armed with rifles and powder and ball to make them strong against their enemies. But instead of listening to her, these pale ones all huddled here without a fire, some of them on the very edge of crossing into the other world.

She knew she'd had her fill of this. A desolating loneliness settled on her, and along with it a yearning for her village, her people. The vision of her father and mother and clan grew so powerful she gasped inwardly, filled with the light, filled with medicine. She remembered the warmth of the lodgefires, and how the cowhide cones caught and held the heat, and vented the pungent smoke through the windflaps. She thought of proud, lean warriors the color of her own flesh, muscles rippling along powerful torsos, warriors who knew how to hunt and kill and protect the old ones and the very young, and bring home gifts to their happy women. Some had courted her once, played their flutes before Fitzhugh had come.

But then the happy imaginings of her mind slipped away, and the dark coldness returned. If she lived through this night, she would leave him.

Chapter Fifteen

The stupid bay offered no help. It had one notion in its thick skull, and that was to turn its tail to the wind and stinging snow. Fitzhugh hadn't any idea where he'd wandered, except that it wasn't far from the camp. He reckoned they'd travelled most of two hours before the oxen gave out.

The wind had sluiced the heat out of him, yanking his coat back and sliding icy fingers across his ribs and down his neck. His leg had stopped hurting and that was always a danger sign. Only the wind gave him direction, but it came in gusts and eddied from the side. He could see nothing: the whiteness of the snow was little help beneath the massed stormclouds. The snow looked as black as everything else.

The horse stopped again and refused to heed the prompting of his heel. He reined the animal slightly left and tried again, and the horse walked forward a few steps. A branch whipped across his face, stinging him. Cottonwoods. He'd probably drifted toward the river. It came to him that he couldn't find his way forward or backward, and might die. He'd been in tight corners in the mountains, more of them than he could count, and he knew this one had turned dangerous. He'd gone to the Rocky Mountain College, as the beaver men had called it—the only college where a student graduated or died. He cursed himself for not taking the simplest precautions, such as bringing a flint and striker, and a coal oil lantern. And for leaving the others and the safety of the canvas-covered wagon with its puckerholes drawn tight against the wind.

Well, the graduating class at that college learned one thing: never to give up. Even then more than a few went under, and for a moment he played the rollcall through his mind, solitary trappers, partnered trappers, men who rode out of the rendezvous in the summer and never came back. He knew his fingers were frostbitten, and the end of his nose, and his toes weren't far from it. It angered him, and anger felt good when he could feel nothing else.

He yanked the horse left until he felt the northwind savaging his right cheek and neck, and then kicked it brutally with his good leg. His horse had to learn to take one-boot commands. The river. The horse shied and stopped. Fitzhugh booted it. The horse stumbled forward, dodged what had to be a great cottonwood, and stopped. Brokenleg kicked again. They made progress through the cottonwoods. He knew they were among them by the lash of branches. Once a limb brained and almost unseated him.

He heard water ahead, a soft mocking ripple, just as the horse minced down a slippery slope and stopped suddenly. They stood on a bank, but he had no idea how it dropped to the river or how deep the Bighorn ran. He cursed, and kicked the horse again. It shrieked, plunged down a black abyss and into water, almost toppling him. Fitzhugh had no idea how high it came, but it wasn't high enough to wet his boots or bother the horse. A path, then, unless he hit a sinkhole and got dead-wet. He sawed the rein, pulling the horse to the right, into the wind, and down the river, and kicked it into a ginger walk. He heard it splash, felt it slide and slip, but each step took him toward his camp and the fire he knew had to be there—if he could see it through the snow. Ten frozen minutes later, by his reckoning, he discerned an orange glow back from the bank on his right, a glow softened by a veil of white. He turned the stupid horse toward the bank and grabbed the horn of his Santa

Fe saddle, knowing what to expect. The horse gathered itself and leaped, throwing him back into the cantle, and then shook water off itself in the middle of some sort of whipping, stabbing brush that flailed the animal and Fitzhugh. A minute later he rode up to the fire and into the stare of Samson Trudeau.

"Thank God, *monsieur,*" he said. "In a few minutes I would have started hunting with a lantern. But no one knew the way—"

Another mistake, Brokenleg thought. Not telling them where he'd shot the buffalo. "Wagon's a mile south, maybe. We'll need a fresh yoke if you can get them. And a lantern." He looked around the camp. Some of his men huddled near the guttering fire, sheltered by the wagonsheet tent. Others peered out of the wagon. "Maxim's hurt. Others half froze. Lost two ox. We got three buffler."

But big, competent Trudeau had already turned away to issue commands. Fitzhugh clambered down, almost too stiff to move, and fell into the snow when his bad leg buckled under him. He got up and limped to the fire, finding little heat in it as the wind flailed it, and more than enough smoke to sting his eyes. He wished he could squat and hold his hands to it. Around him men raced swiftly, good uncomplaining men willing to do brutal work for a pittance. He wondered what brought them here, into an utter wild. Not money, certainly. Something else.

Yoked oxen materialized out of the whirl, and men helped him back up upon his bay, while two of them bearing glass-encased lanterns broke a snow trail south. He followed silently, glad that he'd made it through another final examination at the mountain college. But he didn't deserve the passing grade.

Harried by the wind, they reached the stranded wagon in a short time. The remaining two yoke of oxen had swung eastward, trying to put their tails to the wind. The snowy hulks of the downed oxen lay where they had fallen. Meat,

Fitzhugh thought, if the cold held. Or maybe Dust Devil could jerk it.

Wordlessly, Dust Devil, Guerette, Provost and Gallard clambered out of the wagon, blinking at the lantern-light in the whirl of snow.

"Maxim all right?"

"He's not bleeding," she said.

The answer annoyed Fitzhugh, but he said nothing. Wordlessly, the rescue party backed the fresh oxen into place and attached the tugs, while others cracked whips and yelled at the miserable animals. From behind, the rest of the engagés pushed against the Pittsburgh until it creaked forward, a reluctant monster bucking the gale. They had to keep on pushing because the oxen weren't helping much. Fitzhugh walked his horse ahead, carrying a lantern, following the trail back and breaking it better. The wind tortured his face and hand, but it didn't matter. In a few days it'd be mild and sunny again.

The engagés cursed and whipped the animals back to camp in a few minutes and stopped the wagon at a place where it'd soften the wind that skimmed heat off the fire and flapped the tent. Silently, the engagés unyoked the oxen and let them drift into the cottonwoods, where they'd find shelter and branches to nibble.

"We got to git the meat out," Fitzhugh muttered to Trudeau.

The engagé eyed him sharply, dreading to ask it of the rest.

"If that heap in there freezes solid, we'll never get it out," Fitzhugh said.

Wearily, grunting men lifted the quarters up, and dropped them into the snow, while others dragged them into a line, each giant piece separate. They'd have to hang it all, make it wolfproof, but not tonight. As soon as they were done, they crawled into the other wagon and pulled the canvas shut.

"Maxim, lad. You can stay in a wagon where there's no fire and no wind, or you can try the tent, where we got both. I'm thinkin' you might try the fire, even if she mostly blows smoke at you."

From within, he heard a soft shuffle, and then Maxim's bundled face popped into the firelight, and he clambered out, hunching against the wind. He'd removed his tourniquet and no blood oozed from the frozen bandage. Fitzhugh threw an arm around Guy Straus's boy and helped him toward the fire and the tent.

"I'm so cold," Maxim said.

"Lost some blood."

He settled the lad on the north side of the fire, in the throat of the tent, hoping the fire's radiant heat would warm him.

"I didn't know it snowed so soon here."

"Equinox storm. Common in these parts. We got a fine fall comin' to finish the post."

"Now I'm no good to you."

"What do ya mean, no good? I got to have a herder, lad. Dust Devil needs her a helper, too. She'll jerk meat and you can lay it on the drying racks with your good paw."

Behind him, Dust Devil scraped snow from the ground. "We could be in a warm lodge," she muttered. "This no good for anybody. I'm cold."

Maxim settled to the frozen, snow-flecked earth and drew his capote tighter around him. Fitzhugh added a blanket.

"The cold comes up from underneath," Maxim said.

"Whitemen got no sense," Dust Devil snapped. "Maybe I'll go to my people. They're plenty warm, and happy."

Fitzhugh had heard that often enough before, and ignored it. "We got meat. Now I can help build, Maxim. I'll mix mud and before you know it, we'll have walls, good and tight against the wind. And a pole roof with a foot of sod over it. Big fireplaces that'll take a six-foot log and warm you front and rear, top and bottom. And a bunk of your own."

He dreamed warmth because he needed it himself, the way a starving man dreams of food. And because Maxim needed it, too. Cold and injury, the slow progress of the building, as well as the terrible losses of tradegoods all had taken a toll of Maxim's spirit.

A whorl of arctic air dashed smoke into him, and he coughed. "I reckon Dust Devil's right about a lodge, Maxim. They can be plumb warm in the winter; if the inner lining's up and some robes and mats are on the ground, and a hot little fire burns away at the center. The Injuns got their ways."

"I'll never see *papa* and *maman* again," Maxim said.

Fitzhugh leaned over awkwardly, cursing his bad leg, and found the boy's good hand. Icy. Then he pressed a hand to Maxim's forehead and it burned under his palm. Brokenleg peered into the night, full of foreboding.

In two days the sun returned and pummeled a foot of snow into the earth. The air had turned brisk and transparent, and the sky blackened almost to cobalt, the whiteness of summer gone for the year. The northwind died, after rotating east and finally south. But Maxim lay fevered and black-eyed in the tent, too sick for sun and sweet air, scented with sunbaked sagebrush.

Even before the storm had cleared off, Fitzhugh had put all his engagés to work cutting poles and firewood—better employment in hand-numbing weather than spreading icy mud and pressing sandstone into it. In a single day, they'd felled and trimmed a hundred twenty-two poles, and stacked them beside the rising post. And added a mountain of firewood, some of it still green, to the camp supply.

But it didn't lift Brokenleg's spirit any. Maxim lay fevered, buffeted by harsh weather, protected only by flimsy canvas and a reluctant fire, and not getting better. The boy stared up at Fitzhugh now and then, hollow-eyed and inert, refusing good strong buffalo broth. Dust Devil wasn't exactly herself either; not the lively, funny, fierce Cheyenne sweetheart he'd known. She'd turned solemn and lazy, doing as little as possible, resenting Maxim in the tent.

He'd tried to cheer her up. He'd diverted the engagés from their work to skinning the buffalo quarters and hanging them wolf-safe, and some of them bear-safe, from the stoutest cottonwood limbs. But it didn't soothe her any. She seemed plumb angry about the whole thing—the Buffalo Company, the discomforts, and especially, not hauling the whole mess of goods off to her people, who were probably down on the Powder somewhere, south and east. It didn't seem Injun for anyone to carry on the way she did about the cold and discomfort, but he had to admit they'd made a miserable camp, and a really severe storm could kill them.

Progress slowed down dramatically during the next weeks because of the need to build scaffolding. The walls had risen as high as his men could reach from the ground. They had only rawhide to tie the scaffolding together, but it worked well enough. He needed two more men at the building site to hand up rock to the ones on the scaffold, which meant robbing the other crews. They were further slowed by the need to hew log lintels and set them across the small windows and the two doors, front and rear. Even more difficult was finding and shaping long flawless slabs of sandstone to cap the fireplaces and support the inner walls of the two chimneys. Still, he noted visible progress each day. By late October they were laying up the chimneys at either end of the long rectangle, even as the air cooled and a skim of ice lay in the water buckets each dawn.

Maxim healed slowly, but something in the lad had changed, and Fitzhugh sensed a deep melancholy in him. His hand remained bandaged and sore, so Fitzhugh had him tend stock and bring firewood to Dust Devil, and sometimes drive the oxen tugging the stoneboats. He'd plunged into a profound silence, and worse, an apathy, an uncaring, that suggested his mind drifted far away, back among the comforts of St. Louis; warmth, a soft bed, doting parents, a sister and brother, a variety of meats and greens and sweets, and clean things to wear instead of endless mud and grime and grit, and no place to bathe. The adventure begun so bravely by the sixteen-year-old had become an ordeal and a bottomless pit of loneliness. But the boy didn't ask to go home, and Brokenleg admired him for it.

In spite of the crisp, bright fall weather, Fitzhugh wasn't enjoying good spirits either. Problems loomed at every hand and some of them, such as getting hay put up, involved deadlines imposed by the forthcoming winter. Nothing had gone as he'd planned. He hadn't a single robe to show for his effort, and yet the tradegoods had dwindled from theft and storage charges, and were hostage to the whim of his competitor. He'd expected to walk into old Fort Cass and shelve his goods and open for business; instead, he and his men had toiled brutally since August trying to build a tiny trading house—he couldn't even think of a full-sized stockaded post—that still seemed to be months from completion. The engagés had slid into a skeptical silence, too. At least one of them could well be an agent of Cadet Chouteau, planted to wreak whatever havoc he could. Dust Devil wasn't helping any either, eroding the future trade of the Crows with her fierce Cheyenne partisanship, and more recently her sullen, lazy conduct.

Fitzhugh himself mixed mud and hunted, the only things he could manage well. The nights had grown so chill that they couldn't last much longer sleeping in canvas tents beside dying fires. He wondered if he'd been wrong to turn Dust Devil's ideas aside. Some good lodges, with fires in their central hearths, could be keeping them warm now if they had simply driven to the Cheyenne. He worried about icy fall rains, too, the kind that could fever men and sluice away the mud mortar from the walls before it dried hard and had eaves above it to help keep water off. But the weather held: cold sunny days and lengthening icy nights.

Soon, too, he'd have to plant corral posts behind the rising building before the earth froze. Indeed, he had to complete the roof and get sod onto it before the ground froze so solid a spade would bounce off it. Each day, Maxim was forced to drive his mixed herd of horses, mules, and whatever oxen weren't being used, farther and farther from the building, as the nearby grass gave out.

Well, a man could worry himself half to death! he thought. *A feller could git himself into a lather and quit, like Maxim. A man could say it isn't gonna work, none of it, and think on high-tailing back down the big river. A man could find himself a dozen excuses to give to Guy Straus.*

All these things combined to attack him like an army of biting ants, making him crazy trying to figure out how to do it all, meet the most pressing deadlines, cope with ill-humored men, a homesick boy, and always, the deepening menace of bad weather to men sheltered by flapping duck cloth. But Brokenleg Fitzhugh had a stubborn streak, and he'd learned that there's a big difference between what-ifs and the way things are. A man could what-if himself out of anything worth fighting for. All he could think to do was drive harder, roust his silent engagés earlier, work them and himself later, race against frost and a dying sun. One November day, to the astonishment of everyone, they finished their masonry. The front and rear walls rose evenly to nine feet. Fireplaces with broad chimneys rose at either end, built into the thick, low-peaked walls. Next they would work on the ridge and roof poles, cut them down, hew them to shape, and then drag them out behind three or four yokes of oxen. It would take ox-power and a lot of rope to raise them, too.

That's when Julius Hervey struck. Fitzhugh didn't rightly know that for certain, but what happened certainly smoked like Hervey's fires. One bitter night, when a full moon silvered the frosted earth, some Indians hit the livestock. The engagés, buried deep under blankets and robes in the wagons, didn't awaken until too late. And Brokenleg missed the beginning of it too, perhaps because he usually listened, through his sleep, for the whinnying of disturbed horses or the braying of mules. But the first sound of trouble was the bawling of the oxen, which roamed freely some distance from the camp. The horses and mules, in fact, had been driven into the walled rectangle and kept there with barricades at the doors.

But the night-bawling of oxen usually meant little more than a whiff of wolf, or maybe a black bear, and Fitzhugh hadn't awakened to the sound. At least not until the sound changed to something darker, a bellow that whispered of pain. Then he awoke, listening, and thought he'd better jack on his boots and a capote and hustle out into the meadow, just to check. He was doing that, lacing up boots in the gloom of the tent, when the rest of it hit him: the clatter of hooves and the shriek of panicked horses. Then he knew. He sprang up, fumbling around for his Hawken, and stumbled into a blast of cold just in time to see moon-streaked, ghostly horsemen sweep his horses and mules down the river bottoms. He lumbered toward the half-built building, knowing what the gray light would tell him, and found not a shadow of an animal within, and the pole barricade that had sealed the far door pulled apart.

In a rage, he stomped out upon the meadow, generally toward the bluffs, where the closest good grass remained, dreading what he'd find out there. Trudeau joined him, wearing red underwear and hefting a rifle. Others caught up, making them a well-armed party. He saw no oxen, and heard none. He couldn't imagine they'd run off oxen too—tribesmen scorned the "soft" flesh of whitemen's cattle. The night lacked wind, but still the cold bit at his ears and his balding brow. At last, half a mile distant, on the other edge of the gilded night, he spotted them sleeping, dark hulks on the ground. But it made no sense, oxen bellowing and oxen asleep. And then he knew.

"I think we've bought the store, Trudeau."

"Eh? This idiom I do not know."

"Hyar's damp powder and no way to dry it."

"A man can worry too much, *n'est-ce pas?*"

"Or not enough."

A few minutes later they stood over the bodies of several oxen, which sprawled hot and bloody, steaming on the frosted grass, arrows projecting from them. He knew what the arrows would say to him. Each tribe made arrows its own way; indeed, each warrior marked his own arrows. These would be Crow. He tugged at one, buried up to its fletching just behind the shoulder of the gaunt animal. The arrow didn't yield easily. But it didn't matter. Even in moonlight he could see the fletching was Crow. And whoever had nocked it and drawn the bow had probably been paid by Hervey with tradegoods brought up the river by Dance, Fitzhugh, and Straus.

Fitzhugh and his men didn't have a four-footed animal left.

Chapter Sixteen

When the sun rose like a bloody buffalo heart ripped from the dark carcass of the sky, Dust Devil greeted it solemnly. She petitioned Sun each morning, asking for its warmth and a sweet day, and thanking Sun for all things. But this day Sun would see dark things beneath him, she knew.

Her man hadn't waited for Sun, but finished dressing in the night by the light of a new-built fire, and then hung his powder horn over his shoulder, his sheathed knife and possibles bag from his belt, and checked his Hawken, which gleamed orangely in the flickering flames. He had not said a word, nor did she need to ask him anything. She knew. She'd seen him crazed once before: he became graceful as a cat, silent as a stalking lion, until she swore the mad-spirits let him bend his knee and walk without a limp. Now he walked like that, with the mad-spirit in his eye, his feelings naked before the orange fire. From the back of the tent Maxim watched too, silent and solemn. When the mad-spirit entered her man he became a puma, and now she saw the cat, back arched, tail lashing, silent as rock, claws extended.

He stared briefly at both of them, recognition returning to his eyes for one seeing moment, and then he turned mad again, springing into the blackness. He glided north, without a limp, she thought, and she knew. He was going to walk to Fort Cass and kill Julius Hervey. She wondered if she'd ever see her man again because he was on his way to kill the most dangerous whiteman in all of the country. She knew Hervey would be waiting for him, expecting him, and would probably shoot him down even before a word was spoken between them. And then what? Hervey would come with his men and kill them here, kill the engagés, and carry her off to Fort Cass, a captive woman, a slave. Maybe he'd kill Maxim too, but she doubted it. He would send Maxim down the river.

She did not know what to do. Her medicine wasn't good when she stayed among these whitemen. And she a Suhtai, too, her father a keeper of the sacred mysteries of the Cheyenne. She stared at the roofless building, wanting to despise it but actually sensing its impressiveness. It looked strong and enduring, its eastern flank aflame with the dawn sunlight. She would not cook meat this morning: let the whitemen cook their own. She couldn't fathom her own complex feelings about them, nor about her man, Fitzhugh, either. These were toilers, slaving like animals, and she despised them for it, but admired them too, because they built things her people could not build. She'd been in St. Louis and had seen with her own eyes what these toilers could build.

When she'd been given to Fitzhugh by her father, she thought her man would become one of her people, and live in the villages, and make war and count coup and be a great man among them because of his fierce red hair. She wanted him to be a great warrior of her people, taking scalps of Crows and Cree, capturing more ponies than she could count, and bringing her whiteman things, copper kettles, thick blankets, ribbons and hawk bells. At first it seemed he'd be like that. He had learned her tongue and made friends with her mother's clan and her father's too. But his leg was bad and he didn't make war, and she was ashamed because he counted no coup and had no Blackfoot or Crow scalps dangling from a tripod before their lodge.

But after a winter he'd taken her from her village and joined his trapper friend Jamie Dance, and the three of them had lived alone, far from her people, pulling beaver from the streams. Her life had darkened then because she was not among her people. She kept hoping he would come to live with them, but not until she saw St. Louis did she know it would never happen. He was a whiteman, even if he lived like one of her people most of the time. And if she stayed with him, she'd be like a white woman.

She listened to Trudeau tell his men what they would do. She didn't understand French, really, but still she knew what he was saying: first they'd hunt for the horses and mules, just in case the Crow had not driven them far or had lost some. Then they'd work again, felling the trees to make the roof beams. She marveled that these men would still go on, even without a four-foot in camp. Not even these ten men could lift one end of the massive cottonwood beams they would set upon the walls. This very thing maddened her about whitemen. They would continue on, in their plodding way, and build buildings, plant gardens, make corrals, make *things*. What dogs they were compared to any clean-limbed, muscular, daring, fierce Cheyenne warrior! Whitemen should make war, not love, she thought, thinking of her man's appetites and weaknesses.

The thought of Fitzhugh filled her with joy. As much as she disdained him, she found happiness in him too. What woman of her people was so lucky? Who of her people had been to St. Louis? Who of the Cheyenne women had a rich trapper to bring her silks and wools and skirts and blouses and mirrors and necklaces with shining stones, and tease her and call her Dust Devil even when her name was Little Whirlwind. That was an insult, Dust Devil, his name for the whiteman's underearth-demon. But his bright blue eyes danced when he'd called her that, and he'd hoorawed her and taken her into his arms and made her sing inside. Whitemen were mostly bad, but not Fitzhugh. He made it fun for her to be with badness. He shocked her Suhtai heart, and made her medicine weak, but still she liked him sometimes.

Now she waited for him to kill or be killed. He wasn't a warrior, even though he could be fierce sometimes, so he'd be killed. Julius Hervey was a fine killer, a Cheyenne-heart. The dawn had a nip to it, and she wrapped her blanket about her, wondering what to do. Maxim had left his blankets and disappeared into the river brush. She despised him, a weak white boy without a bit of warrior in him, solemn and blink-eyed. And she wished he wouldn't live in their tent, because Fitzhugh never touched her while the boy lay there, and she didn't want to be touched with that boy there, even in the dark. She found herself alone in the camp, and that was the only good thing about the morning.

She felt the sun gather its muscle and warm her black hair and soothe her amber cheek, and rejoiced. Soon Winter Man would stay, but not yet. She sucked air into her lungs carefully, sampling its texture. She knew air, knew good and bad air. This air tasted good, sweet and dry. For confirmation, she scanned the heavens and saw not a cloud. A good sky. She sucked in another lungful and exhaled slowly, sampling its smell. She did not smell snow on it. She wasn't sure she would do the right thing, and that was the trouble with living among whitemen. Her medicine had died. She needed medicine now, the sure knowing given to the Suhtai. She peered about this camp, cleaved once again by her confusion: despising and admiring, loving and hating, willful and afraid. This could not be, all these voices and feelings.

She filled a doeskin pouch with strips of buffalo she had jerked, as much as it would hold, and added small waxed-paper packets of whiteman's sugar. And a sack of coffee beans. To this she added a steel striker and flint, and a tin cup. She packed her calf-high winter moccasins because she would need them soon. She remembered to take a little spare hide to repair soles. Swiftly she plaited her long blue-tinted jet hair into two braids, and tied her yellow ribbons around each end. She wore a long, soft doeskin skirt, fringed at the bottom, and a blue flannel hip-length blouse which she cinched at the waist with a beaded belt, which also carried a sheathed Green River knife. She rolled a small canvas groundcloth-poncho Fitzhugh liked to have under him because it turned moisture, and then tied the cylinder with thong. She didn't want to take much; just enough to spare her life if she were caught in the clutches of Cold Maker. Then she slid into her new blanket capote, Fitzhugh's gift to her when they'd left St. Louis. This one was scarlet as blood, with black bands at the top and bottom, and had been sewn into a slim coat with a hood on it. At the last moment she remembered mittens, ones she had lined with rabbit fur.

Then she walked east, toward the amber bluffs, never looking back but not really knowing why she was going. It confused her. Was she abandoning her man? She couldn't say. Maybe she was. Did she plan to find her village? Yes, surely that was what led her footsteps lightly through dead, frosted grass toward the east or maybe the south. Did she plan to go on a vision-quest, climb a mountain sacred to her people and fast until she received a new spirit-helper, now that the one she'd always known, crow-bird, had abandoned her? Perhaps she would if the spirits said she must. But other things churned and crowded the edge of her thoughts, too. Sweet Medicine. Among her own people, she could remember Sweet Medicine again. And pray to Maheo, the over-everything spirit. And see the lodge of the sacred hat, brought to the Cheyenne by her Suhtai. She wished to see the four sacred arrows again, but the Southern Cheyenne had them now. She wished to be renamed, after receiving new medicine. Let her not be Little Whirlwind any more, but something else, something that Fitzhugh would not turn into a joke. Visions of her parents and sisters danced in her mind, and lovers too. Would the ones who played the love flute for her, before Fitzhugh came, still play it?

She turned to look back. The roofless post stood solemnly not far from the river and its naked laced cottonwoods.

Nearby the wagons hulked, their white sheets glaring in the early sun, the way her tent did. She didn't see a soul at the camp, and everything stood unguarded, but she supposed Maxim would be there. The rest had scattered, some south and some north, looking for tracks and stock. She smiled contemptuously at that. They would waste the morning. The Crow dogs were expert horse thieves, and would herd the animals far away, across the wide river, and close to the foothills of the great mountains, where they lived.

She climbed the steep bluff, up a long coulee dotted with jackpine, feeling winded by the effort, and at last topped the rim and peered out upon a great rough plains, under a blinding sky. Somewhere far away, she didn't know where, would be the village of Chief White Wolf and her people.

Guy Straus decided to walk. The offices of Chouteau and Company weren't far; down near the levee. The air felt languid, and he'd need nothing except his light cape. He'd waited until tea time, the social hour, not wanting this sally to appear to be business. He and Pierre Chouteau, Jr., had done business many times, and Guy's father had done business with Pierre's father, Jean Pierre, almost since arriving in St. Louis. Straus arbitrage and brokering had been an important factor in the success of the Chouteau interests for many years.

But this call would be a little different. Guy slid his black cloak over his solemn suit, and left his house, hearing the door softly shut behind him. Gregoire always seemed to know where he was and what he'd do next. Guy felt a certain tension this time, not because the Chouteaus, along with the Lecledes, Prattes, and Gratiots, comprised the most powerful clan in St. Louis, but because he faced the possibility of unpleasantness. He did not particularly like Pierre; the man seemed a bit cynical and overbearing. But he admired the man who'd brilliantly built the family fortune, and towered at the apex of the fur trade. Pierre and his brothers were not content to mastermind their empire from St. Louis, but travelled frequently to their farflung posts to see things firsthand. Guy was going, actually, to listen: Pierre was a gentle boaster, so subtle that unsophisticated mortals often missed it. Guy had a good ear, and that would be more important than a wily tongue.

One of Chouteau's numerous clerks escorted Guy to Cadet's battered office, and disappeared within. A few moments later Guy was summoned into Chouteau's rough lair, a menage of curiosities from the wilds, scalps, lances, medicine bonnets, albino robes, along with portraits of his father, uncles, and cousins.

"My dear Straus," said Chouteau effervescently. The man approached amiably, patting Guy's shoulder and arm. Chouteau was a patter and toucher, and Guy supposed it was a form of ownership rather than some sort of affection. "We'll have tea, unless you'd prefer something else?"

"Tea," Guy said, handing his cape to a waiting pox-scarred clerk. Another flunkey had already appeared with a silver tray bearing a steaming teapot and china cups and saucers.

"Come tell me your news. I've scarcely seen you since you went into opposition. How I miss your services, Guy."

"I have very little," Guy said, taking a cup. "Letters from my sons."

"Ah, the waiting! It's unbearable. But my people send down a winter express, and I'll get a report early in the year. And of course I send back my instructions."

Guy smiles and sipped delicately.

"Ah, Guy, what a pity you plunged in just now, and half-capitalized. There's a glut of robes. Ramsey Crooks can't sell his, and neither can I. We tried the Germans but they want sheep. Prices barely holding—forty-eight dollars for a twelve-bale in New York, eleven winter and one summer robe. Crooks and I are holding some back to keep the price up. I fear your returns will fetch less and drive the prices down."

"I'm looking into it. I've approached General Clark about turning some into greatcoats for the army, and bedrolls. Maybe ambulance robes."

Pierre Chouteau looked amused. "Good for a few hundred at best. No, carriage robes are it. But tell me, how goes your enterprise?"

"I wish I knew!"

Chouteau paused, amiably. Then, "I hear you lost all your blankets. From LaBarge's boat."

It didn't surprise Guy that Chouteau knew it. The Chouteau company made it its business to know everything. "Perhaps you can give me some clues, Pierre," he said softly.

"Ah, a bad business. Blankets are at the center of it. They must have their blankets. Good warm Witneys, white so they can steal horses without being seen. We trade mostly the white, Guy. A few indigo, an occasional scarlet. And greens are coming up a little. We've some warehoused, and I'd sell you a hundred or so, a small profit. It's quite a wait when you order from Early."

"I've already ordered next year's."

"Ah, if there is a next year. But that's a tragedy indeed. Why, if some lackey stole ours, I'd have him flogged and brought down the river for justice. You must be wondering about your engagés."

Guy smiled and said nothing.

"A mean business. I've alerted my traders. If any show up for sale, they're to hold the man. A common thief. And of course, not shelve a one. I suppose you're stocking the same ones as we are, though. Hard to tell them apart. Did you put a label on?"

Guy decided not to answer that. "It's good of you to instruct your traders to keep an eye out. But I gather from LaBarge that they're probably skimming the bottom of the river."

"A bad business," Chouteau said, but his face said otherwise. "You'll lose trade to us, except maybe the Cheyennes. We haven't Dust Devil to help us with them. Oh, a lovely lady, she is. Stirs the juices of a man. Culbertson wrote me she's a bit of a partisan, you know. Offending the Crows up at Fort Union. But that's no loss for you, I imagine."

Guy waited expectantly, because Chouteau was about to boast again. "Oh, it's a loss," he said slowly.

"Ah, Straus, we locked up the Crows before Fitzhugh got there. Cass, you know. We should have burned it. We always do when we abandon a place. But we didn't, and now we're back in, and doing a business. No one's traded much with the mountain bands for several years. Some of the river Crow came in to Fort Union, of course. I put Hervey there and sent him an outfit on the *Trapper*."

Fort Cass, Guy thought, alarmed. They'd known where Brokenleg was heading, known our plans, and reopened the old post. And with Julius Hervey running it. Something sagged in him. "Hervey's an able trader," he said quietly.

"Oh yes, one of the best. A bit headstrong some times, and given to madness when he's taking spirits. But a fine man."

And a murderer, Guy thought, suddenly worried. Maxim, Brokenleg, Trudeau and the rest. A slaver, too. Stories had drifted down the long Missouri of the women he stole, kept and sold.

"You'll do well with the Cheyenne, I imagine," Chouteau continued cheerfully. "Fitzhugh's got a ticket there I wish we had. He's probably setting up his store on the Tongue or the Powder somewhere, or maybe they've headed for the Black Hills country. My, how fortunate you are to have Dust Devil. We have Natawista Culbertson, of course, and with her, the Blackfeet."

Guy returned the pleasantry. "If I know Fitzhugh, he'll be right there on the Bighorn now," he said. "Building a post."

Chouteau's eyes were merry. "Well, now, how are you progressing against the Bents? Is Dance set up? Now down there, it's the opposite, with Charles Bent's wife a Cheyenne. But Dance's wife is Mexican, isn't she? A good help for getting a license in Santa Fe."

Guy shrugged. "No word as yet," he said. "A letter from David en route, delivered by eastbound trades."

"I must say, Guy, Dance, Fitzhugh and Straus is a strange outfit, going against us in the north and the Bents down there. Why didn't you slide in between, on the Platte, and try the Arapaho and Utes?"

"My partners like to bloody noses," Guy said, ambiguously.

"Theirs or ours?" Chouteau smiled and sipped.

They talked a while more, but Guy learned nothing. And what he did learn alarmed him: Chouteau back in Cass, and Hervey the trader there! Fitzhugh scarcely had men or tools to build a new post, and lacked furnishings for it. Where was he? What would he need? Would Brokenleg need supplies by packtrain?

"Ah, my *cher ami* Straus, come again, come again. I enjoyed our visit," Chouteau said, as his minions materialized from somewhere, bearing Guy's cape and gathering teacups.

A moment later Guy stood on the doorstep, peering across the bleak Father of Waters, noting the iron-gray sky—did the sun never touch St. Louis?—and began his journey home, a chill on his face and in his soul. Maxim there, and Julius Hervey prowling. Hervey sober was one of the best men to go up the river; Hervey drunk didn't know good from evil. No blankets, no fort. Dust Devil alienating every tribe except her own. Had he been mad to listen to his young partners? A fatal moment of weakness?

He found Yvonne in their bedroom, being fitted by Mme. Ledoux, her dressmaker. Her camisole popped out from opened seams of a watershot green silk dress.

"Guy! I'm getting plump."

"You're beautiful."

She sighed. "My looking glass doesn't flatter the way you do."

Mme. Ledoux curtsied and excused herself.

"No, stay. Finish it up, madame. What did you learn from Pierre, *cher?"*

Guy peered out of their window, across the black rooftops of the bustling city to the Mississippi running a gray streak across the east. Several packets bobbed at the levee, their chimneys spiking the clouds. This was the city of the west; it pulsed with the trade of the west, up the Missouri, out to Santa Fe. The west had been his income and his father's before him. His plunge into a robe venture had been as natural to him as the fur talk at the Planters House, something entirely known and understood, every risk and every possibility. Almost.

"Our northern outfit's in trouble," he began, reluctant to worry her. But he hadn't kept secrets, and her pessimism had often been a valuable anodyne.

She sighed, but didn't tell him she had known it all along. He felt grateful for that. "What did he say?" she asked, her gaze settling on him.

"He said there's a surplus of robes, and he and Ramsey Crooks are holding some back to keep prices up."

"Ow!" she cried, glaring at Mme. Ledoux, who cowered back like a whipped puppy.

"He's put Cass back into trade, and put Julius Hervey there."

She remained silent, and he admired her for it. Yvonne had developed qualities of character over the long years that made her more endearing than when he'd met her. But he knew her mind whirled with disasters, and Maxim was among them. "I hope I can pay Mme. Ledoux," she said.

"He had a full report on Dust Devil's conduct," Guy added.

Yvonne snorted unkindly. She was always less kind to women. "I could have told you," she said, succumbing at last.

Guy smiled faintly.

"What are you going to do?"

"Go up there, I think. I'm not sure yet. I would have to leave my business for months. But I need to know what Brokenleg's doing, whether there's a post, whether he's got robes, whether I should cancel next year's orders. How much I've lost. Whether Maxim's safe."

"Will you ever come home?"

He didn't reply. "I'm not sure what I could accomplish up there," he said at last. "Maybe I should have a talk with Robert Campbell. Cadet toys with us. I feel like a marionette. Like a fly he's brushing off."

He had the sensation that the whole west, clear to Mexico, clear to the British possessions, belonged to Cadet Chouteau; that the lord of St. Louis was lord as well of a domain beyond the grasp of the human mind—and that he knew of every sparrow that fell within it.

Chapter Seventeen

The thing had to be settled. Either he'd see the next sunset, or Hervey would, but not both. Brokenleg didn't know what he would do or how he'd do it. He limped north through the night, letting starlight guide him, cradling his Hawken. He had that and his throwing knife. His leg ached. He'd rarely put four miles on it since it'd been wrecked, and even the half mile he'd come had tortured it, building sharp pain at his hip and in his ankle as well. Walking humbled him, and only his smoldering anger propelled him onward.

He turned over the possibilities as he walked, so absorbed that he didn't feel the frost nipping his cheeks and piercing through his elkskin jacket. It'd been Hervey's work all right. The usual horse-stealing party wouldn't have bothered to slaughter the oxen. Tribesmen didn't care about oxen, but they cared plenty about horses, and the squaws loved mules to pull their travois. These Crow had been paid to do it, probably with the very tradegoods Fitzhugh was storing at the fort. That'd be a typical Hervey stunt, he thought. Hervey's mind ran that direction, finding amusement in it. And Julius Hervey would be expecting him and would be ready. In fact, one devilish thing about Hervey was that he knew exactly how people reacted to anything he did. He always knew who wanted to kill him and why, and the knowledge had been fatal to several men.

Brokenleg realized he probably was marching to his own

slaughter, just the way others had, in a rage. It didn't matter. When his leg began torturing him, he found a boulder and sat down, studying the streak of gray perched on the eastern bluffs. He'd arrive at Cass in full daylight. If he survived, he didn't know how he'd walk back. Maybe he'd ride back, he thought. Cass had a few horses. As few as possible. At most posts, horses were a luxury. It was so difficult to lay up fodder for them, winter them, keep them from being stolen, that no post could manage more than a few. It meant cutting wild hay some place far from the post because the grasses closer in were all eaten down by the herds of the tribal villages that had come in to trade. Hauling oats up the river was equally tedious and expensive. Even so, most posts had a couple of absolutely essential saddle horses, and a team or two of draft animals for a wagon or plow.

After he'd killed Hervey he'd commandeer one to carry him back. Preferably a draft horse they could use to drag roof beams. But first things first, and his business was murder. He stood, stomped on his bum leg until he felt savage pain lance through, and knew it to be alive and taking him on his death-trip. Pain felt right, and he welcomed it. The sheer hurt kept his mood vicious and his mind as keen as a butcher knife. Then he limped north and east again, in a quickening blue light that turned obscure shadows into trees and slopes.

The Hawken felt good, a trusted friend he loved more than Dust Devil. The throwing knife, sheathed at his waist, felt lithe and ready. It would be one of these: with his bum leg he would be no match for Hervey in a brawl. He didn't ask himself why he walked, or whether it was right. He knew. He didn't ask whether he had proper proof that Hervey had set the Crows upon him. He knew. And if he was wrong, he still knew. It made no difference whether he was right or wrong. Let lawyers debate such things. He'd worry about it after Julius Hervey lay cold on the bloody earth—if he worried about it at all.

At length he raised Fort Cass, glowing in a low sun that gilded the Yellowstone River gold. and blazoned the bluffs on the far side of the river. Everything had turned to gold. Only three lodges, Crow he thought, were pitched nearby. Nothing moved. Life at a fur post did not begin at dawn. All the better, he thought. He paused, letting his leg-pain sandpaper all his body until everything hurt, his calves and chest and biceps and neck, all of it enraging him like a picadored bull. He peered about, hoping to find some hobbled or picketed horses, or a milch cow or two, but he spotted none. They'd been run into the fort for the night and would soon be driven out to a distant pasture by a herdsman. He felt disappointed, for it had been in his mind to shoot them all, one by one.

A peculiar light caught the silvered cottonwood palisades and plated them gold, until the east side of the fort looked like it had been erected of precious metal. He paused, just within effective rifle range, and lifted his Hawken, aiming at the heavy double doors. Then he squeezed, and the hammer clapped the cap, and the rifle jammed into his shoulder, spewing blue smoke and a fine boom. He could not tell where the ball had smacked the shadowed gate. He set the Hawken on its crescent butt and opened his powderhorn, pouring a practiced handful into his palm and then down the barrel. He rarely used his measure. He was more interested in watching the fort than in his familiar labor. He saw no movement. He dug in his possibles bag, ignoring the contents of his patchbox, and found a soft patch and a ball, and jammed them into the muzzle, driving them home with the hickory rod that fit under the rusted octagonal barrel. Then he checked the nipple for fouling, and slid a fresh cap over it.

He waited, feeling the sun warm his buckskin, feeling pain radiate out from his leg, pour from his eyes and out upon his gaze until it smacked the fort. He felt his pain savage the fort, probe it, pierce its cracks, jab at those within, and home of its *bourgeois,* who probably still lay abed, with another stolen squaw. It pleased him, the reaching fingers of his pain, here upon a cold morning in a place unknown to the world, unknown to his innkeeping family in upper New York. It pleased him to think of cowing a fort, and murder, and willfullness and doing exactly as his whim dictated.

Nothing happened. But a head or two poked from a lodge door, only to duck back inside. He lifted his Hawken again, feeling the faint residual heat of the last shot in the fine thirty-four-inch barrel, planning to make more heat. The day had grown brighter, and he could make out the crack dividing the two heavy plank doors, and he sighted the weapon at the crack, and squeezed.

He made a fine racket, and he thought he saw splinters fly from the massive doors where the half-inch round ball struck. But no one moved. He loaded again, picking his fouled nipple clean, watching Fort Cass, but nothing happened. The weak sun promised warmth, but didn't deliver. If it warmed him, it'd ease his pain, and he didn't want that. He waited, watching the fort, knowing that it watched back. A pair of black and white magpies burst upward from the stockade, and flew away chattering. Minutes passed, or at least what he reckoned to be minutes. He'd been a long time away from clocks. Fort Cass watched and waited. He walked to and fro, out of boredom, to keep his leg hurting and his temper mean. Off to the east, several Crow women scurried from their lodges toward the river, and into its brush, peering back at him. He spat.

"Hervey. Julius Hervey, come out," he yelled.

The fort watched him.

"You're a coward, Hervey."

He thought he heard his yell echo from the stockade, and thought he heard muffled laughter. The sun lit a log bastion in the northeast corner, and lit the brown suiting of a mortal peering from one of its slit windows.

"Go away," said Julius Hervey.

Brokenleg fired at the voice, which rose from the slot in the log blockhouse. A white dot blossomed in the water-stained gray log inches away. He heard laughter.

He loaded his fifty-two caliber mountain rifle, the handiwork of Samuel Hawken of St. Louis, taking his time about it, letting the sun blazon him. He wished to be a temptation.

"Go back to Missouri," Hervey yelled. "Leave the squaw."

Brokenleg lifted his Hawken and aimed the blade at the slot, and fired. Gray powdersmoke bloomed, and the butt bruised his shoulder. In the fading echo, Hervey laughed. Brokenleg cleaned the fouling from the nipple again, reloaded, and let the sun warm him.

"I have your profit," said Hervey. "And I'll have your woman. Your beautiful brown woman. Your wife, Stiffleg."

From within the post, a stars and stripes rattled up the staff above the bastion, but no breeze teased it. On a staff anchored above the massive gates, a Chouteau and Company banner rode upward, scaring off two angry crows. A mysterious dog appeared from somewhere, trotting along the palisade, lifting its leg to establish proprietorship. Brokenleg followed it with his Hawken.

All the eyes of the fort watched.

"Come out, Hervey," he yelled.

Some catcalls.

Black barrels poked out here and there, several from the top of the palisade, two from the bastion, and one from a small port near the gate. Sunlight magnified the ones projecting from the bastion, turning them into cannon whose bores pointed at Brokenleg. The rest lay in blue shade along the north palisade, and were almost indistinguishable. Brokenleg turned his back on them and studied the river, flowing aquamarine in the bright morning. The waters would eventually flow past St. Louis, and then past New Orleans, carrying any blood spilled on its banks.

"Hervey: Stay inside of there," Fitzhugh yelled. "Don't ever set foot outside."

"I have your outfit," Hervey replied. "And Dust Devil next."

Fitzhugh sighed. Hervey wouldn't come out. Maybe he could keep Hervey in. Keep them all in. Keep the Crows away. He'd think about it. Meanwhile he had to build his fort, somehow. Tiredness hit him. He walked west, toward the trace up the Bighorn.

Behind he heard laughter, and a ragged volley of shots. Balls plowed the naked yellow earth near him, but none came very close. He stopped. He was not inclined to give the appearance of fleeing. A ball singed past him, whispering through the fringes of his elkskin coat, followed by a familiar laugh. It didn't matter. Hervey wouldn't come out. Brokenleg felt nothing, and limped away.

Maxim surveyed the camp solemnly, not knowing what to make of it all. Save for the sound of distant axes among the cottonwoods, the morning lay deathly quiet. The engagés had given up on the livestock, and returned to construction work. Dust Devil had vanished somewhere. She probably was digging roots along the river, he thought. She did that often, patiently extracting a thick brown root full of white meat, something like a carrot. Or perhaps she'd gone out among the dead oxen, butchering. And Fitzhugh had vanished in the night carrying his rifle. It struck him as foolishness. The man was supposed to be a trader.

The youth sighed, not knowing what to do or think. He ached to go home, to warmth and soft beds and regular baths with hot water. He felt grimy and cold and constantly tired from sleeping on the ground, where the cold seeped upward and numbed him in the night, stealing rest. The hunger to go home had become desperate in him. It began long ago, when the blankets had vanished from the tradegoods he was watching over. He'd emerged from that feeling too young, too small, for the tasks assigned him. His homesickness had deepened when they'd discovered they couldn't just move into old Fort Cass, with its comforts, but had to build a new post out of nothing. And then the rest, the wound, the fever, the despair of seeing his father's wealth swallowed up by Fort Cass, had plunged him into a melancholy he couldn't shake off. Monsieur Fitzhugh did not have a single buffalo robe to show for all of this expense and labor.

Dust Devil was probably out butchering an ox to make jerky. He wandered that direction, over frosted grass, in heatless sunlight, looking for her. He dreaded being anywhere near her when she was using her knife, but he forced himself. He could hang the thin strips on a pole rack she'd built for drying. He wondered why they bothered. The only thing impelling him out into the meadows was his father's admonition to be helpful, and learn, and give of himself in all the ways he could.

But she wasn't there. He walked among the corpses, lying so still and cold, the Crow arrows still poking from them. He could never get used to death, and it frightened him. He'd scarcely thought about it until the fever burned him up and his young body refused to work, and then it had terrified him. He wanted to see *papa* and *maman* again; he wanted to go home.

The oxen wouldn't rot, he knew, not as long as the nights were icy and the days not much above freezing. They'd save Fitzhugh some hunting. But it was odd she wasn't here, slicing meat before the crows and magpies and coyotes got it. He hated butchering, and was glad he didn't have to help. He hated the sight of organs, of heart and long pearly guts, and purple things, which brought the gorge up in his throat. All those things were inside of him, too, and he knew someone could butcher him the way an ox or a buffalo was butchered.

Desolately he walked back to camp. He had no livestock to herd, no camp chores to do, and for once he was at loose ends. He peered darkly at the sturdy amber walls of the post, hating it, knowing how much of his family's treasure had been expended on that rock and mud. He nourished dark thoughts about Monsieur Fitzhugh and that Monsieur Dance, too, who'd lured his *papa* away from the family business into—this. Into disaster. What did *papa* really know about running a fur post? And competing with the Chouteaus, lords of all the western wilderness? Nothing!

Even while he stood solemnly before the tent and the ashes of the last fire, the object of his thoughts limped grimly into sight, looking haggard. Fitzhugh glared at him from pain-fired eyes, and at the cold ashes, and Maxim glared back at this man who would be the cause of his family's grief.

"What're you lazing for? Where's Dust Devil?"

"I don't know."

"Find her. Git me some vittles."

"I looked for her."

Fitzhugh muttered something under his breath, and glared at the cottonwood forest, where the sound of axblows drifted to them.

"Where did you go?" Maxim asked.

"Had a score to settle at Cass." He took a step toward the woods, and Maxim saw his lips writhe with pain. Then Fitzhugh deliberately stood on his bad leg, throwing weight on it, while the features of his face hardened into a kind of granite, and his eyes laid sparks upon Maxim. Fitzhugh stepped toward the cottonwoods, at whatever terrible cost to his body. Maxim followed, admiring the man even thought he'd come to despise him.

They found the engagés near the river, debarking and shaping a long twisted cottonwood limb with their axes and the adze. They'd felled a ridgepole, Maxim realized. But cottonwoods were thick and crooked and perverse, and this ridgepole needed the improvements of the axe and adze to thin its thick end, flatten a hump, and reduce its diameter. The ten men had whittled the huge log like furious termites, until now it had become a proper ridgepole.

"Ah, Monsieur Fitzhugh," said Trudeau. "The cottonwood, she is not the best for this. But we have no choice, yes?"

Fitzhugh stared at the giant white pole, virgin white in the gray woods. Beside it were a half a dozen short lengths of log stripped of bark. "I didn't get any stock," he said shortly. "It's penned inside Cass."

"Ah! Monsieur, you don't know what beasts Creoles are. We pole the *bateaux*—the boats up the river. We drag them on ropes if we must. We are ox."

Trudeau grinned, but Fitzhugh's face remained solemn and haggard.

"I read in the books when I am little, monsieur. The ancient Greek, the one called Archimedes of Syracuse, he says that if he had a lever long enough and a fulcrum, he could move the world, *oui?*" Trudeau waved his hand grandly. "We make the ridgepole. We cut levers from saplings. We make rollers. And we're like the ox. Now you'll see!" He waved at his men. *"Allons, allons."*

The burly men jumped into action. Several grabbed long poles, while others carried those short lengths of wood that Maxim had supposed were for fires. Another tied a stout manila rope to the lighter end of the ridgepole, and tugged on it. In moments, eight men had jammed their levers as far under the ridgepole as possible, and set the levers on log fulcrums. Then, without command, they tugged downward on their levers, lifting the ridgepole easily, while the remaining engagés shoved those white rollers underneath, until the ridgepole rested on a set of them.

"Ah! We will roll it now to the post!" Trudeau cried. Eight men grabbed the rope, hunkered low, and pulled. The ridgepole rolled easily. The remaining two lifted freed rollers from the rear, and ran forward with them to drop ahead of the sliding ridgepole. Maxim gaped. Even Fitzhugh's flinty gaze seemed to soften as the great log slid easily out of the woods and over meadow, drawn by laughing, joking engagés as if it were a mere stick.

"We are better than oxen, *n'est-ce pas?"* cried Trudeau.

Maxim felt a stirring of pride in them. Excitement flushed the despair from him as the naked beam bounced and bobbed clear to the post, never halting. He ached with the need to believe that everything would work out; that loss of all the stock would not defeat them. But he couldn't. Even this miracle would come to nothing.

There remained the awesome task of raising the pole to its final resting place at the peak. They would have to do it without the help of block and tackle, and without much help from levers, either. About this the engagés argued furiously. Some wished to build a ramp of poles and roll the ridgepole up it with ropes. A ramp would be an enormous undertaking. Others wanted to stand the ridgepole on one end, using levers and ropes, and then maneuver that end into the hollow prepared for it in the peaked chimney wall, using the longer wall as a fulcrum. Then they could lift the other end with ropes, they argued.

Maxim listened, fascinated, while the ten engagés debated. He had no idea which would work, or whether neither would work and they'd end up where they were before the oxen were slaughtered.

Fitzhugh listened to the bedlam a moment, obviously not grasping the rattle of French, and turned instead toward the camp, puzzlement in his face. He was plainly wondering about Dust Devil. He limped toward the frayed wagonsheet tent, and clambered awkwardly inside, something he could manage only by bending at the waist because of his stiff leg. Maxim saw him flailing about in the creamy light within, pawing at parfleches and trunks, muttering angrily. Then he crabbed back out, looking bitten.

"Capote's gone. Winter moccasins gone. Little doeskin tote bag o' hers gone. Some other stuff. Blouses, and all that." He glared icily into Maxim's eyes. "Don't you got eyes, boy? Don't you keep track none? My squaw's took off and lit out to her people, and you let her go."

Chapter Eighteen

She would take her name back. She was Little Whirlwind to the Tsistsistas, the People, not Dust Devil. At the top of the bluff she turned south and began the long walk, the walk that might never end. She didn't expect her man to come after her, but she would be wary anyway. He was a cunning tracker—not like one of her people, but good enough for a pale-skinned man—and might catch a glimpse of a faint moccasin print. That's why she had climbed the bluff before following the Bighorn river south.

She couldn't fathom her own complex feelings. She loved Fitzhugh; loved his vast red beard, and his half-bald head with red hair cascading from the back half down to his shoulders. She loved his hard blue eyes, bits of sky painted like two chips of rock in his freckled face. She loved his flinty laughter and the tenderness of his lovemaking, a gentleness she knew wasn't common among the men of her people.

Her marriage to a trader made her a great woman among her people, too. Not a girl of her village didn't envy her the marriage, and the things it brought, such as all the bright flannels she could ever want, and brass cooking pots, and keen knives. But above all, it brought her prestige. She had become as important as Owl Woman, of the southern Tsistsistas, who had married the great trader, William Bent, thereby cementing an alliance between the southern Cheyennes and the Bent family. In 1837, Bent had gone to Owl

Woman's father, Gray Thunder, the keeper of the sacred arrows, and asked for the hand of his beautiful daughter. And so it had been arranged, even as her own father, One Leg Eagle, the keeper of the medicine hat, had arranged her marriage to Fitzhugh, although Brokenleg had been a trapper then, and not a trader.

Still, she thought, he had his weaknesses. She wanted slaves, lots of them, to lord over, to treat like dogs, to do the drudging, the hide-scraping, the cooking. She didn't mind cooking—that was her time-honored task—but it would be more fun to make slaves do it. All she wanted was a few slaves, a couple of clumsy Crow women, and maybe a Cree or Blackfoot too. But the more she nagged him about it, the more he laughed and told her he didn't like slavery. What strange notions white men had.

She came to the place where Fitzhugh had killed the three buffalo, and decided she'd walked far enough from camp so she could slip back down to the river bottoms. She hiked down the long grade where the wagon had stalled in the muck, and then turned south again. It felt a little warmer in the bottoms, and the wind didn't cut through her capote so angrily. She would have to be careful now: a lone woman would be prey to any of the enemies of her people. She would be safe only among the Tsistsistas or the Dakota people, the allies of hers. The others might make a slave of her, but she would be a very bad slave, and kill them.

The moons of time spent in St. Louis had changed everything. She had seen things beyond her wildest imagination, and more of the pale-skinned people, and black-skinned too, than she thought could exist on the earth. She saw buildings of rock and brick, and carriages, and shops full of whiteman's magic, where one could get things by trading gold metal, or silver, or colored paper for them. She had seen pianos and harps with her own eyes, and whole shelves of books with mysterious symbols in them. She had seen the place on Washington Street where the rifles were made. She had seen them building with red bricks, all alike, and a gray mud that turned to rock when it dried. She had listened to a group of men, all dressed in blue, who played gold-colored horns Fitzhugh called brass instruments, trombones, trumpets, tubas. And on the great Father of Rivers she saw more of the fireboats than she'd ever imagined. She could not tell the Tsistsistas the smallest part of all she saw because they'd call her a liar. But that isn't what disturbed her. She had glimpsed the future, the medicine beyond the imagining of her people, and it made her wonder about the Four Arrows, and Sweet Medicine, and the Sacred Hat, and all the wisdom of her Suhtai. She had come away from St. Louis changed, unsure whether to return to her people, unsure whether to remain with Fitzhugh.

He'd hated St. Louis, and itched to escape and become like the Tsistsistas again. But she'd seen it—she knew he couldn't escape his origins. He had been a whiteman in St. Louis, even if he was like herself here. At any time he could go back, or become the way he was. She dreaded that: she'd always thought he had become like her and her clan. But St. Louis had changed that. She knew he would never be like her. She ached to see her people once again now, and seek out the medicine men, Big Dog especially, and find out if she needed a new name and spirit-helper. Then maybe she could decide about Fitzhugh.

She set an easy gait south, wishing her blanket capote weren't a bright scarlet, with black bands at its top and bottom. Most of the blankets that capotes were sewn from were white, and good camouflage, especially in winter. But not this: anyone could see her. She had let her vanity overcome good sense. She hadn't the faintest idea where she'd find her village, but it probably would be a long way. Maybe near the Black Hills, what the Dakota people called Paha Sapa, a place sacred to her own people, too, because of Bear Butte. She could not speak the tongue of the Dakotas to ask them where her own village might be. And she didn't know all the finger signs either, but a few: enough to tell them who she was.

The land lay brown and gold and tan and gray in this Freezing Moon, just before Big Hard Face Moon, when the Cold Maker could kill her with his breath out of the north. The birds of summer had fled, and she walked through a surrendered land, when all living things had fled, burrowed, or begun a long sleep. Still, her spirit-helper, crow-bird, flew about, sometimes bursting up ahead of her, angry at her intrusion upon the somnolent quiet. And she knew coyote slinked and wolf stalked, and the deer and elk grazed.

All the day she walked toward her people, drawn as surely as the magical compass needle Fitzhugh had shown her pointed north. What medicine white men had a needle that always pointed north? When Sun began fleeing, she paused, seeking a little shelter, a place she might strike a hidden fire and make a tiny cup of broth from her jerky and berries. She eyed the sky anxiously: the one thing she dreaded was a storm, but she saw only transparent air, fading from blue to indigo as Sun slipped into the earth. Shelter didn't worry her much. With a fire and her poncho over her capote, she'd be warm and dry. She wasn't as soft as whitemen, and didn't need the things they did. She'd walked all day and scarcely felt it, and didn't need much to eat, either. If she found a camping place soon, she'd dig roots and add them to the jerky, and be filled.

The whinny of a pony ahead arrested her. Swiftly she ducked toward the cottonwoods and slid behind a barrier of red-barked brush, and there she unrolled her white poncho and slid it over her scarlet capote, making herself a spirit-person. She would have to find out who these ones were, creep close. The thought that they might be her own Tsistsistas swelled in her, and she dreamed of swift chatter in her own tongue, naming names and hearing names she knew. But it might not be: she was still farther north and west than they came, except to steal ponies from the Crow or Blackfeet.

But it might be dogs. She would have to see without being seen. Her pulse rose with the undertaking. If they were seasoned warriors, they might have keener eyes and ears and noses than she. They might read the sudden lift of a pony's nose, or the rotation of its ears. Sometimes warriors knew without knowing why they knew, their medicine whispering to them, that something lurked beyond the camp, and even what would be found there. And if they were a war party, they might have a sentry posted upon some bluff, who might have long since spotted her in her scarlet capote, walking southward up the Bighorn.

But this was probably not a horse-stealing party, because those walked on foot and rode stolen ponies home if they were successful. They could be anything. She made swift plans: she would need to see them. If they were enemy dogs, she would slip toward the bluffs to the east for safety. Danger would lurk anywhere on the river bottoms. Up on the bluffs she would circle around them, and camp up there, and as far away as she could get with nightwalking. If they caught her, they might use her, or torture her to death as slowly as possible and count it good. She understood these things without thinking about them.

It was not yet twilight but color had bled from the world, and the scene about her had turned gray and blue. She saw no fire burning through the naked latticework of cottonwoods and brush, though she studied everything ahead with care. She slid along the edge of a meadow in her gray poncho, easing toward the single sound that had alerted her, the whicker. The valley bent sharply around a headland ahead, and just there she saw horses picketed on the meadow, dark restless shapes, all of them swinging to stare at her. She froze. They would be closely guarded. She counted only four of them, and felt safer at once.

She walked forward while the ponies watched, and was

rewarded by the sight of a small fire that had been hidden by the long shoulder running down from the bluffs. She froze, not wanting her motion to betray her. Several packs lay on the earth below the sheltering mudstone outcrop, and she recognized some of them as baled up beaver plews. A sheet of canvas had been rigged up into a half-shelter in the lee of the bluff and out of the wind. And sitting crosslegged before it was a bearded whiteman. It paralyzed her. Not whitemen. The few that had come in the days of the beaver trapping had left. She would not stop here, then. She never knew how whitemen would behave. But she always knew how tribesmen would conduct themselves. This one terrified her: he wore his brown hair loose over his shoulders, like her own man; and had a great, curly beard streaked with gray. He wore a flappy widebrimmed felt hat, ancient and dirty. She didn't like his eyes, which peered this way and that, like an evil feather dusting everything in sight. No. She would pass this one, and began to sidle back, so she could head for the bluffs and walk a great circle around this one.

That's when an iron hand clamped around her neck from behind, and the other steely arm patted swiftly for weapons and then clamped around her waist.

"What kinda Injun lady we got here?" the man behind her asked. "Hey, Abner, I catched us a redskin maiden."

She didn't struggle, and didn't respond. Let them think she didn't know their tongue. A terrible despair pierced through her as she felt the hard-muscled arms of the one behind her steal her freedom. He walked her firmly, but not violently, into the circle of firelight that oranged a lavender gloom. He loosed her near the fire, but lounged easily, prepared to leap at her if she tried to flee. White dogs, she thought, but wouldn't give them the satisfaction of talking in their tongue. She wouldn't be tortured to death, but she might be used and thrown aside by these slinking curs.

"You fetched us some comp'ny, Zach," said the one at

the fire, slowly eyeing her. "I can't rightly make out what tribe she is. Can you?"

The one that had caught her like an eagle snatching a minnow had black hair he'd plaited into two braids, like those of her own people. But he wasn't one. He was a square-faced white, with a wide mashed nose that had seen many a brawl, and curious brown eyes that peered intently at her.

Trappers. She saw it now. A pair of them, not unlike her man, and Jamie Dance, with a load of stretched beaverskins and ponies to carry themselves, their catch, and their supplies.

"Maybe she's one of Bug's Boys," Abner said thoughtfully, his gaze feathering over and around every naked cottonwood in sight. "But I don't reckon it. They'd have our poor old scalps danglin' from their lances if they was."

Zach tugged aside the poncho, revealing her scarlet capote. "She's got her a nice outfit, seems like. I don't reckon she's alone, though. I guess mebbe we should douse that fire and be a leetle keerful."

The one called Abner made sign talk: Who are you? he asked her, and waited easily. She didn't know whether to answer. But then she made the sign for her people. With her right forefinger she drew three sharp diagonal slashes across her extended left forefinger, and waited proudly. The sign said Cut Arms, the term that all the plain tribes used to describe the Tsistsistas.

"Why, I reckon we catched us a Cheyenne lady," said Abner. "And plumb alone. Do you think she's friendly?"

Robert Campbell drained his coffee cup and peered vacantly through the rain-dashed window of the Planters dining room. Guy knew he was seeing things, remembering rendezvous fifteen hundred miles away in the Rocky Mountains, conjuring up trips down the great rivers in mackinaws, with bales of beaver in the bellies of the boats. Campbell had been there, and had turned that intimate knowledge into a fortune. He'd become the great financier of the opposition, including Dance, Fitzhugh, and Straus.

"Don't," he said at last, his piercing eyes turning at last to Guy Straus, across the white-linened table. "They need you here."

Guy sighed. He'd been torn between the need to race up the river and the demands placed upon him by Straus et Fils. He needed also to be on hand to send urgently needed goods out the Santa Fe trail. The Yellowstone operation was only a third of his business. "But they'll have to build a post. And I want to bring Maxim back down—"

Campbell smiled bleakly. "The waiting's terrible, isn't it? But Guy—don't go yourself. It'd take four months at least—four months of hardship, danger, and the possibility of illness. You're a city-bred man. You'd make it up there in good enough weather, but coming down, Guy—what if the river froze? Can Fitzhugh spare the men to build a mackinaw for you, and man it?"

"But Chouteau's got Hervey at Cass, and heaven knows—"

"We in St. Louis wait. And wait," Campbell said. "It's part of the fur business. No, Guy. You, too, will learn to wait."

Guy grew aware of his own helplessness. He'd done all he could, selecting men he knew would act wisely. But now doubts caught him: would Brokenleg Fitzhugh be a good man out there? Would he care for Maxim? Would the entire effort collapse and ruin the family wealth?

"He's got to build a post somewhere," Campbell said, intuiting some of what was in Guy's mind. "That'll mean delay and difficulty. He can't possibly be trading. Not with only ten engagés."

"There aren't any other posts they can occupy?"

Campbell shrugged. "Lisa's has disappeared. Others burnt."

"He wasn't well equipped for building. He doesn't even have hardware. Hinges for the gates and doors. Nails. Tools. A drawknife, hammers. A serious omission on our part."

"Send them."

"An express?"

"You want information. You also have a unique trade item to send up the river. And if worse comes to worse, you want an experienced man to bring Maxim down the river. But it won't be cheap."

Campbell was alluding to several hundred osage orange sticks, each carefully selected and prime bow wood, a prized item among the northern tribes.

"The bow wood," Guy said. "What about blankets?"

Campbell shook his head. "It's an odd thing the Lowell companies don't make them for the trade. The Indians want the point bars, the stripes at either end, and the thick weight. It'd be a waste of space."

"But the osage orange bow wood would be worth it?"

"Who can say? We don't even know what it'll fetch. Maybe a stick a robe, maybe two or three. But you've almost nothing in them. What'd you figure it—ten cents?"

"About that. I found a French-Osage to cut them for thirty dollars. That plus some warehousing at Westport."

"An express then, Guy. I know a man. Several men. A dollar a day for four months. And more. You'll need about four packmules. He'll have his own horse. He can take hardware, tools, and maybe three hundred of the osage orange. Plus his own outfit. Let's call it five hundred dollars."

"That'd raise the price of the bow wood."

"Good robe's worth four in New York."

Guy Straus leaned back, wondering if he could stand another five hundred dollar cost on top of everything else. "Robert," he said. "How sure are you about the bow wood?"

Campbell shrugged. "You can never tell with the Indians.

They prize the wood. They prize the bows. But there's medicine. If they think it's bad medicine to buy bow wood from a white man, you've hauled those sticks up there for nothing."

"They buy trade rifles from us."

"No choice. But bows are their own weapons. That's different."

"It might save us. The blankets gone, and all."

"For one year, Guy. Until Chouteau catches on."

Guy smiles. "Then this is the year. Send me your man, Robert."

That very afternoon, one Ambrose Chatillon arrived at the offices of Straus et Fils. The man was wiry and short, and swarthy; so small that doubts flooded Guy.

"Are you sure you can do this?" he asked.

"I am twenty years in the mountains."

"Who did you work for?"

"I am a free trapper. I work for Rocky Mountain Fur, some. Sublette brothers. Monsieur Campbell much. I do many things—mostly come and go, like a ghost across the grass."

"You've run expresses?"

"Many times out the Platte road. Some times up the Missouri."

"How do you deal with Indians—alone out there?"

"Deal? Deal? They almost never see me. I am a creature of the night, Monsieur Straus. I even like night, eh?"

"But you've had encounters."

Chatillon shrugged. "Who has not? I make the gifts. I pour spirits. I show fangs."

"What do you think of American Fur—of Chouteau's outfit?"

Chatillon's dark face turned bleak and hard, his liquid brown eyes froze over. "I do not think," he said quietly. "You are not trusting. If you ask me of this again, you must find another man."

"Campbell recommended you," Guy muttered, chastened. He made up his mind. "I have an express for you. I'm not even sure where it's going. It's for Brokenleg Fitzhugh and my company near old Fort Cass, but they're not at Cass. You'll have to find them."

"Ah, Brokenleg! We made beaver together."

It took a while for Guy to explain what he wanted. The last packet of the season would be leaving in a week, as far as Bellevue. Beyond that, water ran too low. Chatillon was to be on board with his own outfit, plus four packmules, plus some selected hardware and tools, and the osage orange, which was to be picked up at Westport, en route.

"Osage orange sticks, monsieur?"

"Bow wood. The northern tribes covet it. They haven't a very good bow wood. We'll try some trading."

Guy was rewarded with a vast smile.

"Now there's something else, Monsieur. I need information. I wish to know what is happening, every bit. And not just from letters. I want you to be my eyes and ears. Tell me how many robes they've traded. What they are doing for a fort. How far along they are. What they lack. How they're getting along with the tribes—and which ones. And my Maxim. Everything. His health. Spirits. Worries. You may need to bring him back, Monsieur. And if so—that is something you and Brokenleg must decide—my son is in your hands."

The wiry man proved to be a bright listener, grasping his task, asking questions, mastering his mission. Campbell had sent a seasoned, intelligent man.

"You can handle four packmules?"

"It is nothing."

Guy felt a pang of fear. "Very well, then. Very well." He couldn't think of anything to say, and fumbled his words.

"Ah, Monsieur Straus. Trust Ambrose Chatillon, yes? I will return maybe in January, maybe later."

"And if the river's frozen?"

"I am a walker, monsieur. And light on a horse."

Guy paid him half, gave him papers empowering him to pick up warehoused items at Westport, and gave him carte blanche to pick up hardware that would be needed at a post.

"Oh, Monsieur Chatillon—there might be a bonus for you."

The French Canadian smiled and was shown out by Gregoire. Guy watched him go, half afraid that he had thrown more money away. But he had to trust. He had to trust Robert Campbell's judgment, and this man.

Risk, he thought. For years, his firm had operated with minimal risk, exchanging coin and notes. Then with more risk, brokering money and goods. And now with terrible risk, investing in a ruinous business that either broke men or won them a fortune. But he liked it, even though the risk loomed like an evil monster just beyond his vision. Risk. If Fitzhugh could get a dressed robe for a stick of wood, they'd recover most of the loss of the blankets—and profit on the rest. He stared out his window, aching to know the future. Risk added some pepper to his bland life. He knew his father would have been horrified by such a thought.

Chapter Nineteen

Gone. It hurt. Brokenleg glared at the empty camp, finding it smaller and meaner. Something intangible had left it. Life had shrunk down. Dust Devil had brought something he couldn't quite name, something female to the place, making life good.

He limped toward the river, mauling his leg on brush and logs, but heedless of the pain. He'd brutalized his leg this day, and had ceased to register it. He crashed through brush that sealed him from the others, from Maxim, from his engagés, and headed for a barren bankside place he knew where eagles fished. Behind him the cottonwoods sealed off the others, and he was alone.

The hurrying river, burly here, helped him think. Life was like a river, unstoppable, cutting through the canyons of tribulation, flowing leisurely through broad meadows. It gave him an handle on life, seeing all that restless water, coming from somewhere and going somewhere. This strange river drained a vast area, the Wind Rivers and Absarokas to the west, and the Big Horns to the east, and changed its name along the way. Far to the south, it had sawed and hammered its way through the very bedrock of the earth, purple and red, in a place where Jim Bridger swore the water ran uphill. He and the other mountain men called it Wind River above that point, and they had rendezvoused near its banks, on the Popo Agie. And before it arrived here, at the confluence, it punched it way through a solemn yellow canyon that could frighten a man witless for no reason at all.

He watched a yellow leaf ride the current, and knew he could no more stop it than stop her. She'd fetch herself back to her people, purge and sweat herself, consult the shamans, take a new name, and anathematize whitemen forever. He thought she'd loved him, but maybe the Cheyennes didn't cotton to feelings like that.

St. Louis had done it, he thought. All that stuff she'd never seen and hadn't even imagined. She had been like a frightened sparrow there, beating a cage with feathered wings, wanting to fly free. It'd plumb changed her, darkening her mood, cooling her ardor. She'd eyed him narrowly, discovering him among his own kind, scarcely realizing he'd been feeling half caged up too, and itching to escape. It'd damaged something in her, something to do with her pride, her Suhtai heritage, her being at the center of all the secrets and wisdom of the world she had known. She'd become subdued and angry, but he'd reckoned she'd get shut of it once they got up the river again.

He remembered the first time he'd seen her. She was sixteen winters then, and living in her pa and ma's lodge, living the chaste life of a Cheyenne maiden waiting to be married. That was up the Tongue a piece, on a creek near the Big Horn Mountains. He and Jamie Dance had come for a visit, a bit of yarning over a fire, and maybe some trading. Dance never went anywheres but he got busy laying out some tobacco or tin looking glasses or ribbons for some pelt or other. And there she was, standing there beside the lodge, taller than the rest, and solemn. It struck him that she was a right pretty child, that one, but she wasn't laughing and giggling like the other dainty girls, wanting to fetch themselves a ribbon or a glance from the white trappers.

She stood solemn, as if she figured she had some kind of duty or obligation in her to stay solemn and superior-looking, no matter how the rest of the young ladies whickered and whinnied. That wasn't long after he'd busted up his leg, or the grizzly sow had, and he figured she just wasn't having anything to do with some stiff-legged smelly trapper who rode a horse with his bad leg poking out like something obscene that should have been cut off. It wasn't just seriousness in her, either. She stood sort of arrogant, her fine clean jaw cocked high, a faint disdain marking her features and a flat challenge to her eye. He figured she was seeing some caterpillars crawl by. So he looked again at her, puzzled, and that's when he'd been struck dumb.

She was the prettiest thing he'd ever seen, and that included all the white girls he'd ever seen. She'd reached womanhood; that was plain to his alert eye, with a proper swelling of breast and hip beneath her loose doeskin dress. Like all the maidens in that chaste tribe, with its rich taboos about marriage, she would be wearing the cord, a kind of rope tied around her waist and knotted in front, with the two lines running to the rear of her thighs and wound around her legs as far as the knee, making a sort of chastity belt that no proper Cheyenne male ever violated. For Cheyennes, marriage and all that went with it was a plumb serious business, serious enough to gladden the heart of a preacher.

But it was the chiseled planes of her face and her honeyed flesh that kindled something berserk in him. Her cheeks lay broad and prominent like those of her people, but her nose fell thinner and aristocratic, and her jawline sang of clean grace and strength. He didn't meet her that time: she proved as elusive as doe with a spotted fawn. But he vowed he would fetch her up the next time, if she hadn't been married off. And while he waited, he began mastering the Cheyenne tongue, which was something like the Arapaho one he knew. A Cheyenne grandmother living among the Arapaho taught him through that winter.

The next spring he caught up with White Wolf's band on the south fork of the Powder, hunting winter-thin buffalo. She was there, in the lodge of her parents, Antelope and

One Leg Eagle. He liked her father's name; he had about a leg and a half himself. That time she met his gaze with an unwavering one of her own before vanishing. In halting Cheyenne, with an assist from his fingers, he offered a bride-gift: a new Hawken he'd got at rendezvous; powder and ball; two four-point blankets; a pound of coffee; a pound of sugar minus the weight of a trader's thumb; and the entire bolt of scarlet tradecloth. Then he waited outside the lodge on his good leg, while pining Cheyenne girls stared and flirted and giggled, and a boy or two glared angrily.

Little Whirlwind—he hadn't known her name until then—had been given to him in marriage by her parents the next day, along with a dowry of horn spoons, fine robes, several parfleches, a high-horned woman's saddle, and a sacred Suhtai medicine totem, a red pipestone buffalo. Her Suhtai were the red pipestone people.

"I knew it would be so," she said to him. Those were her first words to him, and they spoke nothing of joy. But an obscure light shone in her eyes, which could have meant anything. She seemed pleased, but he didn't know for sure. Her bridal gown had been the softest white doeskin, belted at her slim waist. It hung just below her knees, longer on the right. The whole of its loose bodice had been quilled and beaded into geometric rainbows, and trimmed with elk teeth. On her calves she wore bright yellow-dyed doeskin leggings, and below these, exquisitely shaped moccasins that lay like onionskin over her small feet. She'd brushed her black hair until it shone, and then braided it, and wrapped the braids in yellow tradecloth. On her apricot cheeks she'd rubbed bright vermilion, and along the part in her hair as well. She'd bathed, as all Cheyenne did daily, and scented herself with the smoke of sweetgrass, and sage. When the moment came, her friends carried her bodily to Fitzhugh's lodge, and set her down there for him to gaze upon, thunderstruck.

They'd spent the night in a borrowed lodge set apart from

the village, while Jamie Dance made himself scarce, and the first night had been a torment. She had the right, along with all Cheyenne maidens, of wearing her loin rope for a few days, as long as half a moon if she chose to. That night she chose to wear it, driving Brokenleg to gibberish. She knew it, and smiled gently, and shook her head softly when he clawed her close.

But they'd talked. They had little else to do but palaver, he scratching up words with his broken tongue, barely expressing himself, and she solemnly and slowly, like the twilight song of a bird, so he might catch her thoughts. It occurred to him when dawn probed the eastern side of the lodge that they'd become friends, a little, even if his loins ached and his temper ran as sore and brimful as a flooded river. The elders had told him about the rope custom, revealed to him the wisdom of it; that it gave a newly wed couple the chance to become friends, be at ease, learn how to please the other. He'd thought to pitch it to the winds and snag her into his arms until she went mad with a passion like his own, but once they had sequestered themselves, he knew he wouldn't. One thing for sure; this tall Cheyenne girl had a will of iron and a way of looking at the rest of mankind—himself and Dance for example—that wasn't exactly friendly.

He spent a foul-mood day with her, following her about like a starved pup, and the next night, scarcely after sundown, she'd turned her back to him, slid out of her whitened wedding doeskin with its quilled bodice, tugging it over her black locks, and untied the sacred knot at her waist, and unwound the woven ropes that ducked between her legs, as solemnly as receiving a communion wafer on the tongue, and stood lean and honeyed and arched as a foot-caught hawk. Then she'd turned and smiled, a wildfire burning across her face.

Oh, the feel of her! Oh, the wrap of her slim arms and the velvet of her belly, and all the joys that raced those moments by! Oh, the strength in him that renewed itself faster than it was spent! With the next red dawn, he knew he'd fallen in love. Either that or had rendezvoused in heaven.

"Now you will be a great warrior," she said. "I have made it so. I am Suhtai."

He'd scarcely known what all that was about, but he made haste to find out. Later, Dance peered at him smirkily, but he ignored his old trapping pal and sought the elders, bearing a twist of tobacco, so he might fatten his knowing about the Suhtai and their medicine hat and all the rest. He figured he'd gotten him some kind of priestess.

"You'll make a great warrior and bring me many scalps," she said the next night, her face alive with triumph after they'd coupled.

"Me, I'm a trapper, Little Whirlwind. I'm a trapper. I got a stiff leg."

"You are stiff, yes," she said solemnly, and only her shining brown eyes betrayed her mischief. "Make war again."

He didn't think he could, but he did.

He stood on the bank, his weight off his bum leg, remembering all that and the strange corkscrewed union that had followed for several winters more. They'd fetched no child, and he wondered about it, and thought she might be drinking some herb tea—or something. He'd an inkling she didn't want his miserable whiteman blood mixed with her own. But it had never been addressed, and he didn't want to probe.

He'd been a squawman, all right. And it hadn't been all that close, this union of theirs, at least not the way whitemen make out a good marriage. He wondered how other squawmen fared, whether the same rocky walls existed, or whether it was just him and his Suhtai Cheyenne who inherited all the mysterious distances. How did Alec Culbertson up at Fort Union fare with his Natawista, daughter of Blood Indian chiefs? How did James Kipp and Malcolm Clarke, the other American Fur traders up there, do with their Mandan and Cree ladies? Had they confronted barriers as vast and mysterious as the ones cleaving his own marriage?

He peered angrily at the roiling water, at life flowing by with helpless leaves on its breast. He desperately wanted her back. He'd gone hollow in the moment when he had found her gone. He'd scarcely known, until now, how much they'd become one in spirit and soul, as different as they were. They'd been knitted by something that transcended language and custom, and it was enough, ample, that she presided in the lodge, like an anchor on his restless life. He'd win her back; he'd find a way. He'd light off to her village somehow and knuckle the shamans, spread tobacco, sweat the grease and armpit stink out of him in a steaming lodge, whip his hot flesh with sweet sage, and ask her to be his lady again. But even as he thought these things, he understood their futility. She was gone. And more than loss, he felt anger rising in him, as dark and hard as basalt.

Dust Devil relaxed a bit when they handed her a generous slab of meat, charred black on the outside from its crude roasting on a spit, but juicy and tough inside, so that she had to chew endlessly to reduce the meat to something she could swallow. She saw a doe hanging with its haunch cut away.

"She don't speak English none, but maybe you could try some of that Cheyenne you got on her," Abner said.

"I forgot it, and my jaw's plumb rusted shut if it's Cheyenne's talk," Zach said. "Odd she's alone. Like she was going for a hike. You suppose she's got relatives lurking around?"

"None as I could see. She'd be on a horse if they was, most likely, and not dressed like some Injun princess. She looks like some trapper's woman to me."

She pretended not to understand, but their speculations

worried her. She was carrying too many whiteman things. At least they seemed to mean her no harm—so far. She didn't like the way Abner's gaze feathered over her, settling lightly on her capote, obviously curious about what lay within. She chewed the tough meat, and stared into the flames, letting herself be night-blinded by them. The warmth felt pleasant, and the meat satiated her hunger.

"You reckon she'd enjoy some little fun tonight," Zach?"

"Cheyenne," Zach replied.

"Scratch my eyes out," Abner said, thoughtfully.

She felt grateful for that. She'd have cried Suhtai at them rather than Cheyenne. She wasn't like those easy Crow women, who'd lie on their back for a ribbon or a mirror.

"I'm not one to twist arms and go where I ain't wanted," Zach said. "I'd plumb feel bad doin' that."

Abner nodded, but never stopped gazing at her. She gazed back at him imperiously, letting her eyes tell him she didn't traffic with smelly verminous dogs.

"I suppose we'll git a notion about her when we reach Cass," Abner said. "Maybe she's some engagé's woman, all decked out like that." He turned to her. *"Parlez-vous Francais?"*

The tongue of the engagés. She stared at him dumbly, and then tried her Cheyenne on them. "I am Little Whirlwind, of the band of White Wolf, and a Suhtai, daughter of medicine man of the Tsistsistas'," she said.

"You make sense of that, Zach?"

"Only two words, Suhtai and Tsistsistas."

"You suppose we ought to take her on up to Cass? Like she's maybe runnin' off from one of them traders up there?"

"It don't figure to be our business, Abner. Maybe she's just going to her people."

She listened intently. These two didn't know of Fitzhugh's new post, nor was there any reason they should. The post was scarcely built, and wouldn't be trading for a while anyway. But they would discover it en route to Fort Cass, where they obviously were going to trade their beaver skins. They would discover her man, and would tell him about her. But it'd be nothing he didn't know. Fitzhugh knew exactly where she was going.

She addressed the black-braided one called Zach, in English. "I am Little Whirlwind—Dust Devil—and my man is Robert Fitzhugh," she said quietly.

They gaped.

"I am going to my people," she added.

"Fitzhugh! Brokenleg!"

She nodded solemnly. "Tell him I have come this far safely," she said.

"Where's he? How come you to be here—"

"He's building a post a day's walk north. Near Fort Cass."

"Fitzhugh's trading? Jamie Dance with him?"

She shook her head. "He's gone out to the Comanche and Kiowa."

"Jamie's tradin' too? How come—"

"They have a buffalo robe company, Dance, Fitzhugh and Straus," she said.

"Well, hyar's news!" Zach said. "How come ye not to have a pony, Dust Devil?"

"All were stolen by Absaroka dogs."

"Ol Fitzhugh—he's in some fix, is he?"

"He needs ponies."

"He's alone up yonder?"

"He has ten engagés and the boy—the son of Monsieur Straus."

"How come ye not to speak plain English at first?"

"I do not know who you are."

Zach stared at her, understanding her caution. "I mind the time him and Dance and me lifted a mighty jug or three at rendezvous," he said. "Fitzhugh, that was how he made his bad leg quit hurting a whiles, with the jugs. He'd come to the rendezvous, and dicker for a few jugs, and then he'd not have a hurting leg for a few days. You his woman, you say?"

She nodded, not sure inside of herself. "I am going to my people."

"You runnin' from him?"

"He knows," she replied. She wouldn't speak to these smelling dogs any more, and drew her capote tight around her. The night had begun to bite at her neck and ears.

"Well, ain't this just like old days. I reckon we'll go piss up his rope tomorrah. He tradin' yet by any chance?"

She shook her head. "I will go now," she said, rising.

"I reckon you can stay here safe enough. Warmer, too, with heat from that fire catched up the half-shelter."

She eyed them carefully, seeing no harm in them. But one never knew about whitemen.

"I am Fitzhugh's woman," she said, and sat down again.

Well before dawn she slid away from them, through a biting cold, feeling a scab of frost on the wounded earth. Abner watched in the dark, his gaze feathering over her, but didn't stop her. He slept the way most mountain men slept, instantly awake at the slightest change in the rhythms of the night. She stepped south, with no dawn to guide her, but only the cold star of the north bearing icily on her back. That and the soft rustle of the river now and then, and a star-shadowed trace.

She walked up the Bighorn River that day under a carpet of scudding clouds, seeing no one. Vees of geese honked over her, fleeing the Cold Maker. The damp wind cut through her capote, but it harried her along. She slid the canvas poncho over her scarlet coat, as much to subdue the wind as for camouflage. The world had turned vast, stretching beyond the imagination, and she didn't know where her people might be. All the day she didn't talk to a soul, though she paused to invite a crow-bird, her medicine helper, to lead her. But crow-bird wasn't hearing, and cawed away, indignant at the intrusion into its dominions. She didn't feel hunger until late in the day, when light simply faded from the gray overcast. She found a place easily, a hollow in the wind-sculpted rock back from the river, well concealed by a copse of jackpine, which dulled the relentless blade of arctic air as well. Back on the river, in a slough, she found a whole hollow of frost-murdered arrowhead, or tule potato, and these she pulled upward from their cold slime beds, until she had all she could carry. These she washed carefully, and toted to her camp, where she set her tiny cup over a fire, and roasted one cut-up tuber. She had enough to last for days.

She sat subdued in the dark, her back against the hollow of rock, wanting wisdom. Each day she walked, the world seemed only to grow larger until she felt she had accomplished nothing but was only making the endless world larger by adding steps to it. Beyond her glade, wind gusted through the long-needled pine, shivering it, and she saw that the overcast had slid away, going south like everything else. She could not see out upon the river valley, so she let her tiny fire die so anyone out there could not see in. Above, she saw winter-stars, harder, whiter, larger than summer-stars, which lay soft and blurred. She knew time ebbed away, and she was not as wise as the geese that had honked their terror of the north as they flew over her.

She didn't know where to go. She had looked for signs along the river, signs of her people, the cairns and feather-symbols of passage, and saw none she could identify as the Tsistsistas. Her village could be twenty sleeps away. Did Sweet Medicine watch over another land now, or had Little Whirlwind's long congress with whites destroyed her knowing? She'd lost the knowing, the knowledge that came without thought, of where her people would surely be. Her hands had numbed under the subtle chafe of the icy air, and she tucked them under her capote, and pulled its hood over her hair. These were poor defenses against Cold Maker compared to the warmth of a good Cheyenne lodge.

She decided to keep a vigil this night and think only of the medicine things of her people, and trust that by dawn she would know, the sacred knowing would tell her where to go. She missed her man, Fitzhugh, but yearned for her people, and feared she might fall into some terrible fissure in the earth between her man and her people, and never again be seen.

Chapter Twenty

That afternoon, in cold dying light, Brokenleg watched his wild past trot into the present on ponies. He recognized them far off, and hailed them in. Abner Spoon and Zachary Constable had been free trappers back in the sweet singing days of the beaver, and a decade or so ago the pair of them, Jamie Dance, himself, and others had headed out from rendezvous into the aching wilds, a small company sticking together for protection, gathering the precious plews from icy creeks and whiling away the firelit nights with mad yarning and woolly good humor.

"Brokenleg, ye old coon," said Zach. "I figgered ye'd hightailed outa the mountains years ago."

"Me? Why I don't fit nowhere in the States," Fitzhugh replied, his heart gladdening at these spectres from the dead. Around him engagés paused and stared amiably from their precarious perches on the roofbeams.

"What ya got here, Fitzhugh?" asked Abner, gazing across the rising post.

"A ticket to the mountains is what," Brokenleg replied. "I'm a partner in a robe outfit. Jamie's another, but he's down pestering the Bents."

"Well, hyar's news," Abner said. "Findin' your ugly busted carcass here. They all gone away, at least mostwise, when the beaver wasn't worth nothing, and half trapped out anyway. All the porkeaters took off like scairt rabbits. But me and Zach, we just got the itch to stay and we git on, one way or another, half-starved mostly. In thirty-nine, we couldn't even find the rendezvous, and got half-scairt when nary a coon set foot on the Green. Like we was out here all alone, two stray geese after the rest flapped off to the south. Baddest moment we ever had. But we trade a little. We get enough plews for powder and shot, a little coffee and sugar, and a jug or three."

"You're staying in the mountains?"

Zach turned solemn. "Brokenleg, this hyar land's bit us. We're land-bit. The pair of us, we got to starvin' after the beaver went under and all the old coons took off for Oregon or Taos or Santa Fe, and we get to thinkin' we're plumb alone, and maybe we'd better git on back like some civilized folks, and get us a wife and farm, and all—well, you know how that went. We got as far as Westport, and some sharpers cleaned us of drinkin' money, and some other gents tells us we could hire on for a dollar a day doin' this and that. And I looks at Abner and he looks at me and we rode back out the Platte trail, worrying Injuns all the way, and now we're free trappers with hardly a dime betwixt and between."

"Get off the ponies and have some ox—that's all we've got, and it's getting boiled up. Too tough for steaks, but just right for crowbait like you."

He watched them slide off their gaunted ponies, his heart gladdened by the sight of them. It would take his mind off Dust Devil. The pair of them had seen better days, he thought, and both had aged and weathered terribly, harried to an early death by the hardships of the wilds. Abner's hair had been a lustrous brown once, but now was streaked with gray, and receding back, like his own. He'd always been lean, but now that hard leanness had sunken into creases that whispered of starvin' times. Zach wasn't much better, he thought. But one thing hadn't changed: like most men of the mountains, they wore fringed leather britches and elkskin coats, with gaudy flannel shirts underneath, and wide-brimmed beaver hats, sweatstained and filthy, and rabbit-lined winter moccasins. They both carried Sam Hawken's product, Abner's a flintlock, and Zach's a percussion lock, along with powderhorns, possibles bags, and sheathed Green River knives.

"It ain't like the beaver days, is it," Abner said sadly. "They's gone forever. We go wanderin' through the parks and around the creeks and we don't see none of 'em anymore. Like summer birds, come and gone, and nothing's left around but winter all the time. Where'd they all go? It's plumb lonesome. Last rennyvous, in forty, wasn't even a real one, just old Lord Stewart back from England and spendin' a pretty penny to revive the past. Hardly nobody I ever swallowed Taos lighting with was there anyways, just them porkeaters he brought, and a few artists paintin' us all for posterity."

Brokenleg felt their sadness. He felt it too, the passing of the high wild times, when a man was not beholden to anything or anyone or any idea, but was his own master in a natural world beyond law and churches and wives. Especially wives. It'd stamped him, and it'd stamped a few others like these, and now they could never return to the States and the dull march of days clerking in some town or plowing up some farm. "Well, get the ponies fixed up and unloaded and come dip into the stewpot," he said.

In a few minutes Spoon and Constable had picketed their horses and dropped their packs beside Fitzhugh's campfire, while the engagés folded up the day's labor and clambered down from the naked beams of the roof.

"This hyar's Maxim Straus," he said. "He's the son of my partner Guy Straus, and he'll be clerkin' when we get this outfit perking. And this hyar's Samson Trudeau, my number-two, and he'll take you yonder and you can meet up with my engagés."

Fitzhugh watched them thoughtfully as they made their way among the men, some of whom they knew from the old beaver days. Many a Creole had trapped the plews and drunk away the profits at the rendezvous. But it was their horses that started him thinking; horses he desperately needed, along with their labor. Horses for hunting. He'd been able to salvage some meat from the slaughtered oxen, and keep it cold enough these frosty days, but that would come to an end—and he didn't have a pony to hunt on. If they'd stay, sign on for the winter, he'd have men and horses he needed so badly he'd offer them anything.

But that kind of dickering would wait until later. Maxim had dug up a spare bowl and spoon for each, and they'd ladled out the ox stew, and wolfed it down heartily, along with the engagés, until the entire fire-blackened kettle had been emptied.

"I forgot how ox tastes," said Zach. "Sorta glad I forgot. Not up to buffler, but plumb tasty."

They'd all settled around the fire, huddling close because of a sharp malevolent wind from the northwest that tormented their dark sides while the firelit ones warmed.

"That's some place going up thar," Abner said, eyeing the building, which ghosted amber in the firelight. "You gonna get her sealed up before the bad stuff hits?"

"We'd hope to move into Cass," Brokenleg said.

"Culbertson beat ya. That's where we're a-going. Hervey's there trading. Some Crows told us last summer sometime. We reckoned to fetch us some galena and DuPont, and a few doodads and a jug, and maybe winter there. Beaver don't bring nothing but grief no more, but we'll trade the grief."

"Abner, Zach—" Brokenleg began, urgently. "If you'd stick around some, I'll trade for those plews and winter you. And pay you right proper for some work."

Zach studied the half-built fort rising in the gloom beyond the fire, and glanced at Abner. "I don't see no tradegoods on no shelves, Brokenleg."

"At Cass. I'm renting roof. We'll be in business first of the year."

"Cass? You parked your outfit with Hervey?"

Fitzhugh shrugged. "Not much choice."

"Hyar's damp powder and no way to dry it," Abner said.

"I need hunters. I need horses. I'll keep you fat all winter."

"We heerd your horses and ox was stole," Abner continued nervously. "We met up with your little Cheyenne up the river a piece and she tole us."

"She's off to visit her people," Fitzhugh said uncomfortably. "She say anything else?"

"Truth is, she didn't say much of anything, let us think she's only a Cheyenne speaker. But we cottoned on to all her duds. Too fancy to be a lone Cheyenne girl wandering round and about. We thought mebbe a trapper's lady from Cass—"

"Well she wasn't, and she was just goin' on a little visit, and I think she can take care o' herself pretty fine."

"Don't git your bowels in a roar, Fitzhugh. We caught her snoopin' around and brung her in, and fed her some meat, and she took off before dawn. She told us you'd be here, and about losing the ponies and oxen, and all."

"I'll fetch her later, after we get settled in," Brokenleg said tartly. "Now I need me some men. Are you agreed?"

The pair of them glanced at each other, and then out into the night, and looked uncomfortable.

"Well, you old coon, we ain't exactly wage men. It comes hard to be takin' orders from a boss. Hell, you know what it's like out here—"

"Well, just hunt. Go off and hunt and I'll pay—'

"We ain't taken orders from no one for years, old coon. Not from a *bourgeois* at some fort, not anyone. Not God even."

"But you've worked harder and starved worse as trappers—up before dawn, seeing how the stick floats, pullin' up beaver and skinning 'em, fleshing the hides, stretching, and—"

"Sure, and there wasn't no one telling us we had to."

"How could you pay us anyway? Hervey's got your outfit locked up tight," Zach added.

"We'll pick it up."

"Wagons? Without oxen?"

"I was hoping you'd hire on—"

"Brokenleg," Abner said gently. "For ole time's sake we'll do anything we can. We won't be far away. But Hervey's got him a warm place and a mess of goods we want for these hyar plews. We'll come visit and tip a jug if ye got any juice."

Brokenleg knew he'd failed. They hadn't quite said what was on their minds, but he'd read it plain enough: this was a bellyup outfit, and they'd take their chances on a winter with Julius Hervey and American Fur. It was common enough for trappers to winter at the posts, where they were welcome because men and talk and high times were scarce in all that wilderness. And so it would be.

The next morning he watched them ride out toward Fort Cass. Those two weren't close now, the way they'd been years earlier, back in the grand, wild days of the beaver men. They were half-starved coons lookin' to hole up safe. He ached, not only because he hadn't been able to snare them and their horses, but because the old days were gone and buried, and hardly even a memory in the heads of the ones who'd lived in those times. Abner and Zach were like him: a mess of driftwood, he thought. River-worn and all the bark off.

They could camp in tents and covered wagons no longer. A brutal blast of arctic air, heavy and penetrating, caught them in late November, bringing work to a halt. The men's hands were too numbed to hold axes and saws. The ground froze into a steel plate which mocked spades and shovels, and radiated a cold that pierced upward through robes and blankets, robbing everyone of sleep and making the long nights even more miserable than the short days. Brokenleg had no mercury thermometer, but he knew the temperatures were sinking well below zero at night, and not much above by day. At least, he thought, the skies remained blue. A storm could kill them.

The roof was well underway. The carefully shaped ridgepole stretched across the building, and so did a lower stringer on either side of it, and adze-squared logs lying atop the sandstone walls, all of them forming the framework for the innumerable small poles, lying side by side, that would support the sod—if they could dig sod now. Each of those poles had to be squared carefully so that it would snug into the one beside it, and that labor consumed the energies of all his engagés. By mid-afternoon the sun was fleeing, robbing them of the light they needed. Fitzhugh kept them toiling until the last lavender twilight faded into wintry blackness, and sometimes they continued with the light of a fire built in one of the fireplaces at either end. But the light was so fickle it helped not at all, nor did the fire warm them.

The lack of horses and oxen slowed the labor. Each pole had to be carted out of the woods by two or three engagés, and lugged across the broad meadow to the trading post. Worse, now that Fitzhugh lacked a horse to hunt from, they all had to stop periodically and track down game on foot, sometimes dragging it back for miles—when they were lucky enough to find and kill any. Some days they starved, and turned sullen.

And then the cold came, sneaking silently into them like an icy knife. They rose quietly that morning, into a world that had turned brittle and evil, a world utterly silent because life had fled south or into hibernation. Fitzhugh's leg ached and wouldn't stop aching. He had the feeling, that morning, that he'd lost the race. He found a spade and banged it into the earth. It bounced like a hammer off an anvil. Maxim watched him, wrapped in a blanket, hollow-eyed and shivering. Not even a roaring fire helped them warm, because this sort of northern cold penetrated down to bones and into marrow and left fingers hurting and ears stinging no matter what layers of cloth and leather encased them. Making things worse was a steady arctic wind straight out of the north, not a gale but a ruthless invasion of polar air probing southward in triumph, murdering life before it.

At least they could get out of that flow, he thought.

"We'll move in," he told Trudeau. "Next to the fireplaces."

About half the roof had been poled, and they moved themselves and goods under the scant protection it offered. It contained no heat because of the open cracks between the poles, but it and the walls would baffle the wind, and the fireplace would radiate heat better than an open campfire. They had firewood enough, the detritus of their building, but it wouldn't last long. He scarcely knew what to do next: gather firewood, continue building, try to make some sort of shelter before the winter butchered them.

He had to think about a roof. There'd be mud on the banks of the river, at least for a while, warmed by the passing water. Maybe they could shovel that slop out and drag it somehow to the post. He pulled his spare capote tight, and clamped its hood down and limped toward the river to see what he could see. He found unfrozen mud, at least a bit of it, in a few spots, but what caught his eye was the acres of sedges, brown and sere, along the riverbanks. He wondered if sedges could be cut and thatched. A foot or two of thatching above them would hold heat, and turn water too, if anyone knew enough about thatching to do it right. He didn't.

He didn't like the idea much. One fire-arrow from one

angry Indian who didn't like the way a trade had gone could burn the roof down, turning the whole post into an inferno. One needed a fort here, not a thatched cottage. But he didn't have much choice at the moment, not with the ground as hard as a frying pan and he and his engagés on the edge of frostbite, lung sickness, and ague.

For two days they huddled around the fireplace while the wind mauled the walls and eddied through the windows and doors. Not even a roaring blaze kept them comfortable. At night they posted a watch whose sole task was to feed the fire. Their meat dwindled alarmingly, and men turned surly with hunger and boredom and discomfort, and some engagés talked of walking the four miles to Fort Cass, and its warmth and food. Brokenleg knew he was a poor one to lead men, cheer them on, rally spirits, but at least he could set some kind of example, so he braved the wind as long as he could each day to chop firewood, and even worked an adze over a roofpole or two before the numbing cold drove him back.

Then the wind stopped. The third day bloomed bright and cold. Men could work short shifts before warming. He set half to cutting poles, and took the other half hunting through the bottoms to the south. They found no game. It was as if the cold had driven every four-footed creature south before it, but Fitzhugh knew it was not true. In the winter, deer and antelope gathered into huge herds, emptying the country of solitary animals. They would have to find one of the herds and somehow stalk it, evading its numerous sentinels. But between the brutal cold, and the lack of horses, they couldn't walk far enough.

They came back emptyhanded, and into the accusing eyes of the others, who'd added twenty more roofpoles to the total, and advanced the roofcover several more feet. They were down to coffee, sugar, and tea, and resorted to steaming cups of well-sugared coffee to keep them going. It helped not at all, and Fitzhugh knew his ravenous belly felt no different from that of every man there. Some of the engagés eyed the barrel labeled vinegar longingly, but Fitzhugh resisted. Not now. He would need that for the trade in any case.

They spent another miserable night feeling the cold claw through their blankets and robes and clothing and skin, claw toward their vital centers, where they made the heat that kept them mortal. In the morning, after more sugared coffee, Fitzhugh divided them into three parties of three, with the remaining men to stay at the post and cut firewood and tend the fire. He chose to stay himself, knowing that his bum leg would badly slow one of the parties. He detailed one of the hunting parties to head south, up the bottoms again, but sent the others toward the eastern bluffs to hunt for an antelope band. They bundled into capotes, stuffed their feet into layered moccasins or added stockings if they had them, and walked off into a blinding morning, while magpies heckled and crows mocked.

He busied himself cutting sedges with a sickle, and hauling armloads to the post. He knew intuitively they'd be too coarse to make a proper airtight thatch, and he suspected that the roofpoles lay the wrong way for thatching. There should be horizontal stringers to anchor the bundles of thatch to. Still, he thought, a layer of sedge over his poles, plastered with a thin layer of mud dredged up from the riverbottom before it froze, might give them something, anything, to contain warm air. A lot of decent dwellings were made of reed and daubed mud.

He stood watching while Maxim clambered up onto the roof and spread the sedges evenly over a small area, especially in the hollows between the poles. He liked what he saw. He toted a bucket back to the river, feeling the rock-hard earth maul his bum leg, and painfully scooped up some heavy river mud, feeling his hands go numb. It took all his strength to carry the single heavy bucket back, and he wondered at it, wondered what had weakened him so terribly.

Maxim trowelled it into a thin layer that covered scarcely a square yard, and then fled back to the fire. Within minutes the mud froze in place, anchoring the sedges, and Fitzhugh decided it looked hopeful.

He spent the rest of the afternoon waiting for the hunters, his stomach protesting. To deaden his belly-pain he cut sedges from a swampland that had frozen solid. By mid-afternoon long lavender shadows stretched across frozen ground. The hunters who'd worked up the riverbottoms returned emptyhanded and dour. The shadows lengthened when the sun slid behind the western bluffs. The two remaining parties descended the eastern bluffs together, bearing nothing.

Maxim handed them sugared coffee as they huddled silently around the roaring fire, their gaze averted.

"Maybe we should go to Fort Cass, yes? asked Trudeau, knowing well the implications. "Before we faint?"

"Hyar, now," Fitzhugh said. "warm your butts at the fireplace a moment, and we'll have us a regular rendezvous."

They stared at him, anger and pain radiating from cold-savaged faces. From the small store of camp supplies hulking along a wall, he rolled one of the two barrels,the one marked lamp oil, toward the fireplace. Engagés watched, like rabbits watching a rattler, while he tapped it with an auger.

"This hyar's pure spirits," he said. "You may want to add a little Bighorn River to her—but not much, I'll reckon."

"Sacre blue!" bellowed Samson Trudeau.

"If ye don't want it, I won't pour it."

"I never tasted lamp oil before," Trudeau added.

"Rendezvous!" cried Bercier.

He filled cups. Men sipped and yelped and spat, and added a cautionary dilution, and then settled down to bone-warming and the renovation of the soul. Within an hour they'd forgotten their hunger. They didn't remember it all night. And by dawn, unknown by any of them except Maxim, a chinook had eddied in, and the temperature had risen into the fifties.

Chapter Twenty-one

She felt the caustic black gaze of crow-bird upon her, but she did not see crow-bird. Then she knew those bright eyes gazed upon spirit, and their medicine-helper had come to her. She stretched, trying to drive away the stiffness of her body. Her capote and poncho did little to shield her from the bitter air. She stood up in a gray haze of dawn and knew where she would walk. Her people would be many sleeps away, but crow-bird would lead her.

She wondered whether to build a fire and boil one of her tule potatoes, and decided against it. Maybe later. She must use every moment of daylight during these short days. She gathered her small possessions, slid from her bower, and studied the riverbottoms. Dense fog lay in patches. She turned south and walked, feeling the protest of her cold muscles. But she knew the walking would warm her.

At noon that day, under a hazy and unfeeling sun, she bowed to her hunger and cooked a meal in the lee of a cutbank, safe from prying eyes and the wind. The little roots didn't ease the torment of her stomach much. She walked southward, the unbleached canvas poncho over her scarlet capote to hide her from the wind and from eyes. Many miles, she thought. She wasn't really sure how long a white-man's mile was, but she knew she'd set her moccasins over many of them, up the endless river that ran through broken plains.

That night darkness surprised her without a camping

place, coming suddenly while she trudged across a vast, open flat, some distance from the coiling river. Enough clouds hid the sky so that she could steal no direction from the stars, and could see no place to stop, so she kept on walking, harried more by wind than anything else. She grew weary in the blackness, but her keen night vision told her she walked a long way from anything, across barren grassy basins, and so she pressed on through an endless tunnel. She felt more than ever that with every step the world grew, and her journey lengthened, and she was making no progress at all. Once she fell when her moccasin slid into a hole, and it hurt. The cold made a bruise more painful.

In the landscape of her mind, crow-bird led her forward, and she didn't question it, but followed. She would trust in her medicine. Still, her body rebelled: she felt famished and her strength ebbed. She would need shelter, sleep and food soon. But she found none.

"Crow-bird helper, you must lead me to a safe place now," she whispered into the blackness, and she saw her helper before her.

She sensed the river angling toward her, or perhaps she angled toward it, and soon she pressed through brush that whipped and clawed at her poncho. And then she stepped into nothing, tumbling down a sharp rocky grade into gravel. She skinned her palm in the landing. The rest of her hurt, too. She slowly realized she had fallen into the bed of the river itself, dry here because the waters ran low. A few steps away water murmured.

She made out a looming rock cutbank just ahead, and walked toward it, discerning a great hollow where the raging river had undercut a cliff. The hollow rose so tall she could stand in it, and the air lay so still she felt warmer. At its rear wall, she found soft dry sand, and her nostrils registered the faint smell of animals. She settled into the gentle sand gratefully, falling into a troubled, tormented sleep in moments.

She awakened in full daylight, numb again but rested. The low sunlight of *Hikomini,* Freezing Moon, struck sparks on the river, like the scrape of her oval-shaped steel across flint. She decided to recruit her strength, and gathered bone-dry driftwood to build a fire. She dashed sparks into her charcloth until it glowed, and then her cottony tinder caught, and she had a fire. She boiled all of her tule potatoes, one by one, and ate them, and then made tea, mixing a bit of her precious sugar with it. The sun probed into her hollow and warmed her.

She felt comfortable at last, and even warm. But she was many sleeps from her people. She thought about her man, Fitzhugh, oddly missing him even though he lacked the strength and beauty of Tsistsista men, and never followed the warrior's path. She needed him badly, and it angered her that she should. She didn't need him! How could these things fight inside of her? When she got to her village she would lay a gift before the grandfathers, and listen closely while they explained the Way.

For days she trudged southward through deepening cold, bruising her moccasins, feeling hunger gaunt her even though she found a steady supply of nourishing food in the rootstock of frost-tanned cattails. Her people had always gathered these roots, pounded and dried them into a fine flour. Even when the ground froze as hard as a rock, she could find cattails in unfrozen sloughs along the river. In all these short days and long nights she saw no one. The creatures of the earth, including the peoples of the tribes, seemed to stay close to their dens, preparing for the winter. She came at last to the place where the Little Bighorn flowed into the great river, and she followed it south, along a place her people knew as the greasy grass. The smaller river would take her to her people, while the great one would soon plunge into a terrible canyon.

The soles of her winter moccasins wore out, and she stopped one afternoon in a hollow of a cutbank to sew on new ones from the bit of buffalo rawhide she carried in her bag for just such an emergency. She had to work close to her tiny hot fire to keep her numb fingers nimble while she poked holes with her small awl, and threaded them. Her mind turned often now to her parents, Antelope, her *nahkoa,* and One Leg Eagle, her *nehyo,* and their warm lodge, perhaps still home to one or two of her sisters or brothers. She wasn't sure they'd welcome her gladly. They might find scandal in her flight from the whiteman. They and the *namshim,* the grandfathers, might send her back into the cold, and tell her to return to her whiteman. Her people divorced one another sometimes, but they might see her flight from such an important man differently. She'd tell them she wouldn't marry again. She'd become a medicine woman, if her helper-spirits beckoned!

The moon waned to nothing but a cruel sliver, and then grew again like a pregnant woman, and she knew *Hikomini,* Freezing Moon, had passed, and *Makhikomini,* Big Freezing Moon, had begun. Her man called it December, the last moon of his year. And with it came more cold, this time cruel and murderous, freezing the banks of the Little Bighorn solid so she could gather no more roots of the cattail. It became important now to find a sheltered camping place well before night caught her; a place out of the wind, with ample dry wood, where she could build a fire that would truly warm her. The valley narrowed between pineclad bluffs, and more often than not she found a campsite halfway up them, and far from the dwindling creek.

She topped a low divide and continued southward, weakening each day from a lack of food. Once she found a vast thicket of buffaloberry, and patiently harvested the small red berries while her fingers numbed. These tiny fruits clung to the bushes long after other berries had fallen to earth, and made a winter food for birds. She gorged herself there, but knew the bitter fruit wouldn't help much, or chase away the faintness that made each step harder, day by day. She resorted to prickly pear, cutting the new joints loose and roasting them directly on the fires to burn away the prickers. She downed the hot pulp, knowing it'd fill her but wouldn't give her strength.

The Big Horn mountains loomed to her right, a vaulting wall that catapulted bluely into a white blur above, where heavy windwhipped snows shrouded the peaks. The days grew even shorter, and she spent large amounts of time gathering the few things that might keep her alive in a cold that burned like fire wherever it caught her flesh. She ceased to think about anything except food for her pinched stomach; and all visions of Fitzhugh, of her parents, of her village, faded before the reality of her misery. Still, she reminded herself, she was the daughter of the keeper of the medicine hat; she would trust her crow-bird medicine helper; she would live.

Springs froze; open water grew scarce, and sometimes she had to chip ice with her awl and melt it in her metal cup to quench a raging thirst. One night a skiff of snow fell, whitening the dawn, clinging crystalline on her poncho. She watched the skies anxiously, wanting not clouds but sun because a blizzard would trap and kill her. Cold she could deal with; waist-high drifts she could not.

The wind died, and the next four days brought her much closer to her destination. The air lay heavy and bitter, unmoving, scalding her lungs when she exerted herself, but at least it didn't probe and slice and numb her with its fingers. Something drew her eastward, away from the Big Horns and out upon the broken plains, and she followed without questioning. Crow-bird hadn't appeared in her mind's eye for days, and yet he hopped ahead. She knew where she was going now: Crazy Woman Creek, where her people often wintered in wind-sheltered flats rich with cottonwoods, abounding in deer, and sometimes buffalo.

She worried her feet over the thin ice of Clear Creek, feeling it bend and snap under her soft footfall, but it didn't collapse. On its south bank she found a half-eaten carcass of a mule deer yearling with its throat torn out, downed by a wolf. But something had driven off the wolf, and it had frozen. She sawed away at a flank patiently, and soon was devouring the good flesh—her first meat in over a moon. It did not cure her deepening weakness. She cut away as much as she could, sometimes having to chip it out, while a treeful of crows watched solemnly. The rest she wrapped in her doeskin bag: it would keep her two more sleeps.

She struck Crazy Woman Creek well above its confluence with the Powder. It had snowed there a little; enough to show her the passage of many hoofs and moccasins, cut in an angular pattern that lifted her spirits. Still, she didn't know which way to go, upstream or down. She found a cutbank—this river had carved itself deep below the level of its scooped prairie valley—and built a fire there and ate the last of her meat, and waited. Overhead, corrugated streamers of cloud, infinitely higher than most, scrubbed the low sun from the world.

Brokenleg Fitzhugh awakened warm, wildly thirsty, ravenous, and with a sullen throb in his swollen head. He couldn't fathom the warmth. But yes indeed, he could wave his palsied hand through air that didn't bite him. Then he understood: strong drink had destroyed his carcass. He'd lost sensation. He always knew it'd happen some day; he'd sip too much and wake up a ruin. And now it'd happened. He threw his robe and blanket off and stood, and then toppled to earth over his bad leg, sledged back down by nausea and dizziness. This was serious: he felt warm in the middle of December, and he couldn't stand up.

He discovered Maxim staring maliciously.

"You and Trudeau will have to take over," Fitzhugh muttered. "I'm going under. Tell Jamie. Send an express."

"What's the matter with you?"

"What's the matter! Can't you see? I've lost my senses!"

"Lost your senses?"

"I quit. Tell your father I failed. Bury me on a platform, Injun style, so the wolves don't eat me."

"You look all right to me. A little green."

"Green! I can't feel nothing. I should be froze up solid."

"I'm starved," Maxim said, unfeelingly. It angered Brokenleg. The boy was thinking of his stomach instead of the dying man before him.

Around them lay corpses, sprawled like victims of a massacre. Fitzhugh eyed them suspiciously. Daylight abounded and not a one of the engagés had reported to work.

"I'm going hunting. I'm so hungry I'd eat anything," Maxim said. He picked up a company carbine, his horn and shot pouch, and walked up the river bottoms.

"Hey, you forgot your capote," Fitzhugh yelled. The hollering started his head to throbbing again.

The boy turned and stared, and then continued on his way.

"He'll fetch himself the lung sickness," Fitzhugh muttered. He settled back into his robes to await death. Time had run out, he knew. Anyone who couldn't feel the cold was on his way to hell for sure. He'd heard the last part of dying could be blissful.

Thus he lay for some while, feeling his head expand and contact like a bellows. It was plainly a part of his demise, this throbbing. He cursed the engagés, sprawled around him and craftily avoiding work. They knew. They all lay in their robes knowing he was dying, so they didn't have to work. Worthless. He pitied the boy, who'd be the one in charge after he breathed his last.

He heard a distant boom rolling down the bottoms, and then a second. But it didn't matter. Not even Dust Devil was here to comfort him through his last hours. He allowed himself a vast self-pity, dying alone, dying in the brutal cold, dying without seeing his maw and paw and sisters, dying defeated, not a robe traded.

"I need help," said Maxim.

Fitzhugh turned, startled. The boy peered solemnly at him, his carbine cradled in his arms.

"Help? You want help from me when I dying?"

"I shot a cow elk. A fat one."

Meat. Fitzhugh's stomach growled and howled. "I'm a dying man, but I'll help ye, boy."

He lumbered to his feet, and stood dizzily, the throbbing wild in his brain, his vision blurry. He tottered around, hunting his Green River knife and sheath, and some manila rope, finding both along a wall. A vast, benign joy settled over him. He'd croak in the middle of this, but he'd do it while he'd make meat, and they'd remember him for it, making meat while he croaked.

"How come you aren't in your capote, boy. You'll catch a death of a—"

"It's warm. Is this a chinook?"

Fitzhugh gaped. He stabbed the earth under him with his knife, cutting a furrow through mud.

"Trudeau!" he bawled. "Git 'em up. Git to work. Git them poles on and lay up a sod roof!"

Trudeau stirred, groaned, and stared.

"A chinook!"

"Monsieur, we are starved—"

"Maxim shot us an elk."

Minutes later, three yawning, unhappy engagés followed Maxim and Fitzhugh upriver to butcher and haul the meat, while the rest guzzled river water and tried to subdue their nausea. By noon, the engagés had gorged on elk and were hard at work laying up poles and covering them with sedges cut from riverbanks, and then dragging tarpaulin-loads of thawed earth to the building, and wrestling them up to the roof.

They had this little reprieve, while benign westwinds held

winter at bay, to finish their task. Each of them knew it, and worked furiously, some cutting and trimming poles, others scything sedge grasses, others digging up clay and sod, others hauling and lifting and tamping earth in place up on the roof. Fitzhugh toiled as hard as the rest, sweating the last of the spirits out of his carcass, limping along with tarp-loads of cold moist earth dragging behind him.

The early dusk settled but no man stopped. Maxim built a half a dozen fires for light, and scrambled around keeping them all fueled. In the midst of that he cooked a great haunch of elk on an iron spit, which the engagés devoured on the run. The night air bled heat swiftly, and Fitzhugh knew it'd reach freezing again.

When he reckoned it midnight, he called them off. In the flickering orange light, his men looked exhausted and gaunt.

"You'll work better with a decent rest," he said. "We'll start again before dawn."

Most of them cut cooling meat off the haunch and devoured it before rolling into the blankets.

Fitzhugh limped about, delaying his appointment with his blankets, reluctant to surrender to his tiredness. A fine thick layer of sod covered a third of the roof. But the other end was not yet covered with poles, and cold stars shone from where he stood within the walls. It'd be a desperate race, he knew.

He awoke without feeling rested, and with every muscle disobedient. A streak of gray in the southeast announced the next day. He'd come awake before the rest, some internal clock driving him now, when time was so precious. He limped toward the river, where they had mined the good clay and sod, and banged the spade into the ground. It bounced off frozen earth.

He rousted them all then, and set them to cutting poles while he and Maxim cooked. The westwinds stirred a little after the laggard sun finally poked over the eastern bluffs, and he knew this day would be warmer than the last. But it was close to noon before their spades cut easily into the cold earth and they could continue with the sodding. The work went swiftly, as men toiled in a mad rush to beat winter. Poles nestled into place, extending the roof, shrinking the open end; armloads of sedges nestled over the poles, and slowly the thick earthen topping crept toward the unfinished end.

He realized suddenly mid-afternoon that little remained of the elk; a dozen men had devoured it in scarcely twenty-four hours. Hunger loomed. He sighed, hating to stop his own labor, and gathered up his Hawken and possibles, and limped north into the bottoms again, worry gnawing at him. He trudged for miles, finding nothing. No sign. Not even a rabbit. By late afternoon, with dusk harrying him, he knew he'd been skunked. He hacked a stick from a willow and whittled a point on one end and angled back from the river, toward open prairie, hunting for the frozen hairy-leaved remains of the breadroot, the *pomme de prairie* of the French Canadians, a tuberous root that grew abundantly in the area. He found scores of them, and had no trouble unearthing the one or two-inch carrots with his digging stick as dusk settled. Those and the bones of the elk would give them an abundant stew that night.

They toiled by firelight again deep into the ominous night, until the earth resisted their spades and exhaustion slowed the work. When at last they surrendered, the final hewn pole had been lashed place, but a third of the roof lacked its sod topping. He didn't sleep much; worry haunted him, along with some deep mountaineers's instinct that the chinook had run its course. A different air had begun to eddy in, sharper and moister.

He reckoned it was only four or five when he rousted them out. The silent engagés had barely rested, but none complained. The air had definitely changed.

"Maxim," he said, "build a bunch of small fires around the sod. That clay isn't froze up too bad."

He labored alongside the rest, feeling his muscles complain, measuring his weariness against the haggard faces he saw around him. The frosted earth yielded swiftly to the fires, even while a northwind eddied icy air into their valley. Two men sickled sedges, having to go farther and farther upriver for each load, while the rest greeted dawn with brutal labor, dragging half-frozen earth to the roof, and stamping it down. Dawn broke under an ominous overcast, the sun gold and bright for half an hour, painting the world with its last gasp only to vanish as King Winter ruled again. By noon of that raw, gray day, they jammed the last of the sod into place on the eave overhanging the far wall. Without stopping, they sawed and adzed frames for the small windows and the two doors. While the light faded, that bleak December day, they were hanging two crude doors held together with whittled pegs, on leather hinges anchored with horseshoe nails, and hanging thick shutters on the window-frames.

Inside, twin fires roaring in the wide fireplaces at either end warmed the long, weather-sealed room a little, but the long cold rectangle sucked up the heat. Engagés gathered around the merry fires, warming hands and backsides, grinning and joking, and pretending they weren't starved when Maxim poured sugared coffee into their tin cups.

It was mid-December, not far from Christmas.

"Hyar now," he cried. "We got something to celebrate."

Chapter Twenty-two

When dawn came Little Whirlwind walked along the Crazy Woman in her dazzling red capote, wanting to be seen. She feared the Absaroka, who might catch her here and torture or enslave her. But this land was shared by her people, the Tsistsistas, and the Lakota, their allies. Her people sometimes wintered here, on the northern edge of the world they made their home, because game was abundant, and buffalo often wintered in the bottoms of the prairie streams.

If she met Lakota, they would take her to their village and make her welcome, and some would speak her tongue and tell her where her own band had wintered. And if she met Tsistsistas, she would learn at once. So she walked down the cupped valley of the Crazy Woman, en route to its confluence with the Powder, and hoped to meet someone. She knew her strength had ebbed dangerously, and maybe the lung sickness would consume her. But she gained nothing staying still, so she put one moccasin ahead of the other, and pushed into arctic wind that quartered into her from her left.

For half a cloudy day she walked alone. But some time after she had rested her cold legs, she discovered two horsemen ahead of her, coming at a trot. She stood calmly, awaiting her fate, her scarlet coat a banner on a gray day. Two young men with broad faces and prominent cheeks, lightly dressed considering the weather, pulled up on shaggy ponies. They'd been hunting, and had a doe slung over the back of one uneasy pony. She studied them even as they examined her, and the knowing came from the style of their moccasins, the dye marks just below the fletching of the arrows poking from their quivers, and the quillwork designs. Her people. But they were slower to react, and she knew it was because she wore costly trader's things.

"I am Little Whirlwind of the Suhtai," she said in her own tongue, and they exclaimed. Who among all the Cheyenne people had not heard of this daughter of One Leg Eagle and Antelope who had married the white trapper?

"Ah, we did not know for sure. You aren't dressed the way the People do."

"I wish to be taken to my village, and the lodge of my mother and father."

"It's half a day's ride. Our own is back where we were heading. You didn't see it? This is a good thing. I am Lame Buffalo Calf and this is Laughing Coyote."

The one who'd greeted her slid from his pony and helped her up, ahead of the slain doe. She had to hike her skirts to sit on the pad saddle, but her capote kept her legs warm. He trotted ahead tirelessly as they rode toward the village of White Wolf. She bounced along, feeling no hurt, because her spirits sang, and crow-bird had led her truly.

Near dusk the village wolf-police discovered them, and let the threesome pass, sharp interest in their faces. Moments later, the village crier swept ahead of them, announcing the arrival of Little Whirlwind and young men from Blue Heron's band up the creek.

Oh, the joy of it! Here stood the lodges of her people, their cowhide sides golden with the fires burning within, their tops blackened and bleeding blue smoke, which drifted southward. They formed a crescent in a park on a wooden flat beside the creek, well shielded from the winds. Heads poked out of lodge doors, and the People watched as she rode by, eyes beaming, recognizing her in her scarlet capote.

Some she knew, and she cried out to them as her shaggy pony clopped past. She would see them later, but before that she would greet Chief White Wolf, as custom required.

Furry gray dogs circled the procession, bolting around lodges, overturning medicine tripods thick with black-haired scalps, barking a welcome and begging scraps. But few people stirred because of the bitter cold of the Hard Face Moon, and the endless night. Only the village women braved weather like this, in their perpetual quest for firewood they cut with whitemen's steel hatchets. She saw red and white quarters of frozen buffalo hanging from heavy tripods, and knew her village was fat this winter, and the sacred buffalo, *Pte,* had given their spirits to the People. The cottonwoods nearby were alive with ponies, making a living from bark and twigs.

The young chief did not keep her waiting in the cold, but beckoned her inside his lodge. Little Whirlwind enjoyed the smack of warmth within the cone, produced by a tiny fire at its center. In this relatively permanent winter encampment, the lodgefloor was covered with old buffalo robes, and sleeping pallets and mats lay well above the earth and its grinding cold. But she realized her people could not walk about their lodges in light clothing, as the white people in St. Louis did in the middle of winter.

He motioned her to the place in the lodge where women sat, and she settled herself beside the chief's wife. He eyed her a while, saying nothing, studying her bright capote. "You have come to visit us, Little Whirlwind. And what of your man?"

"He is building a trading post on the Yellowstone," she replied.

White Wolf nodded, saying nothing. "He has sent you," the chief said at last.

"I have come to visit my mother and father."

"Your man did not send you."

It was her turn to say nothing. The sudden warmth was making her sleepy.

"Why does he make a post there, in the land of the Absaroka? It is far from us."

"I asked him to come here to trade."

"He will trade with the Crow, then. Will he trade rifles and powder and knives for robes?"

"Yes. He was going to make Fort Cass his trading post. But American Fur came back, and he is building one nearby."

"It is where the Crows trade," White Wolf said solemnly. "Does Brokenleg Fitzhugh no longer care about the people of his wife?"

"He said he would come with wagons to trade," she said.

"Have you left him?"

"I don't know. My medicine was no good there, with him."

He nodded. "You'll see your Suhtai relatives and learn about your medicine. Are you staying?"

"I don't know."

"Tell me everything about this new post and what we may get for our robes, and what he has to trade, and who is with him. And everything about Fort Cass as well."

She wished to leave. She wished to find the lodge of her parents and eat a large bowl of buffalo stew and make herself strong. She wished to be among her Suhtai, not with this Omissis chief. But she could not leave, and he would hear all the news, and ask questions, because it would be a matter for the headmen and shamans. For only ten winters had the Suhtai shared camp with the Tsistsistas, and she didn't forget that. She eyed this chief with a certain hauteur.

She told him everything. She told him about St. Louis, knowing he wouldn't believe any of it. None of her people would believe what she had seen with her own eyes. She told him about the Buffalo Company, and coming up the great river on the steam boat, with a mountain of tradegoods, wagons, horses, oxen, and those whitemen called French. She told him how the blankets had vanished, and about the long trip in wagons to Fort Cass, and what they found there. And how her man had been defeated at every hand, and ignored her wishes to bring everything here, to the People.

"I think he needs the river to bring those things," White Wolf said. "You did wrong, nagging him. We can go to the Yellowstone to trade."

She felt rebuked. A chief's rebuke weighed heavily, even if he was Omissis. She ached to escape and join her people but strict duty required that she continue. She told him of the Crow horse theft, and Fitzhugh's suspicions about it.

"They have no horses or oxen to draw the wagons? How will they get their things from their enemies at Fort Cass?"

She remained silent.

"This is a serious thing. They have taken or killed the horses for his wagons. Maybe the Crow will get those rifles. We have many robes here. Many buffalo. More than can be counted. But the posts are a long way away. Laramie, far to the south, Fort Union far to the north where we would be in danger from the Cree and Assiniboin and Blackfeet. I will think about these things. We will have a council."

She said nothing. He eyed her sharply. "Are you leaving your man or are you going back? I must know that."

"I will consult with the medicine man," she said, her voice combative.

He did not dismiss her. "Fitzhugh is no longer a trapper; he is a rich trader, willing to take our robes and give us things we need. What you do concerns the People. You will think long and hard about the good of the People," he said.

It was a command. With a nod, he dismissed her.

She whirled out, no smile on her face, into snow. It surprised her. The young hunters who had escorted her had vanished, no doubt into the lodges of friends in this village. The people who had followed her to the chief's lodge had vanished in the whirl of white.

Home! Everything she saw lifted her heart. About her lodges glowed, the fires radiating amber light through the lodgecovers, sweet against the lavender sky. The whirl of wet air captured the smell of cooking buffalo meat, tongue and hump, or white backfat, a prized delicacy, flavoring a stew. And in the midst of these happy smells lay the acrid one of cottonwood smoke, not as aromatic as pine or juniper.

She knew where her parents' lodge would be: winter villages were established in a certain order. She walked swiftly that way, knowing they had heard and would be waiting. White Wolf's village would have about sixty lodges, six times the fingers on her hands, and each would house five or six of the People. Her band was strong, with many great warriors, the best of all.

She wove between the cones along Cheyenne streets better lit than the ones of St. Louis, each lodge a gentle amber lantern in the dark. She found the one her parents owned, its white and ochre horse designs faintly visible on its snow-crusted sides. She scratched the lodgedoor softly, joy building within her. Here she would find her mother and father; her grandfather the medicine man; a sister, Sweet Smoke, and perhaps one of her unmarried brothers, Night Runner, or both. A married brother, Badger Nose, lived with his wife's people.

Her mother slid the flap aside and bid her in. In the soft glow of a tiny fire she found them all, waiting, their faces alive with welcome. They would listen to her describe her journey, and learn of honor or dishonor, divorce or marriage, and the omens good and bad, before all else, such as rejoicing. She took her place, the daughter's place, and stared back proudly at them, letting the snow on her scarlet capote melt into beads. She forgot her need for food and rest; the esteem of her people and her grandfather would have to be won.

* * *

No food again. Brokenleg stared helplessly at his engagés, who were awaiting the day's instructions. Feeding twelve people had become impossible. They'd had only coffee that morning. Even the sugar was gone.

"Trudeau," he said. "I'm going to Cass and palaver with Hervey. We've got plenty of staples in their warehouse, but no way to bring them here—but maybe I can hire it done."

"Some of us should hunt, monsieur."

"Yes. Send as many out as you see fit. Put others on firewood. And the rest to making a comfortable post out of this cave."

He waved his hand at a cavernous rectangle, ill-lit by fires because no window shutters were open. They were far from done: a trading room with shelves had to be carved out of one side, and behind it a warehouse for robes. And on the other side of the building, an engagés' barracks and kitchen, with bunks, plus private quarters for himself and Dust Devil—if he ever saw her again—along with an office. Another month of work, even without the brutal labor of cutting and chopping enough firewood to keep two huge fireplaces roaring.

"It is exactly as I would do it, monsieur." Trudeau turned to the unhappy engagés and began issuing directions in voluble French. Their stomachs pinched as empty as his own, and some of the Creoles looked gaunt.

"Any kind of food—not just meat, Trudeau. Fish. Any roots they can pry out of the river. Birds. You know."

Trudeau nodded. Men began clambering into capotes and hats and gloves.

"Maxim—you want to come with me to Cass?"

The boy was obviously suffering even more than the men, but he had contained everything tightly inside, determined not even to whimper. Brokenleg liked that in him.

"I'll come," he said tautly.

"I may need help. Four miles on my bum leg is a lot.

And if we have to carry some vittles back, I need you for a mule."

Fitzhugh and Maxim headed out into a vicious cold that lacerated their lungs and made breathing hard. Two or three inches of squeaky snow dimpled the ground, enough so maybe they could skid something back from Cass. Dance, Fitzhugh and Straus stored large quantities of staples there, beans, flour, sugar, intended for both trade and the fort's commissary. He glanced longingly at the wagons, hulking useless at the side of the post, and set off. With a little luck he'd have some horses.

The more he limped, the less he noticed his pain, but the air bit his face and frosted his beard, turning it white. The boy looked miserable, gasping cold air that wouldn't go down his gullet, each breath steaming.

"We'll get us warmed up in a bit, Maxim. And we got the blow pushing on our tails comin' back."

"I'm not thinking about that. I'm thinking about Julius Hervey."

"Oh, he's a devil. But I got this hyar devil-chaser," he said, waggling his Hawken.

"He won't let us have anything."

"He might say it, but I got ways of persuadin'."

"What?"

"I got a couple of friends in there. Slicker than Injuns with knives and 'hawks. And besides, Hervey's not so bad. Just when he's drinking he's bad. And he's got bosses, y'know. He can get hisself booted out of the comp'ny. Your pa, back there in St. Louis, he's got a few levers to pull with old Chouteau. And I got me a few levers to pull, too. Old Alec Culbertson up yonder knows how the stick floats."

"What does that mean?"

"Beaver talk. If there's a beaver down in the trap, the stick's floatin'."

"Hervey won't let you in."

"Haw. He'll clap a hand around my shoulders like I was

some long-lost brother. That's winter, boy. That's how fur men git themselves through the long dark."

The river had frozen over, maybe enough to walk on. But he stuck to the trail that ran nearby, through a lattice-work of black branches meshed into a gray heaven. He stopped periodically, more to let the boy rest than to pamper his game leg. In fact, the cold just stiffened his hip worse when he wasn't swinging that ungainly leg ahead of him constantly.

The trail swung east, paralleling the Yellowstone, and then Fort Cass loomed before them, silvery in the dull light, bleeding smoke from all its pores like some dragon. Only half a dozen tawny Crow lodges clustered there, all of them belching pillars of smoke, their flaps fastened tight. There'd be no trading at all on a day like this one, he thought.

The trading window was shuttered and the gates closed, but they'd come running, he knew. Anything for a robe or two. He banged heavily on the gate, the noise magnified by the heavy air. Maxim looked upset. Brokenleg banged again, imperiously, announcing his presence upon this bitter day.

The trading window shutters creaked open and Hervey himself peered out.

"You," he said, a sudden grin widening his lips.

"I come to fetch us some of our goods, Julius."

Hervey laughed. "I told you you'd never see them again."

"Open up, now. I got Dance, Fitzhugh and Straus stuff to git, and I want to hire it hauled. You got a couple friends o' mine in there with horses."

Hervey smiled easily, his hand never far from a sheathed knife at his waist. "Who says you've got friends here?"

"They're in there."

Hervey chuckled. "We're not trading today. Too cold. And you don't have robes anyway."

Fitzhugh edged closer to the trading window, intending

to grab the man by his shirt and drag him out of there, but Hervey glided a step back, his face mocking.

"Getting hungry, Stiffleg? I hear the Crow made off with your livestock. Hard to hunt with a bum leg."

Fitzhugh slowly went cold, draining his soul of doubt, feeling the deadliness of his intent steep his numbed muscles. He'd felt this thing a few times in his days in the mountains, usually just before something died.

"Maxim," he said, "you go try that gate there. I reckon it's unlatched, or about to be. And we'll pick up our goods peaceable."

"What goods?" said Hervey. "I've traded them away."

For a terrible moment Fitzhugh believed him. "Go, boy. Git. Open the gates yonder."

"Your concern about his safety is touching, Stiffleg. He'd be safer in here, don't you think? We'll keep him fed and warm. I'm sure his father'd be grateful and happy to oblige us with a few tokens of his esteem—"

Fitzhugh swung his Hawken up, waist high, and pulled the trigger, even while the massive shutters slammed, cutting off Hervey's heckle. The recoil of the unshouldered butt yanked Fitzhugh's arm back, and almost toppled him. Powdersmoke drifted. A yellow gash, gouged by a half-inch ball of lead, marred the dark surface of the righthand shutter.

"You were going to kill him!" Maxim cried.

Fitzhugh didn't answer. His blood pulsed wildly. He unplugged his horn, measured a handheld charge and slid it down the barrel. Then he swiftly patched a ball and rammed it home with the rod he plucked off its clips. He pawed around for a fresh cap and slid it over the nipple without checking to see whether it had fouled. And all the while he watched for the slightest movement of the shutters and the thrown knife that would zip through the widening crack. But all he heard was laughter. Cass stood tight, with a fortune in Dance, Fitzhugh and Straus tradegoods and commissary in its belly.

"They'll shoot us when we walk back!" Maxim cried, staring at the top of the palisade.

Fitzhugh ignored him. He'd become too mad to speak. He was primed to shoot again at anything that moved. He glared at the boy, demanding silence. Maxim stared back, terror all over his young face. Fitzhugh knew he had yellow-eyed murder in his gut just then. Hervey did it to him. He stank of it. He felt the bile build in him, hating himself as much as he hated Hervey; hating himself for storing the whole outfit in this place like some sheep being led to the slaughterhouse. Hating himself for trusting that Hervey would abide by the few whiteman rules fur men heeded, arrangements that kept the trading wars a notch or two less brutal than savagery. He'd let Hervey mock and goad him over the brink, and knew he'd only opened himself up to his own murder, as well as charges against him back in St. Louis. For there had to be witnesses, probably several engagés out of sight, watching it all.

From behind the shutters, Hervey's muffled voice. "I never forget, Fitzhugh. Sooner or later, you're dead."

"Open them shutters and make it sooner," Fitzhugh said.

"Maybe I will."

But nothing happened. Fitzhugh waited murderously, waited for the smallest shiver of movement. He intended to catapult himself right into the trading room if anyone inside unbarred those shutters. But no one did.

"Mister Hervey," said Maxim, "those are our goods inside, and we have a right to them. We want to employ some men to help us take things to our post. We're paying you rent. You're responsible for keeping our things safe from all harm. If you keep them, we'd bring you into court. My family will. If you steal them, it's on your conscience. I think you're an honorable man, just the way we are, so let us in to pick up our goods. We won't cause you trouble. I don't think you'd really want to be called a—"

"Come in and warm up, boy," Hervey said from behind

the shutters. "We'll send word down to your pa." His sardonic laughter eddied through the shutters.

"You're not a good person," Maxim said solemnly.

"Let's git afore we freeze, boy," Fitzhugh muttered.

"I'm afraid—"

"They ain't goin' to shoot us."

"I never forget," Hervey said, enjoying himself behind there.

But Fitzhugh dragged the terrified boy back, away from the palisade. No rifles poked out, no head peeked over its top, and a minute later they'd scrambled beyond rifle range.

"You tried to kill him," Maxim accused.

"I got that in me, boy."

"He would have opened up. He was just toying with us until you—"

"This isn't St. Louis, boy."

"It doesn't matter where you are! There's right and wrong wherever you are!"

"I reckon you're right. A feller can be daid right. I prefer to be hellish wrong. Out here, Bug's Boys and the like don't have our notions. There's prizes to take and they get took. That's how come your pap joined up with Jamie Dance and meself."

He felt no pain at all during the long limp home because his blood pounded through him. But Maxim had turned silent and hostile, and Fitzhugh felt a kind of pity that a lad with such ideals had to see life without law, both God's and men's.

He found the engagés had built some rough slabwood bunks and cut some firewood that day. But the hunters had stumbled back with nothing—not an elk or deer or antelope or buffalo, no roots or berries or seed; no fish or ducks or geese or crows. And every one of the twelve, himself included, felt faint with hunger. In a day or two it'd anchor them to their pallets.

Hervey had laughed, knowing all about it.

Chapter Twenty-three

The terrible thing about starving, Maxim discovered, is that it doesn't go away. The craving consumed him wherever he was. It assailed him when he rested quietly on his pallet; it agonized him when he walked or sat. The smallest exertion set his heart to racing, and a dizziness engulfed him.

Some engagés had boiled rawhide and wolfed its bitter broth, but most stared gloomily at the new day, a bright one with the low sun blazing off snow.

They glared at Fitzhugh, who'd stored so much of the fort's supplies behind the impenetrable palisades of Fort Cass. Any one of them could desert Fitzhugh's company, show up unarmed at Cass, and find a berth and plentiful food there. Maxim wondered how long their loyalty would endure, how great the temptation would become before they staggered the four miles to the American Fur post.

Silently they shrugged into their capotes and hats and mittens, and gathered their powderhorns and mountain rifles. One took the company's sole fowling piece with him. Another found an ax to chop a hole in the gray ice of the Bighorn, and a sharpened willow wand he'd fashioned into a barbed spear. Maxim watched them hopelessly, knowing their stomachs hurt as badly as his own—maybe worse because they toiled constantly.

He drew inside of himself and searched his soul, trying to find the fortitude to endure. He couldn't find anything in himself to allay the hunger. He closed his eyes and desperately invoked the help of God, turning his back upon the others so they might not see him and laugh. No comfort came to him, but he had the haunting feeling that he had been heard by some ear, some majestic force he could scarcely fathom.

"Maxim, boy. These hyar are starvin' times, and we got to hunt. Let's you and me go fetch us some vittles."

Maxim turned to find Brokenleg behind him, outfitted for the cold, his Hawken cradled in the crook of his arm.

"I can't," Maxim mumbled. He wanted to save his strength. Exercise would make everything worse.

"Fetch that sack along. We'll fill it afore the sun sets," Fitzhugh said, but Maxim knew empty talk when he heard it.

They braved a vicious cold, but at least one without wind. The air lay quiet and heavy as lead, and the sun kindled no warmth with its glaring rays. Maxim followed Fitzhugh wearily, feeling shaky, caring nothing about where they were going because only his stomach filled his mind. But Fitzhugh surprised him, limping gingerly out upon the river ice, testing with each step, listening to the ominous cracks and snaps. He motioned Maxim to stay well behind and spread the weight. But eventually they stepped onto the western shore, a forest of naked cottonwoods similar to the eastern one.

"Nobody's fetched himself over hyar," he said. "From now on, don't talk unless you got to. With this leg I'm not much of a stalker, but don't make it no worse."

Fitzhugh trudged straight through the wooded area to the open flats beyond, heading for the whited bluffs. Maxim watched alertly, but the hunger seemed to weaken his eyes so thing swam. He spotted nothing: no slinking coyotes, no winter-white hares, no geese or ducks, not even a crow in that silent deadly cold. Fitzhugh began puffing up the bluff, and then halted suddenly.

"Hyar," he said softly.

Maxim stared, puzzled. Fitzhugh pointed at a thicket of prickly pear.

"Git your knife out and cut them. Get the pears."

"But—"

"Cut, boy. The pears can be et up. They got to have their stickers roasted off. It fills a man but don't put any strength in him."

Maxim stooped, felling dizziness engulf him. He knew Fitzhugh couldn't bend over. A sticker jammed through his mitten, biting him. He cried out, but kept on sawing and hacking. Cutting a cactus lobe turned out to be harder than he'd imagined. He kept at it, though, while Fitzhugh studied the open country. By the time he'd filled the sack, his hands trembled and he could barely stand.

"I reckon neither of us oughta haul that sack. Leave her sit, and we'll go fetch us some meat."

Maxim followed silently across snow-caked flats, wondering where Brokenleg found the energy to limp forward. They struck a rabbit track, its orderly dimples plain in the light snowcover, and Fitzhugh muttered, backtracking toward the river and a vast thicket of red-stemmed brush there. Closer to the thicket the tracks multiplied, and Fitzhugh mumbled incoherently.

"Hawken'll blow it to pulp," he said. "Boy, you git yonder to that end and start thrashin' through that stuff. Me, I'll poke this old thunder-stick at anything that skitters."

Maxim circled north to the far end of the brush, and then pushed into it, feeling the whip and insult of the branches. The hunger-weakness engulfed him until he could scarcely move, but he thrashed onward, gritting his way. Midway through, he halted, utterly spent.

"You in there, boy?"

"Tired," Maxim said.

"Nothing poppin' out hyar. Git agoing."

It seemed endless, the twisting and ducking, the slash of bowed branches across his frozen face. He paused, a sob caught in his throat, not wanting Brokenleg to know how close to collapse he felt. He broke out, at last, scarcely twenty feet from Fitzhugh's grinning face.

"Shoulda scared the bejabbers outa them hares. I guess you aren't ferocious enough."

Tears welled in Maxim's eyes, and he brushed them aside angrily with his snowy mittens.

"I'm plumb done in, boy. Enough for a day. We'll fetch the sack and have us a prickly pear feast."

They stumbled home through a deepening cold, the day more than half consumed. The dead quiet of winter lay everywhere, and all the while they saw not a living thing; not even a crow circling in the ice-hazed bluffs. At least until they rounded the rear of the post and discovered four mules and a horse tied carefully to a wagon, for lack of a hitching post.

"Be damned," Fitzhugh muttered. He eyed the mules narrowly. "Meat," he said. "They been packing, by the looks of 'em. Whoever it be, we're going to borrow them."

He burst through the thick door, his Hawken lifted, just in case, and Maxim followed. At the fire stood a solitary traveller warming himself, wiry and dark and smiling crookedly.

"Ambrose Chatillon!" Fitzhugh yelled.

The name meant nothing to Maxim. But the newcomer peered closely at the boy, as if he knew him, his dark eyes registering Maxim's pinched look.

"Brokenleg. It has been many years, *n'est-ce pas?*" He peered about, noting the desperate emptiness of the post. "How goes it—you are hungry, *oui?*"

"I got them all out hunting—"

"On horses? I see nothing outside that tells me you have horses."

"Stole," Fitzhugh muttered. "But Ambrose, you old coon, how come ye to—"

"Express."

Fitzhugh gaped. Maxim couldn't fathom why, nor did he understand the word.

"This hyar's from your pa, Maxim."

The young man felt a sudden welling of wetness he couldn't choke back. The small man glanced at him, and sprang toward one of the new packs lying near a wall.

"I think maybe I'll slice up some tongue first, and then we'll talk, eh, Fitzhugh? Guy Straus, he worries himself half sick, so I come to tell him it's good, it's bad, it's all gone to the devil. Which is it, eh?"

In a moment Chatillon handed them slick slices of buffalo tongue, which Maxim wolfed down like a berserk animal. Fitzhugh did the same, and snapped up each slice as fast as the messenger could hack it off the heavy tongue.

"I shot it yesterday. A pity to leave the rest to the wolves. But there's many more a day's ride east, *oui?* We'll save this for the rest. It's hard to make meat on foot."

He set the remaining tongue aside, while Maxim watched like a ravenous dog.

"Now then, *mon ami,* tell me everything. Beginning with your beautiful Dust Devil."

"She's took off for her people," Fitzhugh said shortly.

Maxim realized Brokenleg didn't want to say more. He listened while the company partner described the trip, wagoning up the Yellowstone, the discovery that American Fur had put Fort Cass back in business, and the decision he had to make then.

"You left the outfit with Julius Hervey?"

"Yup. He's got roof. I had seven wagonloads of truck and nothing to protect it and us, when you git down to it."

Chatillon sighed. "I hope the man is reformed, *oui?"*

"We'll git it out."

But Maxim thought not, and boldly said so. He described their recent attempt just to get at the staples stored there, while Fitzhugh listened sullenly. Chatillon heard him out, his attention fully upon the young man.

"When does the rent end?" When do you pick up—"

"First o' the year."

"Soon, then. Without wagons, Brokenleg?"

"Got the horses stole. That's fixed us good. Can't make meat and can't haul the outfit to the villages to trade."

Chatillon nodded. "I think," he ventured, "it's plumb gone to hell."

Little Whirlwind stood outside of the door of a small lodge at the edge of the village, waiting patiently to be invited in. The voice came, eventually, just when she was feeling the cold pierce through her winter moccasins, and she entered into the bare warmth of Hump's dark home, and settled herself in the place where women sat, near the door. No ground robe protected her from the icy earth.

"I've been expecting you, Little Whirlwind. It has been many winters since you've come to me," said the ancient shaman, greatest of all the Tsistsista medicine men, who had lived in solitude since the death of his wife many winters ago.

"You are a Suhtai, and I am a Suhtai," she responded proudly. "I've something for you."

She handed him a small leather sack of roasted coffee beans, a rare and sacred gift that lifted a man's pulse and took the weariness from his bones and helped him be fleet in war or hunting. Not often did a Tsistsista sample the brown decoction of the whiteman's coffee bean.

He smiled, eyeing the beans with rheumy black eyes. "We will purify us with sweet grass, and then you will talk. You've been among the whites. Your medicine is gone."

He tossed small twists of grass on a fire so tiny that it lived on twigs. Its heat barely kept the frost at bay, but he seemed not to notice. A thick pearly smoke swelled from the low flame, and whirled loosely around the unlined lodge. She breathed it into her lungs, and let it flow through her scarlet capote, scenting it. He added dried sagebrush stalks, silvery in the dull light, and more pungent than the grass.

Then he closed his eyes, vanishing into himself, while she sat crosslegged before him, feeling cold creep through her capote. He wore only an elkskin tunic and leggings, unadorned, as if the medicine he possessed lay wholly within him, and was not something to be displayed. Not even his long graying hair had been braided, but hung loose, as if he scorned the vanities of the earth.

"Our friend Fitzhugh has become a trader, and everything you do affects the People," he said at last. "I hear you have left him. Were you thinking of the People?"

She heard rebuke in his tone. She'd come all the way to her village, following the guidance of crow-bird, her heart filled with eagerness, only to hear rebuke. But Hump knew her heart and she had to respond truly. "I am sick of living among them. They will not hear Suhtai wisdom. I told him to bring the things here and trade with the Tsistsistas, but he refused. He said a post must be neutral, and he would trade with the Absaroka dogs."

"Ah," said Hump. "You told him these things. And a lot more."

"They don't live according to our Way," she said. "He doesn't keep himself clean with morning baths as we do, and neither do the rest, the French he has doing the women's work. He does not greet Sun, or care about Sweet Medicine or the sacred ceremonies. They're like the Absaroka dogs, like all the rest, like—"

He cut her off with a wave of a hand. "You are too proud," he muttered.

"I'm Suhtai," she retorted, amazed at her defiance of him.

"You went with him to the whiteman's village called Saint Louis. And came back up the river on a fireboat, it is said. What did you think of the white man's village?"

"It was strange. They have medicine, but it is all because

they are weak. They build huge lodges—bigger than Mandan lodges—and keep them too hot. They are nothing—full of sickness."

"You saw no good in them?"

"I wanted to return to the land blessed by Sweet Medicine."

Hump closed his eyes and sat, communing with himself, while she waited, on edge. "It is said that crow-bird brought you here safely. Why do you doubt your medicine helper?"

She hadn't expected this. She'd expected this great medicine man to welcome her joyously and share her disdain of the dogs she'd escaped from, and all the others, including the Omissis chief of the village. She'd expected him to conduct purification ceremonies that would scrape away the winters of life with Fitzhugh and renew her to the People.

"Crow-bird brought you safely through the winter to us. Yet you want new medicine. You want approving words from me. But when I listen to my voices, they tell me things you wouldn't like to hear."

"I trust your wisdom, Grandfather."

"Then go back to the trader," he said. "Go to the Omissis chief you disdain, and the village headmen and tell them I have spoken, and what your medicine will be. And live no longer without knowing."

"Without knowing?"

"You live without knowing," he said. And he dismissed her with that placid wave of his gnarled hand.

She stepped into a blinding light wrought by sun on snow and stood staring at her cold village, which seemed no longer hers. Not even her parents' lodge seemed to welcome her any more.

She walked over well-trodden snow toward the great lodge of White Wolf and waited outside. A voice bid her enter, and when she stepped in, she found all the elders gathered and waiting, as if they' d known in some mysterious way she'd be coming. They loved to gather and talk and augur the future, and pass the slow days when Cold Maker ruled the earth.

She surveyed their blank faces, and found the same distance among them she'd found in her own family, as if they all were waiting for something. For two suns she'd stayed with her mother and father and grandfather and relatives, and it was as if the hoop of family had been broken and she didn't belong within it. She didn't know what she'd done. She knew of nothing that condemned leaving a man if she must. She could put him away, and he could put her away. And she wasn't running off with some other man, which might have caused a scandal.

"Little Whirlwind, what are your intentions?" the chief asked without preamble.

"I haven't decided." She disliked being grilled, especially by an Omissis. Every headman present peered at her through the smoky amber light, weighing her answers as if they had some right to disapprove of her. She wanted to snap at them, but such a thing would cause a scandal.

"The whiteman Fitzhugh who lived among us as a friend. He is a trader now? Has he many things on his shelves for us?"

"He has nothing on his shelves. He has no shelves. He has only a few men to build a trading house," she replied tartly. Let them see how little it all meant. "They have wagons but nothing to pull them. They let the Absaroka steal everything or kill what couldn't be stolen."

"Fitzhugh is in trouble, then."

"I think he will fail. He might not get his trading goods out of Fort Cass. Julius Hervey won't give them back," she said. "And he's weak and they are hungry."

"A post run by our friend Brokenleg is very important to us," the chief replied coldly. "You left him in a time of his troubles."

"I follow my medicine," she said, her voice razored.

"Did he do you harm?"

She could not answer, and remained silent. They waited for her response.

"Did you learn his ways?"

"Yes, but they are strange."

"You've told all this to Hump, a man we prize above all others in our village. And how did he reply?"

She hesitated. "He said I have not lost my crow-bird medicine. He said I must return to Fitzhugh. And he said—I lived without knowing."

No one spoke. A stick in the fire snapped. She saw eyes turn inward in thought, their focus away from her face.

"Hump's wisdom rises above the wisdom of us all," White Wolf said gently. "We will go back with you. It's best to travel in large parties in the winter. This trading house your man is making would help the Tsistsistas in several ways. It is closer. It would compete with Fort Cass and American Fur, and each would seek our robes and try to offer more than the other—and that would be good for us. But there's more, Little Whirlwind. If we don't trade for his robes, then he will trade with our enemies. The Absarokas would bring robes and take his guns and powder."

She listened silently, discovering that her flight from Brokenleg had become important to all the Cheyenne. It annoyed her.

"Our friend Brokenleg needs horses. We have many, and some warriors who would gladly trade ponies for guns and blankets. He needs to have strength with him when he is ready to get his things from Fort Cass. We have strength; many warriors. He has nothing to pull his wagons. We don't have horses that pull wagons, but we have horses that pull travois. We have thought about all of these things, the council you see here. Hump has told us that it would be a wise thing to go to Fitzhugh with ponies, robes to trade, and our warriors ready to help if Fitzhugh needs us. If he's starving, we'll hunt for him too, and some time he'll pay us with tobacco and vermillion and copper kettles. If we don't help him, Little Whirlwind, then we aren't being loyal to our own—"

"But he says a post must be neutral! He wouldn't let me bring the things here!"

The chief let this extraordinary outburst pass. "His plan was to bring trading wagons here to trade with us, didn't you say? He was planning to trade with all the peoples, but he was also planning to come here and trade with us in our own village."

She declined to answer.

"You're our connection to this new trading company. Up at Fort Union, the traders are married to Blackfeet, Assiniboin, Mandan, Cree. But what great trader of the north ever married a Cheyenne, like Charles Bent in the south?"

"I'm Suhtai," she reminded him.

"In two or three suns a strong party will leave for Fitzhugh's Post, with many ponies and robes. And you'll be with us, Little Whirlwind. Visit your family while we prepare, and then we will go."

Chapter Twenty-four

One by one, Ambrose Chatillon plucked treasures from the panniers he'd dragged into the post. Hinges! Nails! Bolts! Latches! Brokenleg gaped at the sight of iron implements, brought two thousand river miles from St. Louis on the backs of mules. These well-chosen items were the small makings of comfort and safety and convenience for the new post.

And three hundred selected, dried osage orange shafts, an ideal bow wood carried patiently up endless miles of river, past hostile villages, through storms and cold. Fitzhugh studied them, hefted them, admired the care with which they'd been selected and cut. A treasure in a northern land without a first-rate bow wood to be had. A gamble, perhaps. No trader had offered *bois d'arc* for robes, and no tribe had ever traded for the unfinished wood, though warriors of all the northern tribes treasured the orange bows above all others.

One by one the gaunt engagés stumbled into the fort, astonished at the livestock tied outside, and more astonished by the man within, who cut fat slices of buffalo tongue for each with a dapper joy, while joshing them all in voluble French.

"The tongue, it's only a mouthful for these. Just enough so they aren't so faint," he said to Fitzhugh. "We'll go kill buffalo."

Brokenleg peered at his desperate engagés, who slumped

hollow-cheeked and bag-eyed before the fire, warming themselves with a hardy tea brewed from Chatillon's stores. A few mouthfuls of tongue hadn't helped much; and some of them seemed close to collapse.

"We'll start first thing," Brokenleg agreed. "You know where they be?"

"This tongue, it is one day old. Tullock's Creek, just over the divide and south a way. That carcass, it is in the belly of wolves now, but I saw lots—lots."

Men peered at him, hanging on to each word. *Buffalo.*

"You got a horse and pack mules. You reckon we could haul a carcass—"

Chatillon laughed, and crawled into his heavy white blanket capote. "Meat," he said, collecting his powderhorn and possibles.

Fitzhugh watched him, puzzled. "What are you fetching to do, Ambrose? It's killin' cold out there."

"Make meat. See the moon? Fat. See the snow? Blanc. I am a ghost in the night. I ghost past the villages on the river and not a dog howls. I'll find the buffalo, yes?"

"Any of them mules I can ride?" Fitzhugh said, possibility blooming in his brain.

"Maybe, maybe not. Who knows?"

"I'm thinkin' I want me some liver, hot and raw."

So did six of the engagés, those who thought they'd find the strength to walk eight or nine miles through a December night so cold the snow would squeak under foot. The rest, including Maxim, stared helplessly, hollow-eyed, unable to muster the energy for such the nocturnal hunt. That suited Fitzhugh fine. He didn't want them all, and especially the ones most weakened.

They plunged into a night bright and murderous, the vault of heaven glittering wickedly over them. Chatillon led on his shaggy horse, and the mules followed without tether. Three proved rideable but the fourth humped and rebelled with a human on it, so the engagés traded off rides. Fitzhugh rode one, while the unrideable beast was loaded with Hawkens and axes and rope and tarpaulins.

How strange it was, he thought, to have a wiry man and a few pack animals show up in their midst and instantly change everything for the better. His mouthful of buffalo tongue earlier had done nothing to appease the aching of his belly, and he knew the engagés walking patiently through a whitewashed world of open rough prairie had eaten even less. If they found no meat, they'd be in trouble.

It wasn't a pleasant hunt, and yet every man was driven by the prospect of wild pleasure over the low divide and up the next drainage. Frost bit at his toes as he sat immobilized, his bad leg poking out. One of the engagés, Brasseau, clung to Fitzhugh's saddle, no longer able to stand or walk without that crutch, but desperate for meat, and cradling his frosted mountain rifle in his free arm.

On a snow-gilded horizon, coyotes laughed.

His fingers hurt and then numbed. The bony mule wobbled under him, weary and insulted by this extra unpaid labor. Chatillon hadn't fed them or let them paw up grass from the thin snow.

After the Dipper had circled half way around Polaris behind him, spilling night from its lip, he realized Chatillon was slowing and peering into phosphorescent plains nestled below gentle hogbacks. Tullock's Creek oxbowed along the bottom like a winter snake.

"Ah, my friends, you'll wait here, yes? We are too many, and I am a wolf of the night, a beast of the blackness, dealing death under the white moon."

It rankled Fitzhugh, but he knew starving men lacked a good eye and steady hand and a careful stealth. Chatillon knew it too. And in truth, some of the engagés could scarcely stand up. Bercier and Dauphin slumped over the mules, content to let the newcomer do the hunting. They watched Chatillon arc around to the south and approach a black mass not far away, a mass Fitzhugh was just beginning to understand was a few hundred buffalo standing in the midst of brush windbreaks, asleep on their feet under a December moon. He stuck his numb hands into his capote, and under his armpits, and found only pain there.

Now the dead night seemed alive. He sensed the slink of gray things through light and shadow, and knew the presence of wolves. Stars trembled and shattered. The bottoms below rose and fell, a strange moon-mirage, giving motion to a world. Snowflakes plummeted, decocted out of a clear sky somehow.

A weapon boomed, the quiet of the night absorbing the noise and neutering it, as if a gelded rifle had fired a fruitless ball. It boomed again, and gray things checked and slithered.

Some small part of the black mass sagged, and a second part detached itself like a stray from swarming bees, and then stopped abruptly, diminishing in size. The black mass vibrated and fell to pieces, like pie wedges flying out of the pie in all directions and vanished over a hogback. Two bituminous lumps remained.

Thin on the heavy air came Chatillon's high calling, and Fitzhugh kicked his weary mule down a draw onto the tufted bottom, while others followed, turning alive behind him. Then men stumbled past him, their breath hot in the air, stampeding foolishly, berserk with strange shrieking laughter and howling, like swinging apes gathering for a mating. They swarmed around a half-dead kicking buffalo cow, laughing when a trembling hoof flailed their number away. Cold knives bit her gut, sawing through steaming flesh and matted hair while the creature yet trembled. The rank smell of innards caught the air while blades opened her secrets to the cold universe, and hands tugged gray ropes of intestine, the boundins, out into snow where they steamed in protest.

Brasseau, a man renewed by opportunity, slashed toward the liver and found it, black in the night, vast and slippery and evil under the moon. He tugged it out with bloodied hands, and snapped his jaws over the oozing flesh, and then other hands snatched it from him and other mouths separated hot parts from the whole.

He hankered for some himself, this nectar of the plains. He saw how it was going there and rode, instead, to the second one, where Chatillon had dismounted, and in a few minutes he'd freed himself from his saddle, tumbled on his bad leg, dug up the liver of that young cow and bit into it, feeling hot wet flesh on his tongue and life begin in his belly. Chatillon stood amiably, smiling faintly, amused, his eyes scanning the horizons.

The livers vanished, and then boudins, gulped whole, inch by inch, and then rough raw tongue, blood-black while stars whirled. They sat in the cold, dumbfounded by the weight in their own bellies, while the buffalo cooled beside them.

"I think we maybe cut it up, yes?" said Ambrose Chatillon. He hefted an ax and began thumping it methodically across the back of one cow until bone severed and the animal lay halved fore and aft. Mules watched, their breaths steaming. Wearily, engagés clambered to their wobbly feet and began the harvest in earnest, chopping and sawing, separating hump and boss rib from neck and flank, salvaging bristly tongue, hoisting thigh and rump to the flanks of mules that accepted the outrage with flattened ears, mincing uneasily under the carnage they beheld upon them. They saved out Fitzhugh's mule for his transport, but rigged a drag of canvas and rope which Fitzhugh would skid behind him, laden with hacked flesh and hide. All told, they could carry or drag less than one cow on backs of the mules, on canvas sleds, and on their own shoulders.

A rifleshot away a regiment of wolves gathered on their haunches and watched, awaiting their turn. They always got their turn, Fitzhugh thought, and sometimes made their turn. The engagés collected axes and hefted frostbit rifles and tugged at halters, while the wolves edged closer with innocent craft. The post's hunters attacked their own trail, facing into a stiff northwind that slid through Fitzhugh's beard and froze the blood on his jaw. Behind him the canvas bundle slid and jerked, and the rope abraded his hand.

Chatillon drew beside him, letting the weary horse pick his way at his own pace.

"Monsieur Straus is very anxious about many things, and I am to report in full what I see with my eyes and hear with my ears."

"I reckon he's got a right to be. You plannin' to skedaddle?"

"In a day or two. I must rest the beasts. You will write letters, yes?"

Brokenleg nodded. His bum leg ached.

"He is worried about Maxim. I am to take him back if he wishes to go—or if I think he should."

"And what's your verdict?"

Chatillon shrugged. "He looks weak and pinched. But some meat—buffalo is a strong meat, and it heals a body fast. Maybe we don't need to decide now. I don't want to ride through winter nights with a lung-fevered boy."

"He's been through the worst. Growed a heap. Serious young feller, worries a lot about right and wrong. But he's learnin' it don't mean nothing hyar."

"Ah, Fitzhugh. What am I going to tell Guy Straus about the outfit that lies in the belly of the whale?"

"Tell him that's where she lies. We aren't quite ready for it—got to put up shelves and all. Get the innards built. But we got a few more days for that. I told Hervey we'd fetch it come the new year. Can you spare us them mules? That'd give us a wagon maybe, or at least pack animals."

"Three. I'll need a horse and a packmule. If Maxim comes, another mule."

"He's not comin'."

"I will ask him," Chatillon said. "What'll you do if Hervey keeps your outfit?"

"I don't rightly know, Ambrose. You got any notions?"

Chatillon said nothing.

"This hyar post didn't open up like we planned, with Cass back in business, and us havin' to build. Horses got stole and ox killed. I haven't took in one robe yet. But it's not all bad, Ambrose. I got the outfit safe under roof yonder, and now we got a post, and I haven't lost a man, and maybe with these mules we can get a wagon out to the villages for trading. Not bad."

"But not good, *ami,*" Chatillon said. "You may have to kill Julius Hervey before you can touch your own outfit."

Fitzhugh's Post on the Bighorn

December 21, 1841

Cher Papa,

M. Chatillon arrived here bearing things more precious than gold, sent by you. How glad we were to see him and hear his news! But nothing made us happier than his horse and mules, which enabled us to reach a buffalo herd in the next drainage. We were in a hard way, and his arrival was a Godsend.

We spent the days after he arrived hunting, making many trips to the herd, and carrying back quarters on travois we rigged up. Now we have most of five buffalo hanging frozen from limbs, and we all eat madly, never getting enough even when our stomachs ache. He will leave us some mules so we can hunt some more. But we have no safe place to keep them and little feed for them. M. Fitzhugh has been bringing them right into our new post each night to keep them from being stolen. And by day, my task will be to herd them and shave green cottonwood bark with the new drawknife for them to chew on.

Papa, we have had a hard time, but M. Fitzhugh and M. Chatillon will tell you about that. We built a rectangular post of rock and mud and poles, and got it sealed just when the winter grew bitter. It has wide fireplaces at either end that eat wood, but they don't keep us very warm. There is still so much to do. The engagés are sawing wood into planks for shelving in the trading room; building partitions of squared poles. Soon there will be a dormitory for the engagés, with a kitchen at one end; a separate room for M. Fitzhugh and—I was about to say Mme. Fitzhugh, but she is gone and we have no news of her. And on the other end of the building, there will be a warehouse for the robes at the rear, and the trading room at the front.

All this consumes the energies of us all, *papa.* You can't imagine it. Just sawing plank with the two-man saw is a task that wears the engagés out, but now at least they renew themselves with the buffalo, which is a strong meat and makes them well again. The ironware you sent is magnificent, and you picked it perfectly. M. LaBarge must have told you we would need it. The doors swing on hinges. The nails and bolts are useful to furnish the trading room. We have yet to build a robe press for baling the robes—but then, we have no robes to press anyway. One of the engagés, Dauphin, scraped the rawhide of two does very thin, and then stretched the wet hides on the frames of two windows, one in the trading room and one in the dormitory. Now we can open shutters and get some faint amber light. Enough to see our way around without a fire or lantern. But oh, for glass!

Papa, M. Chatillon came to me privately and inquired about my health and happiness. He said I could go back with him if I wished; that you would approve, and welcome me. He said the trip would be hard and cold, but he could get me safely back, even in winter. I thought about it and said no. I'm well now, though I was very sick in October, and lonely. I wanted to go home then, *papa.* I miss you and *maman,* and the warmth of our house, and my friends, and all the comforts of St. Louis. But I will stay. I am needed. M. Fitzhugh is desperately short of hands. And the whole enterprise is so perilous and close to disaster that perhaps I can be of service. I have learned to cook whatever they bring us, and take care of things that Mme. Fitzhugh took care of before she went to visit her Cheyenne people. We know nothing of that, *papa,* and M. Fitzhugh says nothing.

Neither do we know anything about the theft of the blankets on the riverboat. It is much in my mind, finding who did this thing to hurt Dance, Fitzhugh, and Straus—but nothing is said, and M. Fitzhugh seems to have forgotten it. Thank heaven you sent the osage orange bow wood. M. Fitzhugh and M. Trudeau looked at those dried orange wands exclaiming and smiling. They say, though, they don't know what the bow wood will bring. They hope for a robe apiece, but maybe they will have to give two of the sticks for a robe.

I meant to write a journal, but I have become lazy, and most nights I crawl into my blankets without doing what I intended. I also intended to copy down useful information into my notebook. I got the parts of the buffalo into it, and their utility. And I am making a list of roots and berries and seeds one can eat, with a drawing of each plant. But I wanted to do more. I wanted to list the words I have learned. I have a few under the Cheyenne heading, but I don't have many Crow words, and hardly any Sioux. They called the buffalo *Pte.* I've collected flowers and moths and dried them in the pages, too. I'm trying to learn the trades practiced by the engagés. I can fix my boots if the uppers pull from the soles, and I can square a log with an adze. Some day I will know more than all these men do because I have my schooling, too. I am reading the Psalms, one each night when I can.

Soon they will celebrate Christmas. M. Fitzhugh says there will be a buffalo hump feast, and he will give each engagé a gill of spirits. M. Chatillon promised to stay that long, but he will leave directly after that. There's too much to do, and they will not make a sabbath of the day, except for the feast the evening before. There is much cheer among them, now that we have warmth and food and the mules to hunt more.

After Christmas, we must get our outfit from Fort Cass, and that is something I fear most of all, because its *bourgeois,* M. Hervey, is not inclined to give our things to us, and made a great show of keeping M. Fitzhugh away from our company goods. I remonstrated with him, telling him—through the window of the Cass trading room—how we paid rent; how he must protect our property by contract and by honor, and how he must not do us a wrong. But he only laughed, and I fear M. Fitzhugh made a terrible mistake storing the outfit there, in the possession of our rivals.

He says he had no roof for his tradecloth and ginghams and bed ticking and all the rest, and it was safest there. But, *papa,* I question that. We could have kept the perishable things under wagonsheet with us, and let the rest of it—things like axes—be exposed. But he said it would all be stolen. I don't see much difference between it being stolen by American Fur and stolen by Crows or Blackfeet.

Papa, I have confided some things to M. Chatillon that he is to discuss with you. They concern M. Fitzhugh. Our partner in this enterprise is a violent man who will not stop at murder and seems to know little of the laws of God, of right and wrong, good and evil. He says they don't apply here, and it's every man for himself. But of course they apply everywhere the Eye of God sees mortals. He engaged in certain conduct toward our rival, M. Hervey, that I won't describe here except to say it was lethal. That does not seem the way to engage in peaceful trading, or get along with rivals in a sea of wilderness where civilized men must help each other on occasion and forget their divisions. No, *papa,* I fear we have the wrong man as a principal in this business. You wished me to be the Straus family eyes and ears, and

I am that, and its conscience too. I fear if we are allied with M. Fitzhugh we might find blood on our hands. Indirectly, of course, but still there, staining us. From what I've heard, he is no match for Julius Hervey in that department, but two wrongs don't make a right, and I wish he could find other means. The trouble really began when he stored all the outfit there. It was bad judgment. Now, on the eve of trading, we have nothing to trade with except the osage orange. The Crow are hostile to us, whipped up by Hervey.

I have tried to explain this to M. Fitzhugh, and have urged him to do what is proper, and enter into peaceful congress with Julius Hervey, but he only resists and lets me know with a dismissing smile that I'm not yet a man in his eyes.

So—everything depends on what happens next. The Buffalo Company will get its outfit and begin trade, or it will collapse. It will take in many robes from many tribes at an advantage, or it will lose everything you invested. It is something that awakens me in the night.

I miss you and *maman* terribly, and David and Clothilde too, and our Gregoire, and St. Louis. I am a long way from home. I pray this letter, and our news, and M. Chatillon, reach you safely.

Your son,
Maxim

Chapter Twenty-five

Westwinds robbed the twenty-fourth day of December of its cold, freeing imprisoned men to pleasure themselves in the cottonwoods, cutting fire logs or lumber for the interior of the post. Fitzhugh knew he had a letter to write to Straus, and it could no longer be put off. Ambrose Chatillon wanted to leave at once, Christmas eve, to take advantage of the mild. An express was just that; it could never wait, though Brokenleg desperately wanted Chatillon to hang on until after the first of the year.

He settled himself before the wide fireplace and dipped his steel nib into some thick ink Maxim had concocted from carbon black, water, and some spirits. The task seemed worse than a whipping but had to be performed. He'd written little since his youth as an innkeeper's son, and the nib pen felt awkward in his fingers. But not half so awkward as telling his partner, the company's financier, that he hadn't traded for a single robe, and that the whole trading outfit lay in the bowels of Fort Cass, hostage to the whims of Julius Hervey. And yet—that very information, gotten to Straus, could be valuable. A word to Chouteau might help matters.

He scribbled it out, then, in harsh angry strokes, wasting no words, concealing nothing, not even Dust Devil's desertion, which was mostly his own business. He explained without apology his reason for storing the outfit at Cass. That was his judgment. If Straus didn't like it, too bad. Somehow the drafting evoked a fury in him, so that he glared imperiously about the barracks, daring anyone to say a word. Most were outside, but Ambrose Chatillon had busied himself with his preparations. He'd have his Christmas gill, and slip out into the night to begin a two-month journey downriver in the heart of the winter.

Beside the fire, Chatillon was drying thin slabs of buffalo flesh on a rack, and shredding cooked meat into small chunks, which he mixed with melted tallow and spooned into tied off boudins, making crude sausages rich with fat that would not only last for weeks, cold or warm, but would nourish a man better than plain meat on a winter's day. A growing mountain of the gray sausages rose at his side.

"I wish you'd stay, Ambrose. I got needs. If we can't get the outfit from Hervey, I'd take it kindly if you'd go on up to Fort Union and talk to Culbertson. He'll bring Hervey to heel, I reckon."

"An express is an express. And it's out of my way, Brokenleg."

Irritation flooded Fitzhugh. "If you'd stay long enough to see about this business, you could tell Straus how the stick floats."

Ambrose shrugged, and spooned meat and tallow into a boudin.

Fitzhugh knew he was getting nowhere with his old trapping friend. "Well, at least stop at Cass. I got two friends wintering there. Worse come to worse; I'm counting on them opening the gates for us some night and letting us fetch our outfit."

Chatillon stared. "Who?"

"Abner Spoon and Zachary Constable."

"Ah, names from the rosters of the dead. The beaver days are over, Brokenleg. Gone under. Those two, they winter with American Fur every year now, and trade a few plews with the company." Chatillon said nothing more, but something in his tone left matters hanging.

"You sayin' something to me?"

Chatillon smiled and shrugged.

"We hooted and hollered through many a rendezvous, Ambrose. The beaver men was always true."

"That was years ago. The beaver, they are worthless. Trapped out anyway. We get buffalo robes, now, yes?"

Fitzhugh pondered that, his mind boiling like a teakettle. "Well then I need ye all the more, Ambrose."

"Be careful. Don't let Hervey kill you. And don't kill him."

"I'd as soon shoot him first chance I get."

"My friend, I think Hervey would like that."

Chatillon turned to his preparations, wrapping the bulging boudins in oilcloth and stuffing them into a pannier of his pack. Fitzhugh reckoned the man had cured or cooked about fifty pounds of buffalo meat and tallow. Not enough to get him to St. Louis, but enough to get him to any post along the way—Fort Clark, or Pierre, or even down to Bellevue. He'd forcefed his horse and mule for days, even cutting some tall grass on the opposite side of the frozen river with a sickle.

Fitzhugh attacked the rest of his letter savagely, feeling a need to defend himself to Straus. He hadn't lost a man. He'd raised a post out of nothing. Maxim had been sick but was hardening now. He'd fetch the trading outfit from Cass. He'd bring down good returns in the spring. He'd wagon out to the villages and trade. The osage orange bow wood would help. The ironware brought by Chatillon was perfect.

He couldn't think of a thing more, so he scratched Robert Fitzhugh across the bottom, waved the foolscap to dry it, and folded it up. He had no envelope.

"Put this in oilcloth," he said. Chatillon took it wordlessly and snugged it into a waterproof portfolio, beside Maxim's letter.

"Have you any message to him you don't wish to entrust to paper, Brokenleg?"

"Yeah. I'm bringing down a mess of robes next spring. If I don't get my outfit peaceable from Hervey—the whole thing—I'll steal his robes. But I'll bring robes."

Chatillon grinned wryly, and said nothing.

"And tell him you wouldn't stay here long enough to help bust the outfit loose from Hervey, even after I asked."

Christmas cheer. In the early dark his engagés settled around a feisty fire to feast on succulent meat around the bossribs of a cow buffalo. And to sip the gill of pure grain spirits mixed with riverwater as slowly as possible. And to find things to say to men who'd heard everything they had to say, many times over. Larue, Bercier, Lemaitre, Brasseau, Dauphin, Trudeau and the rest. Men he knew now; men who toiled like mules, starved and froze and bled for Dance, Fitzhugh and Straus. Their sweat had yielded them twelve dollars a month, which they would spend entirely on items from the trading room when it was stocked. There were things about life he couldn't fathom, and brute labor for almost nothing was one of them. And yet, they'd come here not for the wage, but for the tantalizing something that set men of the borders apart from all other mortals. Perhaps they were paid in memories, he thought. Tomorrow, Christmas day, they would toil again.

Scarcely had they devoured the buffalo hump than Ambrose Chatillon slid into his hooded white capote and began saddling his pack mule and horse out in the unheated warehouse area, where he'd kept them nights. The men turned silent. Not many of them would venture into an arctic void upon a seven or eight-week journey. Moments later he led his burdened animals toward the front door, bid his hosts adieu and *joyeux noel,* and slid like a gliding owl into a moonless dark that would stretch ahead of him unchecked by reason.

It shocked them, and a foreboding lay upon the barracks,

not just for the fate of Chatillon, but their own. Not a one of the engagés bantered further, but turned his thoughts inward so that men peered toward the fire, testing the flames for comfort and finding none. Chatillon would not follow the Yellowstone northeastward, but cut overland across a naked emptiness to the Missouri somewhere near Fort Pierre, and then ever south and east, tiptoeing like a soul past the devil.

Maxim looked stricken. The boy was obviously regretting he had chosen to stay.

"It's not too late, boy," Fitzhugh said.

Maxim didn't reply, but sank into his private anguish.

The raw stone room seemed too full of stinking mortals, so Fitzhugh pulled himself up and stomped life into his bad leg. Then he twisted into his fringed elkskin coat and caromed out into the night. He found the air quiet and mild, friendlier than the warmth he'd left. He liked the stillness, the dead-winter hush that let a man think without being hounded by babble and hate and conceit and stupidity. Chatillon had vanished into a moonless velvet void. Fitzhugh sucked torrents of air into the bottoms of his lungs, savoring its purity after the rancid odors inside.

He enjoyed this place they'd ransomed from nothing, though he couldn't say just why. Perhaps because he'd bought it with his blood, sweat and experience. The way things had gone, maybe he was the dumbest ole coon in the woods. From this very doorjamb, terror stretched in concentric circle outward, and he understood that in a way that would elude city-bred people. It sharpened his eyes and smell and hearing. People back in the settled world didn't know how a free land like this honed a man's instincts, turned him cunning and crazy. This post would be his passport to the unmapped beyond. He'd turned wild, like some dog joining a wolfpack, and he couldn't live any other way. He couldn't bring the beaver days back, but this—this was a tolerable imitation of them, and it gave him the thing he wanted most: a few more years, a few more decades, of living free as an eagle riding the unfenced sky, before it all vanished beneath the wheels of Conestogas.

He didn't care much about money, but this—this was almost as fine as plucking fat beaver out of snowmelt streams, skinning and stretching the plews as if they were round dollars, hoorawing the cynical stars, and buying all the fixings a man might need at rendezvous. Oh, the ambrosia of scented pine and balsam on a sundrenched alpine slope; oh, the carpets of lupine bluing a meadow and the whistle of an elk at night. Oh, the senses multiplied and grafted by wilds, the alchemy turning smoke into incense, and every mountain brook a vintage wine, a fountain of youth. Oh, where'd the beaver gone, and the beaver men, and the high times around a thousand joyous fires whipping into a spark-lit black, and the wild walks across the top of the world? Gone, and nothing but the slaughter of buffalo to pinion the memory in his skull for a little while before it all ebbed away.

The void beyond his vision lay dark and evil, and he sensed its menace. It held the terror of total possibility. Nothing here kept Hervey from killing him or him from killing Hervey. He hoped it'd always be that way; as empty a century hence as it was now. It elated him, this triumph of possibility. A man had to turn half wolf just to deal with it. Maybe, just maybe, all the timid souls back east would quit coming this way, just quit, and leave all this to himself and the few who braved this life. Fancy notions on a Christmas eve, he thought.

He grieved on the doorjamb while the stars rotated, and then thought of Dust Devil and he missed her. She of the almond eyes and apricot flesh. She scorned everything not Cheyenne, and among her Cheyennes scorned everything not Suhtai, and among her Suhtai, scorned everything not her clan and medicine. She despised him, plain as the pride on her face. And he loved her for it, the way a man might love a bobcat or stroke a porcupine. And perversely, she loved what she despised. He missed her in some well of soul where she'd festered into comfort. He wanted her, scorning and snapping and teasing. He knew she loved him, in spite of his affliction of being born white.

Fitzhugh studied the silent night, and decided then and there what he would do. Tomorrow, Christmas Day, would hold some surprises—for his men, and for others.

They harnessed the three crafty mules Chatillon left them to a frostbit Pittsburgh wagon with naked bows. The mules had known packsaddles, but not harness. Not even whip and blasphemy could move them much, but at last the wily Trudeau attached halter lines to their bridles and discovered they led easily, trained to come with the slightest tug. That would do. A man would walk ahead of the team and wagon.

"Leave your pieces in the wagon," Fitzhugh told them. "This hyar's a Christmas visit."

He added a crockery jug filled with two-hundred proof grain spirits to the small items in the wagon, and they left, all of them except Bercier, who professed to be ailing, but was well enough to tend the fire. What better time than Christmas to share a cup with Hervey's engagés and—he hoped—enlist them all in a peaceful transfer of the outfit from Cass to Fitzhugh's Post.

They rolled north easily over small crusted snow, the wheel hubs stuttering around cold iron axles, scaring up magpies along the way. The weeping snowblind mules considered these affronts just cause to sulk, and had to be whipped. In a while they found Fort Cass belching sour cottonwood smoke like a dragon, but otherwise benign on a warm day.

Brokenleg saw no lodges at all pitched outside the post, and its gates lay open. A good sign on a day given to peace and goodwill among men. Within they'd find camaraderie.

All fur posts hallowed Christmas, and made a great feast of it to break the monotony, and remind them of nobler callings than the commerce of skins. Even Hervey's post, he thought. He hoped that by the time sunset severed the solstice afternoon in this latitude, all his outfit would rest snugly in his own trading room.

"Drive on in and park the wagon next to the warehouse," he instructed Samson Trudeau. "We'll have us some doin's and then get busy."

They drove the team and wagon through the toothed jaws of Cass, under a log blockhouse perched over the gates, and wheeled the wagon around in the yard, while Fort Cass's men watched amiably. He counted about twenty of them, bearded Frenchmen like his own, gaudy in bright-dyed wool. Even as he watched, Trudeau and the others were greeting each other in voluble French, reminding him that the gallic fraternity of fur company employees was a closed society. English-speaking engagés were rare. The Indians themselves knew French better than English.

Hervey emerged from the comfortable trading room, adorned in blue Christmas finery and fresh-trimmed black beard. He surveyed the arrivals and the wagon, bright mock behind his beard, enjoying the sight.

"Ah, the Opposition. Stiffleg and young Straus and their bravos."

"Merry Christmas, Hervey."

"Come to share the feast and guzzle the spirits and holiday a while. With an empty wagon."

"Brung us some spirits," Fitzhugh said, waving his jug.

"The better to stupefy," Hervey said.

"I thunk to celebrate."

"Indeed, and brought your wagon to celebrate with." Julius Hervey beamed effusively. "Well, come on in and we'll pull the cork."

At one end of the comfortable window-lit Fort Cass barracks a cast-iron barrel stove radiated warmth upon the fort loafers, among them Abner Spoon and Zachary Constable, sprawled amiably on benches. Winter birds. Most forts collected them, and as long as the loafers earned their keep with a little hunting or work, no one objected. Meat cost nothing more than a ball and powder.

"I declare, it's the beaver times all over agin," Constable bawled. "A reg'lar rendezvous."

Fitzhugh limped over and clamped an arm around the trapper, and then Spoon. "I brought us some spirits, if you got the cup."

"I never guzzle water before breakfast," Constable said, while Fitzhugh poured.

Engagés drifted in, both Cass's and his, and Fitzhugh poured a couple of fingers for each. The French settled into their own circle, the language effusive on their tongues, while Hervey, Fitzhugh, Maxim and the rest gathered on the other side of the stove.

Fitzhugh lifted his Fort Cass tin cup. "Well, hyar's to you all, and the holy day, and lots of skins," he said.

Hervey grinned. "Lots of skins," he echoed. "Yours in particular."

"I reckon they's robes for all. Lots of bands hereabouts that haven't been traded with since the beaver days."

"With osage orange sticks," Hervey said, strange light flaring in his eyes. "Sticks for robes. I admire the Opposition. When it's got nothing else to trade, it comes up with sticks."

It troubled Fitzhugh. How the hell did he know that? Was his outfit riddled with gossipers or worse? He sighed. He'd have only this trading season to try out the bow wood. If it worked, American Fur would have its own supply.

"What's that about?" asked Spoon.

"Bois d'arc. Osage orange. A bright idea from the devious mind of Jamie Dance," Hervey said. "How many will get you a robe, my dear Stiffleg?"

Fitzhugh felt himself denuded by the man's knowledge.

Where had it come from? Who knew it had been Jamie's idea? He glared darkly at Hervey, who yawned like a cat. "We haven't tried it yet. Maybe after the first of the year."

"If anyone comes," Hervey said. "You can't count on the Cheyenne any more with Dust Devil gone."

"*Bois d'arc.* I think that'd go a finished bow for a robe, maybe three sticks for a robe," Constable said. "They like that wood. I never figgered they had much of a shootin' tool with juniper or chokecherry or willow."

"I had enough arrers whip into my hide so's I dissent," Spoon said. "I don't reckon a osage orange bow's going to pain me more than a juniper."

"More distance," Hervey said. "Maybe thirty yards."

They argued it while Fitzhugh fumed, feeling naked before the spying of his powerful opponents. The whispering must have started in St. Louis, where someone knew Jamie Dance had thought up the idea. Still, this was Christmastide, and he settled back to bragging and hoorawing like the rest. A man could get right ornery worrying it around.

A roasted haunch of buffalo hung near the stove, near a stack of wooden trenchers and a butcher knife. Men fed themselves that sunny day, sawing off thick slabs of tough meat to chew between their sipping. Fitzhugh felt minutes slide by, minutes when he could be loading up his outfit and hauling the first of it back to his post. But Hervey seemed amiable for a change, watching his guests with bright amusement, and Fitzhugh thought that with each passing sip of spirits, the chances of trouble lessened. So he bided his time. To be sure, Hervey played a catspaw game, sliding his barbs home the whole while, hoping to rile Fitzhugh. But he refused to be riled, and Chatillon's warning hung in his mind, along with his own caution. Hervey would love to murder him.

But the sun was fleeting, and he broached the topic at last. "Julius, I got to fetch my outfit before our agreement expires. We're ready. I come with the wagon to fetch the loads."

"What's left of it, Stiffleg. I've traded it away."

"I think you're provokin' me, is all. They'd be hell to pay with Chouteau and Culbertson."

"It's a Christmas gift," Hervey replied.

Troubled, Fitzhugh clambered up and stamped life into his game leg. Men dozed in the warmth, joked, sipped the last of the fiery spirits. He limped out into the yard, intending to check the warehouse. Maxim, worried as always, followed. The sun had plunged so low that the yard lay blue in winter-shadow. He didn't notice a difference until he got to his big Pittsburgh wagon, and then stopped abruptly. The mules had vanished, along with their harness. The wagon hulked naked beside the warehouse, a helpless giant, its doubletree sagging into frozen earth. Choking, he peered into the wagonbed looking for something else: his rifle and those of his engagés had vanished as well, along with the robe that contained them.

"Ah, Stiffleg," said Hervey from across the yard. "Merry Christmas."

Chapter Twenty-six

Brokenleg waited impatiently for the weather to moderate. For days brief boiling blizzards had swept over the post, interspersed with sunny interludes rimmed by mountainous clouds. A wicked wind howled out of the north. He intended to send an express to Culbertson notifying him of events on the Yellowstone, and demanding relief. But with three mules in captivity, the man would have to go on foot, two hundred miles through drifts in the bowels of winter. He wished he could go himself, but his bum leg prevented it.

He kept the engagés busy, barking at them sometimes because of their lassitude. Things cried to be done: the trading window needed a counter and shutters. His own apartment and office had yet to be partitioned or furnished. The matter of dry firewood loomed large always, with two wide fireplaces eating their daily meals. The post armaments had been reduced to Maxim's old rifle, Bercier's rifle and one fowling piece, and these he assigned to his best hunters and sent them into the cold each dark day. They returned with what they could carry—a rabbit, a duck, once a quarter of a doe brought from a great distance. And all the while the reserves of hanging frozen buffalo diminished rapidly. Without the mules they lacked the means to reach the distant herd and pack more meat to the post.

Something had drained away, and the men eyed him with long dark stares, and idled through their tasks. Trudeau looked worried, and did not press them when they gathered for a pipe, or just collected around a fireplace to stare into moody flames.

Maxim sulked and avoided his duties, and no matter how much Fitzhugh railed at the boy, it yielded no improvement. Accusation filled Maxim's eyes, but he said nothing, and confined his thoughts to his notebook.

Hervey had escorted them all to the gates of Fort Cass on Christmas day, thoroughly enjoying himself. He'd been backed by all of his engagés, though they obviously despised the evil he did to guests on a sacred day. But none resisted, beyond a dark stare at their *bourgeois,* because to do so was to court death at his hands. Fitzhugh had itched to brawl, to pound them, but he'd gotten hold of himself, and with a nod to his own engagés, signaled them to leave peacefully.

Nonetheless, at the gates of Fort Cass, he'd turned to Hervey with an accusation. "You're a thief," he said, his glare upon the amused man. And he'd waited taut for the blow, because Hervey had slid knives into men for lesser offenses.

But Hervey had only chortled easily. "Stiffleg, dummy, you don't understand. We'll buy your entire outfit at cost—for the goods and for your transportation. At cost."

"You're a thief," Brokenleg had repeated.

Hervey'd shrugged. "We're just holding it for you. We'll ship the whole outfit down the river on mackinaws in the spring if you want. That'll cost you plenty for transportation, though. You'd be better off selling."

"This ain't done yet, Hervey."

"I'll remember that, Stiffleg. I never forget a threat. You and your men can pick up your rifles and the rest of your truck any time you quit the country. Or come work for me. I'm just storing them safely for you. A little Christmas service." He'd smirked at that.

Fitzhugh's engagés had listened somberly. They understood English well enough, even if they didn't speak it.

After that, they'd trudged home in violet light, never speaking a word the entire four miles. And they'd hardly spoken in the six days since.

This night would witness the passage of 1841, and the birth of 1842, but no one cared. He thought he'd offer them a gill anyway, even if it cut into one of the two trade items he possessed. It didn't matter much. Or did it? He reminded himself that times changed, and half the battle was to endure the worst, take a loss this year and go onto the next. Maybe Jamie would reap a bonanza in robes down south.

Samson Trudeau caught him outside, where he was pacing out the dimensions of a yard behind the trading post where someday they could keep horses inside of a palisade. Another snow squall blotted the timid sun while he calculated.

Trudeau looked worried. "Monsieur Fitzhugh?" he asked, hesitantly. "I think—"

Brokenleg waited impatiently as flakes melted on his neck.

"I think some of the engagés—we are going to lose them."

Fitzhugh absorbed that, angering. "They signed on for a year," he snapped.

Trudeau sighed. "It is so. But I think some, they will leave tonight."

"How many?"

"Six. They go to Fort Cass. They will work for Hervey. He'll give them their rifles back, *n'est-ce pas?*"

"Six! That leaves—" He sighed, angrily. "Who?"

Trudeau evaded the question. "They would like their wages. It is the end of the month, yes?"

"They're gonna break their agreement and want wages too?"

Trudeau nodded, looking miserable.

"They think we're doomed, eh? Quitting? Well, we might be whipped this year but what about the next? And how's

Jamie Dance doing down south? I need them here. I got a post to build."

"They say you can't feed them now."

"I've got casks of spirits in there, and three hundred osage orange sticks for bows. Do they think those won't trade for ponies—lots of ponies of all sorts? Or buffalo meat?"

"But you have to get to the villages—"

"That's right, we do. And I was going to send runners to bring them in as soon as we had a chinook or a break in this." He waved at the heavy sky.

"Some of us want to stay, Monsieur Fitzhugh."

"Who?"

"To stay with you? Myself. I am a faithful man. Larue. Provost. Dauphin."

"Good men." But one of the departing was Gallard, the one they'd suspected of ditching the Witney blankets; the one the engagés themselves didn't trust. "Gallard going?" he asked.

"Especially Gallard. He was itching to go."

"What do you think about him?"

"I have no thoughts about Emile Gallard."

"I think you do. Bring them in when it gets dark. I want my chance to say my piece."

When early dusk sawed off the day's toil the men gathered uneasily before the great fire in the barracks while Fitzhugh watched angrily. They avoided his glare.

"You contracted for a year," he accused, harshly. "You're deserting when I need you most."

Some of them peered back sullenly. He knew he had no control over them. They had only to walk out the door and trudge four miles to escape him.

"I can't stop you from going. But things won't go easy for you. Julius Hervey's toying with you. He wants to break me down, make me abandon this post. Do you think American Fur'll employ engagés who break their contracts? No.

He'll welcome you with that little mocking grin, and put you to work and pay you a wage—until the day we fold up here. And then he'll discharge you and tell you American Fur doesn't employ engagés who bust an agreement."

"You can't feed us, monsieur." It was Brasseau. "No horse. No rifle, eh?"

That made sense to them, he knew. "See that?" He jabbed his finger at the casks. "You think that won't trade for more ponies we can ever use? I figgered to send you out to the villages to drum up some trade, soon as the weather lets up."

"Always, the desperation, Monsieur Fitzhugh." Brasseau had somehow made himself into a spokesman for the rest, and oddly, Brokenleg honored him for it. It took courage to get crosswise of the *bourgeois.*

"Brasseau," he said gently. "Hervey won't keep you. Oh, you'll git your pieces back, maybe. You walk into Cass and he'll give 'em to you. And that'll feel good. A man feels naked here without a firearm. Plumb naked. But he don't need you none. He's got all the men he needs right there, and a bunch of winter loafers to help out too. He don't need none of you."

"We'd like our wages," Brasseau said, determinedly.

"You're busting your agreement and want wages! I ought to just pitch you out."

"Sacre bleu! We have work hard."

Fitzhugh felt cornered. It wouldn't do to mistreat them, not if he hoped to get enough back to keep his post open. Men were plumb scarce. And they'd worked; God knows, they'd worked themselves down to nothing. "All right. Usually we'd keep accounts and settle at the end of the season, wages on one hand, purchases in the trading room on the other. I'll have to give you drafts payable in St. Louis on Dance, Fitzhugh and Straus. Hervey'll honor them. So will Culbertson. If they don't double their prices on you."

He'd lost them, he knew that. Angrily he dug into his

possibles for the nib and some foolscap. Silently, Maxim handed him some ink in a little flask. Seven months wages. Times twelve dollars. Minus—what? He couldn't remember what had been supplied them from stores. He began scratching angrily, eighty-four dollars for Gallard, eighty-four for Lemaitre, for Brasseau, for Bercier, for the rest . . . He signed them all. The signature was a valid assessment on company funds.

They took their chits with averted eyes.

"Now go ahead," he snapped.

They gathered their outfits and edged out silently into a black night, while the rest watched, mute. One of the post's remaining rifles went with them. Maxim looked stricken. A hush settled in the room, save for the snap of cottonwood logs in the fireplace.

"Happy new year," Fitzhugh said dourly. "There's a gill for any that want it."

But no one moved. They peered uneasily at each other: Fitzhugh, Maxim Straus, Samson Trudeau, Gaspard Larue, Jannot Provost, Corneille Dauphin, each lost in his own world.

Until the odd, shuffling noises of an army outside alarmed them.

In the occasional light, she saw that Fitzhugh had completed his post more or less. It looked like one of the buildings she'd seen in St. Louis, but cruder. Heavy shutters sealed the small windows, but here and there light seeped from them anyway. The northwind whipped sour cottonwood smoke from the two chimneys down upon them as they gathered silently before this surprising post raised up on the bank of the Bighorn.

She felt an odd joy in her return, and an eagerness to nestle in the circle of his strong arms, even if he was a whiteman and not worth her caring. She had been virtually a prisoner of White Wolf this long trip, the only woman among thirty warriors. They had prepared carefully for several days, because the Cold Maker roared and the journey from Crazy Woman Creek would be long and difficult. But her marriage to Fitzhugh, it seemed, had become a matter of tribal well-being, and they had taken her choices from her. Nothing like that had ever happened, and they all knew how unusual it was. She had a duty. They'd brought twenty ponies to trade, and burdening these were many robes prepared by the women over the two winters her village had not come to a whiteman's post. Many more fine robes remained in her village, too.

The front door creaked open a sliver, spilling yellow light across the snow. Someone peered out cautiously. Then the door swung open like sunrise, and she saw Fitzhugh peering out at them, his great red beard and long red hair glowing orange in the doorframe.

"Dust Devil?" he said, spotting her in her red capote, on her brother's buckskin pony. "I reckon you brought your people."

"I have come," she said.

He motioned them all in to the bright room within, but White Wolf intervened, posting two of the younger Cheyenne boys to herd the fifty-one horses gathered there, and keep watch. The rest of her people slid stiffly off ponies, gathered their blankets or robes, and entered. The tribesmen seemed to fill the whole barracks, crowding around the fire while Maxim and the four engagés stared uneasily. She wondered where the others had gone. Could they have left him? The acrid odors of smoke-cured skins and wet wool filled the barracks.

Fitzhugh did not touch her and she did not rush to him. But she had become intensely aware of him, as his eyes raked her and met her own at last, sending a small shock of pleasure through her. Whatever she and her man felt, they would not express it before all of these. The swelling of anticipation surprised her. Oh! Her man! Her Brokenleg! How commanding he looked, here in a post he'd built! He scowled at her but she didn't mind. Later he would clamp her ruthlessly, his loving wild and joyous, like a sky-mating of eagles.

It took her people no time at all to discover that nothing burdened the shelves of the trading room, and no robes had accumulated in the warehouse room behind it, and that whatever this post possessed lay heaped along the barracks wall. They eyed the bundles of sticks with some curiosity, and the wooden casks as well, but said nothing. Gradually her people settled themselves on their blankets and robes around the fire, unable to say much to the engagés already there. She sat just behind the circle of men, feeling the chill of a cold stone wall at her back. These whiteman buildings lacked the comfort of a lodge, she thought.

Her man knew the way of the People, and welcomed them with a twist of tobacco. White Wolf solemnly tamped it into the sacred pipe he'd extracted from its pouch of unborn buffalo hide, and every Cheyenne present smoked it, along with Fitzhugh and the fur company employees. Fitzhugh welcomed them leisurely, in his broken Cheyenne. They would begin trading soon, he said. Even now, he had something that might interest them, the orange wood of the Osage People, the wood the French called *bois d'arc,* the wood that made powerful bows that shot arrows farther than any bow made of the woods here. He had three hundred of these, all perfect, cut in the summer and now well dried. Her Tsistsista people listened intently. This talk was of power in war, of arrows finding their mark while enemy arrows fell short, of power in hunting, too.

White Wolf, who wore his black hair in two braids caught in otterskin sheaths, listened politely. When Fitzhugh had finished his welcome, the chief stood and waited solemnly for the attention of the rest.

Little Whirlwind knew she would translate for Maxim

and the others, but Fitzhugh knew enough of the tongue of the People.

"Our friend Bad Leg Whiteman comes back to us as a trader, and we welcome him," White Wolf began. "He builds a post where the Absaroka are, but we understand that: he needs the rivers nearby to take our robes away and bring his tradegoods to us."

Dust Devil translated to English quietly. The engagés would understand.

"Our own Little Whirlwind returns to us with the bad news that the Absaroka have stolen your horses and killed your whitemen's buffalo that pull the wagons. And worse, that the ones who occupy Fort Cass keep your trading goods from you, and maybe trade them to our enemies. We cannot permit this. At last we have a place to trade. Fort William is far away. Fort Union is far away. Fort Cass is closer but the Absaroka are everywhere around it. But now, Fitzhugh, we have a trading post."

She wondered if Brokenleg would object and tell him that the post would trade with all tribes, not just Cheyenne. He'd told her that often enough, and it pained her. But he only nodded, his blue eyes bright.

"We have come a long way, from our village on Crazy Woman Creek, with ponies to trade, and robes. These ponies are ones that have drawn the travois, and they will pull wagons. They are good ponies. And we have others that are only for riders, good fleet ones. You will see them when Sun comes back, and we will trade. You have the orange wood of the bow, and my warriors will want many and we will be a stronger village if we have them, and many guns. We'll take more scalps, especially Absaroka and Assiniboin. We will trade a pony for twenty sticks; maybe a small pony for fifteen. And a robe for ten sticks. Maybe eight for a summer robe, or a split. I see many orange sticks; enough for a bow for every warrior in our village."

She knew he'd object to that strenuously, but he said

nothing, just nodding his head and licking his lips with his pink tongue. Maxim's face darkened, and she knew he was containing his thoughts. He wanted the osage orange to bring the company a robe for one stick, and not be squandered on horses.

"I reckon we got a little fire-in-in-the-throat to trade, if ye be lookin' for it," Fitzhugh said. "The usual—cup a robe."

"I do not think the fire-water is good, but that is up to my warriors. The ponies and the robes are theirs. I will trade my own ponies and robes for the bow wood, not the water that makes men crazy."

"That's all I got—the bow wood and some spirits. The rest I got stored at Cass. It'll be a while, anyway."

"In truth, Bad Leg Whiteman, you can't get your trading things."

"Not for a while. I need to talk with Culbertson up at Fort Union. Hervey isn't keeping his agreement with me."

"You have only these men? Little Whirlwind said you had as many as the fingers are."

"They quit me. Just now, before you come in. At Cass by now, I reckon. I think maybe they'll come back. It's just vittles they wanted. With some ponies and our goods—we got rifles up there, including mine—we'll hunt the buffler and be in business."

White Wolf considered, silently. "We are many," he said. "We will think about these things."

That ended the night's parleying. In the morning, they'd get down to some trading. Around her, the Tsistsistas and the engagés alike expected her to start cooking a feast, but she scorned them. Let them hack the frozen haunch apart and roast it. She'd be no slave to any whiteman, anyway. She discovered Maxim peering at her shyly, the way a boy does when he spies a beautiful woman, and it pleased her. "Cook the meat," she said imperiously, lording over him with her new power, and watched him turn to do it, a haunted look in his face. For the first time, the white boy had seen her as a man sees a woman.

Fitzhugh caught her by the arm and drew her into the empty warehouse behind the trading room, almost black with night.

"You brought them here," he said. "Is that why you run off?"

"No. They brought me. I was leaving you."

"Whiteskin ain't good enough for a little Suhtai Miss," he muttered.

"I longed to be with my people."

"That's about right."

"But I missed you, Fitzhugh. When I got to my people, I wanted you with me. I wanted you there, trading with them, a great man among them."

"I was getting to it. Going to wagon down there with an outfit, and trade. But you ditched me."

"White Wolf says our marriage is important to the People."

"What marriage. You took off. I think, once you git, you git. You better figger on goin' back with them."

"You don't want me any more."

"Want you! I wanted you too bad to say it. But I was never good enough. Your pa married you off when you were makin' eyes at two, three Suhtai boys, seems like, and you never did like it none, and I never stopped hearin' about it."

"Twice I heard the love flute before you came."

She wanted him to touch her, but he didn't. He stood well apart in the cold dark. She stepped toward him, filled with a sudden yearning, but he didn't move. She stepped again, so close she could feel his presence looming above her, feel the warmth of his body.

"You run out on me once and now you want to fix it, and it isn't fixed," he muttered.

She heard a coldness in him, running deep, from down

in his belly, and beyond the repair of an embrace. She stood close, with a frozen ocean between them.

"I am not wanted." An unexpected sadness grew in her.

"You git it turned upside down. You never wanted me."

"It is true and not true."

"I don't cotton to talk like that. You never wanted me. You had your big eyes peerin' at one o' the other Suhtai. And you never let me forgit it after your pa made the marriage."

"I am not one person inside. I have lost my medicine, in spite of what they tell me. What I said is true: I didn't want you, but I did, and I loved you, Brokenleg."

"You quit me when things was lookin' bad. When it got cold and we had no place, no horses, nothing. Like leavin' a man when he's goin' under. Well, things weren't so bad hyar. Chatillon, he's an express up from Saint Louie, he brings mules and bow wood, and we got back on our feet, at least until a few days ago. But you weren't around to help. I'm going to pry my outfit outa Cass. The first time Hervey steps outa Cass, I'm going to nail him and git what's mine. He can't hide in there forever. And I'll do some good tradin' with lots of tribes, but you won't have the pleasure of it or me because you're goin' back to your precious people. You aren't my wife any more."

Those words shot an unexpected pain through her. She stared, numbly, absorbing it. The pain welling through her astonished her. Divorced, then. She did not know what to do. Had she cared about him much more than she supposed? Slowly she grasped that she wouldn't see him again, or lie in his arms, or receive his abundant gifts, or share his laughter, or present him proudly to her people. Put away by the white trader! And she a Suhtai! It'd be a scandal, a shame, in her village. A strange, unaccustomed sadness filled her.

"That is what you wish?" she asked, hiding her sorrow.

For an answer he swung loose and stalked back into the heated portion of the post, leaving her utterly alone. She stood paralyzed in the unfriendly dark, unable to think. Then she remembered crow-bird, and turned inward to the landscape of her heart, and her people's heart.

"I am put aside by the whiteman," she said to crow-bird, but nothing formed in her mind. She waited for her medicine-helper, but crow-bird didn't come. The coldness of the dark room bit at her. Alone. Tears welled and slid down her cheeks. She loved him wildly, and hadn't even known it until now, too late. He would never touch her again. She'd never feel his iron-hard arms holding her gently, or feel the scrape of his wavy beard on her cheek. She wept quietly, still surprised at what she'd discovered in herself. She wept until she couldn't, and then dried her tears.

She walked resolutely into the warm trading room, where her Tsistsista brothers, including her older brother Waiting Dog, were spreading their robes and blankets for the night. She continued on to the barracks where the engagés and Fitzhugh were slipping into their wooden bunks, and White Wolf as well. She found her scarlet capote and gloves, and her small sack of medicine things, and slid out the door into the dead night. She paused in the quiet, until her eyes focused on the picketed horses. She saw no guard. And she would need her horse. The cold numbed her. Beyond the darkness she saw a night-mirage, her own village glowing on the black horizon, beckoning her to follow up the river, but her heart failed her at the thought of another long winter journey, and she walked downriver, toward the Yellowstsone, unable to explain her conduct to herself.

Chapter Twenty-seven

The massive gates of Fort Cass loomed above her like a giant deadfall, ready to crush her with the slightest knock. In the faint light she made out several Absaroka lodges nearby, wisps of smoke from wood-starved fires drifting from their gathered lodges.

She would not be welcome in them. She had no welcome anywhere, except maybe here. She had been Fitzhugh's wife, the woman of a great trader with a St. Louis company. She had been a Suhtai, proud people of the Cheyenne nation. But her people had not welcomed her either, and brought her back to Fitzhugh. Always, she'd measured her worth by association: she'd been the daughter and granddaughter of great medicine men, and of the clan of medicine-givers. She'd been the wife of an important white trapper and trader. Nothing remained within her but hollowness, and that filled with the cold of the night. She knew she had no name. No longer was she Little Whirlwind to her people, or Dust Devil to Fitzhugh. No longer did she possess medicine. She had become a no-spirit person, worse than the dead and doomed forever. Even now, as she stared at this wall of wood, she could not account for her behavior. No one ruled within.

The night-cold had penetrated clear through her capote and her woolen blouse and doeskin shirts, numbing her limbs and hurting her face. Her lungs ached from breathing air so cold. She yearned for warmth, for Fitzhugh's warmth beside her under the robes, but he had sent her away. This air seemed colder than any, even though she hadn't walked for long. Nothing she wore kept it from stinging and hurting her whole body, even her breasts and her belly. She thought wildly of running from this palisade of silvery cottonwood logs, back, back to Fitzhugh's Post. Ask him to keep her. Do anything. Say anything. Be a slave if not a wife. But she wouldn't. She had seen the look in his eyes.

She knocked hard, but the coldness ate up the noise of her pounding and made a whisper of it. She feared suddenly that no one would hear and come. She hammered again, bruising the bottom of her fist, but the sound magically vanished. No one would hear. She hunted for a stick to pound with, but miraculously someone on the other side of the great wall of planks lifted a bar, and the door squealed open on iced metal. A bearded whiteman she'd never seen before peered out at her, his eye sweeping from her winter moccasins upward along the dim-lit scarlet capote, to its hood.

"Oui? Yes?"

"I want to come in," she said in English.

"We are shut now. Tomorrow," the man replied also in English.

"I am cold."

He said nothing, staring at her. Then, "Who be you?"

"Little Whirlwind of the Tsistsistas—Cheyenne."

"Alone," he said. It wasn't a question.

"Are you going to let me in?"

"Don't know what I'd do with ye. You come vistin' at funny times. You sure you got some business heah?"

"I will go," she said, turning away. Behind her the door creaked, and a massive hand caught her capote, halting her abruptly.

"Dust Devil," a voice said, and she knew the *bourgeois,* Julius Hervey, had caught her. She knew she'd made a terrible mistake coming here, and struggled to free herself, but he laughed and hauled her around. He wore only a blanket, she thought, and his white calves and feet were bare, even in the bitter cold. "Madam Stiffleg," he mocked. Then he dragged her into the fort, a force beyond resisting, and she tripped after him, a prisoner.

Behind her she heard the gate squeak shut and the clank of an iron bar. He tumbled her through a dark door into a heated room, faintly lit by a mass of orange coals in a fireplace. And then he lit a taper, and she saw him grinning widely behind his beard. A giant. She'd never been so close to him, and realized he stood taller than Fitzhugh, two or three heads taller than herself. His blanket turned out to be a poncho, and it became plain from white flesh bared by the open sides that he wore nothing else.

He eyed her wildly, possessing her with a gaze she couldn't return.

She had pushed the thought of this aside all the way over here, but suddenly she could not put it aside. She drew herself up disdainfully. "I have seen what is in your eyes. I will be your woman if you want."

He smirked. "It took you long enough. You've ditched poor old Stiffleg. He's got nothing but woes and a few gallons of spirits and some sticks. Hardly even a man in the place. Nothing for a fancy little filly like you. You've come to enjoy a man for a change."

She didn't like him much, and shrugged.

"I knew I'd lure you in, sooner or later. That Fitzhugh—he's a case." His eyes studied her, his gaze sliding over her face, her blue-black hair, the capote that hid her figure. It bore into the capote where her breasts pressed it, and then her slender thighs. Something feral and dangerous formed around his mouth, building into a smile that seemed cruel.

"Fitzhugh picked a beauty. And lost it."

She waited for him to come to her, but he seemed to be enjoying something that lay in his own thoughts. "You're a bonus. I mean, coming here before I destroyed him . . . This'll just make it easier. He'll be crazy."

She didn't follow all that. "If you don't want me I will go," she said, too weary to care.

She turned to leave, but he caught her again, pinned her easily with arms the size of buffalo hocks. "I got the rest of Fitzhugh's stuff; might as well have his woman too." His voice had turned thick and urgent.

"I'm not his woman. He put me away."

Hervey released her. "Booted you out?"

"I am not Fitzhugh's woman now. I am nobody."

He laughed suddenly, a hard, raucous laugh with no humor in it. "Stiffleg finally got me. He finally got me."

"What do you mean?"

"Stole all the fun of taking it from him—go away. I'm tired."

She undid her capote, instead, letting the radiance from the coals warm her frozen flesh.

"I don't want Fitzhugh's discards. Get your dusky little carcass out of here. Have your fun in the barracks. I'm going to bed."

She stood, paralyzed and empty. Was Fitzhugh's rival humbling her, too?

He was: he bounded at her like a lion, and catapulted her through his door into the snowy yard, where she tumbled into glazed whiteness. Cold smacked her. Above, the door banged shut.

Across the yard, the barracks hulked dark and sinister. It would be warm but she would not go there to be used by many whitemen. She did not know where to go or where she could sleep. She edged fearfully toward the trading room door, and found it unlocked. A faint heat reached her in the blackness, and when her eyes accustomed themselves to the gloom, she discovered the glowing remains of a fire in the wide fireplace. She located a log and laid it on the coals, blowing softly until a small blue flame licked the wood.

The room felt icy, but it would warm. And stacked neatly

on shelves were Witney blankets, dozens of them. She liked the smell of the room, with its wools and leathers and iron and cloth, like some incense in her nostrils. She spread several on the puncheon floor, and made a warm nest of them. Slowly they warmed her shivering body, but not anything else.

The door burst open, and a gust of icy air swept the floor. She discovered Hervey there, a mirthless mock in his face. He closed the door behind him and approached, while she peered up fearfully. He wore nothing but the thin blanket.

"I changed my mind. Anything that was Fitzhugh's, I'll use.

She felt cold. "I've changed my mind also," she said. "You didn't want me. You wanted Fitzhugh's woman."

He grinned, and approached, until he loomed above her, an evil giant in the flickering yellow light.

"I will leave here now," she said. "I will go into the night. I do not want this."

He ripped the blankets from her and peered down, while she withered under his bright gaze. He sank to his knees and yanked her skirts upward. She whirled to the side, kicking him as she did, but his powerful hand clamped her, yanked her back. He was grinning.

"My people don't—"

His massive hand clubbed her, jamming her teeth into her tongue. She felt salty blood. She bit his wrist. He yanked it bank and clobbered her again, making her ears ring.

"Feisty little savage," he said serenely, his burly arms plowing her legs open.

"I am Suhtai," she whispered, unbidden tears welling in her eyes. "Daughter of medicine—"

She gasped.

It didn't take long, and then he lifted himself to his feet, the mirthless amusement still in his face. "I thought you'd be a dust devil," he said, and left.

She had no name. It had never been Dust Devil, but once was Little Whirlwind. And once she'd been a Suhtai. She pulled the blankets over her again, and settled into them, only to have the door burst open. Another bearded man stood there, one she knew well. And when she saw him, she remembered that some had left Fitzhugh, abandoning him when he needed them most. Like herself. Emile Gallard peered at her, his brown eyes alive with amusement. By now she didn't bother to smooth her doeskin skirts or hide the stickiness of her loins.

"Madam Fitzhugh," he said. "Your man likes to share his wealth, *n'est-ce pas?"*

"I have no name," she cried hoarsely.

He turned out to be the last. She curled up in her blankets, letting her tears flow, knowing what she must do. It would take strength. She took hold of herself, and stopped the tremors wracking her body. She mopped her face and dried her tears. She let the quiet of the night catch her up in it. Then she cast the blankets aside and sat cross legged, facing away from the embers in the fireplace, and staring into the darkness. There she sang, her voice low and mournful, her mind focused sharply on Sweet Medicine. She crooned the song of her life, sang the song of her girlhood, and her marriage to Fitzhugh, and the end of the marriage.

She folded her red capote and set it aside. Piece by piece, she undid her disheveled clothing, the woolen blouse, the doeskin skirts, her rabbit-topped moccasins, until she had rid herself of everything. She stood, stared into the dying embers, and gathered her courage. The she opened the door, feeling the shock of air chill her, and walked naked over glazed snow to the great gates. She didn't know how to work the latch, but it turned out to be nothing: lift an iron bar and slide the bolt sideways. Fearfully, lest noise betray her, she pulled the creaking gate open until she could slide through, into the night. Across the starlit flat she saw the naked arms of a cottonwood praying starkly to the night-spirits. She walked there, feeling the icy air cleanse her, like sand scouring her skin when she bathed in a river. At the foot of the cottonwood she settled quietly into the snow, feeling it torture her buttocks, and waited.

The cold eye of self-reproach kept Fitzhugh awake and tossing in his blankets. He hadn't intended to put her away. His ungovernable temper had bested him. His red-haired temper, if there was any truth to it. Not that she hadn't provoked him, he thought fiercely. She and her arrogant ways, lording over him, scorning him, undermining his purposes. And not just him, either: she'd been haughty toward everyone, like some duchess.

But he'd always accepted that, and it'd even been a joke between them sometimes. He'd catch her at it, and bellyache, and she'd pout, and they'd laugh like children, and he'd hug her, feeling his world turn incandescent with the strange joy she kindled in him. He hadn't meant to say those fatal words, even though they'd boiled and bubbled in him all the while she was gone, just waiting to erupt when she returned.

He had some notion she'd slid out into the night, but he wasn't sure of it. He'd unrolled his blankets in the barracks, and looked after his Cheyenne guests spreading out in the trading room, and then crawled into his hard bunk. She'd be somewhere. She'd go on back to her village with White Wolf and find her some suitable man. No doubt Suhtai, since she wouldn't marry beneath her again. The idea left him sour and unhappy. He'd come to—what? He'd come to love the slim little devil, in spite of her endless taunting. Sometimes, some nights, they'd laughed and played and caressed, and whispered, and carried on. Sometimes, after a hard day, they'd clung together desperately, as if they'd be torn asunder the next moment by some war hatchet or iron-tipped lance, while she muttered and crooned in her own tongue, so quiet and blurred on the ears he had no notion of what was issuing from her. He might as well be hitched up to a Chinee, or a hottentot, or a Peruvian, for all he understood of her.

He cussed his tensions that robbed him of a rest, and swung out of the bunk, onto his stiff leg. The fire had died to embers, so he slid a long log onto it, taking care not to awaken the rest. Not that many slept in the barracks, now. Just Maxim, Trudeau, Provost, Dauphin, and Larue. Plus Chief White Wolf and a stout headman whose name he hadn't caught. She'd be over in the other room, then. Probably in some corner near her brother. Or maybe out in the warehouse. He eased toward the trading room and found it well lit by the wavering fire in its fireplace. Several of the Cheyenne peered back at him from their robes, wide awake. He studied the forms one by one, looking for the red capote, the braided hair, the familiar form, and saw only slumbering males. Two of them he wasn't sure about, so he edged closer until he knew, and then left, feeling eyes on his back. He tried the cold warehouse where they'd spat at each other, and then he knew. She'd left.

He limped back to his bunk and eased himself down on it, wondering what to do. He'd said the fatal words and he couldn't retract them. He'd put her out, the way a lot of squawmen had put away a lot of dusky brides. She didn't have many choices, though: not with White Wolf dragging her back here and telling her to stay hitched to the trader for the sake of the People. Sighing, he found his heavy woolen shirt in his kit and slid it on, and laced his boots, and clawed into his cold elkskin coat. He clamped a stocking cap over his balding head and then limped out into the night, which smacked him with its granite cold. He sucked in a breath, feeling the air stab at his lungs, and then trod past the picketlines of ponies toward the Pittsburgh wagons, on the off chance that the crazy woman might be huddled in one. She wasn't.

Cass then. Cass or a deadly walk south to another Cheyenne village. He studied the Dipper, spilling down from the North Star, and knew dawn wasn't far ahead. The thought of her walking into Cass, and curling up with Julius Hervey, curdled in him, until he couldn't stand to think it. But he knew he'd done it to himself, pulled the temple down on him like an angry Samson. He started that direction, hearing the snow squeak under his heavy boots, wishing he could hasten his foot-dragging pace. He'd bygod bang on that gate until they let him in.

He didn't know what he'd say to her, especially if she'd found a welcome in Julius Hervey's bed. Which she would. He had taunted Fitzhugh with it; told him he'd have her, too. Hervey didn't care for her any more than he cared for a hundred other squaws he'd bedded. But he wanted her for darker reasons, and Fitzhugh understood them perfectly. He pleasured himself with theft, and absolute power. For years, Hervey had stolen the wives of his engagés and dared them to do anything about it. The few who tried had vanished from the earth.

Tell her he didn't mean it? Tell her he wanted to reel his words back in? Tell her—tell her he'd been angry. He didn't know. He'd eat crow aplenty, he knew that. He wasn't even sure he wanted her back, the haughty little Suhtai lady who'd been born too high and mighty for a trapper or a trader. But he wanted her back, worse even than he wanted to settle accounts with Hervey. He'd beg. He'd beg like a dog if he had to.

A gibbous moon lit his way across a snowy waste, its cold light mocking the heat of his passions. He scarcely noticed the cold, but knew it could murder life swiftly. The ghostly palisades of Fort Cass startled him. Smoke drifted from several Crow lodges to the west, and from the several chimneys of the darkened post. Knock on the gates. Knock one down. Kick that gate into firewood.

He stumbled toward the post, clearing the last cottonwood—which exploded. Above him, the hard flap of wings. A roosting tree. Black crows thrummed into the stygian night, invisible to him except for the faintest glint of moonlight on ebony. He gaped, recovering his wits, his heart pounding at the commotion of the dead. That's when he saw the small body between the great roots of the tree, its dusky nakedness almost invisible in the decocted light. Her. He knew that, even before his eyes fully grasped the form of her. He vaulted toward her, crashing over his bad leg and down upon her. She lay deathly quiet. Too late.

"Dust Devil!" he cried. She didn't move. He slapped her hard across the face. Her head flopped. He pulled off his glove and felt her flesh. It felt dead, icy, clammy. "Dust Devil," he cried, lifting her cold limp body to him, feeling the death in her. He slapped again, a slap that would sting breath into her. She didn't recoil. His hand smacked clammy flesh.

"Dust Devil!" He fumbled the bone buttons loose on his coat, wrestled it off, and wrapped her in it, feeling her flop and sag as he tugged it around her and pinioned her in it with his arms.

Dead. But the stiffness hadn't taken yet. He lurched to his feet, feeling his bad leg howl, lifting her in his arms, and staring at the gray ghost of the fort before him. Go there? Go to the Crow lodges a quarter of a mile farther? He lumbered toward the gate, his leg skidding under him, capsizing him and threatening his limp burden. He'd hammer that gate down, he'd kick it in.

She flopped in his arms, a corpse, and he raced harder, catapulting crazily off his stiff leg and staggering forward on his good one. He reached the gate, and balled a fist—

Open. Ajar. He understood. She'd left it that way. He slid into the yard, peering sharply at the moonsplashed buildings, the engagés' barracks at the far right, the quarters of the *bourgeois* at the far left, the nearer warehouses and storage rooms imprisoning his own outfit.

He turned left, toward the trading room, and shoved the door open. A wall of heat met him. A long log fed a wavering yellow flame in the fireplace, making the room bob and dance. Heat. He carried his inert burden tenderly to the fireplace, and found fire-warmed blankets heaped there, and laid her gently on them.

He rubbed her limp legs and arms, feeling the terrible cold in the lifeless flesh. He pressed her belly just below the soft vee of her breastbone, feeling the cold skin yield beneath his frightened hand.

"Why'd you do this, Dust Devil?" he muttered, knowing why, and feeling the noose of accusation around his own stiff neck. He rubbed her hopelessly, rubbed and manipulated, and despaired, feeling only the cold nakedness under his rough hands. She lay as inert as when he'd discovered her, her small breasts taut and cold, her slender torso heatless.

"Aw, godalmighty, Dust Devil," he cried, a sob building in him. "I did it to you, I did it to you."

Her mouth sagged open. He stared at it, seeing the seizure of a corpse. He lifted himself painfully and lumbered across the trading room, past tables loaded with gewgaws, trays of beads, boxes of awls and knives, hunting for a thing that all trading posts offered, because the tribesmen loved them. He found the looking glasses they treasured, the little mirrors that let them see their beauty, their lordly manner, without having to peer into a quiet pond to know themselves.

He snatched an oblong glass with a wooden handle, and bounded back toward Dust Devil. He saw her clothes, then: her scarlet capote folded neatly, her doeskin skirt, her woolen blouse, her moccasins in a heap. Right there. He held the mirror close to her slack mouth, hovering just off her lips, and waited, and then pulled it away.

A faint fog was rapidly disappearing.

He held it to her mouth again, and snatched it into the firelight. A new mist lay upon it.

"Dust Devil!" he cried, and fell over her, choking on the fire in his throat.

Chapter Twenty-eight

He could only wait. She lay inert before the fire, some faltering thread of life sustaining her. He held the mirror to her open mouth again and again, and each time he found vapor misting it, though he could detect no heartbeat and no rhythm of her lungs. An illusion, he thought; she's dead. The mists on the glass meant nothing.

He lifted himself awkwardly and dropped another log—the last in the woodbox—into the fire. Heat; more heat. Then he eased down to the puncheons again, damning his leg, rubbing her with his hard hands to force sensation into her. But she lay stupefied, in a place beyond his knowing.

"I don't reckon you can hear me, Dust Devil. But I got to talk! You listen now. You hear me, wherever you are!"

Nothing changed. A cold gray tinctured the apricot of her flesh.

"Bad mistake. I got all het up and put you out, and then I knew I'd done it, done the worst. I got a temper I can't hardly bridle and bit. You got to live, Dust Devil. I want you. Don't you give up, don't you quit on me! You're a strong woman, a Suhtai Cheyenne woman, and don't you forgit it! Hyar now, you got a porkeater pilgrim for a man, you got a greenhorn and a drunken fool, but you got a whiteman that loves you anyway. Godalmighty, Dust Devil . . ."

Nothing changed. He held the mirror to her mouth and mist didn't form, and he knew he'd lost her. But the blaze had heated the mirror. He tried it at her nostrils, and caught a mist again, swiftly vanishing in the radiant warmth.

"I'm taking you home, Dust Devil; home to the post!" His voice cracked. "I reined you in too much; I should have given you your head. All you did was visit your people."

The door swung open behind him, and he heard someone at the threshold, taking him in. Fitzhugh glanced that way, and saw an engagé, and beyond, a ghostly gray light rubbing shape into the world beyond. He grew aware of her nakedness, her taut bared breasts, and he pulled a white blanket over her up to her neck and snugged it down around her gently, making woolen sanctuary for her altar. She did not respond. Would she linger like this? False hope and nothing more?

Behind him the engagé left, but soon more came, opening and closing the door, sending gusts of air boiling along the floor. He ignored them, and drew a second blanket over her. The blanket smelled of things he didn't want to think about.

"Stiffleg!"

He turned and found Julius Hervey above him, a pepperbox pistol lost in his massive hand, and aiming at him.

"Is she alive?"

"Yes."

"I enjoyed her."

"She didn't enjoy you."

"Too bad you put her away. It spoiled my fun."

"That's how you see a woman."

"Property, Stiffleg. I like property."

Fitzhugh clamped down his rising bile. "I'll take her back when I can."

"Take her back? Ah, Fitzhugh, you are as slow as ever. It's all in my hands. She's mine; your outfit's mine. You're mine."

Fitzhugh braced himself against the goading, and found Dust Devil's clammy hand under the blanket.

"The slut won't live. Won't sing songs. You don't want a slut anyway, Stiffleg. She came to me, you know."

Fitzhugh knew.

Hervey turned to his engagés. "Take her outside and leave her." They stared at him. "Now." He swung his pepperbox toward them, a vast amusement illumining his face.

Fitzhugh clambered to his feet, helping himself up with a grip on a table. He had nothing to kill with, except his hands.

"Take him out, too. And shut the gates. And don't give him his coat." He glanced at Fitzhugh. "I might just shoot you. I'm debating it. A thief in our trading room. Busted right in, the Opposition and his lady."

He swung the pepperbox toward Fitzhugh, the madness building in his eyes, a mock Fitzhugh had seen before once or twice, and understood for what it was.

No one moved.

"Why doesn't anyone obey this morning? It must be something about eighteen-forty-two. Something new in forty-two." He beamed. "Well, I'll do it myself."

Hervey swung the pistol downward toward Dust Devil, aimed at her chest, and shot, the explosion deafening. Just as Fitzhugh slammed into him. The ball struck the puncheon, shattered, sprayed lead fragments, and stirred the fire. Dust Devil winced and groaned.

Hervey laughed, delighted, and righted himself as Fitzhugh topped on his bad leg. Fitzhugh landed like a poleaxed ox, and Hervey booted him with heavy square-toed hightops. The blow landed on his bad leg, right at his injured knee, and Fitzhugh felt screaming hurt sail through him, clear into his throat. He rolled just as another shot shattered the air, and felt something pluck at his shirt.

Above him, someone landed on Hervey from behind, like a monkey riding a bear. Lemaitre. And someone pulled Lemaitre off of Hervey. Gallard. Through it all, Hervey laughed and chortled, demonic pleasure lacerating the trading room. They tumbled into a table loaded with gewgaws. Yellow ribbons sprayed outward, and blue trade beads rolled, and a box of awls clattered, along with trays of butcher knives, a silvery cascade clattering over Fitzhugh. He grabbed one and crawled, but flying boots clobbered his ribs, and above him, Hervey roared. A pistol cocked. Fitzhugh rolled into Hervey's legs and sliced.

The pepperbox pistol exploded so close Fitzhugh's ears rang. Blood gouted from Hervey's leg, just at boot-top. Another table toppled, spraying bolts of red and green tradecloth outward, unrolling as they bounced. A blue bolt bounced over Dust-Devil, trailing cloth like a comet, and landed in the fire. The wool caught, pumping acrid smoke into the room, while flame rode down the bolt toward Dust Devil.

Brokenleg's leg tortured him. He peered upward. A melee. His own former engagés fought the others—except for Gallard, who wrestled against his old colleagues. Julius Hervey grabbed a rifle and swung it, its heavy stock scything through the brawlers. He lifted it and bashed Lemaitre in the head, caving in the skull. The engagé crumpled to the floor. Hervey swung around to murder Fitzhugh, but Guerette caught the weapon and yanked it, drawing Hervey off balance. Fitzhugh couldn't stand, couldn't find a purchase to put his bad leg under him, so he crawled where he could, doing what damage he could. Then Hervey toppled over him, thrashing among the tables, clawing away beads and ribbons and combs, laughing crazily.

"Stiffleg!" he whispered, swinging those massive hands toward Fitzhugh's throat from behind.

Fitzhugh felt them on his windpipe, clamp him, crush cartilage, squeeze life out of him. He thrashed under the frightful force, and felt his throat collapsing under the sheer pressure of those thick fingers. He clawed wildly, felt his lungs suck at nothing and knew his eyes were not seeing. With his last strength he sawed at the fingers with his butcher knife, sawed through the back of the hand, down to bone; slashed at the other hand clamping him, knowing a slip would cut his own throat but sawing anyway through tendon and muscle while hot blood splattered over his neck and chest. Hervey shrieked and the useless hands surrendered. Fitzhugh gasped, sucking fiery air into fluttering lungs. Hervey lay beside him, howling, the unearthly sound filling the trading room with pain.

The ghastly howl halted the rest. They stared, stunned, at the giant trader whose half-severed fingers gouted crimson blood into the floor, soaking bolts of cloth with it. Fitzhugh sat up, glaring wildly, daring anyone to do anything, wheezing through the ruins of his windpipe. The fire smoldering in the blue bolt had reached Dust Devil, making her twist and groan. He reached across the floor and batted it away. The room stank of burning wool.

Lemaitre lay dead, his mouth an open hole, his head caved in. The fort's engagés outnumbered the others, but their chief trader lay howling like a wolf, his fingers leaking life.

Painfully, Fitzhugh struggled to his feet, panting. His throat hurt. Everything in his neck felt broken. "Fix him," he said, pointing his bloody butcher knife at Hervey. "Fix him or I'll kill him."

Two of the post's men crabbed over to Julius Hervey, tore up tradecloth, and applied tourniquets to his upper arms, twisting until the bright blood dwindled. Hervey's hands looked ghastly, their backs and fingers severed to the bone and sheeting blood from a dozen slices. His eyelids sagged, and his eyeballs rolled upward.

"Sew him up and bandage him," Fitzhugh snapped. "Or let him die. I don't care which."

"I'll do it," said someone, a thin, blackbearded one who looked like he might have doctored men before. He plucked a packet of needles and a roll of thread from one of the two remaining upright tables. They were popular trade items.

Fitzhugh didn't care. He peered about. The room was a

shambles. Ruined bolts of cloth hung everywhere. Beads rolled underfoot. Blankets sprawled. Sour smoke hung. Bercier knelt beside Lamaitre, weeping, holding the dead man's hand. Emile Gallard eased toward the door, looking stunned.

Suddenly Fitzhugh understood about Gallard. "Stop him!" he muttered.

Abner Spoon and Zach Constable responded, but too late. Gallard bolted into the glare and vanished. Spoon followed, but Zach Constable stayed close, armed and ready. He and Fitzhugh locked gazes for a moment, gazes that spoke of old times, beaver days, campfires shared. A sudden pleasure filled Brokenleg. Constable hulked like an open-jawed trap near the door, his deadly throwing knife in hand, an ally.

"Don't reckon they treated Dust Devil proper, Brokenleg," he said so softly he strained to hear. But Constable had said a lot.

Dust Devil moaned and writhed, alive but unconscious. The door had been left open, admitting arctic blasts of air. He found a blanket and covered Dust Devil again. Outside, in the snow glare, others gathered.

Alain Lemaitre dead. A pity swept through him. Killed trying to help him; killed by the hand of Julius Hervey. He choked back a sadness for the moment, knowing later that he'd weep for one of those whose brute toil had built Fitzhugh's Post for him.

The fight had gone out of the Cass engagés, most of whom were half-dressed and without weapons—and hungry.

"Go eat," he said. They filed out silently, most of them looking relieved. None had wanted to carry Dust Devil back into the cold. But some, he knew, had violated her, and he hated them for it, and he'd hunt them down and deal with them like a seared conscience.

He discovered his own rifle, the one Hervey confiscated from him, in the trading-room rack, awaiting a buyer. He took it, and helped himself to his own powderhorn as well. He loaded his weapon, and felt the familiar heft and power of it in his hands. On the floor, the remaining engagés sewed up Hervey, and every time the needle poked flesh and thread drew finger muscle together, the man winced and groaned. He lay in a darkening pool of his own blood.

Fitzhugh didn't pity him: the man who'd boasted he'd put his hands on everything, had lost the use of his hands. Or most of it. Mountain justice, he thought. A biblical justice. Those hands could never grasp again. Their tendons had been severed. The fingers could not pull a trigger or guide a nib pen or clamp a knife—unless all those severed muscles healed, and Julius Hervey became more dangerous than ever, Fitzhugh thought uneasily. His throat remembered those hands, and burned still.

"Zach," he said. "I owe you and Abner. We'll get our outfit moved to my post. Get my shelves stocked with all the truck, and then you take your pick, and stick for the winter."

Zach nodded. "Like beaver days," he said.

"I'm thinkin' maybe I can put you on the fort roster."

"Aw, Brokenleg—we're a pair of lone wolves. With all the country just out the window, it'd be worse than going back to the States."

"Whatever you want," Fitzhugh said curtly. His head throbbed.

And Dust Devil watched, her brown eyes expressionless.

He spent the morning fighting a headache, hovering close to Dust Devil, who lay silently under blankets in the devastated trading room, and trying to bring some order to a chaotic time. He gathered his own subdued engagés and addressed them roughly.

"I'll put you on the roster if you want," he said without preamble. "I need you. I owe you for helping me—and Dust Devil—and my company. I'm fixing to load up our outfit—what's left of it—and haul it back. I got horses now, passel of Cheyenne back there, Dust Devil's people, come in to trade and see how the stick floats. They got robes, too, and more if we open our window."

They stared fearfully at Hervey, who still lay on the floor of the trading room, under a trade blanket.

"There's nothing he can do to you," Fitzhugh snapped.

Bercier and Brasseau peered at each other, and seemed to come to a decision. "Ah, *oui, monsieur* . . ."

"I don't reckon you want to stay here."

They nodded.

Zach Constable, standing sentry at the door, let two men in, Emile Gallard with Abner Spoon poking his Hawken into Gallard's back. Gallard surveyed the ruins malevolently, his gaze settling on Hervey, and then glancing at Dust Devil.

A shudder and groan erupted from Dust Devil, and Fitzhugh saw the fear gripping her, and instantly knew Gallard had violated her. Gallard and Hervey. Maybe others. He'd find out, and find them.

"Caught him," Spoon said. "He's some runner and got the best of me and I lost him. But he doubled back—he ain't clothed much—and ducked into a Crow lodge. They didn't want none of that and fetched him out when I come back."

Brokenleg felt something akin to murder boil through him. He discovered the bloody butcher knife still clamped in his hand, and lifted it, and then winched his arm down slowly.

"Who paid you? Chouteau?"

Gallard shrugged, fearlessly. That was the thing about men like Gallard: they'd kill and despoil without a second thought, while knowing they were protected by other men's scruples. Fitzhugh knew he wouldn't stick that butcher knife into Gallard, and Gallard knew it too.

"You have help dumping the blankets?"

Gallard smiled.

"You lay with her."

Gallard's face went blank.

"Hervey tell you to go to her?"

Gallard grinned again.

"Monsieur Fitzhugh—we make our own justice, *oui?*" Brasseau addressed him from across the room. "The engagés are—one. We are dishonored, *oui?* The Creole have the shame."

Brokenleg remembered. The Creoles would undertake their own justice upon one of their number who dishonored and betrayed them. "Take him. Do what you want," he said.

Fear showed at last in Gallard's pocked face, and he eyed his former colleagues carefully. The engagés stared back, and Fitzhugh saw unspoken agreement among them, though he didn't have any notion what they'd agreed to, or what Gallard feared so much his face ticked and spasmed.

Guerette tied his hands together with manila trade rope, and Fitzhugh wondered whether Emile Gallard would jump and struggle. He didn't, but the temptation rode his face. Spoon grinned and lifted the bore of his Hawken. The remaining engagés led him out into the bright cold, and Fitzhugh watched from the door, not wanting to interfere. The Cass engagés watched alertly from their barracks door. Guerette separated, walked toward the small stables and pen, and returned with a coiled bullwhip in his hand. Then Fitzhugh knew. They tied Gallard to the robe press in the middle of the yard, his chest to the post, and then Brasseau sliced Gallard's blouse away with his Green River knife, being none too careful about it.

Brokenleg expected Guerette to begin, but they did a strange thing: Bercier and Brasseau returned to the trading room and gently lifted Lemaitre, and carried the body out into the snow and the glare. They laid it close to the robe press, where Gallard could see his dead colleague. Lemaitre's head looked ghastly, with the skull caved in on one side. Fitzhugh remembered that Gallard had pulled Lemaitre off Hervey's back, freeing Hervey.

The whip cracked across the man's naked back, the sound like a shot. Gallard's body spasmed and tugged at its bindings like a distempered thing. He screamed, a bloodcurdling howl that didn't stop, but wailed like the whistle of a steamboat. The second lash smacked home, cutting flesh and drawing redness with it. The third followed, renewing the howling, and the fourth, snapping Gallard's body like a rag doll. Fitzhugh watched from the trading room, subdued and sickened. On the tenth or fifteen or twentieth lash—he didn't know which—he peeled his gaze from the mesmerizing sight and turned into the room. Julius Hervey stared, ashen-faced.

And Dust Devil wept silently, her tears welling large at the corners of her eyes.

He settled to the wooden floor beside her, each crack and howl outside a toll on his sanity. The bum leg had always made sitting an ordeal, but he ignored the hurt, and the ringing in his head, and the ache of loosened cartilage in his throat.

"You don't have to say nothin'," he said. "I got hotheaded with you, and said things I didn't mean none, didn't mean at all. And I feel so bad I can't put it in words."

She said nothing, but her unblinking eyes were bright with tears.

"You come so close. It scares me. Your ole medicine-helper, them crow-birds, they saved you. They come nesting in that cottonwood you lay down under, and when I walk by, not knowing you was there in the dark, they busted the top of the sky out, takin' off."

"My medicine?" she whispered.

"Yeah, the whole ball o' wax."

"What does that mean, ball o' wax?"

"The whole package. Whatever you got arranged with the universe in your Suhtai heart, it was mighty big medicine."

"My fingers hurt so much."

"Frostbit. Toes too, probably. Ears and nose, I reckon. you'll be hurtin' plenty."

Outside, the cracks of the lash stopped, but the howling didn't.

"Take me from here," she whispered.

"Soon. You need to get your strength up. We got to get wagons loaded, get out outfit. See them blankets?" He waved at stacks of them shelved at the rear. "I'm layin' half over you and half under you when we go. They owe me them blankets."

"Hurry, Brokenleg," she said, and he heard urgency in it.

Chapter Twenty-nine

Brokenleg stood before the robe press in the Fort Cass yard, noting the splatter of bright blood in the glazed snow. They'd taken Gallard somewhere; he didn't care where. An eerie silence pervaded the American Fur Company post, even though it thronged with men. The bitter cold of new January had driven them to their fires, he thought. That and the morning's terrible events. He peered into the frosty Pittsburgh wagon that hulked before the warehouse right where Hervey had confiscated it a week earlier, and in its bed he found the body of Lemaitre, carefully wrapped in a shroud of bed ticking from the trading room. The drive back to Fitzhugh's Post would be a sad one.

He wondered whether to take Dust Devil with the first load, and decided not to. Death's angel had hovered too close. She would go last. He crossed the yard, the snow squeaking under his boots, and entered the Fort Cass barracks, discovering most of the fur company engagés around a pot-bellied stove there, shipped clear up the river. They looked pensive, having witnessed the flogging of Gallard, but not hostile. Except for two or three who glowered at him.

"Who's your top man? Your assistant trader?" he asked.

One arose, a small, wiry man, and Fitzhugh knew him at once from the beaver days. "Sandoval?"

Isodoro Sandoval smiled. "Brokenleg. A long time from the wild days, *si?*"

Sandoval was one of several Mexicans in the upper Missouri fur trade, and a veteran employee of the Chouteau companies.

"Amigo," Fitzhugh said. "You mindin' all this?"

Sandoval shrugged. "Most of these hombres, they are happy. They never like keeping your outfit from you. They never like Gallard spying and ruining your trade."

"You mind helpin' me? Need a couple of your men to carry your *bourgeois* to his house, and look after him."

"Hervey." The word burst sour from Sandoval's mouth.

"Then I need help with my outfit. Hervey's got the inventory somewhere. I want to do it proper, see what's there, what got took out, and get the papers signed proper by you—long as Hervey's got no signin' fingers at the moment."

Sandoval shrugged into a capote, asked several engagés to fetch Julius Hervey from the trading room, and then they braved the bright cold morning.

"You think I could borrow some ox or draft horses, Isodoro? Or get the mules Hervey stole from me?"

Sandoval grunted.

In the bright yard, they watched the Cass engagés help Hervey toward his quarters. Incredibly, the pale *bourgeois* was walking, in spite of all the blood he'd lost. He held his hands, swathed in crimsoned bandaging, upward to slow the throbbing. Hervey paused before Fitzhugh. "I never forget," he rasped.

"I don't forget, either."

"I'll even things."

"I think they're even now."

"I need one finger to pull with."

Fitzhugh didn't say anything more. He couldn't think of anything to say. Hervey apparently couldn't either, and wobbled off, supported by his men.

Sandoval said, "He'll grow a finger, just to pull the trigger again. A dangerous man, Brokenleg."

By noon of that long New Year's Day, Fitzhugh had a good idea of the condition of his outfit. Working with Sandoval, the inventory, and several engagés, he'd dug through heaps of merchandise. Just as he feared, Hervey had helped himself here and there, wherever he'd run out of items in his own inventory. The American Fur trader had never let himself get too greedy—stealing another company's outfit would be too blatant, even by fur trade standards. But he plainly intended to commandeer bits and pieces, and call it spoilage or maybe even theft by parties unknown, such as the winter loafers. The stores of vermilion, fire steels, two-pound lead bars, bullet molds, skillets, silk ribbons, mirrors, tortoise-shell combs, soap, brass and copper kettles, Havana brown sugar, calico and gingham, hawk bells, and coffee beans all had been pillaged.

Fitzhugh fumed when Sandoval and he tallied the result. Hervey had made off with another ten to fifteen percent of the outfit, beyond the rent that had been paid in kind.

"You reckon I could repay me outa your trading room?"

Sandoval bridled at that. "It is," he began lamely, "a matter for the *jefes* in St. Louis, *si?*"

"You figurin' to stop me from takin' it out off the trading room?"

Sandoval looked trapped, and if Fitzhugh hadn't been so furious, he might have pitied the man.

"Amigo," Sandoval began. "I will bring this up with Alec Culbertson at once, with a full written report. Today, you take what is yours here, *si?* And I will see about repaying the rest from Fort Union—"

"I'm takin' the Witney blankets, the ones that didn't get ruined." Fitzhugh's tone dared Sandoval to do anything about it. "Gallard dumped every bale we brought with us," he added.

Sandoval hesitated. "My eyes will not see this," he muttered at last. "It might cost me my contract."

"If it does, I'll sign you."

His engagés loaded the big Pittsburgh, reverently leaving a space at the front for the shrouded burden lying there. The Fort Cass engagés harnessed Fitzhugh's three mules and one of their drays to the wagon. Fitzhugh selected Bercier to come with him and asked the rest to stay for the time being. He'd need a crew here and another at the post to load and unload. And he wanted a little additional protection for Dust Devil, who was being guarded and cared for by Abner Spoon and Zach Constable.

He halted the wagon beside the trading room door, and slid down, wincing.

Then he stood over her, peering into a taut face that contained no joy within it.

"I'm takin' a load over. Leavin' you with Abner and Zach. If I take you along this time, it'd kill you, I think. I truly don't want that, Little Whirlwind. Truly don't."

She gazed up at him, expressionless.

Bad feelings clawed at him as he steered the drays out of the gates and down the trail. Maybe he'd lost her after all; maybe this whole thing would collapse still. He knew he'd keep this wagon rolling between the posts nonstop, into the night, until he had his six loads out of there and in his own post. And he'd set his men to stocking all night too, and then open trade the next day, with Dust Devil's people doing the honors, and receiving the opening-day gifts from Dance, Fitzhugh and Straus. It was always a big thing, the opening of trade, with plenty of speeches and gifts and a few shots of a mountain howitzer for good measure.

They encountered Samson Trudeau on the trace. He stopped and gaped at the specter of the wagon loaded almost to the top of its naked bows.

"Sacre bleu!" he exclaimed, his gaze on the familiar draft animals, the Pittsburgh wagon they'd lost, and Bercier, one of the ones who'd abandoned Fitzhugh. "I come because they are restless at the post. White Wolf, he asked where

you are and I don't know what to say. And Maxim, he's cross as a sore-tooth bear."

"Hop up here, and I'll tell it as we ride," Fitzhugh said.

Trudeau swung up and stopped suddenly, surveying the shrouded body at the front of the box.

"Mon Dieu! Dust Devil—"

Fitzhugh sighed. "No, it's Alain Lemaitre, who was clubbed by Hervey, while fighting for me—for us."

"Jesu," muttered Trudeau, blessing himself with an instinctive sweep of his hand from forehead to belly, and then across his heart.

Quietly, as the wagon rumbled and squeaked its wintry way south, Fitzhugh described events: finding Dust Devil, the open gate, the brawl at dawn, the wounding of Hervey, and the lashing of Gallard.

"Chien!" Trudeau cried. *"Merde!* We knew it was so. But we lacked the proof. He muttered once in his sleep, *oui?* But why does Dust Devil go naked into the night?"

Fitzhugh let his sadness guide him. "There are things, Samson, that should not be spoken of, ever again."

"Je comprends fort bien," he muttered.

They raised the post a few minutes later, and beheld the tranquility of the place in the low solstice sun. Fitzhugh had never imagined his post to be beautiful, especially in the dead of winter, but now the golden glow lit its chimneys and slanted through naked black-limbed cottonwood forests beyond, and glinted off the ice of the river. The Cheyenne ponies stood against their tethers, their shaggy coats absorbing the faint heat, their breaths rising placidly. It choked him, this unexpected vision of peace and warmth and enduring strength, that seemed to rise from the solid rock walls. This post had been erected from rock of the ages; every other post he'd seen had been made of fragile wood.

Men boiled out of the door to see this spectacle, this burdened wagon laden with trading goods. The Cheyenne seemed as amazed as his own faithful engagés. And no one gaped more than young Maxim, who seemed unable to believe his own eyes. Chief White Wolf eyed the cargo, studied Bercier, examined the horses, just as Trudeau had done, and then waited serenely.

"Samson, I got to git back to Cass, before they git their back up and shut gates and all. I want my outfit outa there so bad I can't think straight. I'm gonna pull up yonder, and then leave this here wagon, and hitch the team to one of those others we got there, and start back. You'n Bercier, you tell 'em. Then you, Maxim, and any Cheyenne that wants to unload and shelve the goods, you put 'em all to work. I'm goin' to haul all night if I must and I got a moon, and the horses last."

Trudeau nodded.

"I guess I better talk to White Wolf. I torture the Cheyenne language enough, but he'll git the idea."

He tugged the winter-stiff lines, and the mismatched team halted before the post. Men smiled, but he knew they wouldn't when they saw the first item to be lifted out of the wagon.

"White Wolf," he yelled in Cheyenne. "Much more is coming and I got to drive back. You come along, and we'll talk."

The chief nodded.

Fitzhugh eased to the ground, stomped life into his aching limb, and unhitched the team. He led it to the sagging, snowfilled wagons a way back, and hooked up. Maxim followed, wonder in his face.

"I'm heading back to Cass, lad, for the next. You want to come along and hear it direct? Or would you prefer to oversee the shelving here? You'll clerk, so I guess you'd better shelve and keep an inventory. Trudeau'll tell you what's to tell."

"You—talked Hervey into giving up—"

"Didn't talk, exactly. Made some cutting remarks with a butcher knife."

The remark plainly upset Maxim. "You killed him!"

"No, just carved on his mitts."

That mollified Maxim a little. "Will we have everything back?"

"Naw, not everything. But enough. Lost—lost precious things. Monsieur Trudeau, he'll tell you that. And Bercier, he'll tell it too."

Maxim smiled softly. Fitzhugh swung up on a wheel, brushed snow from the plank seat, and settled down on it, cursing the cold. Then he hawed the team, which jerked the wagon hard to free wheels frozen to earth. The Pittsburgh lurched and its icy wheels protested noisily as Fitzhugh guided it toward the post to pick up a few seat robes, and White Wolf.

"Well, boy," Fitzhugh said to the youth walking the frozen snow below. "We'll be tradin' tomorrow, I reckon."

All night Fitzhugh drove men and mules to exhaustion, shuttling the wagon between Fort Cass and his own post. He had pried open the jaws of Cass, and wouldn't quit until he had extracted his entire outfit. The Cass engagés watched, amazed, as the wagon drew up before the warehouse time and time again, as the moon shot its long arc across the whited dark.

At dawn, Fitzhugh's exhausted men loaded the last of the outfit stored at Cass into the wagon. It came to half a load, which suited Fitzhugh just fine. He wasn't sure the drays could pull more than that, and it left room for his men, and Dust Devil.

Isodoro Sandoval, in turn, worked through the night with his own engagés repairing the chaos in the Cass trading room. Some tradecloth and blankets had been ruined; but mostly his task involved restoring order. All this they did under the watchful eye of Spoon and Constable, who hovered over Dust Devil like guardian angels.

On that first trip back, late in the afternoon, Fitzhugh had explained events to Chief White Wolf as best he could in his broken Cheyenne, and the chief listened solemnly.

"I want your trade, but a post has got to be neutral or else it becomes a target of your enemies. I don't want to donate my scalp to some Blackfeet or Crow," he said. "You could trade at Fort Cass, with American Fur, I reckon. But if I don't get enough trade, and have to quit, they'll fold up Fort Cass. They opened it again because we're here. If that happens your people will be a long way from any post again; you will have to go clear down to Laramie, or up to Union, or east to Pierre. That's a long way from Bear Butte, where Sweet Medicine received the Sacred Arrows."

The chief had said nothing for a long time, and then: "Did you put away Little Whirlwind?"

"I did and took her back if she'll have me."

"That is good," the chief had said.

They'd loaded up the wagon in the gathering gloom and started back without delay. At Cass, Fitzhugh had been pleased to show the chief the mountain of tradegoods still to be transferred to his own post. White Wolf had studied it, studied what was in Cass's trading room, not missing a thing.

"Tomorrow we will open our trading season," he had said. "I'll want some ponies as well as robes. What do you reckon the osage orange bow wood's worth to your people?"

"They are only sticks. Good wood for bows, but sticks. Ten for a horse; five for a robe. We have all agreed not to take these sticks for less. They are not yet good, supple bows that will put an arrow into the buffalo, or into our enemies."

Fitzhugh had mulled that quietly, and decided to do it—for now. He needed horses. Later he'd ask more for a stick of the best bow wood these people could get, brought two thousand miles.

Now, as dawn bleached the sky, he felt so tired he wondered if he should delay trading a day. His men were asleep on their feet. And he had to move Dust Devil, too. That frightened him. She lay weak and unsmiling and death-haunted.

He hawed the weary steaming drays from the warehouse to the trading room, and clambered down stiffly, ignoring pain and cold. Inside, he found Isodoro snoozing, and he shook him awake.

"Isodoro. We got it all now."

Sandoval yawned. "You work like madmen."

"It's Hervey. Old Julius is back there in his room, plotting still, and thinkin' about his butchered hands and wantin' to do murder on me. I reckoned I'd git while the gitting is good. You want to sign this hyar release paper now?"

He shoved a manifest of the goods removed from Cass that night before Sandoval. The man hesitated.

"Does this say what you're taking out of the trading room here?"

"No. I been thinkin' all night, Isodoro. If I help myself to your goods, they ain't going to understand it back in Saint Louis—neither Cadet Chouteau nor my partners. It'll just look like more thievin' back there, only with me doin' it. Hervey, he stole me blind—we got that on paper, the inventories—and the company slipped Gallard into my outfit and he cost me about three hundred trade blankets. I thought to help myself hyar, all this stuff, and you owin' me, but I don't think so. We'll lay it before American Fur in court back there. I got the papers. All I'll do for now is take five, six blankets to keep Dust Devil plenty warm going back. I figure you got no cause to argue that."

Sandoval looked relieved. He dipped a quill pen into the inkpot they'd been using, and scratched out his name on the final inventory. "I hope I don't get into trouble with this," he said dourly.

"If you do, I'll put you on at my post, Isodoro."

The man shook his head. "I always am with the powerful company."

"I reckon you can send a man to pick up your draft horse later. I'm opening trade, and we're going to be busy."

"This afternoon," Isodoro said. "We are tired, too."

Fitzhugh turned to Constable. "You boys ready to go?"

"Got our outfit parked at the door," Zach replied.

"Help me, then."

He eased clumsily down to his wife, cursing his bad leg. She lay under a mound of blankets near the fire, just as she had for a full day now. He couldn't tell, from the blankness of her face, how she felt about any of this. "You ready to go on home, Dust Devil?"

"I am Little Whirlwind of the Suhtai," she whispered.

It tickled him. As full of feist as ever. "I reckon that's what you are. And I'm glad to call you my woman."

She smiled faintly, the first time.

They carried her gently to the wagon, and lowered her into the place reserved for her at the front of the box, and tucked the blankets about her. He knew the temperature wasn't much above zero, and he worried about it. Around him, his four remaining engagés gathered their rifles and kits, and clambered into the wagon behind Dust Devil. Spoon and Constable climbed onto their horses and grabbed the lines of their packhorses.

Fitzhugh hawed the weary mules and the dray belonging to this American Fur Company post, and they lumbered slowly toward the yawning gates, their breaths pluming the air. Around the caravan, the fort's own engagés lounged and watched, ignoring the terrible cold. Fitzhugh drove slowly through the gates, the teeth and jaws of the Opposition, out upon a free land, and when they'd all cleared Fort Cass, he turned back to stare at Julius Hervey's fort, which had hurt and bled them so much. The gates creaked shut behind them, and he heard the mean clank of the iron bolt sealing them out. But this time it didn't matter. He'd left a whipped and conniving engagé behind, and had taken a loyal one's body out, along with about four-fifths of the outfit they'd brought up the river. And Little Whirlwind. They owed him more, he thought bitterly. A lot more.

He couldn't hurry the exhausted drays, as much as he wanted to because of Dust Devil, but by the time the sun rode the eastern ridge of the Bighorn valley, he pulled up before the new post of Dance, Fitzhugh and Straus, feeling a strange joy. They'd shelve this last load, and open trade at noon, a day late, January 2, 1842.

They carried Dust Devil in first, and laid her on a pallet of blankets near the barracks fireplace. Tomorrow, he thought, he'd string up the wagonsheeting into a sort of private place for himself and his woman. Their own apartment had yet to be partitioned off. His men began unloading and shelving, leaving them beside the fire, along with many of the Cheyenne, who waited patiently for the opening of trade. About thirty of them sat quietly, watching Fitzhugh and Dust Devil.

"I reckon this is your home now, Dust Devil."

"Do you want me, Fitzhugh?"

"More'n ever."

"My people are here. It is good."

"We'll start tradin' in a few hours. We'll give 'em a big howdoo, because they come so far to trade in the middle of the winter. And because you're one of 'em and my woman."

"I had no name. No medicine."

"You figure sittin' yourself under a nesting tree full of crow-birds isn't medicine?"

"It is medicine. Will you call me Little Whirlwind? Devil in your tongue is an under-earth spirit, and bad."

"I will, if you remind me when I forget."

"I need a name. If I take a new name, then what they did to me at Fort Cass—it won't matter so much, will it?"

"How about Missus Fitzhugh?"

She smiled again, and slid a hand from under the blankets to clasp his own.

Chapter Thirty

Maxim watched dumfounded as weary engagés shelved the treasure snatched from Fort Cass. The forlorn trading room, symbol of all their defeats, had been transformed through the night by sleepless men, while Maxim himself kept inventory, checking each item against his endless lists. He'd never dreamed this would happen, and had let hope slide from him these last weeks. He felt ashamed of that now, ashamed that he'd lacked the faith that Brokenleg Fitzhugh had. He fought sleep desperately, feeling his responsibility to make sure everything had been done right; that nothing had been damaged. Fitzhugh appeared now and then in the long night with a new wagonload, and paused only to eye the progress of the shelving, done in the wavering orange light of the fire. And then he'd leave, braving the night once again.

Now, at dawn, men Maxim thought had defected were pulling the last of the goods from the Pittsburgh wagon and staggering in with barrels of sugar, sacks of coffee beans, crates of rifles, pasteboard boxes filled with mysterious things. Others, under the experienced Trudeau, laid these things up on shelves and roughhewn tables, until the room bulged with them: hoop iron, blue beads, boxes of tortoiseshell combs, packets of vermilion, hundreds of awls, cartons of oval fire steels, bags of flints, boxes of percussion caps, trays of Wilson Sheffield knives, bolts of bright tradecloth, scarlet and blue green; bolts of patterned calico and gingham. Bolts of unbleached linen sheeting. Double bit and single bit axes, assorted hatchets, rolls of copper wire, brass kettles heaped into nesting piles, iron skillets and pots, dutch ovens, strings of hawk bells, packets of needles, colored cotton threads, mirrors galore in every size, and even a few Witney blankets, mostly three-point white ones with black bands at either end, ones used to cover Dust Devil when they brought her. And when the trading room burst with goods, and glowed with a thousand shafts of light wrought by the cheerful fire at its far end, the engagés removed the rest to the warehouse just behind, and burned cartons and crates in the fire.

Could it be? he wondered. Would they succeed in spite of everything? With dawnlight softly penetrating the rawhide windows, Fitzhugh came into the room to supervise the last of it. He looked hollow-eyed and feverish, Maxim thought; even more worn down with responsibility and his unending leg-pain than the rest. He spoke with a rasp, from an injured throat, barking at men, fingering goods and staring at them, his gaze as unbelieving as Maxim's own.

"You checkin' this off, boy?"

Maxim nodded. "We lost a lot."

"We got a profit here if we fetch the trade. Losses are kinda built into it."

"Built in?"

"Yes, boy. An outfit hardly operates up hyar without addin' in a loss factor to the prices. These things, they'll fetch, five, six, eight times what we gave for them in Saint Louis. But a lot of that's transportation, and we got wages and all the rest."

"Did my *papa* know that?"

"Course, Maxim. He knows the business almost as well as old Cadet Chouteau himself."

Suddenly they were done: a whole store lay before his eyes, transplanted two thousand miles and dropped into a wilderness building where nothing had stood only a few weeks before. They stared at one another, engagés, Maxim, Fitzhugh, and several Cheyenne headmen who'd observed it all. Maxim could scarcely believe it, and some wild pride inflated him, driving his weariness away.

"We'll open the shutters at noon," was all Fitzhugh said.

The men stood expectantly, and Trudeau became their spokesman. "Monsieur Fitzhugh, we have a sad duty now, *oui?"*

Fitzhugh sighed. "We'll do it," he said.

Every engagé present, along with Abner Spoon and Zach Constable, and the whole contingent of Cheyenne as well, trooped into the cold warehouse where Lemaitre's shrouded body lay. The engagés collected axes. Maxim pulled his capote over his woolen shirt, and followed them.

Gently they lifted the body and carried it out of the rear door of the post, toward the river, toward a site they seemed to have selected near the edge of the meadow, where cottonwoods grew rank. They stopped there, a couple hundred yards south of the post, and swiftly hacked limbs, turning them into thick logs which they placed around the shrouded body. They couldn't cut into the frozen earth, so they would build a log grave for him for now, and bury him when the sun warmed the earth. Tenderly they fitted the hewn logs together so tightly no coyote or wolf could disturb what lay within, and then weighted it all down with stray rock they pried from frozen earth.

They paused then in silence, leaning on their axes, letting the silence of the wintry day remind them of the fate of all men and the voyage of the human spirit through life. Fitzhugh removed his stocking cap, and others did as well. The Creoles had no priest for the burying or the prayers, but Trudeau led them through half-remembered verses.

When the Creoles finished with remembrances of their fallen comrade, Fitzhugh cleared his throat. "This hyar man is one I'll remember long as I live," he said. "Back there in the Cass trading room, with Hervey fixin' to murder me, and me sprawled on the floor, Alain Lemaitre leapt up on Hervey's back and rassled him long enough for me to git free. He saved my life. He was a good and brave man. May he be with God, and rest in peace."

Fitzhugh's post had claimed its first man.

They walked silently back to the post, through frostbit air, each man absorbed in his own thoughts, the toll exacted by the fur business and wilderness and hardship a vast distance from the cities and farms and shops and churches of the east, alive in his mind. Many went into the wilderness; a third came back.

Maxim returned to the trading room, his gaze caressing everything, as if only the sights before his eyes could allay the disbelief he still felt within. He yearned to tell his father of this: to say, we are ready now. We have enough to make a profit. We will trade for horses and then take the wagons out, just as we planned. We might succeed.

But his father lived some interminable wintry distance away, months away, and all Maxim could do was think the thoughts and wish they could fly through the ether and into the minds of his parents. He refused to doze. The day had become much too important to miss even the smallest moment.

When the sun had reached its feeble zenith that second day of January, every mortal in the post gathered in the barracks to begin ceremonies that normally would occur in mid-summer, upon the arrival of the year's outfit. Maxim had expected a smoke and a speech; he'd heard about all that. But now before his eyes, every Cheyenne wore his ceremonial finest, which they had all carried clear from their village on Crazy Woman Creek. Chief White Wolf wore his eagle-feather bonnet with fine otter tassels at either side, and hawk bells sewn to the red tradecloth headband. The headmen wore their ensigns of office, elaborate quilled and beaded shirts of leather, medicine pouches, grizzly-bear claw necklaces, scalp-bedecked staffs.

Fitzhugh himself wore a black frockcoat that Maxim never knew he had, a touch of formality that startled the young man and seemed utterly incongruous with Fitzhugh's wild red beard and receding red hair, his fringed britches and scuffed boots. He sat on a stump-chair because he couldn't manage sitting crosslegged on the floor. They did smoke, at least the headmen and Fitzhugh and Trudeau, passing the long calumet with its red pipestone bowl in the circle. Then White Wolf stood and made a considerable speech which Maxim couldn't understand and wished would come to an end; and Fitzhugh stood and welcomed them all, many by name, in English mixed with Cheyenne.

Then the trader distributed gifts. A twist of tobacco to each Cheyenne as a friendship and peace offering; packets of powder and a one-pound lead bar to the chief and headmen; plus a pound of sugar and a pound of precious coffee for White Wolf. It took a long time, Maxim thought, fighting back sleep. But at last the Cheyenne stood, and began to dig through their parfleches.

"Hyar, Maxim, you got to keep a record of all this," Fitzhugh said. "You sit beside the trading window, and I'll dicker. Me and Trudeau."

All that afternoon Fitzhugh, still in his amazing black frockcoat, pulled buffalo robes onto the counter, spread them out for examination, looked for thickness of hair, flaws, color, whether the robe was a split sewn from two halves, looked for thin spots, weaknesses on the fleshed side, lice and bugs, softness of the tanning, and age.

"This hyar's a good one, boy. Mark it to Looks at Stars, and give him what he wants up to two dollars."

Wearily, Maxim scribbled in the ledger. Was this what clerking was, he wondered? Looks at Stars bought powder and ball, a five-inch Wilson knife, a yard of red ribbon, and two mirrors.

The afternoon snailed away at its own slow pace, and Maxim wrote until his fingers numbed. Some times he carried the heavy, acrid-smelling robes out to the warehouse, where they would be sorted and graded, and eventually pressed into bales when they built a robe press. He ran errands for Trudeau and Fitzhugh, scrambled for things off shelves—the yeller calico up there, the ten-inch knives, the ivory combs, not the tortoise-shell—and slowly acquired a sense of prices. He hadn't the faintest idea what a trade item would go for, or what a pelt would be worth. He realized, suddenly, he knew nothing about the trading itself; the values, the ways to tell a good robe from a poor one, the amounts to charge for hundreds of items on the shelves. It bewildered him. He had to learn and fast. A robe usually fetched a yard of cloth—trader's measure from fingertip to neck—or sixty loads of powder and shot, or three pounds of sugar, or two of coffee beans, or one hank of beads.

Mid-afternoon, Fitzhugh turned the trading over to Trudeau entirely, and walked outside with White Wolf. Through the trading window Maxim could see them dickering for horses in the bright glare: the chief, the owners of various ponies, and Fitzhugh, who walked around each shaggy beast, ran his hands down hocks, picked up hoofs, hunted for galling under the thick winter hair, and watched warriors saddle them and ride them, or hook a travois to them if they were selling a draft animal. Maxim got busy again and didn't know how the trading went, but soon he saw Cheyenne warriors carrying bundles of osage orange, and saw half a dozen nondescript ponies, mustang blood, tied separately to one of the Pittsburgh wagons. The post had horses again; one team and two saddlers, plus the three recovered mules. Those as well as the four belonging to Abner and Zach. A joy effused Maxim, because those horses would mount hunters and meant meat, and travel, and the use of the wagons.

They didn't shut the trading window until well after dark. White Wolf wanted to leave for his village at once, but not until every one of his warriors had traded. Then, as suddenly as they'd appeared, they mounted their ponies and rode away, gaudy in their new finery. It astonished Maxim that they'd leave at night, and not spend their final hours in the comfort of the large barracks.

"They're plumb itching to git back, Maxim. They'll spread the word, and we'll see other bands come in soon. They won't freeze, boy. They know how to make good huts outa robes and blankets if it gets too nippy. Now count up, boy. Let's see how we done on our first day."

Maxim began tallying, muttering as he went, blinking back sleep, his eyes blurry, some crazy happiness keeping him going. He checked and rechecked because he wanted his figures to be totally accurate.

"A hundred fifty seven robes, Monsieur Fitzhugh. Twenty of them summer robes. Papa will be so glad."

"He har!" yelled Brokenleg Fitzhugh. "We're in business!"

But Maxim had fallen asleep over his ledgers.

Gregoire let Ambrose Chatillon out upon Chestnut Street, while Guy Straus watched. Chatillon had arrived that very evening, and had hastened to Straus's home after finding the offices of Straus et Fils dark.

Guy returned to his study, and read the letters from Fitzhugh and Maxim, holding them close to the coal oil lamp. Everything in them exactly agreed with Chatillon's account. Good and bad. They were alive and well; they hadn't lost a man; they'd almost completed a new post, even with only the handful they had to build it. But they hadn't a single buffalo robe. Nor any other pelt, such as beaver or elk or otter. Worse, their entire outfit, save for the spirits and the bow wood, had been kept from them by the man whose name most men in the fur trade dreaded—Julius Hervey. It made him faint of soul just to think of that.

It depended on Fitzhugh, he thought. He'd thought it from

the beginning, and had come to believe what the broken-legged rough cob of a man would succeed where a hundred men of fainter heart would fail. Maxim thought they would fail, in spite of their heroic labor. That seemed plain, between the lines.

Late February. Saint Louis lay in the grip of winter still, but soon it would abate. Great floes of ice drifted past the levee, and in the grog shops there, mountain men talked of spring and green grass and the next trip out upon the far-flung wilds.

He stood at the window, peering into a dark night. A few windows glowed up and down Chestnut Street, but mostly a foggy dark possessed the town. He saw no one on the rutted street. He'd have to tell Yvonne in a moment, the good and bad. She had retired earlier, from a habit of going to bed early in winter. Lamplight strained her eyes, she'd always said. She'd be overjoyed with the news that Maxim was well, and growing stronger daily. Good and bad. Probably bad. Snatching the outfit out of Hervey's hands would take more than even Fitzhugh could come up with. Guy thought to pay a visit to Pierre le Cadet the next day, down at his offices near the levee, and say a few sharp things. But it'd do little good, he knew. One did things for the record.

Guy wouldn't know the outcome until late June or early July, when Max and Fitzhugh would come down the river on LaBarge's packet, with the year's returns. A long time to wait, Guy thought. But that was what any business required, and especially the fur business. In New England or New Orleans, daring entrepreneurs sent their fragile vessels out upon a harsh sea, and then waited, day by day, month by month, for news. So it was with the fur business, although the news would come over a sea of land, not of water.

He'd long since trained himself to wait, and be optimistic. He thought of that red-haired lion out there, and smiled.

Author's Note

Some of the background characters in this story were real people. Among them Joseph LaBarge, pioneer Missouri riverman, pilot and captain. Pierre Chouteau, Jr., along with his numerous family and relatives, owned and brilliantly managed the fur company that dominated the robe trade on the upper Missouri, at one time Pratte and Chouteau, and later, Chouteau and Company. He did not actually purchase the name, American Fur Company, from John Jacob Astor, but the name lingered on, and Chouteau's company was informally called American Fur, a convention I have followed in this story.

Alec Culbertson and his Blood wife Natawista were real people also, the royalty of the Upper Missouri. Culbertson was in charge of operations through the 1840s and 1850s.

My fictional character Julius Hervey is loosely based on the real Alexander Harvey, perhaps the most brutal and villainous man ever to enter the fur trade. His conduct was so appalling that it would not be believed if presented in fictional form. The traits I have ascribed to the fictional Julius Hervey were present in much more violent form in the real Alexander Harvey. Nonetheless, Harvey was a competent trader, and was successful in the fur business, both with American Fur and in opposition.

The most notorious of Harvey's many deeds was the revenge he took against the Blackfeet, either for stealing a milch cow, or for the killing of a black slave. At Fort

McKenzie, probably in 1843 or 1844, Harvey and a colleague loaded a howitzer with grape shot—some say nails—and then opened the gates of the post to the crowd of Piegan men, women, and children waiting to trade, and touched off the cannon. The shot scythed them down, including the women and children, and up to thirty died. The exact number is not known. The whites, under Harvey, then apparently shot the wounded and that night forced the wives of the victims to participate in a scalpdance. That episode cost American Fur Company its Blackfoot trade for years. Fort McKenzie was abandoned and burned.

Harvey murdered another fur company employee as well as other Indians, beat up any who opposed him, stole the wives of the employees and dared them to do something about it. My fictional Julius Hervey is a somewhat milder version of an amazing character.